A Kaleidoscope of Masquerades

by
Deborah DR Kralich

A Kaleidoscope
of
Masquerades

Copyright 2015
TX0008216721
Deborah DR Kralich

Published by Ruskras Corner
The United States of America

This is a work of fiction, the names, characters, incidents, events, places, artistic works and locations are solely the product and concept of the author's imagination and are used to create a fictitious story and should not be construed as real.

A note about the Houston/Galveston area. To make room for the fictional colony of Sand Waves and other fictional areas in this series, the map of the area was extensively redrawn, the distance between the cities lengthened and the Gulf of Mexico pushed back, creating new land areas. The geographical areas indicated in this book are completely fictional and are not to be construed as to represent any real communities, areas, streets, or neighborhoods or otherwise existing entities.

A Kaleidoscope of Masquerades, A Lt. Plate in Sand Waves Mystery III
ISBN 9781942542070
TX 8-190-038

All cover designs, artwork and photography by Deborah D Russo, copyright 2015
Holy Bible King James Version 1923- Quotation- Luke 18: 29-30.

A Kaleidoscope of Masquerades

Cast of Characters

Edward York- Planning to run for Senator, his supporters say now is his time, the Presidency his destiny. Cool and smooth like silver, his true passions are few but deadly.

Grace York- Dressed as an empress for the masquerade ball, she will settle for queen consort in real life. God may call her for a different role but she is cold enough to ignore Him. A romantic brush with a middle class police officer has left her equally untouched.

Natalie Wakefield- Sheltered socialite, all she seems to do in life is throw soirées, travel to spas and placate a temperamental cat. Collecting guests as if they were party favors is an entertaining pastime for the beauty who invents her own style of Charades.

Emma Tates- Sloppy in appearance, she is dedicated to her traveling job, but an indifferent stepmother to two kids abandoned by their own. Her schoolteacher husband loves her. But a strange lack of bonding keeps the family disparate and lonely.

Morris Tates- He believes, given time, Emma will fulfill her potential as a wife and mother. He is often left alone when her company sends her far away. After he takes the children away, a strange woman visitor tempts him with a persuasive call to fate.

Doris Marvins- Unreservedly devoted maid to Natalie, she is convinced only her mistress can be queen at the masquerade ball. Others, jealous and dangerous, disagree.

Serena Towers- Rich and successful journalist, cool and strong as her name implies, she finds herself oddly tempted by a middle class lifestyle totally foreign to her. Her reaction to the man behind this lure will change her life forever.

Evelyn Corrigan- A Lady in more ways than one, her youth and inexperience are a danger to her. Ultimately they may cost more lives in pursuit of a questionable cause.

Miranda Watson- Rich and spoiled, she is not above risking her own safety to make sure she gets the most important character at the masquerade ball.

Forrest Pointpar- An upcoming candidate for nationwide political leadership, he is too focused on equerry pursuits, what character he will portray at the ball, and women, when he should be more worried about his life, which others clearly see is in grave jeopardy.

Ernest Wakefield- Married to a younger enigmatic petite beauty, his fear that she is unfaithful triggers a deadly series of events from which he will never recover.

Officer Skaar- Stuck behind the gates of Sand Waves again, once more he is blamed when the lives of the rich and famous are compromised and threatened.

Darica Daniels- A struggling journalist out of place in Sand Waves, her

4

secret sisterhood is a more of a danger and less of a secret than she understands.

Father Patrick Thomas- The bishop commands his attendance, yet the parish priest would rather not go to the masquerade party. Plotting to break the rules, he does not foresee how desperately needed he will be.

Reverend Erick Skrale- Amused by the costume assigned to him, he does not break the rules and as a consequence, escapes a lot of problems.

Frieda Tates- By letting go of her former life in Sand Waves she has found a different way that will bring her back all that she has lost.

Daphne Martin- In love with the only man that has ever moved her, she has to watch him desert her for not one, but two other women.

Lieutenant Plate- He does not let his popularity affect his official duties but he has developed an unhealthy habit of stalking the woman he is most interested in.

Mark Brown- Fearing he will soon lose his seat in Congress, he has no such worries about the devotion of his wife. He is just annoyed at the new sisterhood she has found.

Peg Brown- Bored with Bible class, she's looking for a new fellowship with women on her own level, a group that will take her to new heights socially and emotionally. The Ladies in Disguise charities seem to be perfect for her inclinations.

Chief Brecken- He wants nothing but peace and quiet so he doesn't have to work on weekends but rarely gets his wish in a place like Sand Waves.

Betty Brecken- She is thrilled to get a performing part at the ball, she is ready to do her best to portray the character assigned, not knowing all others on the initial list were removed long before the event. She is the only one left...

Drake Plate- Retired to East Texas, a former lawman with a secret past, he is proud of his son following in his footsteps but annoyed at police in general for not doing a better job.

Vivian Plate- Traditional loyal wife and mother to two generations of policemen, she would welcome a new daughter-in-law but has little hope of acquiring one soon.

Officer Jordan- Suddenly finding himself at the side of Daphne Martin, he wants not to antagonize his boss, but she is a very lovely girl.

Officer Willhouse- Roped into a blind date, he can only play along and hope for the best and play his part in the masquerade.

Ray Cathare- Only tragedy and Grace York can get him to return to Sand Waves from his beloved East Texas but in the end he is there.

Midnight, Catherine, & **Tomcat** do their best to serve their masters and mistresses with honor but it can be hard on self-respecting felines when their humans go wrong...

February 1983

Prologue

A flickering light in the shadows seemed to flutter beyond him with darkness encompassing it. The Lady in Disguise was slipping out of the building.

She walked slowly, with hesitation that suggested walking might be painful for her. Yet she slid behind the wheel of her car with a single motion. The car engine purred quietly and its small frame was easily maneuvered, passing through manicured bushes over the top of the sidewalk.

Safely in the street, the Lady in the Disguise was feeling very clever in her costume, positive it totally concealed her true identity. She seemed blissfully unaware of her shadow as she drove to the first of her three stops. The shadow watched her with curiosity and anticipation.

Her small dark car stopped first at the mailbox which served the estate of Edward York, the prominent jurist and potential candidate for national office. The shadow watched as she opened his mailbox and slipped an envelope inside without emerging from her vehicle and drove on.

Without even moving his car, her shadow could see her little vehicle dipping down over a narrow bridge, then going back up, climbing the road, still on dry land that abruptly ended at the closed gates of Sand Waves.

With some astonishment, he watched as the car seemed to disappear into the woods that skirted the fence that supported the gates.

He waited a few moments, vaguely realizing that her anticipated emergence back onto the road by foot was too simple a consequence of her actions. Without stopping at the York mailbox, he quickly sped silently, no lights on, to the spot where her car had veered off the road.

Sure enough, there it was, sitting dark and empty at the base of a large tree.

The shadowing car rushed back to the mailbox. Risking breaking federal law, the shadower pulled the mailbox handle. It was empty. He checked to make sure it was not one of those types of mailboxes that had a secret depository that locked, allowing only someone with the key to get the mail.

As he feared, it was just an ordinary mailbox, albeit belonging to an extraordinary man.

Scheduled to become a senator in the fall and often proposed as a future President, Edward York eschewed all but the most ordinary security measures despite his fame and controversial positions on many issues.

A strong factor in his strong support from the public was the general knowledge that Edward York did not fear the many volatile people on the other side of those debates.

In all his political and judicial actions, York had won the complete respect of the people with his unwavering positions based on his faith and heritage. His frequent protestations that he did not deserve any adulation only added to his popularity.

The man in the car was somewhat unnerved that, whatever these women were up to, it brushed the edge of York's enclave. But few people knew the politician was actually physically present since his recent remarriage to his ex-wife had left a media trail, still hot in Europe, after a much announced secluded Italian honeymoon.

Few knew the Yorks had never left home, sending decoys in their place.

The man watching knew.

Could this Lady in Disguise have found out? Surely not. This is some type of prank, he thought.

Disgusted, the shadower was about to raise his window back up when he heard the distinctive clack of high heel shoes going over concrete. Sure enough, the same distinctive outfit, holding a fluttering light, was emerging from a different driveway.

The Lady in Disguise did not glance his way but must have been aware of his patrol car sitting near the York mailbox, alerted when vicious dogs, fenced just behind the mail depository, awoke and came running, barking and growling.

As the shadower reached for his communication device, the Lady in Disguise disappeared into the dense woods bordering one

8

side of the York estate.

The shadower sighed in exasperation. He had been tricked. And he knew it.

The Lady in Disguise that had first emerged was not the same Lady in Disguise who had just crossed his path.

Dressed identically, the two were meant to be mirror images, but one of them had bent a little and dropped her shoulders as she walked.

That could have been part of the con, using a minute differentiation and posture to confuse him. But the differentiation was too minute.

He might have missed it.

It had been two different women. He was sure.

Two different women, dressed in identical costumes, delivering envelopes to mailboxes behind the gates of Sand Waves in the middle of the night.

It was hard to see faces. He was almost certain they wore masks.

No evidence that any crime had been committed except the rarely enforced law that prevented use of the mailbox for delivering anything except the U.S. mail.

But still, enough to alert the neighborhood and alarm residents, so that he had been posted to keep watch and try to find out what was going on. And with consternation, he quickly realized he had sat there trying to puzzle this out for too long. He rushed back to the scene where the dark car had been left.

It was gone, too.

Meanwhile, at least one Lady in Disguise was safely outside the gates of Sand Waves and on her way to her third destination.

Her transportation to that destination was as unique and unusual inside the colony of Sand Waves as it was common and ordinary in all the surrounding areas.

She patted the nose of the horse after slipping down. An identically dressed woman came around to take it off her hands.

"Good evening, Mistress," she said softly.

The horse neighed and its hooves click-clopped as it was led away.

9

The Lady in Disguise watched with some admiration as the horsewoman deftly handled the animal, guiding it into the trailer that was to take it away. Her attention was diverted by the opening of the door in front of her.

"Welcome, Headmistress," said the doorkeeper with some amusement. "I hope you had no problems getting here. Password?"

The last word had the lilt of laughter in it.

Going through the nondescript door into small meeting area with cheap furniture and modern office equipment, she was cordially greeted by the small group of people that she had come to meet.

They stood up in respect for her rank and all, dressed identically, echoed the hope of the doorkeeper.

"No problem at all," she whispered, with a smile.

Just for the sake of propriety, she gave the password.

Chapter 1

YOU are career woman.
You are a homemaker.
You're single and carefree.
You are a mother
  with responsibilities.
You're the head of the household.
You're the woman behind the man.
You are liberated and powerful!
Your destiny continues to unfold!
You are a slave to his love,
  looking down at him from above.
You scorn with equanimity
  the rough and boisterous male!
You are female!
  the epitome of 1980s femininity!

AND- deep down you are a lady!

The last line was a purr compared to the singsong cheerleader jingle. It was followed by a professionally sounding female announcer-

This is why Lady in Disguise hair care products are designed for you. You recognize the days of short straight hair and long straight hair, straight hair of any kind- are over! The 1980s woman, has a face surrounded with ringlets and curls-

"Stupid commercial," Daphne griped, as she sat on her den couch eating popcorn. She fingered her naturally wavy long blonde curls.

"Commercials are getting worse and worse," agreed her companion, also unconsciously running her hand down her long straight dark brown hair.

Daphne reached over and switched the television off. The first few seconds of the advertisement, spooky instrumental music introducing a tall, cloaked model on the small screen, had grabbed her attention.

The actress, with graceful movements within a long hooded brownish gray cloak thinly trimmed in red, dark auburn curls and ringlets slipping out and spilling onto her white cheeks, with red lipstick matching the cloak's trim, had been somewhat enchanting.

But then the singsong began. The idiotic jingle had just gotten on Daphne's nerves. The soothing purr of the last line did nothing to diminish the jingle's disruption and the crisp announcer just lowered the pitch to an irritating monotone.

"Nothing in that commercial is going to induce anybody to buy those products. That company will go bankrupt," Daphne declared.

"You're wrong. You are so focused on selling insurance that you have no idea what's going on in greater society," said her visitor. "The Lady in Disguise sales campaign is sweeping the nation. Lady in Disguise door-to-door sellers are blanketing the suburbs. With great success, I hear."

"So that is why I've been seeing this woman in a costume roaming in the neighborhood. She's a hair care saleswoman? That's quite a gimmick dressing them up like that. I thought it had something to do with Mardi Gras," said Daphne.

"Until our advertising manager was telling me all this, I would have thought it had something to do with that upcoming masquerade ball," said her companion.

"That occurred to me, too. But with that ball being behind the gates, and anyone wanting to go having to purchase an invitation, I felt like the woman in the cloak was a little too common to be connected with that."

"They start first in the upper class neighborhoods. So they are probably just now getting to your area and you don't pay attention if you are not on the selling end," Darica commented. "So are you going to this masquerade ball?"

"Oh yes. I purchased an invitation already. Everyone is hoping to draw a character. Are you covering it for your newspaper?"

"I saw something about that. I did not take time to read the fine print since I'm going to be there in a professional capacity. I'm to do a lead-in next week. No use in writing the story ahead of time. Something is liable to change and I have to do it all over again."

"People like me have to purchase a ticket, and when you do, your name is entered into a lottery. And- oh, let me think, they're going to draw names-" Daphne broke off trying to remember the procedure she had read about.

"Didn't you know the charity involved was connected to the Lady in Disguise Corporation?" asked the journalist.

"No, I didn't pay that much attention. I just thought- how thrilling! A masquerade ball! And at Edward York's estate. Darica, you should see it! I've been there and it's beautiful. He can handle several hundred people, indoors and outdoors."

"I know you've been there." The reporter pulled a slick brochure from a briefcase sitting beside the chair in which she was lounging. She handed the brochure to Daphne.

"So the Ladies in Disguise have a lot to do with it?" said Daphne, with surprise. "I just sent in the money and didn't pay that much attention to the brochure."

"It's their charity," said Darica.

"And they're supporting Edward York? I would've taken them for a more liberal group, based on their TV commercial. They play with the words. But to me, they come across as women's lib."

"I don't know. I think they're supposed to be totally nonpolitical. Only a small percentage of the saleswomen are involved in the charity. They go around to Third World countries whenever there's a disaster. Trying to rescue people. They are the offshoot volunteer part of the Ladies in Disguise Corporation. You know how some corporations have their own charitable organization, rather than just contributing to the United Fund? I've got to do a story on the ball and something about each of the characters offered as prizes."

"I'm just hoping for a good character," said Daphne.

"Who is, or was, Empress Marie Louise?" asked the journalist, glancing at the brochure, noticing the drawing of the empress represented a blonde.

"Oh, I know her from college world history. Napoleon's second wife. The one that– she was supposed to die in childbirth and he was asked should they save her or the baby, and he said save her, even though he was desperate for an heir. But then she and the baby both lived. It was a boy, too."

"Didn't do him any good did it?" Darica was trying to recall her world history class in college. She had made an A but did not remember anything about it. "Wasn't he executed?"

"No. They ran him off and he died on an island somewhere," said Daphne.

"I'm kind of surprised you're willing to spend this kind of money just to go to a masked ball."

"I have my reasons," Daphne said.

"Two thousand dollars? I know you can afford it, but still, as tight as you are... It can't be because you know Edward York. Is he your client?"

"Not exactly. I do have some clients behind the gates. And this will make me look good for them. Most people behind the gates only deal with other people that live behind the gates. My clients know that I don't. But they want me for their insurance agent anyway. My going to one of their social affairs can only help me."

"Hmmm, when do you find out if you won a character?"

"I don't know. I'm hoping I don't win Betsy Ross or Martha Washington. Or any other character that I would have to dress really dowdy, with one of those funny caps on my head. I'm hoping for Marie Antoinette. If I don't draw a character, I'll have a costume made. The fancy dress of the era was gorgeous. Most disappointing about not getting a character would be being left out of the one act plays. I would love to do a skit."

"You want the queen who was decapitated by a guillotine? Will your formal be sprinkled with fake blood? Will a severed head be part of the costume? Carrying that around all night would be a drag."

"Don't be macabre! You were always so bloodthirsty. You watched too much of *The Avengers,* when we were growing up. I just want a character that allows me to dress up in a beautiful gown and lots of fake jewels."

"Maybe you could trade if you and somebody else both get a

14

character you don't like."

"No, I don't think so. I did read something like that's going to be against the rules. Let me see. Page 3. Yep, I am right. Plus I don't think we are going to know who the other people are in the character costumes until the ball."

The doorbell rang. Both Daphne and Darica looked at the clock on the den wall. It was almost 11 PM.

"I have a gun. It's in my nightstand in my bedroom," said Daphne. She crept towards the front door.

"You have a gun?" Darica asked. Her tone was surprised, but she did not hesitate to slip down the hall towards Daphne's bedroom door.

"I'm a single woman living alone in the big city," said Daphne automatically.

"I'd hardly call Sand Waves a big city environment. Too suburban."

"Well, I used to live in Houston. I learned defensive tactics there. Oh, I left my office window shade up. Whoever it is, they can see in my office. So there's no pretending that there's nobody home. Get the gun. I don't have visitors this time of night."

"All right, but I do not know how to use it," said Darica.

"Just don't hold it by the barrel. It's loaded," Daphne said.

She hugged the wall between her foyer and her office in such a way as to peek through the window and see who was on the porch.

Darica had the gun and was holding it gingerly in front of her and coming back down the hallway when Daphne said, "Darica, would you believe it's one of those Lady in Disguise women? She's flitting about my front porch like she's a nervous wreck."

"Don't let her in," said Darica, retreating back down the hall and switching off the bedroom light. "And for heaven's sakes, don't buy anything."

"I'll just tell her I'm not interested," said Daphne. She went to her front door and called through it without opening it. It was a solid wood door with an oval stained glass window. She had to yell to make herself heard.

"NO, THANK YOU!"

"Please," a shrill young voice called back. "I haven't met my quota of calls for the week and all I need is your signature on an acknowledgment that I came by and tried to sell you something."

Daphne cracked open her front door without unlatching the chain, which kept it from opening more than an inch. She looked into the face of a very young girl framed by the familiar gray cloak with red trim.

The dusky yellow of her porch light made the girl's skin look blotchy and the overall effect was that of a Halloween costume.

The girl poked a paper through the opening. "Please, can I come in?" she whispered. "It's my first week. And I was not able to make all the calls they wanted. If I don't get at least one more signature before 8 o'clock in the morning, I'll be fired."

Daphne took the paper and read over it quickly. It was indeed a simple acknowledgment that a Lady in Disguise had come by and attempted to sell her hair care products. She quickly scratched her signature and handed it back through the open space.

The trembling gloved hand took it reluctantly.

Daphne looked at the girl and felt a wave of pity. It was a cold February night.

"Come on in. Quietly, hubby is asleep already," said Daphne, lowering her voice so Darica wouldn't hear.

The girl came in. She looked around as if confused.

"I'll buy that hairbrush you have there in your basket. How much?" Daphne asked.

"Four fifty," said the girl.

Four dollars and fifty cents for a hairbrush! No wonder she hasn't sold anything, thought Daphne.

Daphne fished in her pocket. "Here's a five. Don't worry about the change."

"Thank you," said the young girl, still glancing around. She bent over the small marble section of the hall tree and began to write.

"Here use this book," said Daphne, grabbing a book from a nearby bookshelf. Daphne feared the girl would damage the white marble or somehow get ink on it.

The girl slipped the book under the paper and used it to cushion her pen marks.

"Here's your receipt and some advertisements. You saved my life, what? I really need this job."

Daphne took the brush from the girl and tossed it on the hall tree, without taking her eyes off the vendor.

Without another word, the girl turned and quickly made her way out and down Daphne's short sidewalk that right-angled into her driveway, appearing to almost float as she went down the driveway to her vehicle which was parked at the curb.

"She's gone," Daphne called to Darica, as she relocked her door. "You can put the gun back."

Darica came back into the den, shaking a little.

"You really are scared of guns, aren't you? You'd never know you were raised in Texas. How were we reared in the same house, with the same parents and the same brother and turn out so different?"

"You didn't buy anything?" Darica ignored her sister's reference to their childhood setting.

"No, of course not," Daphne lied.

"Did she leave anything?"

"No, she was just trying to sell me some products," Daphne fibbed again.

How cheap, thought Daphne, *not even a sample*. She recalled when the last cosmetic saleswoman came by, she had left several freebies and Daphne had not even bought anything from her.

"You know, it's really late. Could I spend the night?" Darica asked, with some timidity.

"Of course," said Daphne, surprised by the request.

"I had a friend drop me off, anyway. So I don't have a car here."

"Oh, who?"

"Actually not a friend. Miranda Watson. Also works at the paper sometimes on a quasi-freelance basis. A colleague. I don't really know her. She comes from a really rich set of parents who she still lives with. And I don't want to call her this time of night and I'm not comfortable getting a cab back to the apartment this late at night."

"Still lives with her parents?" Daphne's eyebrows shot up skeptically.

"Yes, but they live in a mansion, so she says she completely has her own space. They are in the upper class for sure. A compound with stables behind the gates and all that."

"I guess that's different. Maybe," said Daphne, thinking of the small house where she and Darica spent most of their formative years.

It was a 1400 square feet house in a small incorporated section of the greater Houston area called Katy. Their parents still lived there.

"I didn't pay any attention that you didn't have a car in my driveway. I guess I figured you just transported in like on the TV show. Or your car was in the blind spot."

"I know it was a shock for me to show up here after all this time. It was a spur of the moment impulse."

"It was a nice impulse," said Daphne. "And to get a cab in Sand Waves this time a night, you would have to call a company in Houston and that would cost a fortune. I could take you home though. But I'll be happy to have you stay."

"I would really like to stay. I haven't slept well recently. Alone in a new place, I guess," said Darica seriously. "Got any good books I can borrow to fall asleep by? I know you don't read much fiction but I sure need something."

"Okay, I'll see what I can find."

"How about this one?"

Stepping onto the foyer, Darica picked up the book from the hall tree.

"Yes! That will really interest you," said Daphne. "I'll put it in the guest room for you."

"That would be wonderful. I do appreciate it."

"Then let's have a cup of hot cocoa. You make it while I get the guest room ready for you. I'm excited you're working here, even if it's temporary. And I'm excited you're going to be at the masquerade ball with me. And we're both going to be in costumes! I can't think of anything more exciting!"

"And remember I'm just going to be going as a servant, while you're planning to be Marie Antoinette," said Darica.

"How I hope so," said Daphne happily, taking the book from Darica and going into the bedroom she kept for guests. It was tucked in the middle of the north side of her house, between a third bedroom used for storage and the attached garage.

She put the book on the nightstand.

This was the first time her guest room had been utilized and it was a good feeling that her decorative efforts were not in vain. As she turned down the bedspread and sniffed the sheets to make sure they did not smell too musty for her sister, she spoke softly aloud to herself. "Marie Antoinette would be a dream come true."

Chapter 2

The Lady in Disguise drove away from Daphne's house feeling relieved. She pushed the cloak off her shoulders and pulled the hood from her forehead. Blonde hair fell on damp cheeks. She had almost reached the main road that led to Houston when she saw a familiar car parked on the shoulder.

She could not go that way.

She tried to recall if there was another way out of Sand Waves. Instead she remembered there was not. She turned her car onto the nearest side street.

It led back into the depths of the colony.

She felt a curious lack of panic even as she became aware the familiar automobile was following her. She eased off the special boots that had given her enough height to be hired by the Lady in Disguise Corporation.

She had sneakers under her seat. She flexed her toes as she forced them into the tennis shoes without taking her hands off the wheel.

A plan was forming.

She drove casually towards the gates of Sand Waves as if she were a resident of the fenced-in enclave, having been out for a late night adventure and was now going home.

At the edge of the woods that bordered the gates on the west side, she veered off onto a small trail, seemingly not designed for car travel.

The design of the trail was deceptive. Tree branches reaching across as if clasping hands in a greeting overhead, along with judiciously placed shrubbery and bushes, made the trail seemed much narrower than it really was.

The Lady in Disguise drove her small car down the trail slightly faster than she would have normally and pulled it into a clearing, coming to an abrupt stop before a small log cabin style building that suddenly loomed from out of nowhere.

The cabin was dark. As her sneakers hit the ground and she pulled herself out of the compact car, she left her headlights on so her way to the door of the cabin would be lit. She pulled out her key.

The larger car that had been following her had just reached the stopping point when she inserted the key into the lock.

Its occupant was much quicker to exit from her vehicle. But she, also in the same costume, stumbled and fell, for she needed six-inch heels to qualify for the part she played.

"Lady," called out the woman on the ground. "You see there is no one here but us. No one to hear the password. And you haven't the authority to have a key."

The Lady at the door ignored her and continued to strive to get the lock to work.

The other woman struggled to her feet. "At least give the password?"

"Why were you following me?"

"Your actions have been somewhat suspicious and there have been some reports against you."

She had just gotten the door open when her fellow Lady in Disguise reached her. The other woman was breathless and still tottering on her heels.

The shorter Lady stopped in the doorway and looked up.

"At least give the password before you enter the building," said the stalker.

"Oh, you have got it bad, what? There's no one here but us two. We've known each other for years and no reason to doubt one another's loyalty. Yet you want the password?"

The other woman took hold of the shorter female by the shoulders. They both tensed and adrenaline surged.

"All right. The password is Bratonn."

The taller woman stepped back. Fear shot through her face. But she did not let go. Her long arms allowed her to make the movement while still clutching the other's shoulders.

"It's been changed," she said in a hoarse whisper. "You would know that if you were still trusted. You have betrayed us! I have to report you."

The shorter Lady clutched the knife she held beneath her cloak and drew a sharp breath.

21

"Can we go inside and discuss it?" she managed to ask evenly.

"We're going inside and I'm going to phone the headmistress. I'm not going to let go of you. You're not going to get away."

With those words, the taller woman pushed the shorter Lady through the doorway and drew a gun from her cloak in a singular motion.

"You cannot shoot me," said the accused, keeping her arms low as she allowed herself to be maneuvered inside the building. "I have high clearance from the headmistress. There has to be a trial first."

Protecting the headmistress was uppermost in both Ladies' minds and they both believed their subsequent actions were in her best interest.

"I know that," said the woman with the gun, her hood falling, sending blonde hair to her shoulders. "But don't try anything or I will shoot."

And the defendant saw the fanaticism in the eyes of her accuser and did not doubt her.

The two women walked past rows of chairs facing a podium. The shorter Lady slightly in front, with her enemy behind.

"You know the phone is just to the left of the podium," the disadvantaged Lady said in a calm voice. "Call the headmistress. She'll tell you my errand tonight was legitimate."

"You trailed a newcomer to a commoner's house, knocked on their door and handed them papers. You have a lot of explaining to do to the headmistress unless you were acting on her orders."

"I was acting on her secret orders," Daphne's recent visitor replied calmly, tightening her grip on the knife.

"Then you won't mind the phone call. I'll stay behind the podium while you dial the number and then hand me the receiver. Carefully."

Gripping the knife to the point of pain, she looked down at the black phone that sat by the imposing structure.

"Okay," she said.

With her left arm, the shorter girl reached for the receiver as her right arm raised the dagger from beneath the folds of the cloak. She whirled around and plunged at the taller woman at the same time as the gun in the latter's hand went off.

After a short silence there was a short moan, then silence again.

The survivor of this encounter staggered only a moment before her equilibrium returned. Taking the time necessary to make sure her adversary was dead, she turned quickly to a computer that took up the larger portion of a desk in a small offset room behind the staged area.

She quickly found its boot disk nearby, slipped it into the slot and turned the computer on.

It whirred and made a lightly grinding sound as it read the disk. It was a fairly new 1982 Franklin Ace, equipped with DOS, designed to do word processing or simple calculations. As soon as it was through reading its boot disk, green flashed on the screen.

Its operator ejected the boot disk and inserted one labeled 'ball'.

In a few seconds the listings of eighteenth century characters, matched with carefully selected twentieth century applicants, appeared on the small TV-like screen in bright green on a dark grayish background.

The surviving Lady in Disguise removed her gloves so as to better type in alterations in the spreadsheet cells. She studied the names of the famous women on the list and those chosen to portray them. She only wanted one changed but to cover better she tampered with several. Finishing quickly, she reviewed the revisions.

The most dangerous female character, Marie Antoinette, now had a new selection beside it.

She took a deep breath, hoping this action would be the key to the success of her plan.

She looked at the male names. The danger there was just as great if the wrong name was assigned to the wrong historical figure. She hesitated. Next time she would tamper with them. If there was a next time. If not, let someone else assume the risk.

She looked at the body on the floor.

She had risked enough already. This was real trouble and she was running out of time.

She carefully wiped the computer keyboard clean with a tissue.

She did not forget to save the file and alert the computer that she

23

was about to shut it down. It whirred, grinding a little more, then gave her permission to turn it off.

She flipped the switch and the little screen went dark. She made sure both disks were returned to the places she had found them and rose to go.

A few minutes later it was the larger car that carefully turned around and made its way slowly back down the slender trail onto the main road.

Chapter 3

"I simply must be Marie Antoinette. I don't care how much money has changed hands. I will get my husband to bribe them, too. It's the dream costume of a lifetime. And I will have it." Natalie Wakefield stood in her dressing room staring in the mirror as her maid, Doris, rehung the discarded dress.

"I cannot wear that one," Natalie said. "I need another dress."

"Yes, Mrs. Wakefield. Another color perhaps?"

"No. It must be the same color, please. I have a certain look I want to achieve at this dinner party tonight."

As Doris searched for another suitable dress, Natalie ran her hands over her abdomen and hips as she gazed in the mirror. She thought of how hard she had worked to be where she was today. Years of starving and exercising, having to repeat that procedure over and over again. Now at last she felt secure.

She realized her position was still precarious in many ways. The wrong move would bring ruination. There were instances when she almost did not mind. Then she would remember the danger. She sensed danger this morning.

"Are you free for the rest of the afternoon before the party?" Doris asked. "It seems to be that you need to get some rest before guests arrive. A nap might be good for you."

"Now, I won't have time for a nap, Doris." Natalie held up the third dress. It was a strapless slim blue gown composed of pale sequins. Not the bright glittery type but those that gave off just a hint of shimmer, creating a subdued affect. "I think this is going to be the right gown for tonight. I know it fits. Just lay it across the bed. Thanks so much."

"I'm sure the caterers have everything in hand for tonight."

"They're dropping everything off and going home early," Natalie confirmed.

"Will you need me?" Doris sounded hopeful. A little overtime was always handy.

"There will be six healthy adults there. We can serve ourselves buffet style."

"Yes, ma'am. If you don't need me."

"Yes, Doris, I will need you. See to breakfast and lunch. Then take some extra time this afternoon to compensate. Then come back."

"You can do without me this afternoon then?"

"Mother hen. Doris, you know the routine. I will be seeing my Lady in Disguise representative this afternoon. Anything special you want for your hair?"

Natalie walked over to Doris and stood close. They were about the same height. Doris was maybe a couple inches taller, depending on shoes and hairstyle.

Natalie reached up and fingered Doris' stringy curly hair.

"Those products are so expensive," Doris began.

"My treat, Doris. I think you could use a mousse and probably some conditioner for dry hair. Any special scent that you like?"

"Lavender maybe. Jasmine if they have it."

"Oh, they have everything we need. Jasmine it is."

"I don't deserve your consideration and kindness, Madame."

"Now remember- no Madame. I'm just plain Mrs. Wakefield. And you deserve a great deal of my consideration, Doris. I depend on you. I especially depend on your discretion."

Doris smiled. "Have you been officially informed anything about your character?"

"Um, no," Natalie said. "But you know I have connections, Doris. I'm going to get the character I want. Marie Antoinette."

"No one would make a better French queen than you."

"I hear my friend, Grace York, wants that character."

"From what I read in the newspapers, Martha Washington would be more suitable for her."

"Yes, she does intend to be First Lady." Natalie reflected for a moment on the recent ceremony that reunited Edward York and his ex-wife in remarriage. She had been a guest. "That is the best she can hope for. This is America. She wore quite a tiara at her recent retaking of her vows with King Edward."

"Is that really what they call him?"

"No, just those of us that are familiar with him. He's got some quality, something about him, that causes otherwise reasonable people to just revere him. It's almost as if he bewitches them. He actually does almost nothing. Yet, everyone is seeing his ascendancy as inevitable. Like he was born to power."

"Wasn't he from the old rich families from the South?" Doris tried to recall the recent newspaper coverage of Edward York. She read all the stories about the people she had occasion to interact with as a servant in the Wakefield home. But she did not commit them to memory.

"Certainly. But why should that make a difference? Why does that make him heir apparent? My husband came up through the oil fields to his position. That shows more diligence than Edward York ever had. What has he done? Served a tour in the Air Force twenty years ago. Served in the state senate in South Carolina. Move to Texas and become a judge. So what?"

"They say he has the charisma. Like President Kennedy and President Reagan."

"Ha. Charisma. What is that? Good looks and charm? How does that qualify a man to be President? Is his silver hair somehow indicative he should wear a crown? No more than Grace York's golden blonde hair qualifies her to be Marie Antoinette. Or First Lady."

Grace York was indeed a golden blonde with symmetrical height and sculptured angled features combined in such a way as to render her beautiful by all standards. Natalie Wakefield's beauty was darker and more exotic. She was only 4 feet, 10 inches, petite but curvy.

Doris had seen them side by side at many formal occasions. She much preferred her employer.

"You would make a much better Marie Antoinette than Mrs. York," she told Natalie.

"If I don't get that character, well, I must, that is all there is to it."

"I do hope so, Mrs. Wakefield. You are so beautiful. Those big brown eyes and perfectly designed face. So slim and petite. You could play any part and do it proud. You will be the belle of the ball no matter what character you get."

Natalie Wakefield surveyed herself in the mirror once more. She so agreed with her maid's assessment, she did not even think to thank her employee for the compliment.

As she again ran her hands across her body, her face reflected the same sentiment towards her form that her maid had expressed. But Natalie's reflections went further than her exquisite figure or beautiful facial features.

I am going to be more than the belle of the ball, she thought. *I am going to be queen.*

Chapter 4

"And will you bring an escort?"

Daphne and Darica were still discussing the masquerade ball that morning at breakfast.

"Don't be coy. I only bought one ticket." Daphne was thumbing through the brochure. "That cost enough."

"What about that cop you mentioned that you dated? Are you going to buy him a ticket? I imagine he's like me. He cannot afford one."

"Oh, he's going to be there. Did you read that book I gave you last night?"

"Really? Your police lieutenant friend is coming?"

"In his professional capacity. Like you."

"That explains it. He'll be in uniform, I suppose? The perfect escort for you."

"He'll be at work but I think he's going to be wearing a costume. Just a simple one. They want everybody there to be in costume. What are you going to do about one?"

"The paper is providing a generic time period costume. I'm pretty sure I'll be dressed as a peasant, servant or something. Nobody will complain. They want me there."

"They want my police officer friend there, too. The book I lent you is actually about his great-grandfather. Or, at least, he is a character in it. It's fiction, I know. But there is some basis for fact, he told me."

"That's very interesting. I read some of it until I fell asleep. Mom and Dad are dying to know more about him. And Scott. Has Daphne finally found someone at last? That is what we are all wondering. You know, I don't know why people gossip that I am a lesbian. After all, I am divorced. It's you they should suspect."

"Oh, believe me they do. The only way not to be suspected of being a lesbian, if you are a single woman these days, is to have a baby," Daphne complained.

"Well, unless you land your cop, you might as well get used to it. Ever since that sex book came out last year, you cannot be single

29

and childless without people saying that. Especially other women that are. I had a female attorney I was interviewing insinuate that my failed marriage was just a subterfuge and deep down I really wanted HER. After having just met me 15 minutes before."

"At least in your job no one would care. It can't cost you any money," Daphne said.

"Not much. Also, it did get the interview to, let's say, produce more substance," Darica said.

"When my clients direct their inclinations that way, you know what I have to do? I have to invent a live-in boyfriend."

"I thought you had an engagement ring you wore to appointments with single men."

"Oh, it's not the single men with their minds in the sexual gutter. Usually middle aged women and the married men. Now you remember our agreement. We forget about each other's professions. You don't try to take advantage of me. I don't try to take advantage of you."

"That's going to be a little bit more difficult now that I've been transferred to Sand Waves."

"I know. I thought about that. We are going to have to establish some ground rules. Pretending we don't know each other at all is not going to work."

"I agree. But I hope you are wrong. I'm in the position that if my superior knows that I have a relative with access to the type of people you have access to, I'm going to be expected to sacrifice my relationship with you for my job."

"You're kidding!"

"No, I am not. It's always just been a job to me. I like it. I do the best I can. But it has become a religion for some of these people now. They think journalism is the Holy Grail and we are to forsake our family and our friends to follow the light. The light of investigative journalism that will lead us to ferret out corruption. As if it needs ferreting out. It's oozing at the seams all over the place."

"Really? It's like that?"

"Yes. And nobody cares anymore."

"Then, what do we do?" Daphne asked.

"We're going to have to go on as before. As long as I was in Dallas, we only saw each other on family occasions. I never spoke of you at my job even when I found out one of your clients was related to Amelia Mattworks. You don't know what a sacrifice that was!"

"You wouldn't have known that if you hadn't seen me in a newspaper photograph of the funeral. That particular client is in Europe anyway right now. Even if she wasn't, you could not get to her through me."

"I know. I don't expect you to tell me anything about your clients. I respect your profession and your obligation to your clients. But I can guarantee you, my editor does not. And neither do any of the other reporters. If my editor knew that I knew somebody that had interacted with Congressman Brown or Amelia Mattworks when they was making headlines and I didn't get something out of it, I would be fired."

"That's horrible. I do not understand why you want to work for such a place. You don't hardly make any money. Mom said you make less than $8.00 an hour."

"And it's not the place. It's the profession. With never any overtime pay, either, no matter how many hours I really work."

"I can get you on at any insurance company-"

"Look, Daphne. I'm nothing like you. I'm not a salesperson. I'm a writer. It's impossible to get published unless you know someone. I can't make enough as a freelancer. I have to make a living somehow. It's all I know how to do. If I weren't doing this, I would be doing little boring journals for corporations and booklets with instructions on how to use chainsaws and the like. Or working at K-mart. It's all I've got. So in order for me to protect my job, I have to pretend that I don't know you and you don't know me. And we can't let anybody know that we're sisters."

"Nobody around here knows anything about me," said Daphne. "I don't bother anybody except maybe my clients. Even when I go to church, I don't associate with anybody. But I have sort of gotten to know a few people in the last year, by accident."

"Despite your best efforts, you mean. You actually know people that have not bought insurance from you? I'm amazed."

31

"Yes, despite my best efforts. On account of being trapped in that flood. And then the Mattworks affair. But I still sold some policies and also kept my secrets."

"You told no one about me? Not even the cop?" Darica asked.

"Especially not the cop. I'm just getting him to trust me. If he knew I had a sister that was a newspaper reporter, I don't know how he would react."

"You know, in the course of my working here, I'm bound to run into him."

"It's a good thing we don't look anything alike," said Daphne.

"And we have different last names. At least something good came out of my lousy marriage."

The conversation paused and Daphne remembered the joy at her sister's wedding and the photos so hastily hidden away at the news of the breakup.

Darica had decreed their destruction.

Their parents had been unable to comply. At their bidding, Daphne had secretly taken custody of the wedding album. She had been happy to accommodate. She had loved the bright photos of the simple wedding at their parents' church with the reception outdoors at the house where the sisters had grown up.

Memories of the pictures of all the family together flooded.

Darica in her long-sleeved white gown with satin cuffs and a V-neck, making her look even taller, next to her short twin in green chiffon with a large brim hat. Their mother in a blue satin formal. Scott and their father in tuxedos, along with the new member of the family, the groom with the humorous name- Dan Daniels.

Everyone laughing, almost ten years younger than today.

Years before career demands, strife between siblings, and then a divorce had disrupted the family harmony.

Not infrequently, Daphne pulled out those pictures and looked at them all over again. But right now they were safely hidden in the attic, popping up only in her mind.

"What's this cop going to think when he finds out you have a twin sister?" Darica interrupted Daphne's train of thought.

"We're not twins," said Daphne, standing up at just over 5 feet tall, her strapless sundress reaching well below her knees. Her sister's long legs, covered in blue jeans that showed her anklebones above 4 inch heels, moved also. She jumped up as well, demonstrating her full 5 feet 10 inch height, not including the heels.

"I can prove it in a court of law," Darica said.

"Ha. No judge would take a look at us and believe it. He would think you falsified the birth certificates. We are not twins, just sisters that happened to be born on the same day. We saved our mother from going through an extra pregnancy." Feeling she had proven her point by the mock confrontation, Daphne flopped back down on the couch.

"So we did."

"And I think you're living in the same apartment complex with him. You must be," Daphne said worriedly.

There was only one apartment complex in Sand Waves. Apartment dwellers were less than welcome. Darica had gotten a one bedroom efficiency only because her company kept it rented on standby for visiting journalists. She was having to pick up the rent. But it was less than retail due to the long term agreement with her newspaper chain.

"I haven't seen any patrol cars in the apartment complex parking lot." Darica did not sit back down but moved into the kitchen.

"Read the fine print on your lease. He's not allowed to take it there. Take those heels off in the kitchen. You'll make punctures in my vinyl flooring."

"Oh, sorry." Darica removed her shoes and went barefoot to the refrigerator. "Why not? A police car is usually considered an asset in the neighborhoods where I've been living in Dallas."

"This is Sand Waves. We have to pretend there's no need for police, firemen, garbage trucks, anything like that…"

"Oh yes. I forgot. Look, I've already applied for a transfer to Houston, or San Antonio, or anywhere in any big city in Texas. I'm sorry Dallas got too hot for me, but I got involved in some, well, some things that we couldn't even print, at least, not yet and I had to transfer for my own safety and the safety of the office and this was the only place that had an opening in the newspaper chain. At least, they took care of me that way."

"Well, I guess no more meeting here at my house. I'm glad you got to see it once, at least."

"No, best not. I'm glad I got to see it, too. It is beautiful. What about your phones?" Darica came back into the den with a Coke.

"What about them? Stay in the dinette with that Coke. Don't you see this carpet is white? How do you think I keep it looking like this?"

"Okay." Darica signed in frustration and sat down at the dinette table. "Your phones. We need to talk about them."

"So I haven't purchased any of those new designer phones. The phone company furnished these when I bought the house. I've been looking at them but I just haven't gotten around to them. I know the old square phones provided by Southwestern Bell are tacky looking but they work great."

"No. I don't care what they look like."

"Then what are you asking?"

"Tapped, you think?"

"Tapped? My God, what the hell do you mean?"

"Probably not, but we need to play it safe. Pay phones. We will use them for any further contact."

"Pay phones? How are we going to call each other through pay phones?"

"Listen, I have a car phone provided by the newspaper. It's not as private as I would like, but I have an idea who's listening, if anybody, and it is not anybody who cares what we do or say. I'll give you the number. You'll be on a very short list that has it. When you call me on the car phone, don't say anything other than tell me where and when you want to meet me."

"Is this how you keep up with all your friends and family?"

Darica finished her drink and came back in the den. Daphne motioned for her to sit on the sofa.

"Only when necessary," Darica said.

"You have direct contact with Scott? Or just through Mom and Dad?" Daphne asked.

"I talk to him occasionally. When I can afford a long-distance call. Sometimes he even calls me."

"Hmm, it's just like the skewed thinking of most men. Our

brother has no problem with you living alone because you are divorced. But he disapproves of my living alone and buying my own house as a single woman."

"It's just that he doesn't see why you can't do your job and live in Katy with Mom and Dad. I had to leave town to get my job. I think he's angry because he suspects Mom and Dad helped buy this house for you. Cosigned your loan."

"Well, that's just great. Where did he get that idea?"

Daphne and Darica were on the same couch but both hugging the opposite arm rests, as far apart as they could get and still be on the same piece of furniture.

"He's not stupid. He knows what houses cost. Most single women could never get a loan to buy a house like this. Most single women don't make enough money to live in a place like Sand Waves."

"Oh, that's just great," said Daphne again. "If I let Scott know I make enough money to easily afford a place like this, his male ego is going to be wounded and he is going to be angry and not have anything to do with me. Otherwise if I let him think I make as little money as he does, he thinks Mom and Dad, or even worse probably some married man, supports me. And therefore, he has nothing to do with me. You don't know how tired I am of that kind of crap. To hell with him."

"Do you really make that kind of money selling life insurance?"

Without a word Daphne got up and went over to her desk and returned with a slip of paper in her hand.

"My paycheck stub, from last month, and it is typical." She handed the green slip of paper to her sister and sat back on her end of the couch. "What I mean is there was no extra large commission from one single sale."

"My God!" Darica's eyes popped open.

"Now, don't multiply that by 12. Some months are slower and I usually take half of November and most all of December off. Sometimes I take a little time off during the summer, too. Business tends to be a little slow in August."

"My God!" Darica gazed at the paycheck stub. It represented more than five times her take-home pay.

35

"And you're right. When I applied for a mortgage on this house I was turned down in spite of making that kind of money. Because I was on commission, they told me my income was too unstable. Yet two insurance agents out of my general office, who I happen to know don't do as well as I do, both got loans to buy a house just about the same time I applied. They were on commission, too. But, of course, they were men."

"So what did you do? Private financing? That's kind of risky. They can sell the loan out from under you."

"I knew about that risk. I looked into it. I didn't go that route. I paid cash."

"What?" Darica turned white.

"I paid cash. I wanted this house. I had been saving since I went to work during high school. And I worked through college. And of course, I saved a lot more when I got into life insurance. The Powers-That-Be in Sand Waves don't approve of single women buying houses. Period. They would like to restrict us to the condos. Scared we won't keep up our yards. I would have still been fighting to get this house. I had the money and then some, so I just paid cash. They couldn't refuse cash. It's a long story and I'm telling it to you in a nutshell."

"Sounds like a good feature," said Darica hesitantly.

"No. No way."

"Any other single women that you know of that got the same treatment?" Darica's voice strengthened at the idea of a new story.

"No. I'm sure there are other single women who own homes here. But they're going to be real estate agents, undoubtedly. You're not going to get anything out of them. They're the Sand Waves minions."

"Rules or no rules, would you let me know if you did find a single woman homeowner willing to talk about discrimination?"

"No, absolutely not. I'm sticking to the rules and you had better stick to them as well. I don't have any contact with Scott. I can do without you."

"Okay. I get the message. Let's not argue. Hopefully, I'm not going to be here that much longer anyway. If there's enough hard news in the area while I'm here, I'm not going to need to dig up any dirt. We don't need an estrangement between us. Consider Mom and Dad," said Darica.

Daphne was somewhat mollified by her sister's conciliatory tone.

"At least we are not as bad as the sisters in that book," she commented.

"Can I borrow that book? I didn't finish it."

"I would let you. But it's not really mine. It's out of print and that's the only copy he has."

"I understand. Well, if things work out, you might have access to it all the time. I'll be happy for you."

"Then, can we stop competing? Can we be sisters and friends for just a minute?" Daphne asked.

"Sure," said Darica. She was suddenly touched by the poignancy in her sibling's tone. "I can't compete with you anyway. What do you want to talk about?"

"I'd like to tell you a little bit about him." Daphne bit her lip. "I don't have anyone else to talk to. He's so special…"

"Of course." Darica moved over to the center of the couch and put her arm around Daphne, dwarfing her a little bit, and tried not to think about her ex-husband, as her sister talked about her police officer boyfriend.

Chapter 5

Lieutenant Sinclair Plate was having stuffed shrimp for lunch. There were not many other people eating at the Toy Museum Restaurant. It was quite expensive and not the place he normally ate.

Today was different.

Lieutenant Plate liked the looks of a woman seated two tables away from him, just over the invisible line that marked the beginning of the smoking section.

He discerned she was a lady with class and just a dash of daring. She was attired in a conservatively styled business suit accompanied by a frill-less blouse telling him that she had taste and that she was a professional at whatever she did.

Yet the blazer and matching skirt were an unconventional blood red, the flamboyant color contrasting with the stark design. She had short dark brown hair.

And she had snappish dark brown eyes that rested on him for a moment with aloofness, then panned down to the food she was nibbling at.

Plate stabbed a stuffed shrimp with his fork and ate as he continued observing. When she stood up, he noticed she was tall and wore high-heeled shoes. She had confidence in her height and did not try to minimize it. She walked well with poise and grace and she was-

It occurred to Plate that she was leaving.

Plate dropped his fork and jumped up from the table.

"Pardon me, ma'am," he said.

The lady in red turned, eyebrows raised.

Plate walked right up to her. "Pardon me, ma'am," he said again. Then he had to pause. He did not know what he wanted to say next.

"Yes?" Her expressive eyes surveyed him with suspicion but they were not completely void of amusement.

"Umm- I'm a police officer, ma'am," he said. He reached inside his coat, pulled out his badge, and handed it to her. "My name is Lieutenant Plate."

Her long slender fingers examined the badge delicately as she turned it over in her hands. She gave it back to him with a small smile.

"What can I do for you, Lieutenant? Have I done something illegal? Surely not."

"Oh. No, ma'am," he said. Plate had to think quickly. And he did. "The fact is we're taking a survey in the Sand Waves Police Department in order to accumulate data which will be helpful in establishing just exactly what the attitude of the general public is towards law enforcement officers here."

"And what role do you play in all of this, Lieutenant?"

"Oh, I'm in charge of the survey. It's being taken under my supervision. Would you be so kind as to help me out?"

"Yes, well, if you'll give me a survey sheet, I'll be happy to fill it out and mail it back to you. I actually don't live here. I'm visiting friends. So you might not want my opinions."

"Survey sheet? No, I mean, I've used them all up this morning. I do want your opinion. Let me just ask you a few questions. I know them all by heart."

"But I don't have much more time left for my lunch break."

"If you will only allow me to escort you to your car. The questions are very short."

The lady in red cocked her head to one side. "All right, Lieutenant. Come along."

Plate was following the lady in red out the restaurant door when he felt a tap on his shoulder. He spun around. A waitress was behind him.

"You neglected to pay your bill, sir," she said, with unquestionable firmness.

The lady in red smiled broadly and coughed a little bit. "I'll wait for you outside the door," she said.

Plate tossed a $20 bill on his table to take care of his obligation.

"Now," said Plate, after he had joined his companion outside. "Just a few basic questions. Your name?"

"Serena Towers."

"Occupation."

"I'm a freelance journalist."

"Are you married?'

"Are you going to write any of this down, Lieutenant?"

"Oh, no need to." Plate pointed to his head. "Great memory."

"I see."

"Well?"

"Well, what?"

"Are you married?" Plate straightened his tie.

"No, I am not."

"Good- um I mean- exactly how do you feel about law enforcement officers? In general, I mean." Plate straightened his collar also.

Serena Towers put her hand to her cheek and cast her eyes downward as though she were deep in thought.

"I have great respect for them," she said seriously. "And I'm sure most of them are fine individuals."

Plate scuffed his feet. "That's wonderful," he said, with all the sincerity he could summon at the moment.

Serena Towers pointed to an automobile. "That's my car over there. I'm afraid I'm going to have to go. My lunchtime has just run out. I have an appointment this afternoon. I don't want to be late."

"Of course not. Thank you so much for the interview," said Plate.

"I'm very much interested in the results of your survey," she said, as she got in her car. "Have you any agreement with any journalist for it to be in the papers or on the news?"

"No, no. It's just an interdepartmental thing."

She rolled out her window and he leaned against the frame of the car. She smiled mischievously at him.

"Are you married, Lieutenant Plate?"

"No!" He jumped back. "No, ma'am!"

"As long as I'm staying in Sand Waves I will be having lunch here every day about this time, every weekday that is," she said. She backed her car out of the parking space, window still down. "Hope your survey works out. I'd be interested in doing a story on it."

She grinned at him and drove off. Plate grinned back and he kept grinning at her car until it disappeared.

Chapter 6

"She slipped out of a small building at the edge of the greenbelt. She got into her car which was parked on the grounds behind some shrubbery. She drove a short distance and put something in Edward York's mailbox. Then she drove as if she was leaving the gated area, stopped at the gates as if she was about to put the code in to open it. Then she quickly veered the car off into the woods. I waited for her to get out of the car and walk back on the road, which as far as I could see, was her only possible choice."

"So then?" Chief Brecken looked at his second-in-command with anticipation.

"Then I realized I waited too long and rushed to the car to try to find her. She was nowhere to be found, that's when I realized she must've known she was being watched. I then rushed back to the mailbox in case she had deposited some type of incendiary device."

"Plate, you are not supposed to do things like that. Suppose it had been a bomb?"

"The mailbox was empty," said Plate, ignoring his superior's critical comment.

"So someone else picked up whatever she left while you were following her to gates?"

"Obviously. And, stupidly, I then rushed back to the car, thinking she would be emerging from the woods by now, knowing she had fooled me. But the car was gone. So then I rushed back to the mailbox again. And there was a woman walking down the road in the same costume, obviously hoping to convince me it was the same person. But I'm sure it was not."

"How sure?"

"Well, pretty sure. It was dark. There was something about the posture of the second one, too subtle to be a deliberate differentiation. The plain truth is- I'm not even sure these were women. They were both very tall, slender, and well built. Wearing cloaks with hoods, I could see some curls around the edge of the hood, I never got a good look at either one of them's face. I would almost swear they had masks on."

"Masks? What kind of masks?"

"Not costume type masks, but full facial masks."

"Oh, this is got to have something to do with that upcoming masquerade ball. It must be some type of a game or joke."

"Have the feds briefed you on the ball yet?" Plate asked.

"Yes, their primary concern is Forrest Pointpar. He has had death threats since he announced he would be running against Congressman Brown in the primary."

"What about Edward York?"

"He is refusing federal protection, as usual. County will have to deal with him."

"Why not us?"

"He has requested we function only as 'local police should'. And that's a quote."

"Oh."

"Probably remembers you were the man in Grace York's life during the time they were separated."

"They were actually divorced, not just separated. And there was no prospect they would ever remarry, I was told then."

"Let's try to keep your personal life out of it all- this time. You are not romancing any of these Ladies in Disguises are you?"

"Not to my knowledge. They are in disguise, you know. They wear masks."

"The regular saleswomen don't wear masks, do they?

"They sometimes do, but not like I saw last night. Those women wear masks over their eyes, with the top edges pointed outwards like those cat eye eyeglasses my mother used to wear back in the 1960s."

"I still say what you witnessed behind the gates last night is some kind of joke."

"If it is a joke, we still need to find out who's behind it and what's going on," said Plate. "We need to because somebody's going to get hurt. Half the people behind the gates have armed security guards and the other half are armed themselves. Anybody wandering around at night for any reason at all is putting themselves in danger even if they don't enter anybody's yard or touch anybody's mailbox. And if it's just some scheme coordinated with the masquerade, why was there nothing in the mailbox when I went back?"

"Who called you in on this?" Chief Brecken asked.

"A man named Wakefield. Hasn't lived behind the gates too long. He's actually suspicious that his wife is cheating on him."

"How does this connect, pray tell?"

"He spotted a Lady in Disguise near his mailbox late at night. Then found a brochure with some handwritten words added next to one of the cream rinse products. 'Sharp delicious thrill'. Finding there is no such product, Wakefield came to the conclusion it was some kind of code."

"Code?"

"Lover's code. He claims there is no way to tell if the costumed person was a man or a woman and suspects it was his wife's paramour, leaving a message."

"Oh, for heaven sakes. This is sounding more and more like a wild goose chase. It is taking too much of your time."

"He's a powerful oil executive."

"I don't care."

"So what do you want me to do?

"Tell Wakefield he needs to hire a private detective. And, I guess, just patrol behind the gates like always. Keep an eye out. And don't tell anybody. I'll be glad when this damn masquerade party is over with."

"So will I," Plate said. "By the way I need a mockup survey about how the general public feels about police."

"What? Why?"

"Just for my own personal use," Plate grinned at his chief uncharacteristically.

The chief did not grin back.

Chapter 7

Darica could not get her colleague, Miranda, on the phone. So Daphne dropped her sister off at the newspaper office shortly before lunch.

She picked up a hamburger and went right back home. She was a little agitated at her sister.

First Darica shows up unexpected, and even more strange-spends the night.

Then after a fairly friendly sisterly time together in which Daphne had confided her feelings for her police friend, Darica had become aloof.

"Lt. Sinclair Plate. Isn't he the one that was involved with Grace York last year?" Darica had said.

"Grace York has remarried Edward York," Daphne had stated in reply.

That should have settled the issue but somehow Daphne felt Darica was judging the relationship before even meeting Plate.

After her sister had left, Daphne changed the sheets on the guest bed. She picked up Plate's book, noting Darica had used a tissue as a makeshift bookmark on page 47, indicating she had not read very far.

Taking the book back into the foyer, Daphne placed it once again on the hall tree. She wanted it there, near the front door as a reminder to give it back to Plate the next time he came by. She debated for a few seconds whether she wanted to reread it one more time before relinquishing it.

If so, she could put it away with her own books in the master bedroom, located in the back center of the house.

It had been a pretty good book. But it was too soon, just a couple of weeks since she first read it. She could always get it back from Plate again, if she wanted. And right now she was more in mind to watch television.

She left it where it was.

Daphne switched on the TV and checked all the cable channels for the type of show she was now in the mood for. Sure enough, she was in luck.

The Old American Movies Cable Channel had *The Mortal Storm* starring James Stewart and Margaret Sullivan. It was just beginning. She grabbed a candy bar and the leftover popcorn and curled up on her sofa to watch it with her cat.

She had seen the movie before but she watched it this time from a new perspective, at the same time reading carefully the rules she had already agreed to when she had purchased her ticket to the ball.

Once payment has cleared for your ticket, your name will be entered into a lottery to win a character. And your prize will be a custom-designed costume re-creating the character you have won. Costumes will be complete with custom makeup and hair styling at a specified location on the morning of the masquerade party. By entering this lottery, you are agreeing to portray the character you win and wear the costume provided for you.

The theme is the late 1700s era of the American Revolution, Constitution and French Revolution, focusing on a period of history of about 30 years.

We do realize some characters were not actually contemporaries of one another or may have just overlapped slightly. We are aiming for the spirit of the era, not a reenactment. However, each winner will be presented an opportunity to perform a short skit that involves an authentic trait of their character at the ball. Details about the skits will be completed before the date.

A set number of special characters are offered as prizes. These are- George Washington, Martha Washington, Thomas Jefferson, Patsy Jefferson, the Marquis de Lafayette, Louis XVI, Marie Antoinette, Benjamin Franklin, Deborah Franklin, John Adams, Abigail Adams, Patrick Henry, Betsy Ross, Gustavus III, Catherine the Great, George III, Queen Charlotte, Molly Pitcher, Benedict Arnold, Robespierre, Napoleon, Josephine, Empress Marie Louise.

If you win the lottery, your character will be assigned on a same-sex basis. However, we cannot consider age, height, appearance, or other physical characteristics in assignment of characters. If you have a physical characteristic that conflicts with your character every attempt will be made to reconcile the attribute via costume and makeup and hairstyle.

45

We regret we have only a limited number of characters. Time and monetary donations restrict us to the list shown above. We realize most guests will not get a character. We are asking guests who do not draw a character to dress in the formal style of the time period in the country of their choosing. If they wish to portray any other character from that time period in history they are welcome to do so, but no special costume or accessories will be distributed. Nor will there be opportunities to participate in the skits for those not winning a character.

All guests who do not draw character must provide their own costumes according to the guidelines on page 2. We are asking ALL guests that do not win a character to please not attempt to portray any of the characters listed as prizes. This would be unfair to the winners and dampen the effectiveness of the atmosphere.

Thank you,

Volunteer Ladies in Disguise Rescuers of the World.

Chapter 8

Forrest Pointpar let out a disgusted sigh when he read the contents of the notification.

This was not the character he wanted.

He wanted a certain character that would fit in with his new passion. He had recently acquired an Appaloosa stallion for pleasure riding around the green belts of Sand Waves.

Living behind the gates, Forrest was able to get a permit to tear down an old structure on his property and erect a stable for the animal.

"I fail to see how my being this character is going to work to our advantage," he said to the small group of men seated with him at one of the round tables in the Toy Museum Restaurant.

"We really don't consider any of the silly playacting to be done at the masquerade to be germane to our purpose," said one of the other men at the table. "The ball is a social event to introduce Edward York to certain powerful people. It's mainly by and for that women's group. They probably won't endorse York. But, judging by their policies in the past, they won't oppose him either."

Forrest looked at each of the five men in turn. He wondered who on earth, or at least who in the United States of America, could be any more powerful than the men who sat at the table with him.

Except maybe the current President himself, Ronald Reagan, ostensibly the leader of the free world.

This leader, sitting right before his eyes, was someone who Forrest had never in his wildest dreams believed he would meet, much less speak to. Yet there he was, behaving almost as an equal, admonishing all of them from the beginning of the meeting to just call him Richard for the conference's duration.

"First names only are to be used all around," Richard had said with an eerily familiar smile. "Just for today."

It was unreal.

The others, Forrest had anticipated meeting someday. Maybe in ten or twenty years, when he was an established lawyer and politician, just to shake hands or get an autograph. That is, if they were still in power at the time.

He had fantasized how he would someday somehow impress them with great works and deeds, serving the public, and he might actually get to have a conversation with one of them.

Instead, while he was still finishing his law degree, they had come to him.

He knew it was a combination of factors.

He was a black conservative politician, holding a minor political office in Sand Waves, running in his first real election.

His late father had been a well loved baseball player in the era just after World War II. Minor league in name only because he had been black. Attaining major celebrity status.

At a time when most of these men had been young baseball fans.

In addition, Forrest's tough reputation as a man who already had a mysterious past had not hurt.

Rumors still flew that he had killed, in self-defense of course, a villain who had been responsible for the death of his woman. This caused certain people, who might otherwise eschew his politics, to completely respect him.

Forrest was well aware that he had become a treasured anomaly by these political power brokers. Intellectually, he understood it. Emotionally, it still astounded him.

He certainly did not mind.

He figured it would all work to his advantage someday. Forrest saw an unlimited future for himself and these men could well launch him on his way.

"All we are saying," said the man whose presence had most astounded Forrest when he had entered the restaurant, "is that President Reagan is very old. He is sure to be renominated, there's nothing we can do about that. But we need a plan to replace him on the ticket when- if, during the campaign something happens and he has to withdraw."

"Wouldn't Bush just become president?" This next man, a known political journalist, was the least deferential to the leader, but nevertheless commanded his full attention.

"George makes a valid point," said the leader smoothly. "Address that, would you Joe?"

"We are not talking about a fatal occurrence," said Joe, whom Forrest knew to be an adviser to past presidents, but could not recall his surname. "I mean if it becomes apparent after the nomination, but before the election, that the president must withdraw from the ticket for health reasons, he would still remain president until the nominee of one of the parties is elected and takes office in January of 1985."

"The vice president would keep his place on the nominated ticket," said another, a New York financial power broker whom Forrest knew by name and reputation but had never even seen a photo of anywhere.

"Just having the vice president step up to the top slot would not work," said a different man, a Washington D.C. behind-the-scenes authority, who frequently made news by giving judicious interviews at crucial times.

"Although, he would certainly try," grimaced the one called Joe.

"We would lose the election," the leader declared. "That is why we need this plan. Our only hope would be a fresh face, known throughout the nation, but seen as a Washington outsider who heretofore had previously had no ambitions to be president. Someone called at a time of national crisis to serve his country."

"That hardly describes Edward York," commented Forrest.

"Not to you, young man," said the leader. "But the nation knows York only as a jurist who became famous because of his Solomon like rulings that went a long way towards keeping the peace in the country after Watergate. He's a folk hero."

"In short, that's right," agreed the Wall Street powerbroker. "The perfect choice if Reagan falters."

"Understand that never in a million years would we want harm to come to the President. We are only preparing for one possibility, which may never even occur. If so, then York will just go on to the senate and if his destiny is the Presidency, that will happen later. No one can escape their destiny. I'm a perfect example of that."

Forrest sat amazed as all the men around him chuckled at their leader's remark.

"Our plan is to run him for senate," said the political adviser. "And make him even more well-known nationwide. We're going to treat his campaign, not as if he were running for office in Texas, but national office. His ads will be seen all over the nation."

"We introduce the public to the private side of Edward York," said the journalist. "As the president is running for reelection. When- I mean if- Reagan must withdraw from the ticket, we have York ready to go to replace him."

"President Reagan," corrected Richard.

"I'm sorry, sir. I mean President Reagan."

"As a conservative," the leader nodded his acceptance of the apology without interrupting his train of thought. "With a name nationally known, and your- er- personal background, we see your endorsement as crucial, especially in the greater Houston-Galveston area. Having someone unique in every large city stepping up to support Edward York at the moment he replaces Reagan on the ticket is fundamental. We have already enlisted most of the prominent and influential conservatives in the nation who think the same way we do and are working on the nuances. What we need to know is, are you on board with us? Of course, we would not be having this meeting if we had not thoroughly researched you and concluded the odds were high that you would be with us."

"I know Edward York personally, sir," said Forrest. "He is a man of honor and integrity and- eh- he's a bit quirky- but I could certainly support him under the circumstances you have described."

"Wonderful!" All the men stood up at once, and each in tern shook Forrest's hand.

"And you will find your future enhanced by your decision today," added Richard.

"However," said Forrest.

And all the men stared silently at him for a moment. Smiles evaporated.

"My problem is I don't think a black man can play this character." Forrest waved the notification in front of him again.

The powerful political brokers, makers and breakers of presidents, all took a few seconds to refocus on the topic Forrest had

50

returned to.

Smiles returned.

"About this masquerade ball," said the former adviser. "It's a trifle. Entertainment for those of us who support this cause. More for the women, the wives of our most important people. And many others who have no idea what we have in mind. Having the ball at York's estate is going to introduce a lot of powerful people to him. But it's really no more than that."

"The thing is, two of my female journalist colleagues are heavily involved in this club and they have pushed this masquerade as a social climax that can yield political rewards," said the journalist.

"And Mr. Pr- I mean Richard, might I add, having it benefit that ladies' charity, the one that goes all over the world to help people, regardless of ethnicity or religion, or political leanings, was a stroke of genius," said the man from Wall Street.

"Thank you," said their leader. "But I cannot take credit for that. The two young writers just mentioned were behind that part of the affair."

"Most commendable," said the one called Joe.

"Then," said Forrest, showing his youth to the other men. "Why can't I have the character I want?"

"Well, if it's that important-" the leader turned in hopeful gesture to the journalist.

"Absolutely. I will get it done!"

"Fine," said Richard, "those in charge of that part of the deal. Find out and get Mr. Pointpar the character he wants."

"Which character was that?" asked the journalist.

"Napoleon," said Forrest.

"Napoleon. Fine. Let me take this notification to the right party and I'll get it changed. If the person who drew Napoleon has already been notified we will tell him it was a mistake and give him your character."

"I appreciate that, gentlemen," said Forrest. "You don't know how much it means to me. I can do Napoleon. At least he was a not a blonde."

51

Chapter 9

Forrest Pointpar arrived slightly late at the Wakefield home. Ordinarily he would have been a little embarrassed by being tardy to a swank social affair hosted by one of his neighbors behind the gates.

However, his early evening meeting at the Toy Museum Restaurant overshadowed everything in his mind and he could hardly keep track of the small talk at the Wakefield dinner table even as his taste buds were registering how wonderful the food was. And it made him sluggish to eat again so soon after eating at the museum restaurant. He felt tired. So when Natalie suggested a game of a type of charades in her famous blue room, he declined and went home.

This left only her husband and the other guests, Grace and Edward York, Mark and Peg Brown, and the maid, Doris, on the premises when Natalie Wakefield disappeared.

It was a parlor game that Natalie herself had invented.

The designated player went into the blue room, shut the bifold stained glass doors while the rest of the players sat in a semicircle on the outside of those doors. The player in the room would then shut off the lights and turn on a spotlight casting a shadow against the stained glass. The player would assume various positions and call out words as clues and the other players would attempt to guess the title of a play, movie or television show.

A shameless imitation of charades, but everyone always seemed to enjoy it. It brought out the artistic side, even in those who believed they had no such facets of their personality.

At the moment she disappeared, Natalie Wakefield was the designated player locked in the room. She was alone save for her solid black cat, whose green and yellow eyes were visible in the dark.

The title she had drawn at random, from a hat filled with popular and classic names, had been *Cleopatra and Caesar*, a simple yet difficult play title to convey.

The last thing the guests had seen was a fan shaped shadow held above her head with one arm as she moved her other arm in classic Egyptian dance style. Her short frame, elongated by the light and the way her dress fit her, combined with her other clues, caused Grace

York to immediately guess the character Cleopatra.

"Incomplete answer," Natalie had called from behind the doors.

Then the spotlight had gone out.

The two couples and Natalie's husband had sat in their chairs for several minutes before they realized the light was not going to come back on without intervention.

"Perhaps we've blown a fuse," said Wakefield, rising from his chair. "Doris!"

The maid had instantly come in at his command and turned all the lights in the den on full. "Yes, sir?"

"Natalie, the lights are on out here. Come on out," Grace York had called to Natalie in the meantime.

"Doris, the spotlight in Mrs. Wakefield's room must've tripped a breaker. Can you check and flip it back please?" Wakefield said.

Not receiving a response from Natalie, Grace had tapped on the bifold doors. There was no reply except a meow.

Edward York and the Browns were still seated. They looked at each other uncomfortably.

"Is there any way to open the doors from the outside? I'm worried that Natalie is not answering me," said Grace.

Wakefield looked at Grace York as if she were speaking a foreign language.

"I think we should open the door ourselves," said Peg Brown.

"Natalie, this is not funny," said Wakefield.

"There were no breakers tripped," said Doris, coming back into the room.

"Is there perhaps a key?" Edward York spoke.

"Doris, get the key to these bifold doors. Mrs. Wakefield is not responding."

"Yes, sir." Doris came back within seconds with the key. Wakefield took it from her, pushed it into the lock that held the doors in place, and turned the cylinder.

He and Grace each pushed back a door at the same time. The cat flew out as they went in. Edward York went behind them and flipped on the light switch.

The room was empty.

Chapter 10

Still dark, it was now early hours of the morning. Plate had already interviewed all of the guests who stayed after dinner, the housemaid Doris, and the husband.

The partygoers had spent three hours searching the house, then the grounds, then the nearby neighborhood before finally calling the police.

Plate was acquainted with all the guests except it was the first time he met Mrs. Brown and Ernest Wakefield. He quickly sent the Browns and the Yorks home.

Plate was glad he had been spared interviewing Pointpar. Keeping the politician's name out of the affair was going to be hard enough as it was.

With everyone else gone, he wanted to re-interview Ernest Wakefield, not in the kitchen seated across from an imposing table like previously, but in the actual room Natalie Wakefield had last been seen, alive and enjoying herself.

As Lieutenant Plate walked into the room, an overwhelming feeling of calm enveloped him. This was no doubt due to the dominance of the color blue. Every object in the room, save for the dark auburn wood framing the furniture, was a different shade of blue.

"This was her private space," said Wakefield.

The entrance was framed by pale blue curtains. The Victorian couch and gentleman's chair were delicately crushed blue velvet. Solid pale blue curtains arched above pure white Austrian proof panels turning the corner as though behind the flowing folds were huge mysterious doors or windows leading to separate enchanting worlds.

"This entire room was her," Wakefield continued mournfully. While Plate had entered, the master of the house stood just outside the doorway as though afraid to go in.

Clear crystal and blue crystal along with small blue and white porcelain figurines, which seemed to have personas of their own, highlighted the carefully chosen accent pieces sitting on the most promising object in the room, as well as the most beautiful, the desk.

"She spends- used to spend- hours in this room all alone."

Lieutenant Plate caressed the top of the desk gently. The desk was the largest object in the room and all other objects were subservient to it.

The mirrored back reflected his gloved hand and the lower part of his dark blue long-sleeved police uniform shirt. Gingerly he examined the glass side panels. Their design was breathtaking.

Plate looked up at the far wall.

"Yes, Natalie painted that," said Wakefield.

The painting of trees against snow white mountains hung above the desk. Painted in tone on tone blue, every color of paint used was a different shade of the color of the sea and sky.

The signature did not belong to a famous designer but to the owner and creator of this extraordinary room.

The missing blue lady herself, he thought. The adjective 'blue' slipping involuntarily into every description in his mind.

Everything about this room reflects her personality. And, Lieutenant Plate reflected, as he reluctantly pried his fingers off the desk, *it will tell me more about her than you ever could.*

Wakefield interrupted Plate's musings with a choked voice. Plate realized the man had been weeping for several seconds.

But Ernest Wakefield gained control, determined to continue.

"She used to stay in this room for hours and hours. She would never let anybody in. In fact, she never liked anyone else to come in and touch anything. She especially she disliked anyone sitting on the furniture. Not that one could sit there long. It makes your back hurt."

"Her behavior varied?"

"Just in the past few weeks, she changed, completely refusing to go in, to touch anything. Yet tonight she opened the room up to the guests for this game, which we had not played in a long time, then vanished. She vanished from this very room without a trace."

Plate perceived Wakefield was being just a bit too melodramatic. "Ah, you mean she was last in this room, then left without entering any other room in the house?"

"No, no. I mean she never left this room. She- as you can see, Lieutenant- There is only one way to leave. Through the doorway which opens to the den. She did not come back out."

"I don't understand. You mean you saw her last in this room?"

"I saw her last in this room. We all did. And she never left it."

"Then, behind these curtains-"

"Behind one curtain is a closet. Behind the other is a window."

"Then it is perfectly simple-"

"Lieutenant! Will you let me state what happened?" Wakefield wiped his for head in frustration.

"Yes, yes."

Get it over with, Plate thought.

And then Wakefield had explained the game.

"Right before your eyes during a game of charades?"

"We could only see her silhouette. The light was sometimes blinding. We may have looked away for an instant. She disappeared. She never came out to the den. We looked in the closet, thinking she was playing a practical joke."

"Then she went out the window."

"Impossible! To go out the window, the Austrian panel must be removed. It is fake, just for show. It doesn't raise up and down. She couldn't possibly have gone out the window without someone noticing. The curtain was untouched. Nothing was disturbed."

The lieutenant frowned. This might be more interesting than he previously surmised.

The idea that Wakefield's previous obsession that his wife's cheating on him was in some way connected to the Ladies in Disguise program seemed to have been left by the wayside.

This was shaping up to be more than just melodramatic adultery.

"No one else went into the room with her?" Plate asked.

"No. No. Well, her cat followed her in. Damn cat follows her everywhere. Black devil. And earlier in the day, her Lady in Disguise representative was in there with her. Natalie spends a fortune on that hair care junk."

"What happened to the cat?"

Wakefield cleared his throat. "In Natalie's absence, I, um, banished it to the garage."

"It did not disappear also?"

"Unfortunately not."

Plate turned back towards the desk. "Mr. Wakefield, would you get the cat for me?"

"Do you want to interview it, Lieutenant?"

Lieutenant Plate glared. "Just examine it."

While he was gone, Plate took the opportunity to verify Wakefield's statement about the Austrian panels. They were fake.

And indeed, the woman could have slipped into the closet easily, but not through the window without making considerable mess and probably a lot of noise.

Plate deliberately sat down in the middle of the blue Victorian sofa. However, he resisted propping his feet on the marble topped coffee table. He might not want to make too much of an enemy of this missing lady. She just might not be dead

Wakefield tossed the cat into the room and it sat down beside Plate's boot, looking up at him expectantly, not without a little hostility in its green and yellow eyes.

"Kitty," he said, "where did she go?"

He pulled out his notebook and, as the cat watched him curiously, he wrote down what few facts he had.

Natalie Wakefield, usually found lounging at her pool, wearing costume jewelry and makeup, entertaining guests in her blue room, or reclusively hiding in same location, cannot be found at all...

Her husband and five guests seemingly above suspicion. No motives. Well, there is $500,000 of life insurance. But the husband is a multimillionaire oil executive... Notation- check Wakefield's finances...

Dinner guests all agreed she vanished into thin air in a small room completely visible from the only opening it had, which she could not go through.

"Damn these modern style houses with no doors," Plate said out loud to the cat.

The blue room, as he was already mentally calling it, was meant to be a study off the den.

Such a room should have had doors to close it off.

No doors to close off. Yet she vanishes in midair in front of five

people, six if you count the housemaid who was on the premises but not actually watching.

Absolutely nothing about this strange story had been determined yet. Lieutenant Plate reflected he had a lot of work to do.

Fatigue abruptly set in. Plate felt he was no longer thinking straight. He had not had enough sleep recently.

I need to look into the design of this house.

His vision suffering some from his exhaustion, he decided he was no longer accomplishing anything by remaining any longer. Before leaving he did get the name of the builder from Ernest Wakefield.

Leaving the gates of Sand Waves, he was even further detained by a traffic jam caused by fire trucks as firemen were engaged in extinguishing a small blaze in the woods just on the outer side of the gates.

He sat watching the firefighting activity that spilled out onto the street, even though the fire was deeper in the dense woods and its actual source was not visible.

Just a lot of smoke.

He was delayed 15 minutes before some of the fire trucks moved enough for him to get by, go home, and finally get some sleep.

Chapter 11

The next morning, near the end of another interview with another husband about another missing wife, after covering all the details normally explored in such an investigation, Plate brought up one more subject.

"Did your wife have any connection at all with the Lady in Disguise advertising promotion?"

"Why do you ask that?" This husband was a very different man from Wakefield. And the small house, where he and Plate sat at a built-in kitchen counter that doubled as a bar, was a much different dwelling then the Wakefield mansion.

This little 1400 square feet home was in the lowest priced colony in Sand Waves. Perky and well kept on the outside, as colony federation restrictions demanded, it was drab and messy on the inside.

About the time the interview was in the concluding stage, Plate noticed two elementary school age children in pajamas peering into the kitchen from the adjacent den, which was separated only by a strip of carpet reducer on the floor that marked where the carpet ended and the vinyl floor began.

Morris Tates noticed them, too.

"Kids, go back to bed. I'm talking to the policeman about Mom. We're going to have a special day together when he leaves. So go back to bed until then," the man barked at the children.

They immediately jumped up and scurried down the hallway.

Plate felt that the house was so small they could probably hear everything from their bedroom anyway.

"Children tend to be fascinated by policemen in uniform," Plate commented. "I can recommend a counselor for the children. Sometimes during these times-"

"They don't need any counseling," said their father. "Emma is not their real mother. My first wife divorced and deserted me three years ago. Deserted the kids, too. If they need counseling, it would be for that. They pine for their real mother."

"Then you have not been married long?"

"Emma and I married about 18 months ago."

"And your children-"

"She is their stepmother. They really hadn't got used to her yet. Her job caused her to travel, you see. So with them being in school and her being gone a lot, they haven't really bonded. No problems, just not yet the depth of real mother-child relations. I was hoping this summer we were all going to be home together as a family. As I said, I'm a schoolteacher and although I normally work a different job in the summer to make ends meet, I was going to stay home and insist Emma not do any traveling either."

A freelance insurance adjuster, six weeks ago Emma Tates had gone to a disaster in Oklahoma to work for companies needing damage assessments in a hurry to process claims for people made homeless by rogue ice storms.

Apparently, she had never arrived in Oklahoma and communications from her via telegram- due to outages of phone lines in the area- had to have been faked.

"I see," said Plate, trying to redirect the conversation now that the relationship of the children to the missing woman did not seem so crucial. "So about the Lady in Disguise?"

"Well, it's funny you should ask that. I had been encouraging Emma to apply for a job with them. They're supposed to be doing fantastic and I hoped maybe she could stay home and not have to travel if she could get that job. But then I found out they only hire tall, thin women. I think they're being sued over that."

"Yes, I heard something about that," said Plate. "You know how far along she got in the job application process?"

"I don't think she ever got around to applying. I do know she talked to the woman that came by in one of those costumes trying to sell hair care products. She told me the one who comes to this block discouraged her from applying because she was short and well, to put it gently, not very thin. Do you think they can have some type of connection to her disappearance?"

"I can delineate no thoughts along those lines," said Plate, with a deliberate vagueness. "However, those women are all over the place and maybe the one that comes to this neighborhood knows something. They seem to have become confidants as well as sales representatives to some of their clients. Do you have any idea who she was? Did your wife perhaps order merchandise from her? Maybe there is a receipt, or if not, maybe the saleswoman left a business card?"

"I can look through her things and see if I can find anything like that," said Morris Tates. "But her purse is missing. And I would almost bet any business card from the saleslady would be there. We don't have a lot of extra money and those products they sell are pretty expensive so I don't think she would've ordered much of anything. I'll look around and see if I can find anything, a brochure, maybe. I know there was one left in the mailbox recently, even though I'm sure it had no stamp or postmark. I'll try to find it."

"Okay, let me know if you do. I'm sure that I can get the name of the saleswoman who had this neighborhood as a territory from the company itself." Plate looked at his notes to see if he wanted to go over anything else.

He did.

"And you said, you usually moonlight in the summer for a genealogy research firm?"

"That's correct."

"What exactly do you do?"

"Pretty much what the title says. I trace ancestors. Family trees. Descendants."

"Sounds almost like private investigating."

"Maybe some similarities, but no, I don't try to find out anything but names, relationships between names, birth dates, dates of deaths, marriage dates. Sometimes there's somebody needing some information for financial reasons. Usually we refer them to private detectives. Our business is strictly genealogy."

"Who then are your clients?"

"Oh, a typical client is someone who has come to a point in their life where they would like some family history. They want to know their roots. Or they'd like to be able to boast of some aristocratic connection in the past. Some religious organizations utilize our services."

"How do you go about finding out this information? Is it expensive?"

"To answer your last question first- yes, it is expensive. As far as getting the information- any way we can. Old books, U.S. government census records in Washington are available if you go there. I travel there at least four times a year, sometimes more frequently depending on business. And there are old newspapers, courthouse records, and the like. A lot of information, also clues, comes directly from elderly family members who people have forgotten about and don't think to ask."

"That's interesting. Rest assured, we are doing everything we can to find your wife. I take it from what you have told me that your occupation hasn't anything to do with her disappearance. And I can't see how her employment as a freelance insurance adjuster could fit in either."

"Exactly. She never works anywhere around here. Larger cities tend to have permanent adjusters and don't need to use freelancers even at the worst times. At least that's what she told me. She's always off to rural areas of Montana for a rockslide, or desert towns in Arizona that suddenly flood, things like that."

"I am still going to need for you to get me the exact name of her employer."

"I know. I guess I really didn't realize I didn't know it until now. It's something like the Insurance Adjusters Independent- no, I don't know. It's got to be on the records somewhere around here. As you can see, I am not the most organized person in the world. I'll go to the bank and get copies of her deposit slips if I have to."

"If it's not too much trouble."

"I tell you, even before this, life has been so hectic, things have happened so fast. I've been so stressed I have gained nearly 40 pounds since I married Emma. Her job was just more burdensome to our family life than I ever dreamed it would be."

"And about your ex-wife," Plate prompted before Tates got into another round of self-sympathy.

"I know it looks bad that my first wife deserted me. It's hard to believe that Emma would do that also. She was a much different person. She was, or is, quite frankly, a social step up from my first wife. Probably even for me. I'm not saying she might not want to divorce me. But I just can't see that she would've disappeared without a trace."

"Your first wife that deserted you- is?"

"Alive and well in Cleveland, Ohio. I have a Texas court order commanding her to pay child support which she totally ignores. All I can do about it is refuse to let her see the children, which she does not want to see them anyway. I can give you her name and address if you need it."

"Please," Plate said, and made physical motions that indicated he was about to leave.

Morris Tates left the room for a short time to get his ex-wife's address.

I just need to make sure your first wife really is alive and well and didn't disappear off the face of the earth also, Plate thought.

He glanced around at the pictures on the den shelves. A wedding picture showed a short plump woman in a skin tight wedding dress clinging to a much thinner Tates, both beaming with the children, slightly younger at their sides, looking fairly happy as well. Flowers all around.

Plate mentally rehearsed his farewell admonition to Morris Tate as he waited.

You realize not reporting your wife missing, not realizing she was not off working at the disaster scene in Oklahoma all this time, is going to make it that much harder to track her down...

"I found it," Tates called from down the hall.

It's usually the husband, Plate told himself sternly. But as Morris Tates came back in with his ex-wife's address, Plate had a sinking feeling the man had no more idea where Emma Tates was then he did.

Chapter 12

"Am I the only law enforcement officer in the country that sees this Lady in Disguise advertising campaign as a perfect cover for a burglary ring, or high class prostitution, or even drug deliveries? And that they are somehow linked to the missing women?"

"Now, Plate," said Chief Brecken. "Just because of the reported sightings of them after dark behind the gates in Sand Waves, it does not mean there is a national conspiracy. Sand Waves is the only place where any suspicious activity is being reported. I cannot find any place else in the nation where these saleswomen are a problem. The company declares it cannot be their employees. It must be impostors. And it may not be criminal. Maybe it's a prank. High school kids. Or some hazing by a sorority. Some Houston college sisterhood dares its applicants to penetrate the gates of Sand Waves. You've got to admit the appeal of that."

"Yes, that would have a certain appeal, all right," said Plate. "Leaving brochures with nonsensical messages in mailboxes at night. But I cannot get beyond the idea that these two missing women are somehow connected to this organization."

"How? They don't seem to have any more contact with these saleswomen than all the other thousands of women in the area. Hell, my wife communes with her representative. They practically have bonded as sisters. Congressman Brown's wife has joined the gang."

"She's gotten a job with them?"

"Yes. She fits the profile and since they've been unable to have children so far, she's got time on her hands."

"Is she involved with this masquerade ball?"

"I don't know. There's been a complication there. A federal operative connected to this event in a peripheral manner has gone missing. They don't think it's anything to do with the party, this agent was deep undercover long before this was planned. But it is something to consider. If you talk to the Browns, do not mention this."

"Why?"

"It is need to know and neither you nor they are on the list. I shouldn't be telling you, so you cannot talk about it."

"I do want to talk to Mrs. Brown."

"Talk to Brown first. At least you know Brown from the flood last year. You know department policy about government reps. Follow it, please."

"Okay, no problem."

I know a lot more about Brown than you could imagine, thought Plate, recalling all the intrigue when he and the congressman were among those trapped at the Sand Waves holiday store known as Innovations.

Plate was not the type of man who would ever use private personal information against anyone under most circumstances. But there could be exceptions.

Despite working with Chief Brecken for several years as second in command at the seven member police force, which served the colony of Sand Waves, Plate knew little of Brecken's personal life.

So Plate decided against asking to talk with Betty Brecken. He did know she was perpetually busy with two elementary age children. If she was already mentally in sync with her Lady in Disguise representative, she was unlikely to be very helpful.

Devotees of the group were sensitive to official inquiries as there had been recent noises made by some prominent citizens concerning desirability of banning of door-to-door sales in Sand Waves.

Plate had overheard a few recent conversations between the chief and his wife. 'Persecuted' and 'sisterhood' had been among the words filtering through due to the telephone's failure to stop very shrill tones from escaping the receiver's earpiece.

Plate pondered other women he knew in the area well enough to ask about their private purchases of hair care products. The chief resumed the conversation, interrupting his mental inquiry.

"I don't think these two disappearing women are even connected to each other," Chief Brecken was saying. "They are miles apart socially and economically and in every other way. Make sure you have proof these two are linked before you connect them in any way. They did not know each other?"

"No connection that we can find."

"Then keep them separate. All we need right now is to start a panic in Sand Waves."

Plate reflected on this as well. It did seem to be accurate.

Natalie was the socially prominent wife of a rich Texas oil executive.

Emma was the working woman spouse of a school teacher who needed a secondary summer job to make ends meet.

Natalie had no children.

Emma also had not borne children but was a stepmother.

Natalie was petite to the point of abnormal. Driver's license height and weight 4 feet, 10 inches- weight approximately 98 pounds.

Emma's driver's license information was floating temporarily unavailable in the system. Her husband described her as five feet tall, variable weight from 145 to 165, depending on how effective the hottest fad diet was for her currently.

Emma apparently had no life insurance apart from a burial expense policy tied to her husband's job, $2500. Less than the cost of a standard quality funeral which averaged $4,000 these days.

Natalie had a $500,000 policy. But on appearance, it seemed it did her husband little more good than Emma's policy. Her trust fund from deceased parents contributed much more annually to the income of the couple and, should Natalie die, some obscure cousin in Europe reaped the benefits, not Wakefield.

Neither woman had enough life insurance to make up for the cost of her death.

There were some other similarities.

They were the same age, born exactly a month apart in 1955.

Both were married.

They both had brown eyes and hair.

The both lived in Sand Waves, albeit on opposite ends of the colony's socioeconomic structure.

They both were Lady in Disguise customers.

And both were unqualified, due to physical characteristics, to actually be a Lady in Disguise.

Neither missing woman attended church, nor were registered to vote, despite both of their husbands professing a conservative political preference.

Both left their homes routinely for significant periods of time, for reasons that seemed obvious at first glance, but upon closer look were ambiguous.

When he was unable to pull up information about Emma Tates, Plate thought of calling Daphne to see if her general manager's insurance computer system could help ferret out a few facts that were off limits to official systems.

Through her primary company, Daphne had access to the nationwide insurance spy computer network that warned companies when persons were attempting to lie on life insurance applications after having been rejected for telling the truth, either about their health or aggregate amount of life benefits. But the two missing women's health conditions or amounts of life insurance did not seem to be factors in their disappearances.

Plate decided more pertinent information would come from Tates, then Wakefield.

"I suppose Emma must not have left much of a paper trail in her life," said Tates over the phone. "She does not like to use credit cards, would not let me put her on mine. She actually doesn't have a bank account. She uses the credit union her company has in Houston. But I can assure you, I know her background thoroughly."

"How is that?"

"After we first met, she gave me the names of her ancestors. She has no living family, her parents being dead in a wreck when she was a child and other members scattered, she was raised in an orphanage right outside Killeen. Anyway, she did have some family names to go on. When I checked the names, I traced her family back to the 1800s. In fact, I was working on going back farther but I was going to have to access European records and that gets real expensive real quick. She was hoping to earn enough money next storm season, if not before, for me to continue. And I have been trying to get a copy of an old book from the 1900s that featured one of her ancestors. She was keen on that but it is so hard to find old books out of print. I had not had any success. So everything is incomplete. I can give you what I

67

have so far if you think that will help."

"Possibly. I'll pick it up from you when I get a chance." Plate rang off, wondering how Emma Tates' genealogical records could help with the mystery of her disappearance.

Probably not much, he guessed, and put the chore of picking them up on the backburner.

Ernest Wakefield was in a business conference, so was inaccessible. Plate was going to have to wait for him to call back.

Plate pulled the manila file folder on Natalie from the file cabinet. County personnel had been thorough with routine tracking of her paper trail. Natalie Wakefield's credit cards and bank statements were all in her husband's name, so told him little. Her name was not even on the deed to her house, although, purchased after her marriage, it was community property in the state of Texas.

Plate recalled growing up in the 1960s and his mother complaining about such things, but supposedly times had changed.

Some changes take longer among the super-rich, Plate reflected.

Plate tossed the folder on his desk and flipped through the file. It had a bulge in one corner. Wakefield had given Plate a number of business cards of the people Natalie patronized. Plate had paper clipped them and stuck them in the file pocket.

He now pulled them out, removed the clip and shuffled. Natalie Wakefield spent money freely and had a lot of the colorful 2-by-3 cards containing mini-logos, advertisements and contact information of merchants and others who served her. Competing physicians, dentists, multiple jewelers, several clothing boutiques, and so forth. His first inclination had been right, he reflected. The pertinent information was here somewhere in the more interesting paraphernalia in the file-

A sales pamphlet from a Lady in Disguise representative, with a hand written name. Evelyn was the first name. The last name was illegible.

A brochure about the upcoming masquerade ball, very detailed.

And a business card for a life insurance agent.

Dedicated to putting the client's needs first, it read,

J. Daphne Martin

Chapter 13

All over Sand Waves ticket holders for the masquerade ball were opening their character notifications.

There were many to choose from in the era of the late 1700s.

It was a time of radical change. The rise of the common man, fall of the aristocracy.

And more cyclical occurrences.

Revival in some lands. Desolation in others.

A cultural shift from the rule of tradition to the reign of emotion.

Persecution of the just and unjust.

Not unlike the previous decade of the modern times.

Most anticipatory ball attendees pulled a generic letter from the gold lined envelope, instructing them in the desired dress of the period and regretting they did not draw a name.

Others were reacting to the presumably more positive news that they had drawn a character.

"I was hoping for King Gustav III," said Reverend Eric Skrale with disappointment. "It would have been wonderful to be able to go as a Swede."

His wife rolled her eyes. "This silly party has just gotten even funnier," she said. "I don't see how you're ever going to pull off that character. You have far too much hair."

The reverend nodded in agreement. "But we have to go by the rules. There's no switching."

"I'm glad I didn't get a character. I wonder how many people got characters really didn't want one," Mrs. Skrale mused. "I considered it was odd that there wasn't a way you could opt out of being in the contest. I was thinking they were going to try to get as many people that sort of looked like the characters matched up."

Reverence Skrale looked at the name again on his notification letter.

"That obviously wasn't the case," he replied to his wife.

"Since I haven't drawn a character, I've been asked to go as a representative Lady in Disguise," Peg Brown told her husband, the congressman, with disappointment. "I wanted to really dress up, not just wear a plain cloak, even if they are going to provide a mask."

"Tell them no, then," said Mark Brown, crumpling up his generic notification that expressed regrets that he did not draw a character either.

"I hate to tell them no. I have just gotten into this organization. It wasn't easy. They're now considering my application to join the charitable branch."

"I don't understand why you think you have to earn any money right now," Mark complained. "I am doing okay."

"I'm not doing this to make money. I told you that when I signed up with them. You're gone to Washington half the time. I don't have anything to do."

"What about your church group?"

"I've got bored with church groups. All we ever do is sit and study the Bible. The Lady in Disguise organization is exciting. If I can get past the first tier, where I don't really do anything except sell hair care products, I can travel with them when they go to the disaster scenes. Now, you know how it will look good for your career."

"It seems a leap. Selling hair care products door-to-door, then off to doing rescue missionary work."

"I don't think there's any missionary work involved. This is a nonreligious, nonpolitical group that just wants to help people. And if you get into the second tier, which means you're officially a part of the charity, you don't have a quota to meet on the hair care products anymore."

Congressman Brown frowned as he attempted to process this information. It all sounded illogical to him.

Women's group run by a group of women, he thought wryly.

Watching his wife nervously fingering her notification, he didn't dare express that judgment out loud.

"Why don't you find out if you can't wear a beautiful costume under the cloak? Would you normally wear dress clothes under the cloak?"

"That's a great idea. We just normally wear street clothes under the cloaks. We're instructed to keep the cloaks buttoned up so that what we wear underneath is not visible. Maybe they would let me wear a period gown beneath and leave the cloak unbuttoned. I'll go call and ask my group leader."

Mark Brown put his hand on his wife's shoulder.

"A word of advice. Don't ask permission. Just do it. If you ask permission, they might say no. If you just do it, what are they going to do? Insist you go home and change? I don't think so. I'll be there as your escort."

Peg Brown smiled happily at her husband. Married ten years, just past 30, she had recently determined she was going to assert herself in her own identity. She wanted some semblance of independence.

But right now she felt very reassured he was going to be standing beside her at the masquerade ball.

Father Patrick Thomas looked at his notification letter in disbelief.

"What is it, Father?" The altar boy, helping the priest with preparatory arrangements for daily Mass, was alarmed as he watched the color drain from Father Thomas' face when he opened his notification.

"The bishop secured this invitation for me," the priest started to explain.

He then decided there was not time to make the boy completely understand what was going on. "Just remind me to phone the bishop after Mass, would you? They've given me an impossible role to play."

"Of course," said the altar boy, and he pulled a string from his pocket and tied it around his finger so as not to forget. He was a very conscientious altar boy and did not like to let the priest down in any way.

"Or maybe Edward York can do something," said the priest thoughtfully.

"Deborah Franklin!" Daphne had no one to complain to except her cat.

This did not cause her to mince words.

"They expect me to portray Deborah Franklin. I didn't even know Benjamin Franklin had a wife. Great. This means I'm going to have to go the library to research this person. As if I have time to do that. Sand Waves Library won't have a thing. It is only really for the children. I'll have to go to Houston."

She glanced over at her cat who was calmly cleaning between her claws as she sat on Daphne's sofa.

"Catherine," she said to the cat. "I'm going to find out if Deborah Franklin had a cat. And if she did, I'd better take you to the masquerade ball with me."

Realizing it had been spoken to, the cat looked up at her curiously.

"Oh, hell!" Daphne's irritation just grew at the absurdity of her own statement. She wanted some kind of revenge against the idiotic organizers of this masquerade party who did not allow any input from people who had paid $2000 for a ticket.

"They're telling me I have to go as a character I've never heard of," she continued complaining aloud to the cat. "I've got to take time and go to the library and research this person. I was sure Benjamin Franklin was single. I didn't even notice there was such a character listed. If he was married, how come we never heard about his wife in school? Great, she probably died young. She probably never had a chance to wear beautiful clothes and all I'm going to get to wear is some type of homespun pioneer revolutionary housewife type dress. Probably with an ugly hood or a peasant cap."

Irrationally, Daphne suddenly felt like crying like a small child.

She rarely socialized except in the course of business. Fun for her was curling up on the couch with Catherine and watching *Columbo*.

She had a closet full of beautiful clothes but never had any formal occasion to attend except annual company conventions.

And those were a form of work.

"Meow," replied the cat.

For once in her life she had elected to go to a truly sophisticated formal occasion. She had paid $2000 for a ticket to this masquerade ball where she planned to truly enjoy herself, eat as much as she wanted, parade around in a beautiful gown and not worry about selling anybody anything. And the man she was cared about was going to be there, front and center, for her to flirt with and charm.

Now she was being told she was probably going to have to wear a dowdy peasant type costume.

"I might have drawn Marie Antoinette, Empress Josephine, Catherine the Great- but no- Deborah Franklin!"

She sat down beside the cat, which crawled up into her lap.

The cat wore a beautiful fur coat of orange, black, and white.

Once again, Daphne pictured colonial revolutionary female costumes in her mind.

She sat there and cried.

Chapter 14

Ernest Wakefield opened Natalie's notification letter.
Marie Antoinette.
How she would love to play such a part.
"Where are you Natalie?" he said softly.
"Don't you worry, Mr. Wakefield. That was the character she wanted and she'll be back to play it."
"No, Doris. This letter was posted before anyone knew of Natalie's disappearance. They won't hold this part for her. They will draw somebody else's name to be Marie Antoinette."
"I think we should get the costume for her and have it ready in case she comes back before that party happens," said Doris.
"Do you really think that, Doris?"
"I feel in my heart, Mr. Wakefield. She's alive. She's coming back to you."
"How could I get such a costume that I know would fit her?"
"You just leave it to me. I have been dressing Mrs. Wakefield a long time. Her figure is perfect. I could fit her the first time I saw her."
"Oh yes!" Wakefield closed his eyes remembering his first sight of Natalie.

He had met her in Europe on a starlit night in Paris nearly five years ago. The exclusive party at the home of a mutual acquaintance had moved outdoors to a yacht deck.
At first mistaking her for a child, he was delighted when she turned out to be a woman of 24. He had loved her petiteness combined with educated sophistication.
Her past was somewhat mysterious. She had been a wealthy orphan, raised in boarding schools with summers at resorts. Yet she was as friendly and down to earth as if she had experienced the all-American rituals of grade school and college.
To a bachelor in his early 40s, she had come along at just the right time. He had spent his post college years building a solid career and was making big money in the oil and gas industry in Houston.

They married, a $50,000 glamour wedding at the Houston Marriot, just in time for the economic boom to take his income up to the stratosphere. They lucked into a small but exquisite mansion in Sand Waves before the housing price bubble peaked.

Her trust fund income added significantly to his earnings and, between them, they made enough money to pick and choose the society in which they played.

Natalie had fit right in with all his social set, already semi-established by his career, and migrating towards Sand Waves and similar command design and master planned communities springing up around Houston in response to the lack of zoning in the big city.

In Sand Waves, the Wakefields were a brilliant success in every way, except one. Sand Waves was family oriented and the standard was one pet and two children, preferably one of each sex.

Same sex siblings were tolerated for the time being but planners among the Powers-That-Be in the colony looked forward to the days when preconception gender selection was perfected by science and all family entities could be uniform.

Occasionally couples exceeded the requisite number of babies. Nothing could be done officially, of course, but in the social sphere, subtle messages were sent in the form of a glass social ceiling for those daring to reproduce more than the acceptable rate of replacement.

The Wakefields had vaguely spoke of children but she was so small, Ernest was cautious about that idea.

Instead, Natalie had found Doris. The maid seemed to placate any motherly instincts his wife might have.

Natalie was still not yet 30. Experiences like the masquerade ball still excited and fulfilled her.

They had time on their side and were busy living happily ever after.

Or so Ernest Wakefield had believed.

And he was used to fighting for his accomplishments. He was not about to give up.

"You just leave it to me," Doris was saying. "I'll find the right costume for that character and I'll get it ready and have it lying on the bed. When she gets back, it will be there for her. Let them give the part to somebody else. They'll just be two Marie Antoinettes at that party."

"Doris," said Wakefield determinedly. "You go ahead and do that. After all, if she does come back and find out she was to be Marie Antoinette and it is too late for her to get the costume, she will be heartbroken. And if we do go ahead and get the costume and she does not come back?"

Wakefield broke off and swallowed hard.

"Don't think that way, Mr. Wakefield. She's going to be found. Some evil man has got hold of her or she's got lost somewhere but I feel in my heart she is alive and that police Lieutenant Plate- he is going to find her."

"There's a credit card on my desk in the living room. Use that, Doris. Find the best Marie Antoinette costume in the entire country! Contact Hollywood. They can come up with a costume that will rival anything these Ladies in Disguise people would offer."

"Yes sir!"

Wakefield stood for a moment as the maid left the room. Then before he could stop himself, he started to sob. He dashed up the stairs to his bedroom.

Chapter 15

An unmarked police car arrived at the Wakefield home later that afternoon. Ernest Wakefield did not expect to be called to identify a body so soon. He was so distraught as Plate drove him to the morgue, that Plate was sure Wakefield was innocent of his wife's victimization. Or he was a near perfectly talented actor.

Sand Waves' Police Department did not have a morgue, forensics department, or anything except a few offices connected to a jail with two cells designed to hold at most four people if the sexes were not mixed.

Ernest Wakefield had kept his composure until leaving the colony, even making small talk with Plate, but then had ridden the distance outside of Sand Waves to the morgue utilized by the county in silence, occasional tears coming down his cheeks.

"The body was badly burnt and a facial identification is not going to be possible. But there were some- uh- features of the body, on the torso, which escaped the flames somehow. The person was wearing extra padding there that was apparently treated with some type of flame retardant."

Ernest Wakefield looked at Plate like he believed the police officer was totally mad.

"The fact is," Plate cleared his throat uncomfortably, "it's a part of the anatomy that a husband might easily identify where is no one else could."

"I think I understand what you're saying," Wakefield managed to say in a choked voice. "You need not go on. I will do my best to give a clear identification."

"I was just trying to prepare you, sir," said Plate. He pulled the unmarked police car into the parking lot of the morgue, sitting quietly behind the wheel, waiting until Wakefield was ready to exit the vehicle.

It was only a moment.

The grim task of identifying the unburnt portion of the murdered woman's body was also done predominantly in silence. Plate and the coroner stood on either side of Wakefield, ready to support him, if he should start to collapse.

A technician pulled the sheet back exposing the mostly charred remains of the woman found in the public access log cabin that had burned to the ground.

The cabins, co-owned by the school district and the colony, were located in random spots along the green belt in Sand Waves. They were usually used by children's scouting and adventure troops or other school aged children for public activities simulating being out in the country. They were administrated by the Sand Waves' Independent School District, but anyone could use them with permission.

Some cabins were easily accessible from main roads. Some were buried deep in the woods, offering a true outdoors experience. Those were always closed from the months of November through March, due to lack of central heating. The district feared exactly what everyone at first thought had happened, someone using a cabin had gotten cold and started a fire which got out of control. So the outlying cabins were locked and unused during the winter months.

It had taken a day before the fire investigation team realized the fire had been arson and that there was a body in the ashes, dead little more than just a few hours before the fire was set.

So badly burned, it was hard to fit any general description, but some singed jewels found amongst the ashes turned out to be precious stones and so the first idea was that this was the body of the wealthy missing woman, rather than the poor one.

Therefore, Ernest Wakefield was given first opportunity to make an identification. No sense in putting more than one human being through that ordeal if it was not necessary.

It was going to be necessary.

"This is not Natalie," Wakefield said. The relief in his voice was undeniable and that he broke down weeping was clearly a sign of joy, not disappointment.

"I'll have to bring in the other husband," Plate told the coroner quietly, as the two public servants and Wakefield left the room.

It was not that Plate was hoping the body had been Natalie. He was just terribly dreading bringing in Morris Tates to do the same chore.

"I need to ascertain from you that you are absolutely sure," Plate said to Wakefield as they were in route back to Sand Waves.

"Absolutely," Ernest Wakefield declared. "My wife's-"

"No need to explain," Plate said quickly.

He accelerated the car a little bit. He glanced around to make sure there were no DPS patrols in sight.

He was not above being stopped. The vehicle had standard license plates. They would not be easily able to see his uniform until after flagging him down. But no flashing lights were in sight.

"I am quite certain that is not my wife," Wakefield reiterated in a calm and controlled voice. He was now dry-eyed but still grim-faced as they approached the entrance to Sand Waves. "Please reassure me that you are continuing to search for her. That the search is not been interrupted by finding this- this unfortunate lady."

"Certainly. We never call off the search before an identification is made. There's been no interruption in procedure concerning the search for your wife."

Plate did not verbalize what was really in his mind.

I just don't have any idea where to search for her and have no clues and no idea what to do next unless something turns up.

"Thank you," said Ernest Wakefield. "I'm counting the days, dreading each day as it passes as this infernal masquerade ball gets closer."

"Pardon?" Plate jerked the car a little guiltily as Wakefield's comment intruded on his thoughts about the hopelessness of finding Natalie Wakefield.

"This infernal masquerade ball," said Wakefield, now feeling more irritable than anything else. "Her maid, Doris, who is really more of a companion as well as a maid, is convinced that Natalie will return to play the part of Marie Antoinette, that she so wanted to play at this shindig. I've even got a costume, as they took the official costume assignment and gave it to somebody else. But I've got a Marie Antoinette costume waiting because Doris is convinced that Natalie will return and will be heartbroken if she cannot be Marie Antoinette at the ball."

"Hmm," said Plate, not knowing quite what to make of his

words.

"And furthermore," Wakefield continued. "Doris is convinced that if Natalie does not return for this masquerade ball, well, that nothing short of death would keep her away. So each day as the ball gets closer and closer, I dread it more and more. I'm praying she returns before that day comes."

"Has your wife's maid got you convinced that Mrs. Wakefield will, perhaps, never return, if she doesn't return in time for this party?" Plate asked.

"I know it sounds superstitious. Nevertheless, I am beginning to believe it myself. If Natalie does not return before the masquerade ball, I, too, am convinced she no longer walks the earth."

"You know your wife disappeared in a room without doors in front of six other people," Plate began reprising the details once more.

"What are you talking about?" Wakefield appeared confused.

"Well, I was just reevaluating the circumstances and, while I know the credibility of the witnesses, it just seems impossible-"

"No! I mean what you said about the room having no doors. That's ridiculous. The room has bifold doors."

Plate drove straight to Ernest Wakefield's mansion. Department protocol and technicalities could wait.

The two men fairly flew into the Wakefield foyer, went straight into the den and turned to the blue room that faced it.

Plate was right.

There were no doors. Examined closely, the 48-inch doorframe showed faint evidence of indentations from missing hinges. The spaces had been filled in with wood putty, sanded and painted so expertly there was barely a trace that doors had ever hung there.

"Lieutenant, you must believe me, there were bifold doors the night Natalie disappeared. There had always been bifold doors on that room." And he once again related in detail the game Natalie had invented, how the guests had sat outside the doorway in the dark with the lights on inside the parlor. Emphasizing the spotlight against the stained glass.

"I wish someone had made this more clear at the time," Plate complained.

"I confess I never noticed the doors being gone. How can they be gone without a trace?"

Plate caressed the repaired doorframe. "Very well done, with almost no trace."

"But how? When? Who?" Wakefield asked, distressed even more.

"When- must be before I came here to see the room. Remember I interviewed you first in the kitchen, then we came to this room. There were no doors then. That was a peculiarity that struck me."

"The doors came with the house, Lieutenant. The room always had doors."

"So we know when. During the time the house was empty. You were off searching for your wife before calling us. And how. Employing expert restoration carpenter skills. As to who and why? I've no idea."

Chapter 16

Daphne rarely had visitors except for her parents and extended family members that she occasionally invited over for dinner. She did not allow insurance clients to come to her home and used a post office box for an address.

She could also use her general manager's office address if she needed to. But it was a pain to go into Houston to get her mail, so she usually used the Sand Waves postal facility for convenience.

Her home was her enclave, a refuge where she opted for inaccessibility.

So she was alarmed when the doorbell rang at midnight.

Unlike previously, Darica was gone.

Daphne was alone.

She pulled her pistol out of her nightstand drawer and cautiously approached the front door. A small clear window in the center of a dense stained glass panel served as her peephole. She had to bend slightly to see through it at a safe distance.

She routinely left her porch light on all night. The figure was clearly delineated. He stood tapping his boots impatiently and reached to ring the doorbell again.

"Plate!" She had rushed to the door and opened it before he got a chance to push the button for the second time. Although there was no one else in the house to wake up, her suburban neighborhood was so quiet at night that she was afraid one of the neighbors might hear the bell and ask questions in the morning.

"I'm sorry. I forgot it was so late," said Plate. "I should have called."

He stepped into the door without asking her if it was okay.

"This some kind of an emergency?"

The phone ringing this time of night would have been equally disturbing, Daphne reflected.

She relaxed and became sleepy again.

"Yes and no," said Plate. "You know how you are always telling me I'm going to need your help in the future. Well, this is not exactly a need, but I think you can help me with something in a way that no one else can."

"Come on in then. Let me go get dressed."

Plate waited in the den while Daphne changed out of her nightclothes and returned her gun to its place.

Both of them were mentally rehearsing what they were going to say to each other during the short interlude.

Daphne's cat jumped down from her perch on top of the television and went over to Plate to sniff at him.

"You know you should formally introduce me to this cat," he said to Daphne when she reentered the room wearing comfortable jeans and a shirt. "Do you mind if I remove my belt and my vest? It has been a long day. And I am tired."

"No, go right ahead, anywhere you like," said Daphne.

As she went discreetly into the kitchen, Plate took off his long-sleeved uniform shirt, removed his belt and vest, and put the shirt back on. He placed his equipment on the abbreviated bar that topped the half-wall that separated her kitchen from the den.

Daphne scooped up her cat and held it in her arms as she walked back towards Plate. "This is my kitty. She is two years old. A very sweet and obedient cat most of the time."

"What's her name?"

"Her name?"

"Yes, don't you ever call her anything besides kitty?"

"True. She does have an official name. But I usually do just call her kitty."

"You going to tell me her name?" Plate laughed, recalling that many times suspects refused to tell him their names on initial contact. "I have my ways of finding out in the end."

Daphne laughed also. "I'm sure you do. Her name is Catherine."

"Catherine the cat."

"No cat jokes, please. I love that name. Naming this creature is the first time ever I have gotten to choose a name for anything. So I named her Catherine. So there."

Plate laughed again and sat down on the couch.

"Now," said Daphne, with affection. "Care to explain why you have woke me up in the middle of the night, interrupting my sleep and

83

disturbing my cat's nocturnal prowling?"

"I want your opinion. No, actually your insight, about a woman named Natalie Wakefield. That's the first thing. Then I have to tell you about a woman named Serena Towers…"

Plate narrated the story of Natalie Wakefield first.

"It's obvious to me that Wakefield murdered his wife," said Daphne, after he finished.

Plate perceived that Daphne was speaking facetiously but not completely.

"And your jump to that conclusion is from what perch?'

Daphne laughed. "I actually considered about calling you up and telling you this when it happened. Another case for you."

"I don't need another case. Let's just stick to this one. Are you Natalie Wakefield's insurance agent?"

"Yes and no."

"Daphne, please. It's the middle of the night. I haven't been home yet. I'm hungry. In case you're not getting the drift, I am in a bad mood."

"You're always in a bad mood when you want my help. Anyway, a few weeks ago a man called up and ordered a half million dollar policy over the phone."

"That's criminal?"

"It was Wakefield."

"Okay. Still, what is your point?"

"You don't understand. People don't buy life insurance. They have to be sold life insurance. The only people who come after us are usually already half dead or plotting suicide. That's why there's the two-year provision in the state law. Commit suicide within the first two years of the policy and all the beneficiary gets back is the premiums paid."

"This is not a case of suicide. Not even death. There's no evidence to indicate that Natalie Wakefield met with foul play. There's no evidence at all. Period. She has just disappeared."

"So you suspect an upcoming case of insurance fraud?"

"Possibly. It hasn't happened yet. But it could."

"They have to wait seven years if there's no body."

"Wakefield is a rich man. He can wait. But he seems genuinely grieved by his wife's disappearance."

"It's an act. No, don't look at me like that. Hear me out. He called and ordered a policy over the phone on his wife. Said he was referred by one of my other clients who later denied even knowing he wanted any insurance. Anyway. She was perfectly healthy, passed her medical with flying colors!"

"Still, that hardly-"

"And it was all done by mail! I didn't even have to go out to the house. Nobody does that! Something fishy. Fishy as cat food. I never met Mrs. Wakefield. I spoke to her briefly on the phone. She took her medical-"

"If you never met her and didn't get her signature in person, how could you verify it was really her?"

"She would've had to have provided identification to the medical technician."

"So you didn't get to see the blue room?'

"The blue room?"

Plate explained what details he knew of Natalie Wakefield's disappearance to Daphne, including the part about the doors being removed.

"A lady disappears from a blue room, and then the blue doors are taken down," Daphne said contemplatively. "Well, how about that. How could it not be her husband? If you ask me. Tell me, was she wearing a blue dress?"

"Yes, as a matter of fact she was. The maid said she changed her clothes three times that night before finally settling on a blue strapless gown composed mainly of pale sequins."

Daphne clapped her hands. "So she was a lady in blue. That's important!"

"Possibly. Women do change clothes. I didn't think that was important."

"An experienced hostess like Natalie Wakefield would have had her dress planned out weeks in advance."

"I appreciate your speculation. But it still adds up to nothing. I have nothing so far. Nothing describes this case perfectly. A background check revealed nothing about Natalie Wakefield. Her maid knows nothing. Nobody knows nothing. And the cat won't talk."

Daphne laughed and scooped up her own cat. "For what all you told me. Nothing is not the right word for all this. Fake is the word."

"Fake?"

"You described a blue Victorian sofa. And a matching chair?"

"Yes?"

"Well, they've either been recovered or they are fakes."

"Why do you say that?"

"I know a little about antiques. A lot of my clients have real antiques in their houses. Real Victorian furniture is either dark red or dark green or a hideous floral pattern or something like that. Never light blue. On the other hand, you can order a reproduction in any color you want."

"How do you know this?"

"I do a lot of shopping. I've been looking at furniture. There's a place in downtown Houston that specializes in reproduction furniture. You can go there and order anything you want. I'm thinking of redoing my office."

Daphne indicated the small room located off the den that served as her home office.

Plate sharply looked around.

Daphne's floorplan was a simple elegant design.

Entering the front door on a slightly raised foyer, bordered on the right side by a wall that harbored a coat closet, a visitor could see parts of three different areas immediately. Directly in front was the large den, to the left was a formal dining room with a small formal living room attached.

Off the den, also to the left, was the kitchen and dinette area. There were no walls separating the spaces. A half-wall partition did give a little semblance of a barrier to the kitchen area and served as a shallow bar.

Proceeding into the den, the dinette adjacent to the den and behind the kitchen was completely open as well. Then turning around, the small room off the front of the den behind the coat closet wall was

Daphne's home office. An L-shaped hallway hit the den at a right angle and led to two small separate bedrooms, the large master being on the other side of the den, centered at the back of the house.

Plate had been in the house before but only had vaguely mapped it out in his mind. But he had memorized the layout of the Wakefield house, a probable crime scene, meticulously.

"Your house is the exact same floor plan as the Wakefield mansion. At least the downstairs. Only, of course, it is much smaller."

"Really? I have the same configuration of space as the blue lady?" Daphne was impressed.

"Yes. Where the wall to the right of your den separates your master bedroom and forms the corner of the hallway, that's where the stairs are that go up to the second floor. Where they have a real staircase, you only have disappearing stairs to the attic. Otherwise except for size, the floor plan is identical."

"That only means the same builder probably built both houses."

"Yes, but it also means if I want to re-stage her disappearance, I can use your house as a miniature model."

"Considering what I paid for this house, I'm not sure I like you using the word miniature in connection with it."

Plate did not reply. He walked into Daphne's office.

"How would you like your office redecorated at police department expense?"

"Redecorated in what style?'

"Victorian reproduction furniture."

"Do I get to keep it?"

"Maybe. Probably."

"Cool," said Daphne.

"One more thing. Can I get you to run this name through your insurance agency computers?" He wrote it down for her.

"Emma Tates?"

"Yes. Another missing woman."

"Okay. I'll check."

Plate hesitated. Daphne was important to him. Her feelings mattered. He treasured her friendship.

"And there's something else. I've met a woman named Serena

Towers," he said.

"Is she missing also?"

"No."

He took both of Daphne's hands in his and took a deep breath. What he had to tell her was simple, old as the sea, but he wanted to make it substantial enough in words that she could absorb it slowly.

And forgive him someday.

"I hope you will understand," he began…

Chapter 17

Daphne called Plate the next day with the information he had requested. No Emma Tates in the state of Texas had ever applied for any individual life insurance in her entire life. A couple of women by that name were found nationwide but their physical characteristics did not match the description of the missing Sand Waves woman.

The conversation was very formal and businesslike.

Emma was listed as a dependent on her husband's group insurance with the school district. Since Tates had elected a small life benefit for the family, she had ten percent of his annual salary as a benefit. Likewise his children had five percent.

"Why doesn't that give me any hard information?"

"Because he enrolled them at the correct timeframe window and coverage was automatic. All he had to do was put down their names and birthdates."

"They did not even have to answer any questions? No health information given?"

"No, if she had wanted more than $2500 benefit or more than $1250 on each of the kids they would have had to. But as they took the minimum guaranteed, all they needed was name and date of birth, with relationship to the primary covered."

Plate felt frustrated. Daphne's information, usually so valuable, was of little use. He did note the similarity in the birth dates of the two missing women. Both the same age, born a month apart. But that was nothing. Natalie's birthdate was 2-3-55. Emma Tates 3-3-55.

Right in the middle of the baby boom, millions of babies were born on those dates and the coincidence could not be counted as significant.

Tates was unavailable to view the body in the morgue.

Before the body had been discovered, he had notified Plate he would be out of town a few days. His school was on winter break and his ex-wife, also a teacher on a similar break, had agreed to see their children. Tates could not miss an opportunity for some contact between his children and their real mother, no matter what was going

89

on with his present wife.

Plate cursed the latent maternal instincts that had surfaced in the former Mrs. Tates, but he had not tried to block the reunion. Tates had left contact information that would become valid as soon as he arrived in Ohio and checked into his hotel.

Meanwhile, he was on the road in his vehicle, inaccessible. There was nothing to do but wait.

Plate returned to the Wakefield home that afternoon.

Once again he observed the Victorian style furniture in the room from which Natalie Wakefield had disappeared. He had already checked with the furniture store in downtown Houston that had specialized in such products.

Natalie Wakefield had indeed ordered Carlton McClendon reproductions of a Victorian sofa and gentleman's chair upholstered in a light blue velvet fabric. And she had ordered a set of matching end tables and coffee table with marble tops.

Doris had greeted Plate at the Wakefield mansion.

"Mr. Wakefield is at work, sir."

"I know," said Plate, as he showed her his credentials again and said all the necessary lines to get her to let him in.

Wakefield had told Doris about the missing doors. She claimed to have had the same reaction as him. In the shock of what was happening to the household, she had never noticed the doors were gone.

"Doris," he said, as they approached the blue room entrance. "Tell me about this furniture. The couch and chair, for instance."

"Mrs. Wakefield did not like anyone to sit on them."

"I know that."

"Oh- you mean, well, they are reproductions. Mrs. Wakefield had them specially made."

"Really? And the rest of this, too?" *So it wasn't a secret that they are reproductions*, Plate thought.

"Now the desk came from Finger's. But the marble topped tables are reproductions as well."

"Did she just go to the store and purchase the desk?"

"No, it had to be ordered. She had to wait a long time for it. It's

Pulaski."

Plate sat down in the gentleman's chair. Doris gave a discreet gasp.

"Sit down, Doris."

"Oh, I couldn't, sir!"

"Sure you can. I won't tell."

Doris sat down on the sofa as though fulfilling a long and painful desire.

"Now, Doris, tell me what you know about Mrs. Wakefield."

"What do you want to know?"

"She changed clothes three times the night she disappeared. Right?"

"Yes, she did."

"Why? Was she usually indecisive?"

"No. I don't know why. She couldn't seem to get the right look for the evening. It was most unusual. She was ordinarily so, uh, you know, organized and decisive. She never changed her mind."

"What else do you know about her?"

"Not much. She was a very nice lady. She hired me about three years ago, like I said."

"Tell me about her habits. Her peculiarities."

"Not much really. Except this room. She had it designed from top to bottom. It was her private part of the house."

"And her relations with her family?"

"She loved her cat. She had several good friends. Other ladies in this area. She was somewhat of a snob, not meaning anything bad by that term. She did not associate with anyone outside the gates normally. Except she was close to her Lady in Disguise representative. In fact, when her ordinary representative failed to show up that afternoon, she was mildly distressed. But she did say she like the substitute very much."

Plate stared at the maid. She was a very short moderately overweight young woman. She seemed very competent and truthful.

"What about Mr. Wakefield?"

"I really don't know, Lieutenant. I never really saw nothing between them. If you know what I mean?"

Plate decided direct questions about Natalie Wakefield's relationship with people were going to go nowhere. He changed his tactics.

"Tell me more about all the dresses she considered wearing that night. Were they all blue?"

"Yes, come to think of it, they were. Is that significant?'

Plate recalled Daphne's positive assertion about the significance of the color of the dress.

"I think so," he said, carefully watching Doris' reaction.

She looked baffled but he also detected a trace of alarm. "How?"

"How indeed?" Plate rose and walked over to the curtains that turned the corner. "I need to see the closet again. Could you raise the curtains for me so I don't do any damage to them?"

"It's only used to store seldom used items."

"I need to list the contents."

"Okay," said Doris doubtfully.

Carefully removing the Austrian poof panel, she spread it on the couch where the blue velvet beneath it gave it a different hue.

Hanging behind where the panel normally draped was a plain white window shade which masked the sheers' transparency. The shade rolled up at her touch.

Plate took out his notebook and made an inventory of the contents of the wide shallow closet.

A discarded chandelier that appeared to be broken.

An extra roll of carpet.

A broken folding chair.

A rectangular frame wall mirror.

Twenty boxes of expensive Christmas cards (The Wakefields sent only the best).

A cardboard box of old and out of season clothes.

Plate had Doris pull the box out and he knelt down beside it.

He knew he would not find any blue evening gowns but somehow hoped one or two might magically appear anyway.

No luck.

There was a pair of distinctive blue jeweled evening slippers. They had satin covered uppers with straps of jewels that wound around the ankles, almost to the calf. The pointed satin toes were closed in. Each shoe boasted a large solitary jewel that look like a deep rich sapphire but was too large to be real. The heels were only two inch square.

Practical evening shoes that also managed to convey wealth and sophistication. And everything about them was blue.

"Was she wearing these shoes the night she disappeared?"

"No sir, I'm sure she was not. She had a pair of spike heels. Madame was quite short and she really didn't enjoy wearing those shoes very much as they didn't give her any height. But she was especially fond of them and frequently wore them in familiar company where height was not an issue. I don't know why they were in that box. They should be in her closet."

"I would like to see the gowns that Mrs. Wakefield rejected that night?"

Doris closed the box, replaced it, fixed the curtain, and led him up to Mrs. Wakefield's bedroom.

As he climbed the stairs behind Doris, he wondered what had he missed in the blue room...

Besides the doors.

Natalie Wakefield's bedroom was impressive, beautiful, ritzy. Yet though larger and more ostentatious, it had nothing of the charm of her blue room downstairs.

She did have an old fashioned canopy bed.

An elaborate Marie Antoinette costume covered the entire bed. On a nearby table a faceless Styrofoam mannequin head, equipped with a weighted base for balance, held a wig of curls correctly formed. Several layers of colorful material draping the table contrasted with the near platinum blonde curls.

The hair was devoid of any jeweled décor as arranging such garnishments before the day of the ball would weigh it down and cause the curls to disarrange.

So while intricately styled, it was bereft of the crown it should have worn. The base of the mannequin head surrounded by cloth, the neck was not visible. Yet it was easy to imagine where the neck stopped and the flat table surface began.

Even with sunlight streaming in the windows of the socialite's bedroom, the wig on the mannequin head managed to be spooky, invoking the fate of the original woman who inspired the coveted costume.

"Knowing what happened to the real Marie Antoinette is what makes the costume so effective," said Doris.

"You're quite perceptive, Doris," said Plate.

"Thank you, sir," said Doris.

And she is right, realized Plate with mild surprise. *If you didn't know the history of the French queen, this elaborate getup would be just another fancy ball gown with an exaggerated Shirley Temple curls style wig. A step up from Halloween but with less elegance than a formal dress should have.*

A search of Mrs. Wakefield's closet revealed no blue evening gowns.

"I don't know what happened to the others," Doris insisted. "Maybe Mr. Wakefield sent them to be cleaned."

"Does he usually do things like that?"

"No."

Plate continued to question the maid about Natalie Wakefield's personal habits, hoping to keep her talking as they left the room. She chattered on as long as they were on the second floor.

As they approached the stairs, the servant's comments became shorter. She stopped at the top and took a deep breath before descending. Silently Doris slowly preceded Plate down the steps, her stout form balancing carefully as she put each foot down. She'd had no trouble going up the stairs, but the reverse seemed to be an ordeal for her.

Plate stopped behind her, to allow some space between them as she continued cumbersomely down. He found himself level with the top of the door frame of the scene of Natalie's disappearance.

Viewing the blue room as a still life portrait from the steps which ended almost directly in front of it, Plate suddenly realized what was missing.

"Why doesn't the desk in the blue room have a matching chair?"

"Mrs. Wakefield did not like the chair that came with the desk.

She tried several others and finally decided it looked better without one."

Doris gave this explanation as she reached the bottom of the stairs.

"How does she use the desk? Or was that the purpose of the folding chair that's now broken?" Plate followed her down quickly to continue the conversation on level ground.

"No, of course not. Mrs. Wakefield would never allow such a cheap looking chair to sit out in her house. Such inferior practical products are always kept hidden. I don't know where that chair came from. The desk is just decorative."

"No one ever sits at that desk?"

"No, it is too beautiful to use. That's what Mrs. Wakefield said."

"I see."

"It is that all, Lieutenant? Mr. Wakefield told me to give you full cooperation but I do have my duties to attend to."

"That's all about Mrs. Wakefield. But I need to know little bit about you, Doris. Tell me about yourself."

"Oh, I'm no one, Lieutenant. Just a maid." Doris smiled secretively as she spoke those words.

"You shouldn't say that."

Pressed, Doris gave Plate a brief biography.

She was from Wisconsin and had left her home state after graduating from high school. Times were hard there right now, jobs scarce. She had come to Houston hoping to find secretarial work but then found most good secretarial jobs in the 1980s required a bachelor's degree in a secretarial field.

Having only a high school education, Doris had applied for temporary work, whatever she could find. The agency had sent her to the Wakefield home and she and Mrs. Wakefield had made a positive connection, resulting in a permanent job.

"Unfortunately, people tend to look down on being a maid these days. Yet I find it fulfilling and satisfactory work. Of course I realize not everyone has a mistress like Mrs. Wakefield."

"What do you think happened to Mrs. Wakefield?"

"I really do think she- now you promise you won't tell Mr.

Wakefield that I said this-"

"Between you and me, Doris."

"I think she has gone of her own volition. I think she will come back."

"That sounds hopeful."

"I am quite hopeful that such is the case. She was very excited about this masquerade ball. If she's gone of her own free will, she is going to come back before then."

"And if she hasn't left of her own free will?"

"Then I'm afraid she's dead."

As he left the Wakefield mansion, Plate was entertaining the same fears. He glanced at his watch. He had stayed at the Wakefield place talking to Doris longer than he had planned. He had a lot to do before he could call it a day, go home and change, then head for the gates of Sand Waves

He had two appointments there.

A date with the past.

And a date with the future…

Chapter 18

"You're not in uniform?" Grace York made this observation as Plate stood in her back doorway.

"Still no servants allowed to stay after six?" Plate was looking at his watch as Grace let him in.

"Edward will never change," Grace said. "When he officially announces his candidacy for senator, he could request Secret Service protection. He has recently received death threats for his stand on abortion. You know he will never do it."

"I'm not in uniform because I'm technically off-duty," Plate explained. "I have a- uh, date with someone behind the gates so I was coming this way anyway."

"A date?"

"Personal. So why did you want to see me?"

The absurdity of the question, had it come only a year ago, struck Plate hard for a second.

A year ago, Plate had believed Grace York would become his wife. He had seen his entire future tied up with her.

Ostensibly it was during the investigation of the Mattworks affair that Plate no longer really thought of Grace as his girlfriend. Grace had been a suspect in the death of Amelia Mattworks' granddaughter.

At that time, she was divorced from Edward York. York was married to someone else and there seemed no chance the two would ever be together again.

Plate had believed he could keep his personal relationship with Grace separate from his investigation of the murder. The line he had mentally drawn to separate his relationship with Grace from the facts of the case, and the pursuit of its resolution, had dissipated.

When he had first drawn that line, he envisioned it disappearing towards the end of the case with the side focusing on his relationship eclipsing his professional duty.

Instead, it was the reverse.

The romance had dissolved. Edward York's second wife had vanished from the scene. Grace had remarried Edward.

All in less than a month.

Yet the breathtaking speed of these life changing events had not phased Plate. Somewhere in the background Daphne Martin had lingered from the extraordinary experiences during the great flood in November of the previous year.

Lingered like remnants of floodwaters refreshed by new rain.

But now there is Serena Towers…

Plate pushed thoughts of Serena from his mind.

He was almost surprised by the sound of Grace's voice as she continued to talk, answering his question.

"I want to speak with you about Natalie Wakefield."

"Just how well do you really know her?'

"She's a new friend. I have not known her long. But that does not make her less important to me. That's why I am speaking to you right now. I suppose I really just wanted reassurance from someone I knew. From you. I wanted reassurance that everything is being done to find her. I don't have many friends. If I lose one, I lose a significant percentage." Grace smiled wryly at Plate.

"I still consider you a friend."

"I appreciate that. More than you really think I do. But there's nothing like a girlfriend."

"I agree."

Plate and Grace stared at each other for a second and then both burst out laughing.

"Seriously, I am concerned about Natalie," said Grace, her mirth subsiding.

"Rumors are these disappearances have happened before and are somehow connected to other men," said Plate frankly.

He did not tell Grace about the body of the unknown woman who was not Natalie. He felt that would indicate to Grace that he was taking Natalie's disappearance the wrong way. Grace obviously felt no distress as to Natalie's physical safety. She just wanted her friend back with as little complications as possible.

Plate saw no need to alarm her.

"I know. I have heard those rumors, too."

"If she is your confidant-"

"She is my confidant at times. I don't think I am hers."

"I see. So she never told you anything?"

"No. I know she has gone away in the past. But not without her husband at least thinking that he knows where she is. And I don't really believe it has anything to do with any other man. I don't have anything to base that on. It's just that she doesn't have that female interest in men that, well, most of us have."

Plate and Grace grinned at each other again briefly, inadvertently. Then both dropped their eyes to the floor and suppressed their smiles.

Plate took Grace York's hand. "You have my word. I am taking Natalie Wakefield's disappearance seriously."

"Thank you," Grace said, somewhat regally.

Plate felt like he was going to be dismissed.

Not yet.

"Can I ask anything about this date behind the gates of Sand Waves?" Grace allowed a little bit of a feline tone to creep into her voice. Her attempt at a warm smile failed slightly.

"No." Plate spoke simply, with respect, and withdrew his hand.

"Well, thank you again." Grace spoke much more coldly and turned away from him.

He reached for the doorknob. This time he had been dismissed.

Chapter 19

Edward York joined his wife after Plate left.

"Why didn't you come out and say hello?" she asked.

"I cannot take these things as lightly as you," he said somberly.

"I don't see how you can think there is anything between him and me after all that happened. He's dating Serena Towers."

"Really? I would not have put those two together in a rational world."

"Yes, I know you don't like Serena because she doesn't share your political views-"

"Religious views," Edward corrected Grace. "Everyone has a right to their political views. Serena Towers disrespects God with every article she writes. If not overtly, then subtly."

"Oh, Edward, you are so old school. You are going to have to broaden your appeal if you are ever going to be elected president."

"I am only running for senator. And Grace, I will never compromise my beliefs to gain popularity."

Grace bit her lip. *If only I could make him see some compromise would help his cause. Would make the opposition seem more radical and obnoxious.*

Instead she said, "Even the church is softening its stance on many issues it was so rock solid on in the past."

"I cannot answer for anyone's conscience but my own," said Edward. "The church may have its periods of leniency, but in the end God's law, the natural law, must prevail. If it does not, all will be chaos."

"We can never have chaos in this country. The Constitution-"

"The Constitution is an instrument of God," Edward interrupted. "Built on God's Holy law and his commandments. Should it ever cease to be thus, it will be worthless."

Grace rubbed her head, which had suddenly began to ache.

Already charges of religious fanatic were being leveled against Edward. Not in Texas where his popularity was unchallenged, but in the northern parts of the country and the liberal west where a presidential bid from him was feared in 1988.

"You have the senate seat, but you are going to have to fight for more."

"Perhaps the senate is all God has planned for me," he said calmly. "You know if I did not believe it was His will, I would not be interested."

Grace knew it.

"I have let God speak to me through others," said Edward. "I feel no great personal calling to the political life. But it comes so easy, it seems so unanimous, that it must be in His plan."

"God must be giving this to you easy so that you will be inspired to fight when the time comes to carry on further," said Grace, somewhat patronizingly.

These words drew Edward's attention to his wife's position. She so seldom stated such opinions and he knew faith did not come easy or complete to her. She had to fight to retain her faith, and although he had never been in such a position, he admired her for persevering.

He hoped the restoration of their marriage was a sign to her of God's will in her life. But his hope was shallow, like that of a man who knows his life's companion is the one God has sent him but that their differences are irreconcilable in earthly life. They must muddle along as best they can until the next world where their happiness will be made complete.

The growing depraved condition of the world weighed Edward York down every day.

Every day he fought it with prayer and almost daily attendance at early morning Mass. He loved God, he loved his Savior, the comfort of the Holy Spirit, the Catholic Church. He loved Grace and he loved, in imagination, the children he prayed they would have someday.

He just did not love life.

Edward endured life. His wealth, work, house, relations with other human beings were all to be endured in this earthly life and he strove to so endure it all. Despite almost constant mental fatigue, he made this effort because he believed God wanted him to.

He had been given great wealth at birth, exceptional good looks and charm, deep intelligence. Now, as a man of 45, he had a beautiful wife whom he loved extraordinarily, even more that they had endured a bitter separation and tragedy which finally brought them back together.

For life, he now believed.

Until death do us part.

And his hopes for the future flourished not in his almost certain election to the senate, or any future presidential office. Those would be more life events to be endured.

Edward had come to the conclusion that only having a child would ever be an earthly experience that would be more than an endurance test.

A fabulous blessing from God.

The only bright light on his horizon between now and the ultimate end in which he would meet his Savior was the prospect of children.

Children to love, play with, make friends with, and as adults, ultimately carry on.

He regarded his wife's slender figure.

He knew it might never happen.

But after once having left, enduring a bitter separation from Grace, and distance from the grace of the church, even undeserved and temporary, he had vowed- never again.

Grace was his wife and only wife and never again would they part. If there were no children blessing their union, nevertheless the union would hold. A union without children could be equally blessed in the eyes of God. This was an acceptance long in coming to Edward.

"I've asked Father Thomas to say another Mass in hopes of a blessing," Edward said lightly to Grace. "I've been feeling a little low about it."

He knew she did not like to talk about infertility but she would know what he meant.

"Wonderful, darling," said Grace, wishing she did not love Edward quite so much. "I got a great report from the doctor last time. Let's think about happy events and maybe relaxing will help."

All tests had been run on both and nothing showed any reason parenthood would be denied them. The memory of the one pregnancy that had occurred was so bitter they had both put it out of daily thoughts. It was almost as though all it had been was a foreshadow of future pregnancies.

Especially to Grace. She saw the shadow all the time.

She went to her husband and put her arms around him, clutching him close to her. The two years she had been separated from him had almost killed her.

She felt like her very life lived within him.

By the end of that hard time, she would have gladly have had that child to have gotten him back, to have escaped enduring those days of anguish.

Now she did have him back.

Getting him back had, for the first time in her life, given her faith that God indeed existed, whereas before, the words 'hopeful agnostic' would have described her. She liked her new found faith. But while outwardly embracing the Catholic Church, she was far from convinced of Catholic dogma.

In this new relationship, God seemed more to her like a friend than a stern Father or Savior. A Friend who loved her and could keep her safe and grant her happiness, while making suggestions on how she should behave.

A Friend who had graciously allowed Edward to return to her and put her world right again.

Grace was grateful.

"You're everything to me," said Grace to Edward.

He smiled and returned her embrace. "Let's take advantage of this time we have," he said, and ran his hand over her breasts.

"Definitely, just let me get something to drink from the kitchen. Go on upstairs and pick out some music, something upbeat."

Edward released her and started towards the staircase. He turned and called back to her, she tilted her head up to him and he was thinking how beautiful she was when viewed from above.

"Could you bring me some apple juice?"

"Of course." Grace had to pick her way by some remodeling in progress connected to preparing the house for the masquerade ball. The men worked only in the daytime but they left their equipment scattered around and their project was not yet complete so the house layout was temporarily awkward.

Alone in the kitchen, Grace prepared apple juice first, then reached on a high shelf for a decorative canister.

She opened the small plastic case she kept hidden inside and punched a little white pill from the package. She counted to make sure she hadn't missed any.

She really wanted Edward tonight but she could always say she felt tired. He never forced her. However, she had been diligent, the right pill for the day was the next one.

Good, she thought. *If only Edward could see our love is all we need. If I can just get him to go ahead with the plans to adopt or just wait a few more years until-*

Grace's images halted there. She did not like to think of herself growing old.

She wondered briefly about Plate and Serena. She had heard gossip. Grace was not surprised that someone more sophisticated than that insurance agent had turned his head.

She wondered how she compared to Serena in Plate's memories.

Never mind, she thought. *I have Edward. He is all I will ever need in this world.*

She swallowed the pill and put the package back in its hiding place.

Wife of a senator, maybe First Lady before she was 40, she wanted to be beautiful, slim, young and free…

Chapter 20

Serena Towers was a guest of the Watson family and they lived behind the gates in a compound featuring a large mansion with several thoroughbred horses stabled there. Miranda Watson had grown up riding and frequently placed in Houston-Galveston area horse show competitions.

She had abandoned the activity upon attaining adulthood but still rode for pleasure.

Plate was taking Serena to dinner. It would be a pleasurable distraction from the anticipation of the upcoming chore of taking Morris Tates to see the burned corpse.

Serena had just come back from a ride so Plate had to wait for her to change. No member of the Watson family was home. Shown to the library by a maid, he had time to take in the 1920s modern style furniture complete with period light fixtures.

The Watsons had an extensive library of historical books, covering all the way from ancient Rome to early twentieth century wars.

Plate was perusing a copy of a text on the rise of Stalin in early Soviet Russia when Serena appeared.

Her fresh and glowing beauty erased all political thoughts from his mind, almost all thoughts of Natalie Wakefield and Emma Tates and their disappearances…

And the inevitable ordeal to come with the distraught schoolteacher.

Plate went to embrace Serena.

Morris Tates loved his wife despite her shortcomings. She had been less than the devoted stepmother to his children that he had hoped for. She was gone for weeks, occasionally months at a time for her job.

Which left him lonely and feeling much as if he was back where he had been as a divorced man.

That she did not fit the 1980s standards of beauty, that she was overweight and never wore makeup or stylish clothes, were the least of his concerns.

She was classy and witty when she wanted to be. More educated than she admitted, he suspected. She was just shy about it. She was an enthusiastic sexual partner and she never failed to make him feel special and appreciated no matter what activity they shared.

He loved her and wanted her found.

So when he reached his hotel, after an exhausting car trip with two children and a difficult reunion with his ex-wife, who was perturbed when the children she abandoned over 28 months ago did not greet her with ecstatic hugs, and found a message from Lieutenant Plate, he visibly sagged. The concerned hotel receptionist offered to send a complimentary glass of milk to his room as soon as he was settled.

He declined her offer but did allow a porter to take his bags, a service he would have ordinarily frugally refused, and tipped the boy $4.00.

What does money matter anymore? he anguished, stretching on the bed with the phone receiver in his hand. *If Emma is dead, I'm not sure I can go on. Frieda will have to take the children if I kill myself. She'll have no choice.*

Yet even as he dropped his head on the hotel pillow, with suicidal impulses flickering through him, he knew they were puffs of smoke. He would never kill himself as long as his children were alive. And his ex-wife would still have a choice. She might refuse custody and let her parents take them.

That would be worse than anything. They were drug addict hippies since the 1960s, who still kept their recreational pursuits just outside the boundaries of the law.

Why did I ever marry a girl with parents like that? he wondered, as he dialed Plate long distance. *And this phone call is going to cost a damn fortune.*

Before punching the last number on the hotel's modern push button phone, he almost hung up, considering the possibility of calling collect.

After all, the cop wanted to talk to him. So why should he have to pay?

But in the end his pride was too strong to try for a collect transfer. He punched the last button of the number the receptionist had given him.

"Sand Waves Police Department. Officer Jordan."

Tates asked for Plate.

"The lieutenant is off for the evening. But if you are returning his call I will page him and have him call you back. I cannot guarantee he will answer his page, but he will get a message from our answering service soon as he checks in."

"Great, no urgency on my part," said Tates, sitting up on the side of the bed and talking as fast as possible to keep the call as short as could be. "The lieutenant knows where I am tonight, and tomorrow I will be at my ex-wife's house, with the number being- hold on, I got it right here."

Tates simultaneously rejoiced and cursed. He would not have to bear the cost of the conversation between him and Plate but he did not have the number of his ex-wife's residence right in front of him, which would have cut this expensive long distance call even shorter.

He did find the number in his billfold after a few seconds, relayed it to the night officer, said goodbye and hung up.

Still sitting on the side of the bed, Tates pulled a laminated sheet from under the phone.

Surcharge of $2.00 per each 10 minutes of all long distance calls, in addition to phone company charges, it said in bold letters.

"Crap," he said, and pulled open the nightstand drawer in hopes of a room service menu. He began to regret turning down the complimentary glass of milk. He did not like milk but it would have saved him having to buy a drink with his meal.

But in the drawer there was no menu.

Just a book.

Turned face down and totally blank on the back.

Tates rarely stayed in hotels. He did not have the money to travel. So he did not immediately know what book it was. He turned it over.

A Bible.

Suddenly tears came to Tates eyes. Here he was worrying about the cost of a long distance phone call, when the call from Plate might be news that Emma was dead.

Surely if the police officer had good news about his wife, he would have left a positive message.

Tates held the Bible in his hand, still closed, and rocked it back and forth, staring at it and feeling its textured skin in his hands.

Then he opened it, not intending to read it actually. He was not a religious man, but not irreligious either. He rarely considered it.

Some of the words are in red, he realized, *wonder why?*

A section leapt out at him.

And he said to them, Verily I say to you. There is no man that hath left house, or parents, or brethren, or wife, or children, for the Kingdom of God's sake,

Who shall not receive manifold more in this present time, and in the world to come life everlasting...

Chapter 21

Darica kept a small unmarked Bible in her desk at the newspaper office.

She had been raised in church but rarely attended anymore. But she liked to keep the Bible with her. It came in surprisingly handy when she was having trouble making decisions about how to write some of the more sordid news stories she was given.

Frequently she had to make decisions that affected other people's lives. Newspapers, especially the chain she worked for, did not need guilt beyond a reasonable doubt to convict people in print.

Working for a small intensely serious paper also gave her more power than many reporters working for the big dailies. She had to do her share of cut and paste editing, assembled in a different location where the paper was actually printed.

In centuries past, journalists had to set type, but the 1980s technology had made typesetting obsolete. Now the text, headlines and photos were printed like pictures on large poster size sheets that became uncut jumbled pieces of a jigsaw puzzle.

Copy was printed in long sheets on slick semi-glossy paper, with pictures and stories mixed. Manually, the paper had to be put together like a predetermined puzzle, a work up of the final product, before it went to press.

The story texts, headlines and photos, along with advertisements, had to be located and then cut from the sheets with Exacto knives. Then the strips of copy were run through hot wax machines, and adhered to slick white newspaper size surfaces in the correct configuration.

This was a slow, tedious process.

A mock-up of each page was painstakingly cut and pasted, with lined tape forming boxes around advertisements, which came out of the printing process the exact sized purchased.

The result was a galley of every page of the whole paper, to be constructed and then proofed.

Before this could happen, all elements of the paper were initially relayed by the new 1980s computer technology to the printer. Special nonprinting characters now sized headlines, captions, and other displays like magic, if those newspaper ingredients were not the default type size.

If a mistake was made in the math, the machine would print the wrong size. Then the incorrect printing had to be redone by hand with scissors. A whole page could be thrown off by one incorrect headline.

Since the final letter sizes could not be changed after printing, whatever could be cut, would be cut to make the page work. Ads were off limits but photos could be cropped or discarded. Story copy was not changeable either but stories could be shorted.

That was why reporters wrote from the top down, meaning the most important information was at the beginning of the story and each paragraph held lessor information. An ending paragraph was always written so that if it were lopped off in the final cut, the story would still be integral.

Of course if the reverse happened and there was too much space, that was easy.

The paper kept classical inserts in every size imaginable to fill unexpected space.

Support the American Heart Association.

Support the American Cancer Society.

Etc...

Attend the church of your choice.

That one had been discontinued recently.

Still working on stories she wrote herself, Darica could also see everything turned in by everyone else that had been selected by the editor for print when it was her turn to do the final read through for missed corrections, new informational additions, and any final editorial change requests.

These did not come from the editor who Darica actually worked with and called boss. That person was really no more than a glorified reporter with a title and a public face.

The real editorial commands came from persons unseen. They came by special messenger.

With markings, identifying them for what they were, known only to the newspaper staff.

110

They were taken seriously.

But even those requests were at the mercy of column space configured in the layout lab.

Darica chewed on her pencil in disgust. She had made the corrections requested to the short society piece concerning the upcoming masquerade ball.

She dared not disobey the orders but maybe there was something she could do.

The Bible said man was his brother's keeper.

Daphne was not her brother, but Darica believed sisterhood counted too.

She deliberately mis-sized the headline so it would be twice as big as expected.

She could not trust that she would be the staff member to lay out that particular page so she was leaving nothing to chance.

Through the magic of computer manipulation the single paragraph concerning well-known investigative journalist, Serena Towers, was moved to the end of the story.

Forbidden to cut it out yet, the least Darica could do was put it at the end, confident that it would be chopped off in layout when space became tight due to the oversized headline.

And well-known investigative journalist Serena Towers is staying for a while in Sand Waves, the guest of the Watson family behind the gates, even though her colleague, the Watson heiress, Miranda, is nowhere to be seen, off on an assignment in Europe.

Taking a short hiatus from work, Serena has been seen about town on the arm of a well-known local law enforcement official, Lieutenant Sinclair Plate, whose name was mentioned in connection with the murder investigation of Amelia Mattworks' granddaughter this past January. Young in years for his rank, Lieutenant Plate is considered an eligible bachelor in Sand Waves. Ms. Towers, winner of a number of investigative journalism awards nationwide, would make for an interesting companion as well.

"Hopefully, the paper will have enough ads that there won't be space for that," Darica said, murmuring aloud to herself.

That SOB cop doesn't need the pleasure of seeing his name in the paper, she thought. *And Serena Towers can kiss my-*

The phone rang shrilly, jolting her musings.

She was the only one in the office at the time, finishing up late typewritten work that should have been turned in before deadline. Fortunately all she had to do was make the corrections in red pencil and drop it in her editor's basket.

It would be there in the morning when the editor got to work and reviewed, then entered corrections as last minute data during the time the computers were hooked up to the phone lines.

The editor would never know Darica had turned it in late.

As the phone continued ringing, the sides of her particleboard cubicle vibrated slightly with each jarring tone. Every cubicle in the small office had a phone.

Unlike most home phones, these square box pushbutton types also had large square buttons at the bottom that were semi-transparent. For each different extension directed to each different reporter's desk, a different button lit up when the extension numbers were pressed directly after the main phone number by the calling party.

Darica was used to such advanced technology. In the cities where she normally worked, the phone system was even slightly more advanced with each extension having a slightly different timed ring sequence.

Here the same bell tolled for everyone. It was necessary to look at the phone to see which button was lit up.

Darica was a bit surprised to see her button glowing. She was so new at the paper, she did not get many calls directed to her.

Moreover, as it was after hours, the console operator was gone, so the caller had to know her extension before dialing to get her button activated.

"Hello. Darica." She spoke simply into the mouthpiece. She did not identify the name of the paper nor give the caller her last name. She would usually have done both.

However, to receive a call directed at her this time of night was a little spooky even for an experienced reporter.

Maybe it was just some kid playing with a series of numbers and

112

just happened to come up with the right combination that included her extension.

Of course, that was ridiculous.

"Darica!" said the voice on the other end of the phone line, "Long time no see! What a coincidence! We're both in this little weird colony at the same time. I'm on vacation. I think it would absolutely be a blast if we got together."

"Serena?" Although Darica was sure the distinctive Northeastern accented voice was that of Serena Towers, it had been so many years, and was such a shock, that the identification was formed as a question.

Darica and Serena had been journalism majors at the same time at the same college and had worked together on the college newspaper.

As far as Darica was concerned, those experiences were the only elements in the world they had in common.

In college, Serena had been slightly older, a rich girl throwing family money around. Darica had been on scholarship, a tight budget, and pulling down a part time job.

"Why don't we meet for lunch at that wonderful restaurant inside the Toy Museum tomorrow?" Serena asked the question just as if they had been good pals all these years and had only a normal amount of differences between them. No more divergent than most people of the same sex and generation in the same society.

Darica was about to decline curtly. Then her journalistic instincts kicked in. She didn't for a second believe that Serena Towers ever took vacations and if she did, the wealthy freelancer went to Monte Carlo or the French Riviera or the like, not Sand Waves.

Darica was tired of writing society news. Maybe this was the break she was hoping for.

Chapter 22

Serena Towers was very pleased with herself.

Approaching 30, she had accomplished a great deal in her life. She was an award-winning freelance journalist, her name not only known to her peers but to a smattering of the general public. She was tall, an accomplishment that she could not claim credit for, thin, she could definitely claim credit for that, and while her facial features were sharp and not sequentially defined, she knew if she dressed well she cut a striking figure in almost any type of society.

She was sure this was why Police Lieutenant Sinclair Plate found her attractive.

Not that she did not find him attractive. She most certainly did. But more than his physical attributes, his somewhat unique place in Sand Waves society made him an extremely valuable contact for her work.

Dating him had been something of a whirlwind affair. Involved in a master's degree program at one of the local universities, he had dropped his studies to make himself available as her escort for any evening she desired him. That impressed her. And he was that rare thing in the 1980s for a man, a gentleman who did not force himself.

This was a relief that Serena was not used to. Dedicated as she was to living in the modern era, she was surprised at first how relaxing it was not to have to worry about performing sexually on demand.

As Plate continued to pay her attention, she got used to it. She began to let her guard down with him in a way that was slightly dangerous, and although she was dimly aware of it, the feeling of acceptance as a human being was so nice that she put the risk in the back of her mind.

So she readily embraced the idea of him escorting her to the masquerade ball. He proposed the combination casually, first asking if she was actually going, without prying as to what capacity- personal or professional. And she did not tell him. She only said yes.

So he told her, since he was going to be there in uniform, but less on duty than as a social obligation, he might as well come by and pick her up.

Why not? she mused. *After all, I have little enough real pleasure in this life. I've unselfishly served my profession since my college graduation and really even before. This cop is fun. Why shouldn't I have a little fun?*

"And she told me right out who is taking her to the ball," said Darica bitterly.

"We are no longer in high school, Darica," said Daphne. "I'm not going to be brokenhearted if I don't get the right date to the prom. This is the 1980s. I can go to the dance alone."

"But you were so sure about him, just a few days ago. One thing- she smokes, so she will probably give him lung cancer if he marries her."

"I realize you think telling me this nonsense is doing me a favor. I already knew about it. These things happen. All's fair in love and war and all that. I really don't want to talk about it. I mean here I am, like an idiot, talking to you on a pay phone at the drugstore. I get a note in my mailbox saying call you on your car phone at a certain time. Like a cloak and dagger spy, I leave a comfortable home and go out into the cold and spend twenty cents to call you when I have a perfectly good working phone at home."

"I told you earlier the reason we need to contact each other this way."

"Okay, fine, so maybe my phones are tapped. I don't know. I don't really care. But what's teed me off is that I had to go to all this trouble just to hear you tell me my boyfriend- my ex-boyfriend that is- is taking someone you know to the masquerade ball."

"I'm doing you a favor. So you won't take him back when Serena dumps him. I know her reputation. She goes through men like we go through hairspray."

"I don't use hairspray. And I don't need you to keep tabs on my personal life. I never interfered with your marriage, did I? I just acted as maid of honor and minded my own business." Daphne bit her lip. She knew Darica's failed marriage was a sore spot. But she wanted her sister to move on from debasing Plate verbally.

"I just wanted you to know what a jerk he is." Darica's voice took on a hurt usually associated with her ex-husband's shadow. But she did not speak of him. Daphne saw her opportunity to force the conversation in a tangential direction.

"Okay, he's a jerk. Let's just leave it at that. By the way," Daphne's tone altered slightly as she attempted to change the subject. "What else did Serena Towers tell you when the two of you met?"

"Nothing that would concern you. How do you know Serena?"

"I've just heard of her," Daphne replied in a light tone of voice. "I have read many of her articles in *Newsweek* and the like."

"You are better off not knowing."

"All I'm curious about is the woman who is taking my place. Oh come on, gossip a little!" Daphne tried to put amusement in her voice as if they were both still in high school talking about crushes on teenage boys with rival teenage girlfriends, after all. "Tell me everything she said."

"Don't be silly, Daphne. The things she said about your ex-boyfriend would only upset you. And nothing else she said would interest you at all."

"Will you let me be the judge of that?" Daphne heard impatient shuffling behind her. Another person was standing in line to use the pay phone. Daphne glanced at the other vacant stall. The woman, who was clutching a toddler, shook her head and drew a line across her throat with her free hand, indicating the other phone was not working.

"At least tell me what is she going to wear to the ball?" Daphne asked impatiently. "Hurry up. Somebody else is waiting to use the phones and apparently this is the only one working."

"You have the strangest questions. Why would you care?"

"Just call it female jealousy. I want to make sure she doesn't outshine me. Come on, I don't care what professional journalistic conversations you had, everybody is talking about this ball. I know it had to have been mentioned. What is she wearing?"

"All right if you must know. We did talk about it. She will be plain and simple Betsy Ross. So just spruce up yourself a little bit as Deborah Franklin and you won't have anything to worry about. Nobody knows what Deborah looked like anyway, much less what

116

kind of clothes she would have worn."

"You didn't tell Serena Towers anything about me?"

"Of course not."

"She doesn't know I used to date Plate?"

"She never mentioned you and neither did I. She seemed to think Plate was previously involved with Grace York during the time period she and Edward were divorced and he married another woman. She knows that woman, too, the one that left Edward and Sand Waves for Hollywood. They all know each other you know. That social set. Anyway, just to cushion it for you, Serena claimed her relationship with Plate was going very well and might even be permanent. But I don't believe it. Nothing is permanent with those people. Look at Edward York's history."

"I know all about that. Well, okay there's a lady waiting for the phone. I've got to go." Daphne hung up the phone and whispered, "Sorry!" to the woman standing behind her. She slowly walked towards the exit door of the drugstore.

Then she had a second thought. She grabbed a basket and rolled it around the store, picking up a few odd items at random, glancing over to the pay phone occasionally as she repeatedly passed it. Eventually it was available again.

She parked her basket on an aisle, grabbed more change out of her purse and went back to the phone to make another call.

Serena Towers has to be rich enough to afford any costume she could think of, thought Daphne, as the muted sound of the target phone ringing came through the receiver at her ear. *Why would she go as something simple? This whole ball must be rigged.*

She had decided to tell Plate everything.

"Lieutenant Plate is out on assignment right now. Could I help you?"

Daphne recognized the voice of Officer Skaar from previous acquaintance but she did not want to interact.

"No, thank you," she said simply, abandoning her resolve.

She hung up the pay phone and went home.

Chapter 23

Lieutenant Plate tried not to spend too much time comparing Serena Towers and Daphne Martin. He believed his relationship with Serena was going wonderfully.

Using the tactic of courting her in an old fashioned way, the same tactic he had once decided would work well with Daphne, was an even more fabulous success with the celebrated journalist.

Serena was relaxing and becoming more and more susceptible to his desires. He had no doubt, barring any outside interference, the time would soon come for him to make his move.

He was enjoying watching Serena from a distance when she was not with him. His job as a police officer made that surprisingly easy. Other than traffic violators and potential criminals, few people in Sand Waves noticed a patrol car weaving in and out of area parking lots and streets. This was normal patrol work seeking to reassure all the residents, whether inside or outside the gates, that the police were vigilantly guarding them from evildoers.

And when he was in plain clothes and in an unmarked car it was that much easier.

If only it could also be productive.

So far the only thing that had surprised Plate about Serena Towers' activities was her meeting with the local newspaper journalist Darica Daniels.

He had known there was a new worker at the paper, one with a car phone, no less. He really had not paid any attention to her. Being familiar with area journalists fell on the periphery of his job. Ascertaining their ambitions and courting their favors fell under the auspices of Chief Brecken's position.

As second in command of the small force in Sand Waves, Plate was more of an auxiliary contact with the local press, furthering relations with them when other responsibilities were slack enough to allow for socializing.

Right now, everything going on was keeping him extremely busy. Work related activities and his time consuming relationship with Serena Towers had already caused him to have to drop his current

118

university class. Serena's work as an international freelance journalist did not fall under the purveyance of Sand Waves press relations.

Serena had already made it clear to her new attendant that his work as a law enforcement officer in Sand Waves was so far outside the realm of her sophisticated high level investigative pieces that he need not worry about any common conflicts of interest he might have if he were dating a local correspondent.

He had really just forgotten about the new *Sand Waves Whisperer* journalist until Serena drew his attention to Darica by meeting with her in an odd location at odd hours of the day.

At that moment he missed just being able to go over to Daphne's and getting her to run the name through her insurance office computers. But although on the surface he and Daphne were remaining friends, it was a little too forward to be consulting openly with her right now.

Serena might misunderstand.

He would have to find out who Darica Daniels was the old fashioned way. With phone calls and paper inquiries directed to past locations about past activities.

He did note with interest when Darica exited the newspaper offices and stopped at the local phone booth just down the street. Granted, in her profession, she might be taking measures to make sure competitive colleagues on the same paper would not get wind of any of her sources. Or the source she was phoning might dictate such procedures.

Why else not use her car phone?

He suspected she may be contacting Serena Towers as the two had gone to journalism school together in college.

And he could not trust Serena to tell him anything. She was a journalist first. She had already made it clear their professional personal relationships would be strictly separate.

So be it, he philosophized.

It would take several days to pull the phone records of the pay phone Darica was using, and if his contact at the phone company was feeling snippy, he might even have to get a court order, which would delay it even further.

But in the end, he would know whom she was calling. It was just a matter of time.

His biggest problem, after Serena brought Darica to his attention, was that he could not follow both women at the same time. Earlier, in uniform one day, he had managed to brush against Darica in the street and she had recoiled from him as if he were vermin. Obviously she did not like the police and was not going to be susceptible to his charm.

It was a quandary and he was not sure what he was going to do about it. He did not want to call in any of his fellow officers. He did not want anyone to know he was keeping the woman in his life under surveillance. And he had yet to think of an excuse for not being able to follow Darica, other than the truth.

That might look like he was putting his personal life above his professional obligations.

Meanwhile, all legitimate leads and all outlandish leads in the disappearances of the two women, Natalie Wakefield and Emma Tates, had completely dried up. Those cases were not taking up any time or resources.

If he were to diligently pursue those cases beyond the normal investigation protocol, he would not have time to follow either Serena Towers or Darica Daniels.

He pondered what to do.

Finally he made a choice as to which woman to follow. When she reached her destination this time, he was surprised to find the choice did not matter.

Both mysterious reporters, the one he was working to seduce and the one he was suspicious of her activities, came together at a small building owned by the school district and located at the edge of the green belt.

This particular building was adjacent to a strip center. Driving deep into the woods was not necessary to access it.

This time, Plate was not in his patrol car nor was he even in uniform. He had surreptitiously shadowed Serena Towers, thinking now that his relationship had progressed, it was important that she not ever catch that he was stalking her.

So in casual clothes, covered by the deepening darkness of the evening as the shops in the strip center slowly closed down and cut their lights, Plate observed Serena arrive.

He watched with great interest as she rapped on the door, spoke softly to whoever guarded the entrance and was let in. Several more women arrived, repeating the pattern, before Darica Daniels entered in the same fashion.

It had all the elements of an old fashioned sorority meeting, yet there was something about the women that was odd. Plate could not quite put his finger on it.

He continued to watch but there was nothing else to see.

Chapter 24

Inside the small building, the largest room had been cleared of movable displays and rows of chairs set up. More than 40 near identical figures settled in the chairs that sat before a small podium. The woman who came to address them from that podium wore identical clothing, also complete with mask and gloves. But she was different.

Her entrance was choreographed. Quickly up sidesteps, her robe flowing, her cloak hemmed the perfect length so that it barely brushed the floor as she strode, it would have taken quick and scrutinizing observation to have noticed the differences in her body structure.

She was not tall. Her arms were not long.

She carried no basket of products.

The expressions and gestures of her arms and hands were so fluid and graceful that it did not give her differences away.

"Ladies, you know why you are here."

There was acquiescent murmuring amongst the women.

"You are the vanguard of our movement. Most of you come from humble beginnings and the upcoming masquerade ball will be your first time inside the gates of Sand Waves. Do not be intimidated. The powerful and wealthy that live there are no more than you. But they are used to their every need being taken care of. And Ladies, that is your job at the upcoming ball, the rich and powerful will be identified to you and you will take care of their needs. You will hover next to them with graciousness and servitude. Detailed instructions will be provided for each of you. When you leave tonight, there is an envelope with your name on it. Take it. Take it home with you. Read it every day. Memorize it. Keep the notion in your heart that by giving your best at the ball, you will be performing a service to our greater cause of serving those in need in the world. These people at this masquerade ball, they are the ones with the money and the power. They are the ones who can make or break our organization. Heed your instructions well, Ladies. Do not fail us."

The speaker tightened her grip on the podium as she watched her audience murmur in anticipation as they rose and made their way to the table with the envelopes. There was a fluttering of papers as they all helped each other find the correct one.

"Remember, Ladies, don't open your envelope until the night of the ball if it has a star on it. This means you have been selected for portrayal of a supporting character or as an extra in one of the spontaneous skits. You will be given a script when you arrive and turn your envelope in. These rules are to ensure that we provide the most spontaneous and relaxed entertainment for our guests. And our skits will be memorable and talked about long after we're gone."

The meeting ended and most departed.

"Headmistress," said a Lady in Disguise to her leader, catching her alone in the restroom.

The headmistress turned, still completely masked.

"I've contacted the two women you have suggested as replacements," said the first speaker. "They are here. I think they will serve our purposes well. Both are eager to join and are willing to serve their time on the sales paths before moving up."

"That's what interested me most about you, how you were willing to come on board at the bottom level. I knew you had to be after a story."

"True, nothing gets by you."

"It did you credit that you did not deny you were a reporter."

"It would have been stupid to deny the obvious."

"And you have been invaluable in setting up this masquerade. Once it is done, I promise you will be free to write your story."

"I have not been impatient."

"Still, I understand secrecy is hard on you."

"Yes, secrecy is hard, but I know what the rewards will be."

"You can relay pertinent information to the new recruits."

"Yes, ma'am."

The journalistic-minded Lady exited the bathroom.

The headmistress sighed. She wondered if any of the women she was responsible for knew anything about the real rewards to come. However, there was no more time to sound out her new recruits.

It was time for the next meeting. No more than twenty women were asked to this conference. As each woman gave the password and was let into the meeting, she detoured through a make-shift dressing room to don her robe.

A serving Lady in Disguise was on hand there, her cloak already in place, to make sure each member exited properly disguised. All the Ladies in this group were in the company costume, but they did not wear the cat-eyed festive masks of the previous group.

They wore full face masks, reminiscent of female princess Halloween masks but much more elegant and expensively made. The masks came in several sizes, had flexible natural material that breathed for comfort with a thin strip of adhesive that kept them anchored in place on the forehead, under the chin, and near the cheekbones. From a distance it would almost appear to be a normal face.

All exterior features of every woman were completely covered except their eyes. Slits for eyes also varied in size, as did mouth and nose openings and once a Lady had been in this level of the organization for the probationary six months, she could virtually order a near custom-made mask by properly mixing the measurements.

Sewn to the edges of the hoods of these garments were auburn ringlets designed to fall down over the cheeks and forehead. New members were instructed how to wear the mask in coordination with the head covering.

Everyone invited was present when the headmistress reprised her advancement to the stage. It was not that most had remained while all the others had left. Rather the others had departed and many of these women had arrived.

They were the highest level in the organization.

"A short technical announcement," she began. "The hair dressing sessions scheduled on the morning of the ball for those assigned characters have been canceled. The participants were given wigs instead. The headpieces were included in the costumes."

"Are we getting more information about the performances?" asked a Lady in the audience.

"We have carefully selected which ladies will be onstage during all the skits," said the headmistress to the select group before her.

"As coordinating committee members, it is your responsibility

124

to contact the women assigned to you and direct them."

A hand was raised in the crowd.

"Headmistress, is there someone to take the places of those missing at the ball?" asked a Lady in a loud voice.

"Is there any news on our missing?" asked another questioner.

"Unfortunately, no word," said the headmistress. "We must keep all our Ladies who cannot be with us anymore, in our consciousness. No matter the reason they are gone, they served and deserve to be remembered."

This statement was met with approving murmurs and scattered applause.

The headmistress whispered to the Lady she had at her side. "That reminds me, I have something that needs to be delivered to Emma Tates' husband."

"Oh?"

"A note that will comfort and perhaps even relieve some of his distress, if you know what I mean." said the headmistress, still whispering. "Can we trust one of the newcomers to deliver it unopened?"

"I think so."

"Remember to tell her the consequences of disobedience."

"She's been asking for an assignment. I am sure she is ready and will do her best."

The headmistress handed an envelope to her compatriot, who then left by the side door.

"Now, back to the masquerade ball," the headmistress spoke up. "Quite right, we have backup plans. This is our chance. Right now, we are a household word in most big cities in America. After this ball, we should be household words throughout the whole of the United States. And may I remind you there is much more to this country than cities like Houston, Dallas, Galveston, or even Sand Waves."

Behind the masks, eyes began to glaze as the headmistress turned the talk from events, which interested them, to the repetitive sales inspirational lines they were so used to.

The meeting broke up with the usual- "Now go out there and make the world your own! Sell, Ladies! Sell! Sell! Sell!"

Chapter 25

Morris Tates arrived back at his house near dawn and in some lower back pain from having driven all the way from Ohio with a minimum of stops.

He had pressed on, despite being extremely sleepy near the end.

It was with some trepidation that he had left the children with their mother in that northerly state.

But when Lieutenant Plate's message had reached him that he was needed to possibly identify Emma's body, his ex-wife had insisted she would keep the children safe while he returned to Texas for that grim chore. Without the children, he could drive nonstop, except to refill the gas tank, and get there much faster.

He had to admit that it was peaceful without the children and the drive had been a chance to prepare mentally, think, and listen.

In the hotel room that first night after receiving the message that Plate was trying to contact him, he had read the Bible until he had fallen asleep. Lieutenant Plate had returned his call early that morning as he prepared for his second meeting with his ex-wife.

Before he told Frieda about the body that had been found, as soon as he had got to her apartment, he had begun to talk about what he had read in the Bible, without knowing why.

Some of it had struck him so he just wanted another adult opinion. He approached the subject shyly at first.

To his surprise, he found Frieda a sympathetic listener, something she had never been when they were married.

"I, too, have done some soul searching since our divorce," she had told him, then apologized for the cliché. "It's more than that. I cannot explain it. It is spiritual."

The conversation evolved into his telling her about the possibility of Emma's body being found.

Frieda's demeanor was incredibly sympathetic and, in addition to promising to keep the children safe, she insisted he return at once and could depend on her driving the children back to Texas, if necessary. She had gone to her closet and pulled out a set of cassette tapes for him to listen to on his drive home.

So he had listened to the Bible all the way back, wondering alternately at the words he was hearing and at the surprising revelation that Frieda was even acquainted with such a book, much less had it on cassette tapes.

It was near dawn when Tates reached his driveway. He was quite sleepy so was only mildly alarmed when a car pulled in behind him.

A woman in a hooded cloak came to his car window. He rolled it down to tell her his wife was away and not in need of any hair care products.

"You may remember me. I am Emma's Lady in Disguise representative."

Morris Tates stared at her blankly.

"I'm not here to sell anything. I've come to lend support during this crisis. I know you are about to contact the police about identifying Emma and I did not want you to be alone."

"I was going to get a couple hours sleep before contacting the policeman," Tates mumbled as he slowly got out of his car.

"I'm just here to deliver this message of sympathy and implore you to read it."

"Okay. Thank you," said Tates, as he took a large envelope from the woman. He walked up to his front door and fumbled for his keys.

"Promise me you will read this message before going to see the police. It will give you much needed comfort and strength for the ordeal to come."

Tate turned and stared at the woman. Her eyes glittered as she held him back from opening his front door.

"Uh, okay, I promise. My absolute word, scout's honor."

And in his state of exhaustion and stress, Tates actually held up his hand in the Boy Scout signal.

The Lady in Disguise relaxed and smiled kindly at him. "You don't know how relieved I am to hear you speak so," she said, then turned and went back down his driveway.

He felt for a second as if she had actually physically embraced him. Yet she had never touched him. Their only contact had been a brief moment when both of their hands had touched the envelope she gave him.

Sleepily, Tates went on into his house and settled down at once on his den sofa.

I didn't realize those Lady in Disguise women were some kind of religious group but that one had a pure fanatical look about her eyes, was his last thought, before he fell asleep, still clutching the envelope she had given him in his hand.

The woman who had just accomplished her first humanitarian mission for the Lady in Disguise charities walked slowly in the cold back to her car, which was parked a block over from the Tates home.

She was so exhilarated that she did not feel the chill in the air as she stepped over the curb. Parking out of sight of the target house was a silly rule, she had believed previously. But she understood it now.

She was proud she had been called upon for this task and was planning to record in her diary exactly the excitement and emotions involved in fulfilling the assignment.

This was against the rules but she felt she would be called upon to testify someday.

And no one knew she kept written records of her few appointments, much less a secret diary. She would not be able to write in that hidden ledger until her husband's job took him away again.

Meanwhile a note in her calendar book would have to do.

She reached into her glove compartment and pulled out her Daily Record 1983. Flipping through its pages, which were mostly blank, she wrote with exuberance the location of the assignment, with a small note for posterity.

On this day in February of 1983, I fulfilled my first Lady in Disguise Charity assignment of taking a sealed note of comfort to a recently deceased customer's husband.

I complied with all instructions and relayed the headmistress's verbal message to him as directed verbatim and got him to accept the envelope with the sympathy note with no trouble.

Signed,
Peg Brown

Chapter 26

"I have a short meeting scheduled with Lieutenant Plate, you know the one that was trapped with me last year during the flood," said Mark Brown.

"What does he want?" It was afternoon and Peg Brown had just risen from a mid-morning nap. She was a little cranky.

"He actually wants to talk to you about the Lady in Disguise group. Come with me and speak to him. He's a nice guy. I told him I wasn't sure you would be available."

"Good thing you did. Absolutely not. I don't have time to mess with him. At the group meeting, we were warned that authorities in Sand Waves are becoming concerned about our success and trying to think up ways to stop us. Like making a rule against door-to-door sales."

"I don't think that would be constitutional," said Mark thoughtfully.

"He's trying to find dirt on our organization. We're doing nothing illegal. I'll hire a lawyer personally myself and fight any efforts to stop us."

Mark rolled his eyes when his wife looked down. Far from making any money as a Lady in Disguise representative, her endeavor was costing them money. He did not need to add lawyer fees in on that.

"I'm sure such a major corporation has plenty of lawyers on staff."

"Must you meet with this cop?"

"It's just a courtesy. He was a great help last year."

"I don't see what he could have done for you, just being trapped in a flood. The killers weren't after you."

"Nevertheless, his efforts were very helpful," Mark said lamely. He recalled Plate's discretion with cautious gratitude.

"I don't want you telling him anything about my activities in the movement."

"I could hardly tell him much. I don't know anything."

Peg sighed happily and gave her husband a sly look.

"It's far more exciting than I had hoped for," she said invitingly.

Mark Brown rose to the bait. "Tell me. Just a little. I am your husband."

"I'm not supposed to be telling you any of this," said Peg Brown, smiling broadly. After years of playing the dull, dutiful politician's wife, staying in the background, making sure she did not harm or distract him from his purpose while others fawned on him and drained his energy, she had his full attention at last.

"Then don't tell me."

"Oh, you're just trying to aggravate me! We're going to have to arrive at the ball separately. You're not to see me in my disguise."

"I thought that you were unhappy that you were expected to wear one of those Lady in Disguise costumes," said Mark Brown.

"I was at first. But I got a star! I am going to be in one of the skits. I will be performing on the stage!"

"What about that special costume we had made for you to wear underneath it? Are you going to abandon it? I like that a lot."

"I'll still wear it. I'll just keep the cloak closed. I can secretly signal you by opening my cloak and you'll know which one I really am." Peg was pleased to hear her husband comment on her wardrobe choices. It did not happen often.

"Sounds good."

She had already decided how she was going to please both him and her new bosses. "I just don't take the cloak off until after the skit that I'm in. I don't want to miss out on being on stage."

"That is all so ridiculous. I know you're wearing the costume underneath. But they don't know that, right?"

"Right. I hate to start out breaking the rules. But that green satin gown is so lovely. They haven't really gone into what's going to happen after these little one act plays over. But I'm sure there is not going to be any reason I can't remove the cloak then."

"So I'm not to see you before, even though all those cloaks look exactly alike? That makes no sense at all."

"It's just a rule. Since I'm going to be breaking the rule about wearing street clothes underneath the cloak, I don't want to break any other rules if I can help it."

"Okay." Mark Brown turned to leave.

"Wait a minute! I haven't told you what I'm going to be doing."

"Well, what are you going to be doing?" Mark asked.

"I'm going to be in a skit with one of the costumed characters."

"I knew that."

"But guess which one? Edward York!" Peg exclaimed.

"Okay, that's good. I'm hoping for his endorsement in my campaign against Pointpar. So what character is Edward going to be?"

"It would absolutely totally be completely against the rules for me to tell you that!"

"Okay, don't tell me. Look, I've really got to go."

"They didn't exactly tell me which one. But he's going to be a king. And this skit is going to reenact his execution."

"Louis XIV! Damn Edward York! He has all the luck! I didn't even draw a character. And he gets Louis XVI!" Mark Brown felt an irrational wave of juvenile jealousy.

"And I'm supposed get some more information on how they're going to do it, right before the ball. And although we were strictly told not to talk about our parts, I overheard one of the other ladies whispering that she was in charge of catching the head of Marie Antoinette."

"I wonder how they going to come up with all of this. Are they going to have a guillotine? They must have a magician involved."

"It's so exciting. I only wish they had not forbidden filming it."

"Nobody wants to carry those cumbersome VCR cameras on their shoulder at an event like that. I don't see where they are an improvement over 16-millimeter movie cameras like we have always used."

"Those old cameras don't have sound, Mark. Remember? And they could've hired somebody. The Hills even had one come to their daughter's wedding and film the ceremony. You can hear the vows, well, most of them."

"Security is going to be extra tight. There's not going to be any press there. No cameras or photographs allowed. Might be able to sneak a 110 in but it will be confiscated if you get caught. No outsiders of any kind. The catering is being done by people that have

131

been screened by the FBI."

"Because of Edward York?" Peg asked, curious.

"Because of Forrest Pointpar. He's just a joker running against me. But there's been death threats and with the recent death of Frenel, the African-American community is on edge. The administration is terrified Forrest will be harmed."

Brown was referring to the recent death of civil rights leader Clie Frenel shortly after visiting Sand Waves.

"No one's contacted me. Surely they are screening all the Ladies in Disguise that are going to be there."

"They know who you are. From my understanding, the regular saleswomen employed by this company are not going to be at the masquerade. The Ladies in Disguise that are going to be there are like you. They are upper echelon women involved in the charitable aspect of the organization. Have they said anything to you about your officially being in that group yet? I think it's ridiculous that you have to walk neighborhoods trying to sell hair care products."

"That's just an initiation period for those of us selected. Sort of like a sorority hazing. I was told that, after the ball, I'll be moving up. There are a couple of other ladies involved in exactly the same way as me. You would recognize their names if I told you who they were. Well, no, I take that back. You would recognize one of them. The other, is- well- being brought up from the middle class. Not that I'm saying anything against the middle class and this girl is supremely intelligent. I think that's why she's been selected."

Mark Brown sighed, thinking, *what a folly these women's organizations are. They may do good charitable works but they can't possibly really be anything but a hotbed of gossipy cliques.*

However, he actually said, "I'm glad you finally found something that gives you some focused purpose on a daily basis."

"Yes," said Peg happily. "I have found my niche. The Bible study group called the other day and asked if I was coming back. I told them no. I just had too much going on right now. I sort of miss them. They've all got children except me. And when we're not studying the Bible, that's all they talk about is their children and I don't have anything to say. I don't ever hear any of these Lady in

Disguise friends of mine say much of anything about children, if they even have any. Most of them are single."

"Being single doesn't mean being childless anymore," Mark Brown commented.

Peg was suddenly tired of the conversation and told her husband he better get going.

The congressman kept his brief appointment at the Toy Museum Restaurant with the policeman, apologizing that Peg was unavailable. And, remembering his lack of loyalty in the past to his wife, he decided to honor her wishes today. He told Lieutenant Plate he knew nothing about the Lady in Disguise organization. His wife was just participating to be involved in that wonderful charity and neither one of them had knowledge of any unseemly activities the group would possibly be involved in.

Rival hair care companies undoubtedly started such rumors, he intimated.

"You know the intrigue involved in these big corporations," said Mark. "They probably feel threatened by the fact that women could be advancing into their market share."

Plate listened politely to the congressman defend the Ladies without much comment. He knew a stonewall when he saw it and knew nothing he said or did would persuade it to come down.

Plate's mind kept wandering back to his earlier appointment that morning at the morgue and how Morris Tates had expressed so little emotion when he had identified his wife as the burnt corpse found in the cabin on the greenbelt.

So he did not tell Mark Brown that word had come down from undercover sources that indeed something had to be wrong with the feminine sales force roaming the streets of suburban America with their incredible products.

Some private testing had determined the miraculous products they hawked were no more than ordinary shampoo and other hair care staples used by most women since the dawn of the twentieth century.

And most interesting, the corporation was on the verge of bankruptcy, the Ladies in Disguise sales force having made a splash

133

in advertising, a fruitful harvest via charity, but very few actual sales of their wares that made monetary profit. The sales force was not paid on commission like most such enterprises. They had a small quota to meet. But it was so low that if they bought the products themselves and collected the salary they would still come out ahead.

The company did not make economic sense.

The congressional representative's high security clearance meant that nothing prevented Plate from revealing these facts to this particular husband of a Lady. But since neither was willing to talk to him, he saw no reason why he should not let Mark Brown and his wife just continue to believe the Ladies were angels in disguise...

Chapter 27

Anonymity was not always the rule when Ladies in Disguise met on company business.

Serena Towers knew exactly who she was speaking to on this particular interview, even if she was unaware of who was serving their lunch at a more remote meeting place, one without heat.

The server was in full disguise, moving slowly as though she had difficulty walking. As she was one of the homeless, taking advantage of the charity of the group and living in a Lady in Disguise facility, the server was on call for such duties as she was performing today.

"I'm hoping your article will focus on how, when women get together, work together as sisters, how much we can accomplish. That's why I think it is imperative you keep your affiliation with our group a secret. If the journalism industry knew you were a Lady in Disguise, the article might not be taken seriously. With you remaining publicly unaffiliated with us, it will be more effective."

"It would also be more effective if I could use your name."

"Not yet. Maybe in the future. Right now I must remain behind the scenes. My husband's position would be imperiled if his associates knew I was very much more than a decorative housewife. But in my heart, I know times are changing. It won't always be this way."

Serena was of the opinion that, as it was 1983, times had already changed. It was no longer a man's world.

However, she wanted this story. So she was going by her agreement with her interviewee not to reveal any names.

"Write about the charitable work we've done. How only we could have done it and the good it has brought the entire world," said the cloaked woman seated across the round table.

"I've seen it first hand in Europe and Africa," said Serena. "That is one reason why this article for a major news magazine is so important. The commercial side of the company blankets the television stations with ads, the women in the street promote the company from within the American home. Yet the charity gets little attention."

"It is the charity that is the backbone of the company. The charity will save us."

"And there will be more attention after the ball is over."

Both women laughed.

"Seriously, though, if you want to do a story, especially after the ball, about us, about who we really are, then you are going to need to do some research."

"Research?" That sounded like work to Serena. She preferred to write her stories from a personal point of view. Full of action, witness, and feelings.

"There's an old book you need to find," said the Lady in Disguise, as she offered Serena a cigarette.

The server hobbled forward with a cigarette lighter and lit both women's tobacco. Serena took a long puff of smoke.

"What book?"

"It's a fictionalized book, but it tells the story of one of our contemporary movement's founders."

This perked Serena's interest.

"Yes," continued her source. "And it was a man, believe it or not. Back in those days, women could not really get anything accomplished without a man behind them. This man, well, the book tells his story before he became involved with the movement and founded our branch. To understand everything, you need to read it."

"And it's called?"

"*Murder as the Organist Plays*. From early in the century. I have not read it myself. I have heard about it, stories passed down through the generations."

"Who wrote it?"

"I cannot remember. An obscure writer who stumbled upon the story and wrote it as a fictional novel. It is out of print. But I have an old book jacket in my safety deposit box. Unfortunately, my family's copy of book itself was lost when I was a small child. And I have never been able to find another copy. Maybe with your resources- No, not maybe. I know you can find a copy somewhere."

Serena requested the serving lady to please get her another cup of tea. The woman made her way stiffly out of the room.

Finding an old out of print book, turn of the century era, was not as easy as all that.

Serena was doubtful.

Just because she worked in journalism, she had no extra secret paths to obtaining old manuscripts. The headmistress had been watching too much fiction.

And not given her enough time.

However, Serena gave an optimistic answer. It seemed so important to her literary benefactor. Serena did not want her discouraged in any way. She knew this woman was extremely private and rarely opened up like this. She wanted to keep it coming.

"Now about the overall goals of the organization," Serena continued, generating ideas for the quest for the book in the back of her mind as the interview continued.

Shortly the servant made her way back with a hot cup of tea.

"I would ask you that when you find the book, you first deliver it to me. I need it before the masquerade ball. I am going to direct some of the Ladies to use it to create some more characters among themselves to slip into on their breaks. I just feel my saleswomen deserve the opportunity to do more than serve refreshments."

This idea sounded like lunacy to Serena but she kept quiet.

"Mistress is so good to us," said the apparently crippled server.

"I want the girls working under me to be happy and feel appreciated."

"Headmistress, I do feel happy and appreciated," she said dutifully.

"Won't it be the wrong time period?" asked Serena.

"Doesn't matter, we'll go with generic costumes that will blend in."

Serena pondered the idea for a time that her source was seriously disturbed and it caused a cold chill to grip her heart.

The server was also looking strangely. At least what Serena could see of her expression, only her eyes visible through the narrow slits in the mask.

"I know I sound crazy. Don't be fooled by my eccentricities. I am perfectly in control. And before you hear it elsewhere, there is something else. I know you are a journalist, but there will be no photography at the ball."

"NO photography?" Serena's journalist instincts automatically rebelled against this idea.

"The organization wants to ensure total privacy for our very important guests," said the headmistress. "And the feds have requested such rules, since Forrest Pointpar will be there."

The server asked if there were any other chores she might do before going home.

"No, thank you, my dear." Her superior waved her off.

Serena argued the verdict against photography for quite some time. Her companion tolerated the argument as something Serena needed to get out of her system and reiterated the judgment at the end with mild amusement.

Faced with this implacable attitude, Serena surrendered.

"Right. Let's leave it at that. I think it is a mistake you will regret," said Serena. "However, I think I should go and get on the book issue right away, if as you say, it is so important to get the book before the ball."

"Fundamental," said the other woman, sipping her tea as her cigarette burned in an ashtray. "And a personal goal for me. For personal reasons. I don't usually indulge myself that way but..."

Having heard the rest of the conversation from behind the exit door the server hobbled out of the building. She had heard very little but she had heard enough. In the car, she removed her cloak and also the stilt like boots that made her tall enough to be a Lady in Disguise.

Her feet hurt, but that was the least problem she had.

She could trust no one but the information was vital. It had to be conveyed. Cut off from her contacts and not knowing who to trust or what was really happening, she thought of the one person she knew was safe. After her attempt to reach that person had previously failed, she had lain low, kept in complete disguise at almost all times, even when she slept in the safe places made available to Lady in Disguise members who were between residences.

Homelessness was high in the area due to the recent economic decline reaching Sand Waves very late in the business cycle, which had been affecting the rest of the country for several years.

In Texas it was only a dip in the surging economic tidal wave of rising oil prices. However, it was enough to send shockwaves across the Houston area. Still no match for the recession up north, the decline had combined with exorbitant interest rates and a bubble in housing prices to catch a narrow slice of socially mobile white collar workers in a homeless trap.

A tiny percentage of Sand Waves residents were swept into the loophole of losing a high paying job needed to sustain the monthly mortgage while still retaining significant illiquid assets too substantial to qualify for any assistance.

This percentage did represent a solid number of people. It was one of the reasons guaranteed salaried Lady in Disguise positions were so coveted. Many men having lost jobs, or in fear of their jobs vanishing, were encouraged by the other adult family member bringing in steady wages.

Sand Waves was an addictive place. With its own separate school district, its own separate places of worship (of every imaginable religion, all located within walking distance of each other), its own shopping areas, even its own hospital system (despite the great Houston Medical Center being just a short drive away), its own dramatic theatre and movie theatre, and just about one or two of any other entity needed for modern existence (all strategically located so as to not mar residential structures), a family could move into Sand Waves and live there for the duration of their lives without ever leaving. If they could afford to.

Most could not. Most had to work either in Houston or Galveston. Few jobs were available in the command designed colony and they were quickly filled, usually by relatives of the rich and/or famous.

Since the Lady in Disguise movement began, there had been an increasing number of couples that had begun to depend upon the income from the company completely, and it was not enough to make ends meet, especially in a place like Sand Waves.

139

In hopes of hanging on until better times, some couples let or sold their homes. Frequently they wanted to keep their children in the Sand Waves schools, which boasted a complex and intricate set of social climbing activities and groups.

The only apartment complex in Sand Waves was a very small set of units hidden in the back of the colony, used primarily by persons temporarily displaced by the uneven buying and selling of their houses.

Rents at these apartments were 50 percent higher than comparable apartments just down the highway and there are no long term leases ever signed. This discouraged riffraff, as did the total lack of hotels in the colony.

So needing a place to stay for a while was not considered unusual and no questions were asked by the benefactors of the group. After all, being a charitable organization was one of their purposes. Why not help their own? Those in need were extremely grateful.

This particular Lady in Disguise, at sea for sanctuary, took advantage.

She knew she would be called paranoid if she openly revealed her fears about what might happen at the upcoming extravaganza.

Maybe she was. Maybe nothing was planned except for reaping the harvest of the avalanche of publicity promised.

She could almost believe it.

Except for the one rule that made no sense. There was to be no photography, no camcorders allowed in. Why, if positive publicity was the goal? Why exclude any way to capture the images of the evening?

She meditated on her own plans and the plans of the group that she really belonged to. Were they any better or worse? Were they all really after the same end, the same effect?

She pulled out a cigarette from her cloak and lit it. She felt very tired of it all, but she was not going to give up.

She recalled the crucial book. Maybe that was the answer. Something about the title was familiar. She had seen it somewhere recently she was sure…

She closed her eyes to think.

Chapter 28

"Must be that they are having their own people photograph the event and want no competition." Darica Daniels was talking to Serena Towers. The two were meeting again to discuss how they would coordinate their stories on the upcoming party.

"I agree. That is the only explanation."

"Sucks. Lots of money lost to our lot." Darica looked glum. "Oh, I know money is not that much to you. But it is to me."

"Listen, since you are pretty much focusing on the ball, you may have a little free time-"

"Ha!"

"Well, a moment or two. And if so, could you search out a book for me?"

"A book? Out of print, I suppose?"

"Of course."

"No."

"Don't say no. There would be a reward."

"Really?" Darica saw extra money and all it could do for her and her pressing bills.

"Substantial, if you come up with it before the event."

"Why?"

"I'm not sure. But I can assure you, if we have the book, our project will be that much better and probably command a higher payment. And as a new member of our organization, it will put you in pretty good standing with the headmistress. It is her who wants the book."

"All right, give me the details." Darica keenly wanted to see the headmistress unmasked. An exposé of who really ran the charitable section and where all the money really went would be a real scoop.

Serena was handling this organization with kid gloves.

Darica had never met a charity she trusted and she was sure one as large as this one would have plenty of corruption to reveal.

She doubted whether Serena had the same ambitions in infiltrating the group. She really didn't care what Serena's motives were.

Knowing the flamboyant correspondent, Darica would not be surprised if they were personal. Serena had been known to go after people she felt had slighted her in the past, to go after them and their favorite institutions.

Working with Serena was like a churchhouse mouse being teamed with the big MM.

Darica knew that. She knew that if a cat sniffed them both out, she would be the one fed to the feline.

Serena would escape with her customary glamour and go off to other international rogue pursuits until she delivered another sensational story to the world.

Getting that book for the headmistress might afford some protection and definitely a step up from the churchhouse.

She might at least get into the bell tower or the choir loft.

Church, choir, bells, music.

Murder as the Organist Plays.

Darica suddenly remembered why the title was so familiar. And where she had seen a copy of that book...

Serena felt sure if Darica found the book, she would contact her.

Darica was too new to be entrusted with contact information for the headmistress. Darica's only way to translate finding the book into positive action was through her.

Darica was only one avenue Serena was going to pursue.

As many people as possible helping her out was always a good thing. But she could not motivate most people with the urgency of her need, lest she aroused suspicions. So her best bet for finding the book, Serena believed, was to find it herself.

She had already tried all of the university libraries, the city libraries, all the libraries she could think of within the geographical area where the book was set. And none of them admitted to having a copy. Her only realistic hope was to scour used bookstores in hopes of accidentally coming across one and there was little time to do that.

The Galveston-Houston area had hundreds of used bookstores. Calling clerks and asking them was a useless endeavor. Not wanting to sort through hundreds, if not thousands of books, to see if the title was on the premises, most would just say no and hang up.

She had to go to each bookstore in person. It seemed an impossible task. She suspected there would be great benefits to finding the book, much more than just pleasing the headmistress. She was determined to try.

"I'm sorry, Sinclair. Unless you want to go to Houston and search through thousands of out of print books in used bookstores, I'm not going to be able to see you. Excepting the ball, of course."

Plate wondered if she was really telling the truth or if for some reason she was stalling him. Plate did not relish the idea of searching for an obscure book in Houston but he did have a suggestion.

"Why don't we meet here and start at the Sand Waves Used Bookstore on my lunch hour? Then you can go on to Houston if we don't find it."

"Fine. I have not much hope they'd have it, but you never know."

"Might as well start there."

"You're not in uniform," Serena commented in the parking lot when Plate stepped out of his patrol car.

"I had a meeting earlier with someone who can't be seen with a uniformed officer without arousing undue interest," he explained. "So I get to stay in plainclothes the rest of the day."

"Good. I don't want the staff at this bookstore to get curious either," she said, as they stepped inside.

"Staff?" Plate laughed.

The sole personage in the store barely glanced at the couple as they entered, noticing only because a cheap bell dingled.

"Looking for a special book," said Plate, in answer to the bookstore owner's faint nod. The elderly shopkeeper was unpacking books from boxes near the front of the store.

"I see the section it should be in," said Serena, and she took off to the back end of the store.

"So," said Plate, looking about at the thousands of books as he followed her. Like wheels from a spoke, multiple aisles of bound manuscripts extended out from a central counter containing a single

143

cash register. "Why is this book so important?"

"Confidential," said Serena. "But you will know after the ball is over. It's a part of my work."

"When is your piece going to be published?" asked Plate, as he watched Serena approach the Historical Mystery shelf with trepidation. It was a smaller shelf in the rear but still held hundreds of books.

"As soon as the ball is over and I write the conclusion. Now, about this book. IF it is categorized right, it should be here. But it might be on the history shelf or mystery shelf. It could even be in the nonfiction section of the store. It's written as a novel, with the writer imagining she was there and could see everything. Or so I was told."

"Really? What book are we looking for?" Plate pretended to peruse the titles on the designated shelf, while surreptitiously casting an eye over to the abundant science fiction department. It was right next door, so to speak. He slipped over there.

Serena consulted her notes.

" *'Murder as the Organist Plays'*," she read. Looking up, she saw Plate on the sci-fi aisle, reaching for a paperback.

Plate stopped, his hand holding the book in midair. He replaced it slowly.

"I know that book," he said slowly and cautiously. This was unknown territory.

A true coincidence, or…?

"You do?" Serena looked at him, alert. "You've read it?"

Plate saw the wariness permeate her body language. His muscles tensed as well.

Both were wary of such a stroke of luck.

"No," he said casually. "But I've seen it at a friend's house."

"Really." Serena paused. "Your friend must have interesting tastes in literature. Must be an interesting person. Who is he?"

"Just a fellow officer," Plate said. "He's from the area where the book is set."

"I'd love to meet him," said Serena quickly. "Maybe he could add some details. Would he think me terribly forward if I asked to borrow the book? Just for a short time."

Plate rapidly created a story. "Uh, no. Best let me handle it. He's, he's undercover right now. Drug case in Galveston. He's on loan to them. So he's virtually incommunicado."

"Oh, Sinclair," said Serena disappointedly.

Her phoenix of hope started streaming down. Fabulous and terrible luck at the same time.

"If you only know what it meant to me to get to read that book." Serena had tears in her eyes.

"I could probably get it for you," said Plate evenly. "We keep keys to undercover operatives' true residences while they are gone. If I could find it for you, I could get it. He would not mind, I'm sure."

A rush of anticipation flooded back in. "I would be eternally grateful," she said.

"Again," said Plate, wanting to leave himself a way out. "If I can find it. He's single, lives alone, place is probably a mess."

"Please try. I could go with you."

"Of course, angel. But you cannot go. I cannot even let you know where he lives. I'll try to get it tonight and let you have it in the morning. It will be way hours of the morning before I will have a chance to try for it."

No sleep again tonight, he thought.

Plate turned to face Serena and gave her a deep kiss. The store proprietor made noise.

He let her go and grabbed the sci-fi book he had replaced on the shelf.

"We found it!" he called out to the bookstore owner. All three people started towards the cash register.

Chapter 29

"Could it be someone is preying on these Ladies in Disguise and some of their customers?" asked Chief Brecken.

It was later that afternoon in the chief's office.

"It's hard to say. You cannot rule it out. But there are so many Lady in Disguise representatives and almost every woman in Sand Waves is a customer. That's like saying someone is preying on women who eat beef. It may let out a few, but by far includes most."

"Morris Tates has identified the body as Emma?"

"Right. And fire department forensics have determined she was wearing a Lady in Disguise costume. Those cloaks are made of quality fabric. It didn't completely burn."

"But Emma Tates was short and fat. These women are involved in a major lawsuit because they are all tall and thin."

"The body was burnt so badly, weight could not be determined, but the woman was short, no doubt, the coroner said."

"Maybe Emma Tates lost weight during her disappearance?"

"Maybe. But she could not have grown taller."

"What was the part of the body intact enough for someone close to identify?" asked Brecken.

Plate told him.

"Oh," said Brecken, wrinkling his nose a bit. "I guess a husband would know."

"Well," Plate began an objection.

"No two sets are alike, Plate," said the chief brusquely. Then he added quickly, "So I'm told."

"Shame there were not enough dental specimens left for a conclusive ID. And you have to have something to compare with. Apparently Mrs. Tates never went to the dentist or doctor."

"If Tates is sure that was his wife, that's where we will let the matter stand. What about Natalie Wakefield?"

"Trail's totally cold. Nothing."

"You've got to come up with something," Chief Brecken insisted.

"I do have an idea but it will be time consuming, require

cooperation of someone who is disappointed with me. Someone I have hurt, I'm afraid. And I would need the morning off to pursue it."

"Any hope it will lead us to Natalie Wakefield?"

Plate shrugged.

"Go on then, what morning do you want off?"

"Tomorrow, the day of the ball, would be best. I'll have to arrange it with my friend. And, Chief?"

"Yes?"

"It needs to be sort of a secret morning off."

"Secret?"

"What I mean is if anyone calls for me or comes by to see me, make up something about how I have to be in Houston to testify or anything to send them on a wild goose chase."

"Okay," said Brecken, looking at Plate thoughtfully. "I'll have Jordan cover for you. And Skaar, if necessary. Go call your friend. Grovel a little if you have to. Be charming and deceptive, if needed. You can do it."

"Thanks for your confidence in me," said Plate.

Chapter 30

Shortly after dawn Daphne's doorbell rang, waking her up.

I'm going to get that damn thing disconnected, she thought, as she made her way from the bedroom to the foyer.

Daphne recognized the Lady in Disguise as the same one that showed up the first night.

"I'm sorry to be here so early but I have several hairstyles to do before tonight and yours is simple enough to hold a good while. Simple and elegant, what?"

"Yes, this is great but I understood the hairstylings had been canceled. My costume came with a wig," Daphne said.

"Just between you and me," said the girl, "they couldn't get enough volunteers like myself to go to everyone's house and do their hair in time. So they did send out the wigs. But there was a few of us still willing and they sent us out this morning. Don't tell anyone. The others will be jealous."

Daphne agreed to keep quiet. It was indeed a blessing not to have the wear the uncomfortable wig.

"Your hair is the perfect color for the time period. And so natural and soft. Do you usually hold your curls well?"

"Er- yes. Normally, I just let my hair hang down. It has a natural wave. I have to use conditioner. Otherwise, I just wash it and keep it trimmed."

"Shoulder length is a good measurement for you. And it will really make it easy for me to style it up in a chignon. Could you just go into your shower and get your hair wet? I have everything else I need right here with me."

The Lady in Disguise pulled out a large valise, opening it to reveal metal curlers, pins and a blow dryer.

She's going to style my hair in Shirley Temple curls and then blow dry it? Daphne mused as she went into her bathroom to get her hair wet. *Wonder if she actually knows anything about hairstyling? She looks like the rich little girl out on a social adventure in the middle class.*

Daphne took her time wetting her hair. She did not want to have

148

to take off all her clothes and she did not want a mess made of her makeup. After a few gymnastic manipulations, she managed to moisten her hair without doing either.

Returning to the den, she found her visitor had all of the rollers and other paraphernalia arrayed out on the coffee table. The Lady in Disguise had pulled a dinette chair over to the den and was holding a gray cape as she waited for Daphne.

"I forgot the little vinyl cover we use. Okay if I just put this cape around your shoulders?"

"Not at all. I don't mind." Daphne sat on dinette chair as the Lady in Disguise began to fix the cloak around her shoulders.

"Hold on a minute," said Daphne.

She took the cloak from the stylist's hand.

"Let me just get a book to read while you are doing this. It will help me to keep still."

Daphne flared the cloak around her shoulders as she stepped up on her foyer and stood in front of the hall tree mirror. She quickly buttoned the top button by the neck and pulled the hood up around her head so she could get a quick look at herself in the Lady in Disguise costume.

It was an interesting effect. The gray brown gabardine material with the thin red line trim framing her wet blonde hair, with the rest of the garment falling from her shoulders in curtain-like folds, was a striking sight.

She looked down at the small marble shelf on the hall tree.

"I thought I had a book over here," she called back to her visitor, staring at the white stone with gray streaks.

"I'm a very quick stylist. It won't take any time. And you don't have to sit perfectly still." There was an impatience in the lilting voice of the sales girl. She was holding up a rattail comb in one hand and a pair of scissors in the other.

"You're not going to cut any of my hair?"

Daphne came down off the foyer and stared face to face with the other person.

"Only if there's a stray lock that I just can't get into place. Here, let me tuck the hood on the inside so it won't be in the way."

Daphne complied.

True to her word, the Lady in Disguise worked quickly and deftly to get Daphne's hair in curlers. While the hair was still on the rollers, the girl manipulated the heavy blow dryer as if it were a lightweight hand fan.

In no time, Daphne's hair was dry, out of the rollers, and being carefully pinned and sprayed.

"This is beautiful," Daphne said, when she was allowed to get up and go look in the mirror.

"Thank you. I've really got to go. My next client is waiting."

"Of course. Let me just get something for you from my purse."

"No, absolutely not. We are never allowed to accept tips. This is a Lady in Disguise company courtesy, in hopes that you'll do all your hair care business with us in the future."

With those words, the girl was at the front door trying to get out.

"I have to unlock the door from the inside," Daphne explained when the girl showed a little bit of panic at not being able to exit immediately. "I have a double deadbolt."

"Oh, yes I see," the girl said shakily.

She hastily exited as soon as Daphne got the door open, her cape making a slight swishing sound as it dragged across the concrete walkway. Daphne called out another round of thank-yous to her as the girl made her way down the sidewalk.

"Look at you," Daphne said aloud to herself

Alone again, she gazed at her reflection in the hall tree mirror and very carefully touched a few of the curls.

My costume may be simple, but it is elegant and fits good. With this hairstyle I'm go to be right up there at the top with the glamour, she predicted happily and felt another surge in gratitude to her Lady in Disguise visitor.

Chapter 31

"Are you sure Lieutenant Plate is unavailable?"

Standing at the reception desk at the Sand Waves Police Department, Serena Towers looked lovely in a striking red and black pantsuit with a diamond pattern gray tone on tone blouse.

Officer Jordan could hardly keep his eyes off her as he tried to pretend to flip through the calendar on his desk.

"I'm sorry," he said, forcing himself to glance down long enough to make it look like he had time to read the notations on the date squares. "Lieutenant Plate is at the gun range, doing routine firing qualifications. He can't be reached right now. I'll leave him a message. I'm sure he'll call you as soon as he is done."

"Did he leave anything for me? Package? A book? He promised to get me a copy of a certain book this morning. And I need it. It has information in it that I'm going to be using in a story that's nearing deadline."

"No, ma'am." Officer Jordan stared into her clear brown eyes and felt himself getting lost.

"Are you sure?"

"He didn't leave anything for you."

"Thank you."

Serena turned away in disappointment.

Somehow, she had failed to get this policeman to take seriously how desperately she needed this book. She was exasperated that the progress of their relationship had seemed to slow in the last few days.

And, even more frustrating, was that she could hardly get the policeman to talk seriously to her at all.

He wanted to laugh, joke and flirt all of the time.

She still needed to find a copy of *Murder as the Organist Plays* before the masquerade ball tonight. She had known she needed it and she had known Plate had a copy so she had worried less about it in these last hectic hours before the ball.

There were so many things to do, so many details to attend to. So much to do. So much to worry about.

The book seemed like a minor point.

She sighed. It seemed ridiculous that this book was so important to her superior. She had no idea what it had to do with the masquerade ball.

There was simply no alternative but to proceed without it and take the consequences.

"Stupid blasted firing range requirement," Serena said aloud, then smiled cryptically at her own wording.

"We'll just have to do without the book. What does it matter what it says in an old book? Why can't we just make it up? Nobody will ever know the difference."

Serena was now on the phone with her boss, who accepted the inevitable with calm disappointment.

"I suppose you're right. Make up a story. I suppose ethics don't enter into this anymore."

"Journalistic ethics died with Watergate," said Serena, slightly off topic. "I'm going to go ahead and prepare without the book. If I turn up a copy before time runs out, I could always make changes."

"Just be sure you make any changes clear and specific."

"No problem."

"I want it published as soon as the ball is over. I take it the bulk of the story is already done?"

"Right." Serena hung up the phone at the Toy Museum Restaurant and asked to be seated so she could order lunch.

Darica Daniels had said something about seeing a copy of that book, but soon it will be too late to include it, she thought, as she glanced over the menu. She had eaten at the restaurant so often, she looked at the list of entrées without really seeing it.

As the waiter came by and took the order and the menu, Serena resolved to contact Darica one more time before finalizing her work. She noted that Congressman Mark Brown was having a drink at the bar alone.

She debated going up to him and seeing if information might emerge. But she decided against it.

It was far more important that she meet up with Plate and she did not want any distractions. She still also had one more hope.

152

Plate had the sweetest way of showing up right as she finished her lunch. She ate very slowly in anticipation of that delightful occurrence happening again today.

It would be a perfect prelude to tonight.

After tonight, there would be no more instability in her life. She could settle down.

Her project would guarantee her future, no matter what came to pass. No matter what judgment it rated from her superior.

Her superior little knew that Serena's project was not only unfinished, she had yet to physically begin it.

Serena always worked that way. She collected ideas in her mind, jotted facts down in her notebook, and then shortly before deadline she wrote her stories fast and furiously.

Working that way had gotten her in hot water with more than one editor who did not understand the time she spent in mental preparation for the writing was just as much work as the writing itself. To editors and other journalists in the same office with her, it looked like she spent many hours doing nothing.

Freelancing was the only way for her to go, she had realized early in her career.

Now that the biggest story of her life was on the horizon, she saw no reason to change the work habits that had been so successful.

Therefore no one knew as she sat at the lunch table, looking so impressively carefree, that while not a word had been penned on paper, she was hard at the task and her preparation for the labor ahead was almost complete.

Chapter 32

A good part of that same morning that Officer Jordan claimed his lieutenant was at a fabricated shooting range activity, Plate actually was locked inside Daphne's office closet.

The closet had been emptied of its contents.

Daphne stood outside the doors with her arms folded against her chest.

"How do you like it in there? I can keep you locked in indefinitely, you know."

"Hush, I am trying to think."

Daphne could hear Plate beating the palms of his hands against her office closet walls.

"If my walls are damaged, you'll be doing the re-papering."

"Two things," said Plate, not stopping his wall examination. "A-nobody normal has wallpaper on the inside of their closet walls. B-have you got all the stuff moved out of your office yet?"

"I am perfectly normal and I have moved everything I can lift."

Daphne gazed with dismay at the mess in her den. To keep them separate, the contents of the closet were piled on her spacious brick fireplace hearth in the far corner. The other contents of the office itself were piled on her den couch, her coffee table, her end tables, and some of it spilled over onto the dinette table. Her desk chair had been rolled down her hallway.

Her heavy desk and pole lamp were all that remained in the actual office space.

"All right, let me out."

"No. Just sit in there and meditate on the cruel way you have treated me for a while."

"Daphne! Now!"

Daphne unlocked the bifold doors.

"Natalie Wakefield's closet had the doors removed. There was a dense window shade, that when pulled down, covered the opening completely. In front of that was an Austrian poof panel, surrounded by moiré taffeta curtains. At the adjacent corner where your window is, the same set of curtains and shade covered the window. The taffeta moiré draperies met at the corner. Walking into the room, the first impression was that it was located on an outside corner of the house with two windows, one on each side. And remember, that floorplan was on a much larger scale in a much bigger house, so it was easy to get confused."

"Well, on the other side of the wall, the closet is off my foyer. Is that the way it was in her house?"

"Exactly the same. The foyer is even raised like yours. Just much larger. You step up onto the foyer and go straight to the front door. There was a spacious coat closet on the left, midway."

Plate walked around a short distance, going out of Daphne's office, a couple of feet into her den, then making a U-turn and stepping up on her foyer. He looked at the front door straight ahead, then to his left at a small door. He opened it.

"My coat closet," said Daphne matter-of-factly. "At least that's what the builder called it. It has enough room to hang maybe three, four coats, depending on how thick they are. And it squishes the garments horizontally no matter what material they are. See. The hangers rub against the inside of the door. It's a nuisance. I wish they had just left it as wall space. Then I could have put a nice shallow table there instead of that narrow hall tree. As it is, when I open the closet door, it practically covers the width of the foyer. It's totally impractical for hanging up anybody's coat, if they have just come in the front door. Because you have to knock the entrant off the foyer to get inside the closet."

Plate paid scant attention to what Daphne was saying as he studied the layout. He took off his blazer jacket and attempted to hang it in the coat closet.

"Has to be what happened," he said out loud to himself.

"And," Daphne continued, "If they had left out this coat closet, they could have made my office closet the length of the wall. Even if the doors remain the same size, I could have a nice little set of cubbyholes to the right that I could store anything in that was long and narrow."

Plate suddenly heard everything Daphne had said. Like a tumbled mathematical formula revisited, all her words became factors which suddenly sat up straight in his mind and computed.

"I know why you have that stupid little coat closet!"

"You do?" Daphne asked.

"I did some digging and found out that after the builder had custom made the Wakefield mansion, he sold the design to the company that built these tract homes in your neighborhood. That company added that design, shrunken considerably, to their repertoire and every fifth house on these streets is this floor plan."

"Meaning?"

"The builder lopped off the upstairs, since they already had one two-story plan and the colony limits the number of two-story homes in the lower end neighborhoods."

"Why do they do that?"

"God only knows."

"Ridiculous Sand Waves authorities," said Daphne.

"So your builder just used the first floor, which was complete in and of itself. The first floor has everything needed for a middle class home, two bathrooms, three bedrooms, kitchen, and den. Since it was based on the Wakefield mansion, you got the bonus of an extra formal living and dining room, with this little odd room off the den that you use for your office. They call it a parlor."

"That's why I bought this house. It seemed to have a lot of extras for the price range. The extra odd little room was perfect for my office. I love having a formal dining room and I know the living room is just large enough for a couch adjacent to the dining room table but it comes in handy when I'm entertaining."

"Rather than do away with the coat closet, which is significantly larger in the Wakefield mansion, your builder just shrank everything."

"Laziness!" Daphne scoffed.

Plate walked down Daphne's right-angled hall into her laundry room.

"Your laundry room in the Wakefield mansion is part of the maid's quarters. Your third bedroom that backs up to the garage is where Doris lives. Your master bedroom is a billiard room with a bath off to the side, just where your master bath is. The den wall that separates your master bedroom from your den is where the staircase going upstairs is. So you see right into this parlor-office when you are coming down the Wakefield staircase."

"Legally, it's a fourth bedroom because it has a closet, so the real estate agents can call this a four bedroom house. But it would be a pitiful bedroom. What about my second bedroom? What do the Wakefields use that for?" Daphne asked.

"I don't know. That door was closed. Wakefield said it was used for storage."

"That's pretty much what I use it for. It's tucked in the house in such a way that nobody notices it."

Plate smiled at her and walked back into the den. "The missing doors. That's where the missing doors are, I'll bet. And other evidence."

"And the kitchen, dinette? Den? All are just like in my house?"

"Yes. Just much larger. There's more furniture, more décor, more confusion. You know, displays of this and that. Distractions."

"Do you think you know how she disappeared out of that room?"

"Yes. And I've been blinded by a distraction. Several distractions. A lot of eclectic junk in the closet. But the main conjuring trick was the vanishing bifold doors. You have bifold doors on the closet inside the office. She had bifold doors on the office itself."

"This room came with two impossible doors that opened out in the den and the one on the left blocked the entrance of the hallway if it was opened, the one on the right covered the return air vent if it was opened. I had them taken off. See where the indentations of the hinges were? I need to get some wood putty and fill them in, but I have never got around to it."

"Heavens! Of course, that's the one difference. You've got the small wall facing your open section starting the den and that's where your airconditioning return air vent is. In the Wakefield mansion, this small wall is much wider and there is a mirrored credenza covering it."

"So their return air vent is elsewhere?"

"It's in the ceiling. I noticed it."

"So the space where my return air vent is- is dead space there?"

"No, it's not dead space. Look at the lineup. You have a wall here about three feet wide. It separates your foyer from your office. In that wall from left to right are three separate entities. First, your office closet, wide and shallow, takes up half the length on that side. Then you have to walk around to the other side of the wall, stand on your foyer to see the front of the coat closet which takes up half of the space left, a fourth of the total. The other fourth is walled in so your return air vent has efficient circulation. Your vent faces the den, preventing you from putting any furniture there. The Wakefield mansion has a totally different airconditioning setup."

"I'm confused as to how this gets you any closer to seeing how Natalie disappeared," said Daphne.

"The bifold doors were removed to distract me. Someone removed the doors to distract me from the dead space in the wall and how the coat closet was only separated by a thin panel from the blue room closet. The elaborate curtain set up was to fool the eye into thinking there was no closet in that room and both sets of curtains hid windows. Well, they knew as soon as I looked behind the curtains I would see the closet, so I was to be distracted by the missing doors and the junk in the closet. Only I had never been there before and Wakefield didn't miss the doors. So trying to draw my attention to the missing doors failed miserably."

"She escaped through that closet, through the coat closet?"

"Yes, pushing the coats into the dead space and slipping out the closet door straight to her front door, straight out of the house. Very simple. The panel inside the closet must have been removable and she came out the coat closet into the foyer as they all sat there just a few feet away, watching the parlor doors."

"Wouldn't you have seen evidence of that when you examined the closet?"

"Everything had been put back exactly like it was. And nobody told me the room had always had doors. From the time she disappeared until I got there, about three hours while the others were searching for her, expert carpenters went into that house, sealed with caulk the secret exit from the room and took the bifold doors down.

They were careful to leave the filled-in hinge indentations imperfect, so as to be seen if looked for, so that it would look as if they got a little careless. That even more focused attention on the missing doors as being key to her disappearance."

"And no one noticed?"

"If they were telling the truth, Doris and Wakefield, both claim they did not notice the missing doors, which, apparently, being left open was their default position, so most of the time they were just pressed against the sides of the doorframe and really weren't very visible."

Daphne looked at her near bare office and tried to image how the Wakefield mansion's equivalent must appear and what it might be like to live in such an expensive home.

"What happened to the makeover for my office that Sand Waves Police were going to pay for? Where's my Victorian reproduction furniture?" Daphne demanded.

"All this has moved along a lot faster than I anticipated," admitted Plate. "I haven't time to requisition money for you to order furniture. It would take weeks. And I originally believed the furniture had something to do with it. I don't know what I was thinking. She hid in the desk somehow? Not enough space for a normal size person but she is supposed to be extra petite. But that was nonsense. The furniture didn't matter. I was making it too complicated."

"Do you know if she left alone?"

"I doubt that. I do know why the items in the closet were left there. I know how Natalie Wakefield either escaped of her own accord or was taken."

"But not why?"

"My best guess is someone did not want her to be Marie Antoinette at this masquerade ball."

"Who is going to be Marie Antoinette?"

"The substitute name provided on the new list is a Miranda Watson. She happens to be the daughter of the owner of the corporation."

"Lady in Disguise Corporation is not a public company?"

"No. And word is it's close to bankruptcy. Or already there.

159

Thing is, the charity is a separate entity. It's rolling," Plate declared.

"Miranda Watson. That name sounds familiar but I cannot place it," said Daphne, with frustration.

"She's not even part of the company as far as we can see. She could not be a Lady in Disguise if she wanted to be. She's only five feet three. And she's got a profession. She's a newspaper reporter."

Daphne digested this information.

Maybe she's Darica's friend? Daphne thought, but actually said, "Miranda's going to be Marie Antoinette?"

"That's just it. Her newspaper says she's not even in the country. She was sent on assignment to Europe. But she is due back today. I would think that would not be enough time for her to play as important a part as Marie Antoinette by tonight."

"No, because she would have to be fitted for the costume, the elaborate wig. She would have to be versed on the skit."

She cannot be Darica's friend if she's been in Europe, Daphne concluded silently.

"What have you been told about your skit?"

"I've just received a small script. There's not really much to my script. And the whole thing doesn't make sense. My character died in 1774. She has a pseudo conversation with a king while he is still young, foreshadowing his execution, which happens later. It's dumb."

"Is there any violence in your script? I've had some inside information there's going to be executions reenacted of the kings and queens of France."

"Why no. Like I said, one of the kings is in my skit with me. We just talk. Of course, he wouldn't have been executed until quite a few years later. I have heard he's also in a different skit further down the line where he does get executed. That is an old technique, you know. Threading some of the characters through the skits and making it more like a real play."

"Who's telling you about the plays?"

"Just someone I know."

"Daphne, this is about more than just selling hair care products."

"High society intrigue? So what you're saying is, the organizers of the masquerade ball have kidnapped Natalie Wakefield so that

Miranda Watson can be Marie Antoinette? Why not just make her Marie Antoinette in the first place?" Daphne asked.

"It seems Miranda Watson doesn't care enough about being Marie Antoinette to even come back from Europe early, although her bosses at the paper said she could."

"And the reason that Miranda's parents, even though they're the owners of the company, could not secure the Marie Antoinette part for her in the first place is because the charity and the company really are not connected?"

"That's what we think."

"But the charity wanted to please the company, so it must be that Miranda's parents wanted her to be Marie Antoinette and threatened some kind of action?"

"They swear, via transatlantic phone calls, they're not involved in any of this. They're elderly people. She came along late in their marriage if you know what I mean. They are very rich and Lady in Disguise is not only company they own. I think it's been a tax write-off for them, truth be known."

"That would make sense. I said all along that company cannot possibly make money."

"I don't recall you saying that."

"I was talking to somebody else."

Daphne debated at this point in time whether she should tell Plate about Darica.

Darica had been so insistent on secrecy. And there was the problem of Serena Towers. "Trouble is, other than these members of this, well, sort of cult, if you want to put it that way-"

"I do."

"But other than them, who would care about all this? I mean, I wanted a better part than I got. But I'm not going to get violent about it or sue them because they said I was too short to sell shampoo for them."

Plate was silent. He had told Daphne all he felt he could reveal.

"Look, I may have some other information for you, too," said Daphne, sensing she was going to have to come up with something else to keep him talking.

161

"Oh?"

"You may already know this, but only the charity section of the Ladies in Disguise is going to be at the ball. All the actual saleswomen have been excluded."

"I knew that. It was because of the Secret Service protection for Forrest Pointpar."

"What you may not know is that there are three newcomers that are being let in for the first time."

"I already know that, too. In fact, I know who they are."

"Well, I guess I can't tell you anything."

"Yes, you can. How did YOU know all this?"

Again, Daphne almost told Plate about Darica. But she did not.

"A client."

"Ernest Wakefield?"

"No. I can't tell you. Client confidentiality. And Ernest Wakefield is not my client. I may never have met her but, on paper, Natalie Wakefield is my client."

"If they divorce, she gets custody of the insurance agent?"

"You joke. But it can be a sticky situation when married clients divorce. But if the Wakefields divorce, it won't matter to me. Legally, I am only Natalie's agent."

"Be that as it may-"

Daphne's doorbell interrupted their conversation.

Plate stepped down her hallway. "See who it is. I don't exactly want to be seen here today. I parked my car on a different street and walked part of the way. I was sure I wasn't followed."

"Serena Towers keep that close tabs on you?" Daphne asked lightly as she slipped towards her front door to try to see who was there. She bent over slightly to look through the window.

"Who is it?" Plate called softly from the hallway.

"It's a Lady in Disguise," said Daphne, with surprise.

"Don't let her in. Step outside on your porch and talk to her."

"It's cold outside!"

"Do what I told you. I'll watch from in here." He came back in the den.

"Are you scared of them?" Daphne smirked. "Better hide."

"Yes," said Plate sarcastically. "I'll go in the bedroom and lock the door. Do you think I can hear from there? Go ahead. Let her in."

"I don't have a lock on my bedroom door."

"You don't?" Plate asked incredulously.

"I'm single."

"I have a lock on my bedroom door."

"A- you live in an apartment where you don't have much choice about the setup. B- you're a cop. This is my house. When I first bought it, I accidentally got locked out of the bedroom and had to sleep on the couch until I could get the developer's troubleshooter out here. The bedroom door lock was defective so I asked him to replace it with a plain doorknob. If you want to lock yourself in, you have to use the bathroom. Please lock yourself in the guest bathroom, not my personal bath."

"Go answer the door!"

"Look, I'm not going to answer the door. The woman can just go away. I don't have any obligation to answer the door if I don't want to. It's locked. She can't get in and I don't care if she does see somebody's here. Just let her get insulted. And speaking of locking people in, I have one more question about how Natalie Wakefield disappeared. Maybe more than one more question. Who removed the doors and how did they get in to do that?"

"I don't know."

"Second, who put the coats back in place?"

Before Plate could answer ambiguously again, the doorbell rang again. The caller leaned on it twice. It sounded loudly.

Persistently. Urgently.

"Go answer the door," Plate hissed. He stepped back into the hall, standing strategically where anyone entering the den could not see him but he would be able to see them.

Silenced, Daphne crept to the door. If Plate wanted the Lady in Disguise let in, that was okay. But she wondered what was going to happen if the woman did come in.

"Yes? I don't really need anything today," she called through the doorway.

Then she stopped short.

The face inside the hood was Darica.

Slightly opening the door, she did not loosen the chain. She had no desire for Darica to know that Plate was at her house and even less desire for Plate to know the Darica was parading around as a Lady in Disguise.

"What you doing here in that costume?" Daphne whispered through the door, realizing with alarm Plate had hung his jacket on the hall tree after his abortive attempt to squeeze it into the coat closet.

"Let me in. I need to talk to you. It's about that book you had here that I was reading. What have you done to your hair?"

"It's styled for tonight. I am not letting you in. I have company."

"Company?" Darica stepped back, disconcerted. "Not that cheating cop?"

"Of course not," Daphne lied. "I have friends. You seem to think that's outside the realm of possibility." Daphne was still whispering.

"I don't see anybody's car."

"Some of my neighbors walk over sometimes."

"You told me you never see them!"

"One of them is here now."

"Why now?"

"A sudden attack of friendliness? I don't know. What are you doing in that costume in broad daylight?"

"How do you think I knew what I told you about the Lady in Disguise group?"

"You've infiltrated them! I thought that you just had a source."

"I'm my own source. Listen. Later today after your friend leaves, call me at this number. Go to a pay phone."

"All right. Now just go on, before somebody sees you that recognizes you."

"Nobody around here knows me. I've been careful."

"Don't forget there was a Lady in Disguise that came over the first night you were here? What kind of a coincidence was that? What have you gotten yourself into?"

"I don't know. Now, call me like I told you."

Darica turned and walked down Daphne's driveway. As far as Daphne could see there was not a car on the street.

Plate came into the den.

"Daphne! I told you to let her in. I wanted to know what she had to say to you."

"She didn't want to come in." Daphne turned, blocking him from the doorway, hoping Darica would get out of view.

"Was it the same woman that came here before?"

Daphne thought for a moment. "I have never seen this person as a Lady in Disguise before."

"Was she short?"

"No she was not short. She had all the physical characteristics needed for a Lady in Disguise."

Plate scowled. "If she followed me here, she has to be one of two women."

"I'm pretty sure this woman had no idea you were here. Can't you accept that some of these women just want to sell hair care products?"

"No. I'm beginning to think that that's the last thing they want to do. By the way, I need that book back that I lent you."

Daphne looked around for the book. "Didn't you ask about that earlier? Did I forget?"

"No, this is the first time I have mentioned it."

Daphne looked around the house quickly. "It must be lost in all this mess. I don't see it."

"No one else has been here asking about it, have they?"

Daphne remembered. "No," she said, "nobody. Why would they?"

"I don't know. By the way, your hair looks great. I can't wait to see your costume."

"Are you still going tonight with Serena Towers?" Daphne asked.

Plate looked at her with sympathy. "Yes. Try not to judge me too harshly. When you find that book, put it someplace safe. And you know, you keep your window shades up."

"They let the sun in. Helps keep the house warm on sunny winter days."

The light blocking shade behind the pouf panel in Natalie

165

Wakefield's closet came to Plate's mind.

"That's it," he said.

Plate went to the front door and looked back at Daphne standing in the center of her den.

"Are you leaving? What about all this mess?"

"Pull the shades down," he said, jerking his jacket on.

Daphne complied.

Plate looked around cautiously before he went out the front door.

"Keep your doors locked. Be alert when you're driving behind the gates tonight. Bring your gun. I'll make sure it gets by security."

"When are you coming back to help straighten out this mess you've left?" Daphne called behind him.

"Later. I know who put the coats back in place and who let the carpenters in! See you at the ball tonight!" Plate yelled back at her and took off down the street in a trot.

Fortunately he's going the opposite direction of Darica, Daphne thought. She planned to look for the book then became distracted as her cat, yawning from the effects of a midday nap, came in and meowed for lunch.

"Catherine, you are the only normal person I know," she said to the cat.

Chapter 33

Daphne had fed the cat and resumed watching out of her front windows, contemplating her deserted neighborhood, not knowing what else to do, when a car pulled up in the driveway, almost disappearing into the blind spot not visible from the front of the house.

With effort she could still see the tail end of a car in her driveway. The full driveway was not visible from the front door as the garage jetted out too far and blocked the view.

Plate had only been gone some 15 minutes and she was contemplating the wisdom of going out to a phone booth to try to contact Darica, as her sister had instructed.

Daphne held her breath. She had her gun in her pocket. She was afraid to move from the window, lest she had already been spotted there. Though the way the light was shining she doubted anyone could see in the house anywhere near as well as she could see out.

In a few minutes, around the corner of the walkway, another familiar cloak fluttered towards her door.

Slowly fluttered.

This Lady in Disguise walked stiffly, whereas most of them that Daphne had ever seen, almost seemed to float in their cloaks. She was half expecting the woman had materialized from nothingness.

She certainly could not have walked far. She must be from the blind-spotted car.

And far from floating gracefully, this woman was walking stiffly, having not gotten very far down Daphne's right-angled sidewalk.

Somebody must've filed a lawsuit forcing them to hire the handicapped, Daphne thought. *That woman looks like she was born with some kind of defect. She's all out of proportion. Tall does not always equal beauty and grace. Maybe she's a leftover case of polio from the 1950s. But she does not look that old. Maybe just an accident case, unique injuries, hard to categorize, difficult to know if she would be rated for life insurance as a higher risk. Probably not, if she had no other health problems.*

With that satisfactory observation, Daphne decided this was a legitimate sales attempt. She grabbed a scarf from her bedroom, covered her curls and quickly sprinted to her front door.

"I don't need anything," Daphne called through the door while the woman was still a good two feet away.

Before Daphne had a chance to walk away, this Lady in Disguise hastened her approach and called out loudly the exact same speech about needing one more contact to meet her quota or she was going to lose her job. The exact same speech as the young girl who had shown up the night Darica had first visited, and then earlier today as a hair stylist.

This woman appeared closer to her own age but she seemed as tense and distressed as the girl had been that first night she had appeared.

Daphne hesitated.

She had her gun in her jacket pocket. If she did not at least open the door and take the paper and sign it, it might look as though she knew she had something to fear.

Plate's warning, fresh in her mind, had been ambiguous.

And she was not sure if she had anything to fear. If Natalie Wakefield had simply been kidnapped to make sure the daughter of the owners of the company got to play Marie Antoinette, all of this cloak and dagger activity was really social stuff and nonsense.

Daphne opened the door.

It was broad daylight.

She was safe in her home in Sand Waves and a female door-to-door saleswoman was calling on her.

She undid the chain and stepped out on the porch. The Lady in Disguise towered above her.

"I'm really not interested in buying anything today. I'm not feeling too well," said Daphne, firmly blocking the woman from entering her house.

"I'm so sorry to hear that," said the woman smoothly. "If you just sign this paper, I'll be right on my way and I won't bother you again."

"Fine. Fine. I actually already have a Lady in Disguise

representative."

"Oh dear. You, you haven't signed anything recently for her have you? Bought anything?"

"No," Daphne lied, thinking, *if I tell her I dealt with another woman, then, she's going to tell me that she has to make a sale. Just the signature on the paper won't count, since somebody else had already been by...*

The woman stepped back a little bit. She appeared as if she was a little surprised. She still held the paper in her hand, making no move to give it to Daphne.

"Where do I sign please?" Daphne made her voice sound deliberately irritable. And tried to look at the paper in such a way that indicated she had never seen one like that before.

"I'm so sorry. Right here," said the woman.

And she handed the paper to Daphne. Daphne quickly scratched her name, making her signature illegible as she frequently did when she was unsure of the situation, and handed it back.

"Thank you so much." The woman glanced down at the paper, then turned away. Then she looked back. "Is there another single woman living around here?"

Daphne thought quickly. She did not like to let strangers know she was single. In fact, she frequently lied about her marital status, using the pronoun 'we' instead of 'I' whenever use of the latter might inadvertently give it away.

Crippled or not, she was now a little nervous about being outside with this woman, glad she had not let her in her home.

"I know who you mean. I'm married myself. Hubby's actually asleep in the master. He works nights."

The woman glanced at Daphne's driveway.

"He's a delivery driver and has to keep the van inside our garage. Having it parked in our driveway violates deed restrictions here. You live in Sand Waves?"

Daphne was one of the few people in the neighborhood that kept their car inside their garage in all kinds of weather. Most couples had children and the houses had sparse closet space. They did not have room for a car in the garage, needing all their bedrooms for people rather than storage.

The empty driveway in front of a two car garage was universally ambiguous. Cars might or might not be inside.

Someone might or might not be at home.

"Yes, I do." The Lady in Disguise replied automatically, then looked alarmed at her admission.

"Then you understand how Sand Waves is," Daphne said.

"Yes, I- uh, I had a referral, then lost the paperwork. All I could remember- she was a single woman who lived in this colony, right around here. I heard she might be interested in joining our group and so was hoping to catch her."

The woman hesitated, not sure it was necessary to explain.

"You are on the wrong block. The single woman in the neighborhood lives two blocks down the side street, I don't know her personally but we all know about her," said Daphne conspiratorially, smiling brightly and putting her hand on her doorknob. The woman stepped unwillingly off the little porch onto the sidewalk. She awkwardly backed up.

"Good luck in finding her," said Daphne, moving closer to her door but not opening it. She put her other hand in her coat pocket that held the gun.

"Thank you." Looking vaguely worried now, the woman continued to make her way down the sidewalk, still backing up a little, but finally turning away.

Daphne jumped back into her house and shut the door and locked it behind her. She took a deep breath, turned and looked through the window, watching until the woman drove away.

Daphne did not know cars but the she recognized the automobile was extremely expensive, with gold plated trim on some of the chrome.

She wondered who lived two blocks down on the side street and hoped it was somebody who, like 99.5 percent of the rest of the residents of her particular colony, worked all day every day during the week.

Odds were overwhelming that she had sent the Lady in Disguise to an empty house.

Pinning the scarf to make sure the wind did not take it off when she went outside, she searched for her car keys. Daphne finally located them in her purse and exited through the garage. Making sure Catherine had not slipped out with her, she got into her car, raised her automatic garage door opener, backed out, also making sure the heavy double wide door closed well before she exited into the street.

She drove to the Toy Museum Restaurant. Since all this had begun, she had been tracking down pay phones that were not so obvious. The Toy Museum Restaurant had a plush ladies' room that had its own foyer plus a waiting room. There was a pay phone in each.

It was now afternoon and there would not be very many people eating. It was a good time to go to the pay phone to contact Darica.

She could not get Darica on the phone. She tried calling the pay phone number Darica had given her. A man answered and said no one answering Darica's description was at the bar.

A bar, Daphne thought without surprise but with consternation. She tried Darica's car phone. No answer.

Daphne considered the options for a moment. She put another twenty cents in the phone.

"What did the woman look like?" Plate asked Daphne.

On her third phone call, she had called the police station. She had actually caught Plate in his office.

Wakefield had agreed to a meeting later that afternoon and Plate was killing time before reporting to the chief.

Brecken was busy talking to his wife about the upcoming evening. His office door was not only closed, but locked.

"She wasn't wearing any makeup," Daphne told Plate. "I think she had brown hair underneath that hood. The hair around the edges was auburn. I think that was fake though. The lack of makeup was first thing I noticed. Most of the Ladies in Disguises wear heavy makeup if they're not wearing that cat-eyed Halloween mask. This woman was wearing neither."

"What else was unusual about her?"

171

"Like I said, she couldn't walk very well. She took short painful looking steps. Reminded me of some of my older clients who had polio and have to walk with braces. Some of them have to use canes but there is a type of brace that if it's only the lower legs that were affected, a cane is not needed. And with those cloaks, those types of braces would not be visible."

"Okay. Thank you, Daphne. By the way, what is that background noise? Aren't you at home?"

"No- uh, I went out for a bite to eat. And this was bothering me so I called."

"You did the right thing. It would make me feel better if you went home and stayed there."

"Uh, remember? The masquerade ball is tonight."

"I know. Until then, I mean. I'll be there."

"With Serena?"

"That's the plan. See you there. Remember what I told you to bring with you."

"Maybe," she said evasively. "It's heavy and I will just be bringing an evening bag. Maybe I won't want to carry it."

Daphne hung up the phone while Plate was still talking. She realized then that somehow she had always hoped the escapades of the Serena Towers relationship would fall through and her original dream of being with Plate at the ball would still come true.

Did not look like it at this late hour.

It was depressing.

"That was an informant," Plate said to Chief Brecken.

"Is the information any good?"

"A little tiny piece of the puzzle perhaps. We need to be extremely diligent about screening all of the Lady in Disguise people. The only sense I can make of it right now is that what the corporation and the charity are saying is true. There's a parallel set of Ladies in Disguise running around. But the question is- what are they doing?"

"Selling bogus Lady in Disguise merchandise?"

"That would make the most sense. But I haven't been able to find very many people who have actually bought anything from any of them. A few women are gobbling up the stuff, but most say all they do is talk to their representative. The only thing the saleswomen seem to want is signatures on statements saying they came by trying to sell."

"Maybe it's as simple as forgery. They're collecting signatures."

"Possibly. Some 20, even 10 years ago that would've been a great scam. But now everything is so automated. Even the grocery stores, some of them, are starting to take credit cards. None of those visited by the seemingly bogus Ladies in Disguise have been the victim of any type of fraud."

"Possible assuming of identities for fraud?" Brecken asked.

"Another good idea. But no evidence that is happening."

"That must be what it is. And the perpetrators are just smart enough that they are not going to show their hand before they have a huge collection of signatures of important people."

"Sounds good again. Except the Ladies in Disguise visitations that had the characteristics of the bogus ladies are not perpetrated on the upper classes, but on the middle class and even lower, if there are any such in Sand Waves. I think there is a possibility some of them plan to infiltrate the ball. But for what reason, I cannot fathom."

"Still sounds like this is two separate parallel cases. Three actually. The murder of Emma Tates, the disappearance of Natalie Wakefield, and the Ladies in Disguises who don't match the company pattern. In short- murder, high society hijinks, and potential fraud. For a few hours, you need to concentrate on this masquerade ball and forget everything else. You don't have time to go back to Natalie Wakefield's house and tear down her walls. Wakefield is insistent on a warrant for that anyway. He thinks you're crazy. So drop that until after the ball. The security of the VIPs that are going to be there has to be at the top of our agenda. And oh, the Secret Service is going to be protecting Forrest Pointpar. Edward York has refused. But they'll still be on the premises, keeping a surreptitious eye on him as well, whether he likes it or not. The county is providing extra men. You're going to be there in a nineteenth century police uniform. Acting like a guest but being a cop."

"The costume period is the 1700s, you know."

"Best we could do. I would send you as a knight in shining armor but you would be too encumbered by the chain mail if you need to take action."

"That would be off a hundred years or more in the other direction. But thanks for the thought."

"Taking the tall brunette?" Brecken asked.

"Yes."

"Too bad. I liked the short blonde better. She was by here earlier, looking for you. The tall brunette, I mean."

"I'll bet she was. If she comes back, cover for me some more. I've been trying to get through to Ernest Wakefield for a couple of hours now. He finally answered my page with a page of his own. So I am going to call and ask- can I come over one more time? I need to try to convince him to cooperate. Even if you don't think I should today, maybe I can see him tomorrow if he's not too hungover from the party."

Chapter 34

Plate arrived at the Wakefield mansion before Ernest could get there from his office. He also wanted to see Doris, so he went ahead and rang the doorbell. But no one answered.

Plate frowned. Even if Wakefield hadn't got there yet, Doris should be on duty. It was too early for her to get off. He tried the front door. Locked. Maybe Doris was in the back of the house.

The Wakefield mansion was fenced but the barrier was mostly decorative. It was only vinyl slats. No match for many enclosures of the larger homes and compounds which ran the gamut from iron bars to stone walls.

The Wakefield place was one of the lesser residences behind the gates. It was simply a mansion with a decent size yard.

Plate plodded around back and peered through the dinette windows, wishing he was in uniform instead of plainclothes in case someone saw him trespass and decided to report it.

Through the second kitchen window, he could see Doris. She had been chopping lettuce. The light green confetti of the chopped iceberg littered the table. Doris sat in a chair facing the windows.

Plate saw her, moaned, and beat his fists against the squeaky clean glass.

Doris could neither hear nor see him because she was slumped face down on the table, a knife in her back.

"I don't care who's dead or where. Turn it all over to the county. You cannot be late for that ball tonight. Does Wakefield still plan to be there?"

Plate reassured Chief Brecken. Ernest Wakefield would still be at the party despite the murder at his house that afternoon.

After all, it was just the maid.

"Then have them cordon off only the room she was killed in. Don't cause any more inconvenience than necessary to Mr. Wakefield," the chief instructed. "Get out of there soon as the county arrives and plan for tonight. Your date has come back again looking for you. Talking about some kind of a book. She is waiting outside my

175

office right now."

Plate's focus left Doris quickly as he heard those words. "Make up some excuse and don't put me on the phone with her. Just tell Miss Towers I will call on her tonight in plenty of time for us to get to the party unless she just wants to meet me there. Tell her I'll have the book with me. I plan to get there at least two hours before the party starts."

Brecken took a moment to step into the hall and confer with the tall beautiful woman waiting there. His phone cord was long enough to stretch from his desk through the doorway so he kept the receiver to his ear as he spoke to Serena.

She conveyed her wishes softly. He smiled and winked at Serena who returned his gestures.

"Ms. Towers says pick her up," he said to Plate, after re-entering his office and closing his door. "She will be happy to be of assistance if needed or she won't mind just sitting and waiting, reading that book."

"Right. She would probably be trying to get more interviews for her story anyway. Tell her I'll pick her up at 6 PM." Plate hung up.

Slipping back into the hallway, unencumbered by the phone this time, Chief Brecken relayed Plate's message and Serena left.

Ernest Wakefield had arrived a half hour after Plate had discovered Doris dead in the dinette. Since Doris had obviously just been killed, her body was still warm, Wakefield could not possibly be her killer.

The county personnel arrived shortly after and Plate gave them instructions as he had been directed.

They were to take care of notifying any next of kin they could find, arranging for the body's removal and all forensics. A perfunctory interview of Wakefield was taken for appearance's sake and he was told he was at liberty to prepare for the event taking place in just a few hours.

Plate went back to his home to do the same thing.

Chapter 35

All over Sand Waves, participants were preparing for the ball.

Forrest Pointpar was extremely pleased with his custom made Napoleon costume. Earlier that day he had attended a second meeting with the same group of people he had met with before in the Toy Museum Restaurant.

They had chosen the morning of the ball to demand a final decision from Forrest on which way he would go.

Forrest had considered the matter settled but this group needed confirmation.

This time the leader of the group was not there. That was to be expected and Forrest was not surprised to see his chair vacant. It was a sign of respect for his position that a vacant chair was placed, as much as possibly could be placed, at the head of a round table.

"I have carefully thought over your proposal concerning Edward York," said Forrest formally, adding silently, *I think all of you are creepy, scary, sinister, and just plain weird, the way you're going about this. If anything happened to cause Reagan to step down I would automatically support Edward York to take his place. He would be the natural choice. So why all this charade?*

But Forrest did not state the obvious. Somehow, he decided, these men were so far removed from the real world that there was no way they could possibly see the obvious. They believed they needed all of this cloak and dagger subterfuge to achieve what would normally happen anyway.

As Forrest listened to them, he reflected on how easy it was to remember what they did and how hard to remember their actual names.

He still could not. Except for one. The absent leader.

"If anything should happen to cause our president to have to step down, I will publicly support Edward York," Forrest said simply.

This met with expressions of approval all around.

"I wanted to thank you all again for getting me the right character at the masquerade ball," Forrest added.

The other men all laughed.

177

"You've got to understand," said the Wall Street man. "We're really not involved in this masquerade ball."

"Some of our supporters offered to underwrite the event and allow it to feature Edward York in such a way that he gets some entertaining publicity that will capture the attention of people who are not interested in politics at all," said the adviser to past presidents.

"It's really just good PR," agreed the Wall Street powerbroker.

"Edward York is the hope of our nation," said the behind-the-scenes authority.

"President Reagan is a strong leader but we fear that due to his age he might not make another four years even if he does go on to be reelected," said the journalist.

"Let's say the very best possibility for the future comes true. Ronald Reagan is reelected and serves as president for another four years in good health," said the behind-the-scenes authority.

"We need somebody to succeed him then, if not before. While President Reagan is a strong conservative and a religious man, Edward York is the man to lead our country away from the pitfalls that began to befall it in the 1970s. His religious convictions are not only strong, they are implacable. He is not only a conservative, but his priorities are in the correct order," said the adviser to past presidents.

"We expect him to take up the mantle of leadership and fight for the return of our society to the days before abortion became legal, divorce became a technicality, drugs became acceptable, and the traditional family began to decline," declared the behind-the-scenes authority.

"There is no other man, particularly of his age and attraction, who can fulfill this promise," said the well-known political journalist.

"There will be many Supreme Court vacancies in the next few years," agreed the Wall Street man.

"We have confidence that not only will Edward York be the strong moral president we are going to need as we approach the end of the twentieth century, but he will appoint the right men or women as Supreme Court justices to carry us forward into the twenty-first century," said the adviser to past presidents.

"Men and women devoted to God and to upholding the

Constitution," said the Wall Street man.

All of this sounded good to Forrest. He did not feel like he needed to give all this social and political stuff too much analysis.

He was looking forward to portraying Napoleon at the ball tonight.

He was really looking forward to his date.

The meeting broke up early and Forrest was free to go back home to get ready for the night. He smiled to himself when he imagined the consequences of what he was fixing to do.

Chapter 36

"What's in the tote bag?" Plate asked casually. Serena bunched up her costume in such a way that she could fit in the front of his personal car.

"The American flag. I am Betsy Ross, remember?" Serena zipped open the bag and pulled it apart slightly. Red and white striped material was clearly visible through the zipper.

"I like your costume. Not as realistic as I was expecting though."

Serena's dress was a traditional Revolutionary War style day dress with a narrow skirt and an apron. She wore a hat of the era, styled in the way contemporary shower bonnets were designed. Her straight hair was visible around the edges, giving her an almost boyish look.

Here the tradition in the costume ended. It was made of satiny red, white, and blue striped material in back, with a large white panel in front, and ruffled lace trim about the scoop neckline and sleeves. Over the front panel a knee length apron of white lace was trimmed in red ruffles.

"I didn't think they had such police uniforms in the 1700s," Serena commented.

"It's a police style uniform from the 1800s and I think it's based on the British version. My costume is realistic for the time period. Just the wrong one."

"There were several international costumes, remember? You should be okay."

"Yes, I know." Plate was watching Serena out of the corner of his eye as he drove towards the gates. Thinking, on the surface at least, her demeanor met her given name.

It's the perfect name for her, Plate analyzed. *She's always calm and collected. And Towers fits her also. She's kind of like a tower, obviously strong minded, erect. Posture great, never hunching over or leaning in, like so many tall women. She bears her height like a queen.*

"You look lovely," he said.

"Thank you. You look very nice yourself."

As they were stopped at the gates, waiting for their credentials to be checked before they were let in, Plate leaned over and kissed Serena.

She had been completely understanding about his not having been able to produce the book.

"My project is going on without it," she said.

She reached her arm around his shoulders, soft material of her dress smooth against his neck. He had his cape folded in the backseat. It was too cumbersome to drive in. So his arms were free to embrace her.

A horn honked behind them. The embrace had lasted longer than they had realized. The car ahead of them had pulled forward and been waved through.

Plate pulled up.

"Good evening, Lieutenant," said Officer Skaar. "I know you. But your companion?"

With a smile, Serena handed over her identification. A driver's license and a press pass.

"I didn't think there would be so many people here this early," Plate remarked, as Skaar took Serena's identification.

"So far mostly official personnel," said Skaar, handing her property back to Serena. "Just a few guests. People who are gluttons for punishment, I guess. None of those costumes look very comfortable."

"If I didn't have the cape, I'd just feel normal," Plate said. Then he added casually, "Grant, what recognizable costumes have you seen so far?"

Morris Tates should already be here along with Congressman and Mrs. Brown, Plate thought.

"I've seen some pretty weird costumes, so far. One was a bride who came in with a dress that had bloodstains on the front. She was carrying a plastic dagger."

Skaar was in the dress uniform of the Sand Waves Police. He did not look out of place.

"You're kidding."

"I am sure that is not one of the official costumes," commented

181

Serena. "But you know that those who didn't draw a costume didn't have much time to prepare."

"There was a short stout guy all in black with a hood, carrying a very real looking sword," Skaar continued.

"And they were at liberty to come in time period outfits like you did, Lieutenant." Serena winked.

"Right. Okay. Don't rub it in all evening, okay?" Plate requested with mock severity.

Serena laughed gaily.

"Pass on through, Lieutenant. More people are getting in line behind you," said Skaar. He waved the car away.

Plate was right in surmising that the costume Skaar described worn by a short stout man was Morris Tates as Robespierre.

As soon as he and Serena had entered the ballroom, she had excused herself to go to the restroom and he had a chance to pull the list of characters from his cloak pocket.

Various informant communiqués, sifted and analyzed, had produced a final list, the last of many changed documents, revealing exactly who was supposed to be what character.

Even so, Plate felt it had probably been changed again.

Morris Tates, who as far as Plate could see should not even have been invited, had been finally assigned, of all possible historical figures, Louis XVI.

However, Plate knew that Tates was in a different costume. He had courteously traded with the Catholic priest who had been, maliciously in Plate's opinion, cast as the character Robespierre.

Finding out from his parishioner, Edward York, what other men about the same size had been assigned costumes, the priest had contacted Tates, whom coincidentally he also knew through his genealogy work.

Fortunately, Tates had been assigned a character respected in the Catholic Church. Seeing the simple costume of black satin with an executioner's hood that purported to represent Robespierre, Tates was more than happy to swap. He felt the elaborate Louis XVI costume was too decorative for his tastes, not to mention uncomfortable.

Both men agreed to keep quiet about the switch so as not to step on any toes of those who made the rules. But in his official capacity as security, Plate contacted everyone on his list.

A last minute upgrade in security had earned him the latest list of who should be who and he had tried to call them all for confirmation. He had no reason to distrust anything anyone said about their costumes. Not everybody answered their phone. In fact, most people were too busy to take his call.

Plate noted with interest that both the priest and Tates had been accessible the morning of the ball.

Both claimed they were coming as Louis XVI.

The priest explained he had traded but did not want to mention the name or identify his previous costume as he did not want to get anyone in trouble.

Tates did not mention Robespierre.

Plate believed the priest and very much wondered if the only reason Tates did not reveal the change was fear of the authorities behind the ball and the consequences for illicitly changing costumes.

Plate folded the list and returned it to his pocket.

On his own, while Serena powdered her nose, Plate spotted Tates almost at once, but kept back a little, hoping the schoolteacher didn't notice him as being any different from the other uniformed officers checking out the York compound prior to the bulk of the guests arriving.

Plate also noticed Peg Brown in her Lady in Disguise costume. She winked at him and flipped open her cloak to show her more fashionable attire underneath as she passed by with a serving tray full of drinks to offer to the few guests already straggling in.

She knew Mark Brown had told Plate about her surreptitious costume. The congressman had told her to touch base with Plate for security reasons and not to say anything about it to any other Lady. She had agreed with a pout, but now that the ball was underway she found herself enjoying the intrigue and Plate knowing her secret was part of it all.

Time was passing. Security checks began to be continuous. The area was beginning to fill up.

183

The substitute Marie Antoinette arrived with a little fanfare. She had a hard time walking in the stiff costume which extended almost four feet each direction sideways. People had to move out of the way to let her pass. She almost knocked Morris Tates down, and he overreacted, being thrown off balance, so that he actually did fall after she'd left him behind.

Marie Antoinette took no notice that several Ladies in Disguise rushed to the man, fearing he had struck his head or fainted, as his eyes appeared closed.

Plate didn't get there right away as several more elaborately costumed partygoers suddenly appeared in front of him and he had to take a few minutes to get around them. By the time he got in view of Tates again, the school teacher was on his feet and assuring everybody he was all right. In fact, he was smiling and looked very happy.

Too happy for just having identified his dead wife as burned to death in a horrific manner just a short time ago, thought Plate.

But maybe the gaiety and color of the costumes was taking his mind off the tragedy. Plate felt a little guilty for judging him.

He looked around for Serena. The red, white, and blue on her costume should make her easy to spot but he didn't see her.

Most of the costume colors from that time period were shiny satin look pastels. Or gray gabardine cotton, like the Lady in Disguise cloaks with hints of brown and beige. There was homespun which had a color all its own, if it could be called a color.

But like jewels scattered among sand, some of the costumes were in brilliant hues and they livened up the atmosphere, more flamboyance arriving as the evening progressed and time spun faster to herald the masquerade ball's official beginning.

Chapter 37

Napoleon made quite an entrance.

On horseback.

Yet it was his date that stole the show.

After standing back for a few minutes, numerous guests, mostly male, surrounded the tall shapely long legged woman dressed in a low-as-possible-and-still-hold-em-up strapless leopard skin minidress with a very short uneven hem.

Looking majestic at first, the horse soon hung its head as all attention focused on the female human.

"Did my best research efforts," Forrest was explaining to everyone within listening distance. "This would be an authentic 1700s costume in tribal Africa. Actually she is overdressed. But I didn't not want to scandalize anyone."

The tall sleek woman had a black cat eyed sequined mask, similar to those worn by the Ladies in Disguise saleswomen. She was balancing herself carefully on six inch heels which made her certainly qualify to be a Lady in Disguise.

Several people looked like they wanted to offer her a cloak right now.

Virtually ignored, the horse was led away in disgrace.

A few Lady in Disguise servers were also crowded around Forrest's date, as if seriously trying to get a new recruit.

They were all wearing full facial masks for this occasion and if they had all been lined up side by side on stage they would have been as near identical as the chorus dancers in the Ice Capades.

One of them had to be Peg Brown.

Plate no longer had any idea which one.

As they crowded around the athletic looking beauty accompanying Forrest, Lieutenant Plate looked around for Marie Antoinette. He wanted to keep her under surveillance also.

Supposedly Miranda Watson, daughter of the couple that owned the company, was in the doomed French queen's costume. He wanted to talk to her and to the parents.

He had no idea what costumes the Watsons would be in. Or if

they were even going to attend. But he figured he would watch Marie Antoinette and see if she spent any time around an elderly couple and take it from there.

In such a costume she should be highly visible.

But he didn't see her, either.

He was also trying to figure out where Darica Daniels was. If she was there in her journalism capacity, he wanted to know how she was dressed. The big loophole in trying to keep track of who wore what costume was that all the people who didn't draw specific costumes, like Forrest Pointpar's date, might come in anything traceable back to the 1700s.

Or even like himself, just something that looked old fashioned.

The Secret Service and the county were looking after Forrest Pointpar and Edward York, respectively, and clandestinely together.

So Plate did not need to try to pay attention to them.

Besides the women he wanted to watch, he was interested in Ernest Wakefield and Morris Tates. He'd already identified Tates but he wasn't sure which man was Wakefield. More and more people were arriving and it was getting harder and harder to pick out individuals.

Another realization dawned.

Plate had no idea how Wakefield was dressed.

Exasperated, he felt a surge of relief when he finally did see someone he recognized.

He started in her direction.

Chapter 38

The York mansion looked nothing like Daphne remembered. She had plenty of time to survey it as she waited in line to be checked out by security before she was let into the main room.

The furniture was removed from the spacious den and the forward wing of the house, with the front door opened now to the world.

It was unrecognizable as the house that had hosted the funeral receptions of so many famous personages such a short time ago.

Walls had been knocked down to connect the den with the spacious front section.

Chandeliers had multiplied in the ceilings.

All that seemed familiar to Daphne were the miniature figurines so prized by Edward York. These were still standing on the built-in shelves in the den where the line of people waiting to get to the main room curved.

She stared at two very different figurines in surprise.

Daphne was very pleased with the pale mauve satin gown sent to her. Although she was not crazy about the color, it fit very well and was becoming. It could have been a lot worse.

Now she saw someone had studied Edward York's collection of the 1700s figurines in formal dress and modeled her costume on one of those prim and proper ladies of the era. Based on her own research she was not sure Deborah Franklin had ever worn such a dress, but there was nothing to prove she had not.

The hairstyle that also flattered Daphne was definitely not a Deborah Franklin original. It was copied from a different figurine obviously representing a gaudy lady of the day. Again, however, no one had any expectations and would accept the resulting effect as genuine.

The lady figurines stood side by side on the shelf with French and German soldiers of the 1700s.

Daphne laughed. Music began and she moved ahead, leaving the miniatures behind.

Still in line, Daphne could see further ahead as the line crept on.

The whole downstairs interior of the York mansion had undergone such significant renovation for the event, it was able to accommodate a live orchestra tucked in the northwest corner of the room. Buffet tables containing every type food imaginable graced the sides of the spacious hallway and the large living room now combined with part of the den.

Walls dividing them, still leaving some visible scars on the floors and ceilings from where they were detached, were gone.

The front hallway had also been opened up wherever possible to allow it to connect with the living room. Walls, that had once made these totally separate rooms, now were no more and a good section of that large room was visible from the hall and living area. Only bathrooms, two on each side of the hall remained intact, with those on the west side now becoming little isolated sections.

As would happen, one was already sporting an 'out-of-order' sign.

At the very end of the living room, a small observation platform had been erected with a rail across it. This rail ran to the far corner and down the side wall leading to a large stage erected against the wall. It was a complete theatrical stage with curtains all the way around, a backstage area, and side wings for effective entrances.

The stage floor was a good five feet from the ground, enabling an excellent view from most anywhere in the room. Steps came down from either side and the observation platform became a ramp as it approached the back area. Jutting about eight feet into the room and ten feet wide, the stage nevertheless took up less than a fifth of the space made available to guests.

Part of the den was roped off, as was the area that led to the stairs and elevators. A small section by the fireplace was accessible, as caterers had to be able to pass through to the kitchen on the back corner of the house. The two huge side wings of the house were closed off, leaving the heart of the mansion as the primary area for guests to mingle.

High end folding chairs lined the walls. Small tables on the left accommodated guests who wanted to sit and eat. The area before the stage was open like a dance floor, with people milling about.

After the ball, plans were for the stage and observation platform to be removed and the original walls restored, save perhaps for the ones that so isolated the den. Grace and Edward had not decided if they liked the new accessibility to the den or not.

"Quite a change," said a familiar voice at her ear. Then the voice addressed the nearest security agent. "Officer, I know this lady. She can pass."

"Good evening, Lieutenant Plate," Daphne said formally, not looking at him, but staring straight ahead, as he came up beside her.

"I think they've remodeled the entire downstairs of the house. Added some more space to it. It's less the living quarters of a home, than it is a banquet hall." Plate took Daphne's arm and led her around the security line, causing not just a few jealous looks to be shot her way by the impatient members of the lengthening queue behind her.

"Should I be talking to you?" Daphne sniffed.

"We're supposed to be remaining friends remember?"

"Won't your current date be jealous?"

"I assume she's watching me somewhere from a distance. I brought her here tonight, she excused herself, and I haven't seen her since."

A masked Lady in Disguise came by with a tray of food for them to select from. Each took an hors d'oeuvre, thanked the server and moved slightly away from her.

"Do you recognize that one?" asked Plate.

"I don't recognize anybody," said Daphne. "Looking around, I think I must be the only woman here not wearing a mask."

"Your costume does not call for a mask?"

"Interesting you should mention that. My research on my character, Deborah Franklin, was such that I felt she would never have worn a mask, given her personality. When the costume arrived, there was a mask with it. And a wig. But then one of the Ladies in Disguise came around to do my hair this morning-"

"Did you bring the mask?"

"Yes, it's in my handbag. I feared maybe there was a requirement to wear a mask that I had overlooked in the instructions, so I brought it just in case. I didn't want to get thrown out."

"Put it on, Daphne."

Daphne looked at Plate for a moment. Their eyes met. Then she followed his instruction.

"Keep it on," said Plate seriously.

"All right."

"Did you bring your gun?"

"What? And break the rules? There was a 'no weapons area' sign posted a mile from the entrance. You're asking me to admit a felony to someone I cannot trust?"

"Never mind. Grace York is Empress Josephine. She's wearing-"

"I see her. I know that style of dress, the empire line. She's the only one in the room wearing it. I recognize her posture."

"Good. The woman carrying a large water pitcher in the plain dress, that's the chief's wife, Betty Brecken. She's Molly Pitcher. He didn't come, so she is solo. You might spend some time with her."

"Okay." Daphne's eyes followed Mrs. Brecken as she disappeared into the growing crowd.

"My date, Serena Towers, is dressed as Betsy Ross. She's wearing a colorful dress with an apron, and a hat with a ruffle trim. Parts of her outfit is composed of American flag material."

"That's interesting."

"Why?"

"I heard she was wearing something plain and simple, that's all. A lot of color in that dress for colonial times. I saw her, just now as I came in."

"Where did you see her?"

Daphne reflected, remembering.

"She was going backstage. She had a pencil and pad in her hand. She must mean to get a story about the skits."

"Who told you anything about her costume?" Plate asked.

"Just someone I know. Listen, Plate, I cannot stand here all evening chatting with only you. There are eligible men out there, waiting for me. I should mingle." Daphne sniffed again.

"Edward York is wearing a powdered wig and a 1700s suit, with a cloak. His mask is almost lifelike. Impossible not to recognize him.

190

He's supposed to be a Swedish king from the 1700s. Natalie Wakefield was to have been Marie Antoinette. But there is a Marie Antoinette here with a mask on. We're not exactly sure who she is. Not anyone you would want to trust."

"That's the Marie Antoinette person over there."

"So I see. I've been looking for her."

The French queen stopped briefly on her way to the stage. She pulled her mask off for a second, long enough only for someone staring right at her, like Daphne happened to be, to see her face. Then the mask snapped back in place and she continued.

"Natalie Wakefield? Swedish king?" Marie's face was like a snapshot in her mind. Daphne was so excited, glancing all around as the security line was being processed faster now and more people were making their entrance into the room. She quickly filed the image away without comment.

"I told you that's not Natalie Wakefield," said Plate. "We think it's the daughter of the people that own the company, Miranda Watson."

"I know that name from somewhere. Look, there went Marie Antoinette, in the direction of the stage. Are they going to start everything this quickly? My skit doesn't come up for a long time. I am way down the list."

The short figure with the towering hairstyle quickly crossed to the stage but had difficulty getting up the steps. A Lady in Disguise grabbed her and she vanished behind the curtains.

"Reverend Skrale is Benjamin Franklin," Plate continued.

"I should be paired with him in the skits!"

"Who are you paired with?"

"Louis XVI. Which is ridiculous because Deborah Franklin never went to Europe. Ben left her behind. She died 20 years before the time period of this affair. Louis XVI became King of France in May of 1774. He wasn't even crowned until the next year. Deborah Franklin died in December of 1774. She would've never met Louis XVI, certainly not as a king. Whoever wrote this stuff didn't do any research. I spend a whole day in the Houston Public Library. All the information is there about all these characters. They were fascinating

191

individuals."

"What materials did you bring out? I may want to see them later."

"Nothing! I just read books and looked at pictures there. Do you know how much they charge if you don't live in the city limits?"

"I figured you could afford it."

"They only let you take away worthless books, anyway. You cannot check out reference books at all anymore," Daphne complained.

"I think accuracy was not the goal here. They were just trying for a general atmosphere. Father Thomas was supposed to have been Robespierre, but he's Louis XVI now. He traded with Morris Tates who, quite frankly, I don't understand how he was even invited, much less awarded a character."

"Still investigating his wife's murder?"

"Yes. And from what I can see, he doesn't have any ties to anybody here. But that's too complicated to get into now. Just remember what I'm telling you. Stay close to Louis XVI or Molly Pitcher."

"You're making me nervous. Now about the Swedish king-"

"All these masked affairs should make you nervous, should make anybody nervous. Everyone going around in disguise like this. Definitely enough to give any cop indigestion." Plate had eaten half of his hors d'oeuvre. He looked at the other half and tossed it into a nearby potted plant.

Daphne had a sudden acute desire to relieve his suffering. She patted his arm.

"Peg Brown is here as a Lady in Disguise," Plate continued.

"What?" The volume of conversation seemed to have increased and the music was louder, also. Daphne watched the emergence of Marie from behind the curtain, feeling something was wrong about it but could not see what it was.

Marie vanished behind the curtain again. Then she reappeared a few moments later. The music diminished.

"Marie is involved in an intense conversation with Robespierre," Daphne observed.

"They are probably going over their lines. I said Peg Brown is dressed as a Lady in Disguise. She's one of the servers. It's her initiation into the group."

"And the Congressman?" The noise came back and Daphne had to shout a little again.

"He didn't draw a costume. So, he could be any one of these men in a powdered white wig with a mask. Be careful. It's hard to tell some of them apart." Plate raised his voice as well.

"Getting back to the Swedish king. You said that Edward York was a Swedish king. Which Swedish king?"

"I forget the name. It doesn't translate directly into an English name. Forrest Pointpar is Napoleon." Plate drew his notes from an inner pocket of his cloak.

"Your costume is interesting, if uh-"

"I know. Wrong time period. Just skip it."

The music died down a little once more. Voices became close to normal again.

"Forrest Pointpar's date is a 1700s version of what a female from Africa might have worn back then," said Plate in a lower tone.

"That's obvious, Plate. Everybody can see that interesting lady with him. She must be cold."

"Looks like there is a delay onstage," Plate commented, looking in a different direction.

Forrest's date was already forgotten.

"I can tell you about somebody. Now see that Lady in Disguise? The one standing near Forrest? Since we are identifying everyone," Daphne said, pointing, "that's the newspaper reporter, Darica Daniels."

"How can you possibly tell?" Plate was astonished.

"I have to say I know her very well. Well enough to recognize her body structure even under a cloak."

"How do you know her? How do you know this?"

"It's a long story. You just have to trust me. I'll tell you after this is all over."

"I've been keeping her under surveillance as a suspicious operator."

Daphne laughed with great pleasure. "Really? Well, I suppose it's not beyond the realm of possibility that she is a suspicious operator. But she's on the side of the good guys."

"And how do you know that?"

"Trust me. Listen you're always asking me to trust you. And you would know the answers to these questions if you had not let Serena Towers lead you astray."

"I haven't been led astray."

"I know you're worried that you cannot find her though. It's no smoking. Doesn't she smoke? She's probably slipped out. I saw 'no smoking' signs posted next to all the 'no guns' signs. Posted due to liability insurance requirements, no doubt."

"Are these women your insurance clients? Is that how you know so much about them? How did you know Serena Towers smoked?"

"No. Not exactly clients. At least in Darica's case. She can't afford life insurance although she probably needs it. And I've never met Serena Towers. I just heard things about her. Mostly from you."

Loud preliminary fanfare sounded.

"The skit with Marie Antoinette is beginning," Plate said.

Daphne and Plate moved closer to the stage but too many people were standing in front of them so they remained nearer the middle of the room.

Most everyone stopped where they were and stood still, watching.

Daphne took Plate's hand and he did not pull it away.

The lights dimmed and a drum roll sounded.

Chapter 39

" 'Natalie Wakefield as Marie Antoinette with Father Patrick Thomas as Robespierre'," intoned the announcer.

As everyone stood still, silence followed.

"That's wrong," whispered Daphne.

"Apparently, the scripts were not changed when characters were switched. Marie Antoinette should be Miranda Watson. Did you say you know her?" Plate whispered back.

"No. I'm trying to remember. I've heard the name. It'll come back to me. So we don't know who's up there playing Robespierre and Marie Antoinette?"

"Morris Tates for one. As to who the woman is-" Plate paused.

"She looks different on the stage, even her dress looks different. Must be the light. Not trying for historical accuracy are they?"

"Try to remember where you've heard the name," Plate instructed Daphne, his voice now louder.

Other people had begun whispered conversations. And a few others were now speaking out loud.

Everyone paused again as the two principal characters came on stage.

Another drum roll signaled the beginning once more.

This time the skit proceeded.

The women in the Lady in Disguise costumes played the subordinate characters in the skit. They had no lines, but merely moved in tandem as Robespierre denounced the tyranny of Marie Antoinette's reign and ordered her decapitation.

How is my skit with Louie XVI going to make any sense after this? Daphne wondered as she watched with fascination. *People are going to laugh at us.*

She whispered as much to Plate.

"Shush," he replied, scowling as he squinted his eyes at the stage.

Daphne did become quiet, more because the dialogue coming from the stage had caught her imagination, than because of Plate's admonishment.

The lines were poetic and whoever was portraying Marie Antoinette had incredible grace, especially considering the bulkiness of her costume and weight of her wig- a headpiece with a colossal crown that looked to be metal, not plastic, sparkling with the blinding glare of real jewels, and piles and piles of white hair in twists and turns to bind it to the heights it aspired.

As the music became more integral, an animated interaction ensued between Robespierre and Marie Antoinette in near pantomime.

There was a smattering of appreciative applause when it ended.

The lights dimmed as one of the Ladies in Disguise stepped up to Robespierre threatening him with a long sword at the pinnacle of the play. Somewhat less graceful than the women, Morris Tates nevertheless did an excellent job of conveying acquiescence. He backed off, declaring the superiority of the female beside him and her right to judge her fellow woman, who arrogantly claimed the title of majesty.

The Lady in Disguise quickly denounced the French Queen as a traitor, not only to her people, but also to womankind everywhere and sentenced her to death.

Being significantly shorter, Marie Antoinette only had to bow slightly to be at the correct angle for the Lady in Disguise to successfully wield her sword.

The lights in the room flashed off, with a spotlight only on the two women. One towering. The other bowed.

The Lady in Disguise raised her sword, the crowd ooohed and gasped as the weapon came down.

The lights went totally out for a moment.

There was another loud drum roll.

Then the spotlight came on and followed the severed head as it rolled down the stage and toppled over the side.

A few screams sounded before all the bright lights went back on.

Marie Antoinette stood, fully intact, holding hands with both Robespierre and the Lady executioner.

They took bows.

Meanwhile, a different Lady in Disguise grabbed the wax head that had rolled into the crowd and held it up in triumph, separating it from another bouffant platinum wig skirted with draping ringlet curls, bereft of any ornamentation.

Plate studied the wig. It looked very familiar.

Applause shook the room.

It grew into an accolade, especially when Marie left the others in the background and moved center stage. She spoke no words and did not remove her mask, as did the other participants in the theatrics.

Instead, she held her arms up high stretching so strenuously that her heavy court gown lifted up briefly from the floor and the tips of her shoes were visible.

"My God, the wig!" thought Plate. *"And now her shoes."*

Even several seconds later, after the players had left the stage and the curtain was drawn for the next skit, there was a great deal of applause all around.

"You never did tell me about the Swedish king that Edward York is supposed to be portraying!" Daphne rapped Plate on the shoulder impatiently.

"That is Natalie Wakefield!" Plate rushed from Daphne's side and forced his way rudely through people in front of him to get to the stage. But before he reached its edge, Marie Antoinette disappeared behind the curtain, which now enclosed the platform from all sides and had no visible split.

Deciding to follow, in her slim satin dress Daphne was able to quickly pass more cumbersomely costumed participants. But she was unable to catch up with Plate who had slipped behind the curtain, finally having found its opening.

Daphne stopped at the edge of stage, which mirrored her height.

Behind the curtain, Ladies in Disguise surrounded Plate and demanded he leave at once. No disruption was going to be allowed before the start of the next skit. Seeing the stern look of the main participant, Edward York, Plate reluctantly exited to the left side of the stage.

Ernest Wakefield, unmasked, in an ordinary business suit, greeted Plate as he ascended the steps.

"Natalie has come back!" he exclaimed. "I've just been with her.

197

She sent me to find you."

Daphne watched as the two men made their way into the crowd. She decided not to try to follow. Too many people were in the way and she wanted to see the next skit, with or without Plate.

If he had police business, it was best to leave him to it.

She turned back to the stage. At least she was closer now. She could not have a better view unless she was on the observation platform which was extremely crowded. And too far away to get to in time.

Plate and Wakefield reached the specified restroom. Several cloaked Ladies surrounded the door. They stepped aside reluctantly for the men.

Music for the second skit began.

Wakefield knocked, then assuming the noise was too loud for Natalie to hear, he pushed the door open.

The room was empty.

"Where is she?" yelled Plate. "I saw her, too."

It was too awkward to explain he had identified her by her shoes.

"She was here!" Wakefield exclaimed, yelling at the top of his lungs. "RIGHT HERE!"

The music got even louder and, although both men were trying to ask the nearby Ladies where Natalie had gone, neither could make himself heard.

Plate did get gestures from one that indicated Natalie had gone towards the viewing platform. But Wakefield had gotten a different indication, so they went opposite ways in their search.

Plate spotted Grace York, regally dressed as Empress Josephine, watching from the observation platform in front of the far wall to the left of the stage. With a small out-of-date camera, she was openly preparing to film her husband's performance in defiance of the rules.

Ignorant that Natalie Wakefield had vanished again, able to see the observation platform and the stage perfectly from her new position, Daphne caught a glimpse of the man she loved as he forced his way in the direction of the woman who had so recently rejected

198

him. Daphne's eyes followed Plate as he made his way up the platform to Grace.

Wonder if he is going to take away her camera, she thought sarcastically.

She looked away as Plate reached Grace, not wanting to watch them together.

A drum roll sounded.

" 'Edward York as King Gustav III of Sweden at the Masquerade Ball'," the announcer called the title of the skit, as the curtain parted once more.

Chapter 40

"Oh my God!" Daphne gasped in panic and looked around frantically for Plate.

However, the lights had dimmed at the far ends of the room, the observation platform was now in near darkness and she could not see him.

Fearing to make a fool of herself in front of hundreds of rich potential clients, she twirled about in the center of the floor beneath the well-lit stage, looking for somebody she could recognize. She spotted Forrest Pointpar several feet away from stage right, heading in Grace's and Plate's direction. Her eyes adjusted to the dimmer light and she could just make out the policeman and the politician's wife he had so recently loved.

Forrest reached them on the platform.

"Mrs. York! Mr. Pointpar!" Daphne yelled in futility, knowing they could see her but not hear her.

Edward York's introductory music was too loud to hear anything, as she struggled towards them, amidst the now stationary crowd whose attention was focused on the stage.

The masterful politician made his entrance as a king.

The music drowned out Daphne's words. She took a deep breath and stopped. Maybe she was just feeling irrational paranoia.

On the stage, Edward York did a short semi-ballet, yet completely masculine dance, incorporating sword fencing movements but without a weapon in his hands. A combination of militarism and grace envisioned by the choreographer to convey the glory of King Gustav's progressive reign in the faraway age of Enlightenment.

Two Ladies in Disguise knelt on either side of the stage, silently indicating Gustav's exalted status as ruler. They remained stationary. Four other Ladies in Disguise, danced lightly around Edward as he portrayed the king, a combination of bows and curtsies indicating their appreciation for his magnanimity.

Daphne felt cold fear and rejected any irrationality.

For out of the corner of her eye, Daphne saw something odd about the woman kneeling stage right. The anomaly registered in her

200

mind and she once again tried to get Plate's attention. He was scanning the room visually while physically holding Grace's arm.

As she yelled, Daphne caught the eye of Grace York for a second and waved frantically, jumping up and down. Grace looked at Daphne, puzzled. But Grace was distracted by something amiss with her camera and she held it up to Plate. He took his eyes from the crowd and fiddled with its controls. Daphne went silent, feeling helpless.

The music suddenly changed from an optimistic minuet to a somber march and drew most everyone's attention back to the stage.

Forrest Pointpar reached Grace and Plate on the platform.

Another drum roll distracted them all.

Only Daphne's eyes were on Plate and Grace when the lights flickered off and then on in a flash, before completely going out except for a spotlight directed at the stage.

Like everyone else in the room now, Daphne turned to the stage. Her eyes became trained on the only light, focused on Edward York in his kingly costume as he turned in puzzlement at the unexpected direction the theatrics had taken.

All energy drained from Daphne as the light dazzled the crowd.

From her Swedish grandmother's bedtime tales, Daphne knew what would come next.

Most of the Ladies in Disguise had abandoned their dance due to lack of good vision, required when dancing intricately in floor sweeping cloaks. They were just standing there.

All but two.

Two women did not let the spotlight blind them. In seconds, in unison choreographed movements, the two women who had been kneeling on either side of the stage jumped up.

They pulled long shining knives from beneath their cloaks and jumped at Edward. The one from stage left circled behind him, the other, stage right, came straight at him.

He turned instinctively to the woman on his side as the one behind him made her plunge into his lower back. As he staggered slightly forward, the woman at his side struck her blow into his abdomen.

He cried out as the spotlight failed completely.

The crowd, now in complete darkness, could only stand still in their restrictive costumes as they heard his body hit the wooden floor of the stage with a loud hard knock that seemed to vibrate across the whole dark room.

Chapter 41

No one thought it was part of the show.

Somehow, everyone understood at once.

Whether due to the bright red that appeared on Edward's torso in seconds as he clutched his lower midsection with one hand, raising his other hand upwards, before the light vanished and he fell.

Or the calculated gymnastic movements of the female killers just prior to their strikes.

Or some sudden collective memory of the highly educated audience of the events of 1792 in a faraway land in another world and time.

Or from an unfathomable transcendent spirit of comprehension blanketing the room.

No one believed the violence was faked.

Amidst the chaos and screams in the dark following the assassination, Daphne would always remember the cry of Congressman Mark Brown being louder and more persistent than all the others.

"Help! An ambulance! Please, help! Somebody call an ambulance! Get a doctor!" he called.

Repeating his words in different sequences over and over, long after the lights had come back on.

On the platform to be near Forrest, federal agents had acted as swiftly as possible, reaching an electrical box, reversing the tripped breaker.

The spotlight also came back on, temporarily blinding everyone in its path until someone on stage rationally reached up and switched it off.

Daphne found herself at the very foot of the stage, looking up at Edward York's limp hand, fingers ringed with jewels, as it fell over the edge, blood dripping from his fingertips, a puddle forming underneath him, also overflowing the smooth edge of the stage and beginning to run down.

In horror, she recoiled and turned back to look in the direction that she had last seen Plate. He was still there on the observation platform, staring beyond her, holding Grace York with both his arms thrust to the side of his body where he had caught her.

She was limp and her eyes narrowed to a slit. Forrest Pointpar was one of the few people moving with any rapidity at all. He bounded over the platform railing, rushing across the room pushing people out of his way, federal agents trailing behind him.

He jumped up on the stage, not bothering with the stairs, while the agents trotted in line up the sidesteps. Deftly, Forrest grabbed each of the onstage Ladies in Disguise, in turn, and pulled off their masks. In shock, none of them resisted him, and Daphne had a clear look at their faces.

One of them was Darica.

Chapter 42

In a spectacle that any unknowing bystander would have believed was rehearsed, a federal agent had taken each Lady in hand as soon Forrest had ripped her mask off. In sequence, each was pushed backstage into the hands of more security men.

"Daphne!" Plate was now yelling her name while he still held Grace York, limp in his arms. And on his other side had appeared Serena Towers, out of nowhere, her contrasting red, white, and blue costume sharp amidst the mostly sedate pastel colors of the more authentically crafted 1700s garments.

The red on her costume stood out as glaringly as the red blood on the stage.

Daphne watched as Serena, taller than Grace and as tall as Plate, reached out to them with comforting gestures. Daphne turned her attention back to the stage. Forrest now knelt before Edward York, reaching under his shoulders, gently turning him over, attempting to hold up his head. The orchestra music had stopped and sirens could be heard in the distance.

Daphne looked directly at Edward's profile. Forrest gently removed the powdered wig and the thin, almost transparent mask of Gustavus III, which had only changed Edward's features to a pseudo portrait.

Lifelessly inclining towards the stagefront, Edward's handsome face became shockingly normal again amidst the entire theatrical kaleidoscope around him. His gold speckled silver hair fell downward, locks caressing his forehead, which betrayed no lines of stress. His eyes were closed and his face was peaceful, his skin even paler than the white makeup on his neck.

He's gone, Daphne thought with clarity. *He's dead.*

By now, Grace York, supported on either side by Plate and Serena, was making her way across the room. The crowd divided to let them pass as if making way for true royalty. Some people even sank to their knees, more than one audible prayer could be heard, others wept and turned away. One or two saluted.

Father Thomas and Reverend Skrale appeared from different

directions, came together and followed.

The widow taken to her husband's body, Daphne pondered, without feeling any emotion other than stunned surprise.

Grace York is a widow now.

Without bothering to try to analyze what that meant for her life, or what it meant for the country's future, Daphne turned her attention to smaller drama being played out not far away, but with few watching.

Congressman Brown was huddled on the floor, shaking and crying as a couple of the Ladies in Disguise hovered over him. Not wanting to watch Plate, Serena or Grace any longer, and knowing for certain in her heart that Edward York was beyond any help, Daphne started towards the congressman, remembering a previous time she had encountered him weeping and not known what to do.

She had a stab of fear that he had been attacked also but no one seemed to be concerned for his physical well-being. Only his emotional state aroused the curiosity of the Ladies.

She felt a little more normal when she reached him, faster than she thought possible, and knelt down to ask him what happened. He was obviously unharmed, if distraught.

It took a minute for Daphne to realize his distress did not come from having observed Edward's death. His attention was focused on the opposite direction. He pointed mutely to one of the hall bathrooms with an out-of-order sign, where several other Ladies in Disguise were blocking the doorway.

"Can I get through please?" Daphne said with the authority of someone not unused to forcing her way into an area which she had no right to enter.

"Are you a nurse?" asked one of them anxiously, as she made way to let Daphne in the bathroom.

"Yes," Daphne lied, pushing the others aside, thinking, *they dare not refuse to let a nurse pass.*

Sprawled across the bathroom floor was a stricken Lady in Disguise. There was blood to her waist, visible as the cloak had fallen open to reveal an elegant dress from the 18th century style. Blood also ran out onto her cloak's hood from a gash above her mask which was slightly skewed to the side. Moreover, there was a little drop of blood at the side of her mouth.

Although the manner of attack was uncertain, that the Lady in Disguise had suffered a potentially mortal wound somehow, was obvious.

A barely perceptible movement caught Daphne's attention. The woman's chest fell and rose very slightly,

"At least get that mask off her face. She is alive. She needs to breathe," Daphne commanded.

A cloaked figure, trapped between the stricken woman and the far wall, immediately reached over and ripped the mask off the face of her fallen comrade.

It was Peg Brown.

Chapter 43

Daphne felt her heart pound hard in her chest. Then she pushed her way back out of the room where the congressman's wife was stricken. She needed to find someone with some authority or at least find a telephone. It was so obvious to her that Edward York was dead that she feared no one would bother to call an ambulance.

For the distant sirens had ceased before ever coming near.

Only a hearse would arrive at the mansion and there would be no one to help Mrs. Brown survive.

"If anyone a physician? Are there any nurses here?" she yelled as she made her way back down the hall, pushing people out of the way.

She weighed what options she could possibly select in the chaos, which could be most effective in getting help for Peg Brown. By now Lieutenant Plate, Serena Towers, Grace York, and Forrest Pointpar were all on stage. But they had backed away from Edward's body where he had fallen at centerstage front.

They formed a semicircle in behind him.

Before them, in a Louis XVI costume, kneeling over his parishioner, Father Thomas was reciting the Late Rites of the Catholic Church for Edward York.

"Is an ambulance coming?" Daphne yelled as soon as she hoped Plate could hear her. He handed Grace York to Serena Towers and bent over to speak to Daphne before she could ascend the steps at the side of the stage.

"He's dead," Plate said grimly in a low tone, the singsong voice of the priest still intoning the Catholic ritual in the background.

"Make sure an ambulance comes," Daphne said urgently. She grabbed both Plate's arms, almost pulling him off the stage. He came down a couple steps, stared at her for a moment, then bounded around her.

"Is the ambulance still coming?" he yelled, as he ran towards a group of men surrounding the fireplace in the den, somehow isolated from everyone. Daphne did not recognize any of them.

"It was canceled. The coroner is coming in an unmarked car," said one. "We are trying to keep it low key right now, and not alert the press."

"Get the ambulance back on its way," Plate demanded and immediately one of them picked up the phone. "Why?" he asked Daphne, in a voice only she could hear. Daphne had followed him halfway into the den before Plate turned back to her to continue speaking to her. "Someone else's hurt?"

"Yes. Peg Brown. She's in a bathroom off the hallway. It has an out-of-order sign. She was dressed in one of those costumes. Congressman Brown is nearby but I think he thinks she's dead. He's helpless, in shock. Some of the other Ladies in Disguise are with her."

"Get back to her immediately. Tell them all you're with the police. Get the other women out and shut the door and don't let anybody in until help arrives. Do you have your gun? Don't look at me like that. It's no time to quibble, do you really have it?"

"Yes." said Daphne simply, not bothering to explain that one of the main reasons she had broken the rules and followed his advice was because her research of Deborah Franklin indicated Deborah would have always had a gun nearby.

Daphne was not a nurse and had no medical training. She had no idea how to help Peg Brown survive her injuries. But with her gun in her hand, she could make sure there would be no more violence done to the woman.

At the sight of the gun, the cloaked women scattered and left her alone with the injured wife of the congressman.

Mark Brown was still incoherently wandering in the larger area somewhere.

It seemed an eternity before Plate rapped on the door and she had to not only open it but hurriedly get out of the way of the EMTs who rushed at Mrs. Brown with the speed of an attacking army.

As Plate led Daphne back out into the ballroom, she was struck how a swarm of uniformed police officers had replaced the elaborately garbed, powdered wigged aristocracy and the cloaked, hooded female servers. The costume of the constabulary had become the dominant wardrobe on the scene.

Forrest Pointpar had joined the men by the fireplace, as had some of the other VIPs. His scantily clad date was left abandoned at a table. County officers were corralling her and most other guests on the opposite side of the room from the stage.

One of the officers gently directed Mark Brown back to the room where his wife was stricken.

A uniformed officer conferred quickly with Plate.

"Do they know who did it? Did they catch the assassin?" asked Daphne.

"They have apprehended someone. It was a woman who came with a Lady a Disguise cloak covering red clothing. She apparently infiltrated the group on the pretext of getting a news story. The journalist that you mentioned earlier- Darica Daniels."

"No! Impossible!" Daphne felt faint for the first time. She swayed a little bit and Plate caught her.

"What is it?" he asked. "What do you know about this woman?"

"She's no assassin!" Daphne cried.

"She's a friend of yours? A client? You told me no- before."

"She's my sister."

Chapter 44

Plate did not have time to react to this statement before all people still in the center of the room had to move aside again to let royalty pass.

Marie Antoinette, walking slowly and awkwardly in her huge costume, was being led across the floor.

She was gripped by her husband, who had pushed the dress askew to clutch his wife by the waist and support her as she made her way.

When she passed Plate and Daphne, the former reached out his arm and stopped her.

"I will need to speak to you soon," said Plate.

Natalie Wakefield nodded silently, her tall piled hair wig precariously shaking as she did so.

"My wife is been through a great ordeal, Lieutenant," said Ernest Wakefield. "She was just attacked. It was another attempt to kidnap her during the second skit. Fortunately the attacker was beaten off."

"Nevertheless."

"I certainly understand," said Natalie, in a hoarse whisper emanating from stress rather than vocal problems. "Considering all that has happened, Lieutenant, as soon as I get some rest, I will be at your disposal."

Plate stepped back and let the Wakefields pass. He glared at Daphne. "I'd better talk to you right now."

"Don't you have things to do here? Natalie Wakefield said she was attacked. Edward York-"

"You saw those men in the den with Forrest Pointpar. They are federal agents. The assassination of a candidate for federal office is their department."

"They have Darica?"

"Under arrest. Or at least being held as are all the other women on stage at the time of the murder."

"Oh Lord."

"Come on, let's get out of here. I can get us out. It's probably not

211

a good idea that you be found with a gun. Even if I did give you permission to bring it."

"What about Serena Towers?"

Plate had forgotten about Serena. He looked around in surprise. Serena was no longer in view.

Two men in dark suits walked up to Plate and Daphne. "I know this woman. She is with me," said Plate.

"We're trying to clear everybody as soon as possible who couldn't possibly have had anything to do with it. If, Miss, you will give your name and contact information-"

"I have it," said Plate. "I told you I know this woman personally."

The two dark suited men looked at each other.

"Okay, Miss, you are cleared to go." One man grasped Daphne's hand and put a blue band around her wrist, similar to a hospital band. "Don't cut this off until you get out of the gates. Unless of course you live behind the gates-"

"No, I don't," said Daphne.

Both men nodded respectfully to her and turned away, grabbing the next person they came to.

"Do I have to go?"

"Soon. Wait until I have a chance to take you out to your car. Just kind of hide the bracelet up your sleeve, and then show it to any of them that stop you again."

Daphne pushed the bracelet up under her cuff.

The crowd moved in waves once more.

"Who is that?" Daphne exclaimed, as two stretcher bearers came out with another body covered in a sheet to the neck. The face of a very pale blonde girl, her eyes closed, ominously still, was all that was visible. "It looks like that young girl that came to my house as a Lady in Disguise."

A county officer conferred with Plate briefly.

"No," Plate then told Daphne. "That can't be right. Why would you think that? No. That was not a Lady in Disguise. That county officer just told me that was the first Marie Antoinette. She was found in a closet backstage attacked the same way Peg Brown was. She's been identified as Miranda Watson. Also, apparently Morris Tates had been injured. I knew he should not have been here."

"Still, it looks like her," Daphne insisted stubbornly. "She was attacked during her skit?"

"Could not have happened during the skit. The only fatal skit was the one reliving the death of Gustav III."

"Oh, I was trying to tell you," Daphne began.

"I know. I know now. One of those men in the den is a historian as a hobby. But even he never dreamed-"

"My Swedish grandmother- but it was so complicated and the noise was so loud and we had so many things to talk about..."

"I know. There wasn't anything you could have done. I don't even think there was anything I could have done even if I had known."

"Darica knew! She heard the same stories from my grandmother, our grandmother! Plate, I think she must of been undercover all this time. I know she's not an assassin."

"Don't panic. I'll contact them as soon as I can. Is your car here?"

Daphne nodded.

"You probably cannot get to it right now. Let me take you home and on the way you could tell me everything you know about the assassination of King Gustavus III of Sweden. Then I've got to get back here as soon as possible."

Chapter 45

"King Gustavus III of Sweden was assassinated in a masquerade ball in 1792. He was all dressed up in a costume, but the costume was such that it was distinctly him and everybody knew it was him. So he was an easy target for the assassins who surrounded him and one of them shot him."

Daphne told the story as they drove out of the gates on the strength of Plate's authority.

Outside the gates, no one knew anything yet. An ambulance quietly going in, passing them, was not abnormal. Many elderly lived in the enclave and they frequently needed assistance.

Everything was being kept as calm as possible for as long as could be sustained.

"Shot him? Not stabbed?" Plate knew that would not be long and he needed to get back as soon as he could. He was speeding on his way to Daphne's as they spoke about international history.

"No. He was shot. He didn't even die right then. In fact, they believed he was going to live. But being way back then before modern medicine, his wound got infected and he died a few weeks later or something. I remember my grandmother telling me stories about it, passed down from her family who'd been in Sweden several hundred years before then."

"Several hundred years?"

"I don't know. Something like that. Anyway, they were there at the time. Family lore is that even one of the family members was actually in attendance at the ball. That's not too farfetched when you realize what a small country Sweden is and that they had a fairly, for the time, egalitarian society under that king, and there was some upward social mobility."

"So he was a popular king?"

"Yes and no. Like most politicians, I guess some people liked him and some people did not. Anyway, he made enemies of some sect or other and they killed him."

"Actually killed him at this masquerade ball?"

"Are you listening? They shot him at the ball, sort of point-

214

blank, in the lower back or in that vicinity."

"Religious sect?" Plate asked.

"No," Daphne replied. "Political."

"Did he come in on a horse?"

"What?"

"Never mind. Go on."

"Well, the wound was mortal but they didn't know. He didn't die then and there. He lived a while."

"Sort of like President McKinley," said Plate.

"President McKinley?"

"Yes. Our generation doesn't study any assassinations except Lincoln and Kennedy but McKinley was assassinated in 1901. He also lived a while and there was hope he would recover. But he died. That's how Teddy Roosevelt got to be president. Remember the book I lent you, that was written about my ancestor. Or sort of about him. It mentioned the McKinley assassination."

"Oh yes. And you know there was something else about that book. Something that Darica told me. It rang a bell at the time that I didn't put it together till later."

"What? How could she know about the book?"

"I showed it to her. Well, she is a writer. She was interested."

"Go on."

"She told me about this meeting of the Ladies in Disguise. She was very closed mouth about her work but she told me about this later, over the phone, because she remembered one of the characters in the book. She remembered his last name because it was weird."

"Bratonn?"

"That's it. That's the one. To get into this meeting she had to give a password. And that was the password."

"Bratonn was the password?"

"Yes. And on another occasion when they met and they needed a password they used a different character from the book. But I can't remember which one it was."

"Cambray?"

"No, nothing like that. It was feminine sort of."

"Elicia?"

"No, closer-"

"Coria?"

"That was it. Coria, just Coria. Darica thought it was strange because the word actually is a scientific word that refers to a layer of skin and then when she flipped through the book and saw that it was a character in the book, she was sort of freaked out."

"Let me have the book back. I want to look at it again."

"That's the problem. I still can't find it. I looked for it and it's gone."

Plate felt a shower of fear. "Missing from your house? You're sure we did not just get it mixed up with your stuff when we moved it all around."

"I looked through everything. It's gone. I never took it anywhere. I never even showed it to anyone except Darica. I did read it. And I showed it to Darica and she just flipped through it that one time. She spent the night and took it to bed to read. It put her to sleep. It's a good book for that."

"You sure Darica did not take it?"

"I am sure. I put it back on the hall tree the next morning."

"She never came back after that?" Plate asked.

"Yes, but she didn't get it."

"Anybody else been to your house since you last saw it?"

"Nobody- wait- except-"

"I want you to stay home. I'll have patrol officers drop off your car as soon as possible. Give me your car keys."

"I was going to say, there was someone else. One of those saleswomen. A Lady in Disguise. I never saw it again after she came."

"Do you know which one?"

"Yes, as a matter of fact, I do."

They had arrived at Daphne's house and the conversation had to be cut short. Daphne handed him her car keys as he saw her to her door.

"I'll contact you as soon as I can," he said. "Stay inside, keep your gun close by, and don't open your door to anyone but me. Promise?"

"But, my sister-"

"NOBODY ELSE," he yelled at her.

"Okay," she said meekly, as she stepped through her front doorway. The difference in the height of her foyer versus the ground outside the door put her slightly above him.

As she reached to shut the door, Plate pulled her forward and kissed her quickly.

Then he pushed her back inside her house.

"Lock the door!" he commanded.

Stunned, she did so, seeing that he did not leave her porch until he heard the deadbolt cylinder click.

She took her gun out of her purse and set it on the hall tree.

Feeling utterly exhausted, she flopped on her couch and turned on her TV with the remote, putting on the 24-hour news channel which was talking about a new type of rabbit trap.

She muted the sound and sat there staring at the screen, still in her costume, tears in her eyes, waiting for the inevitable breaking news signal to come...

Chapter 46

Plate returned as fast as possible to the scene of the tragedy. Morris Tates, Peg Brown, and Miranda Watson had been transported to hospitals.

The news was about to break. A few facts were already known.

Both women critical. Tates' condition unknown.

Peg's attack was a complete mystery but some details about Miranda's attack and Morris' situation had surfaced.

Officer Skaar reported to Plate what he had overheard from the federal authorities in the den. "Natalie Wakefield decided to change her costume after the first skit. She said she was in a restroom when the lights went out. She had gone to a different restroom because the first one was on the fritz. When the lights came back on, not knowing anything that had gone on out in the ballroom, she decided she better not take the dress off, in case there was another power failure, and she didn't want to be caught in the middle of changing clothes. And she stepped out of the restroom, she claims Morris Tates confronted her and pushed her back inside."

"Who else is saying all this?" asked Plate.

"The witnesses. There were plenty. And Natalie went to a hospital but apparently she is on the phone with feds right now."

"Go on," Plate instructed.

"Fortunately for her, a Lady in Disguise had seen where she had gone and told Ernest Wakefield when he came looking for her. He saw Tates attacking her. This was after the lights came back, after the second skit had, uh, stopped. Wakefield and a nearby Lady in Disguise managed to grab Tates and subdue him, during which time he suffered one of those strategic blows to the temple. Not sure whether it was Wakefield or one of the ladies who struck him. One grabbed a wrench which happened to be under the bathroom sink. Natalie Wakefield was wearing a heavy medallion as part of her costume. She said she ripped that off and struck him with that. Wakefield says he was only using his fists. My money's on the wrench."

"So she was planning to change out of her costume, because it was so difficult to move around in," Plate repeated thoughtfully.

"Doesn't that make sense?" Skaar asked.

"But she did not. And what was she going to change into? Any news on the other victims?"

"I've been briefed. All victims were viciously attacked and left for dead. No news on Tates' condition." Chief Brecken arrived at that time with this news. "Skaar, go back and help the feds if you can."

"Did they say what has become of Mrs. York?" Plate asked when Skaar was no longer in hearing range.

"She was taken upstairs to the third floor."

Oh, yes, recalled Plate, *there is extra security up there…*

Where Amelia Mattworks had lived.

So much change in such a short time.

"Federal investigators want everyone above suspicion to leave the premises as soon as possible," said Brecken. "Except us, of course. They've got everybody else lined up. I just talked to the head man. This looks like a well-planned conspiracy. They are furious."

"I need to find my date, Serena Towers. And another woman named Darica Daniels. Is she still being held?"

Brecken gave Plate a puzzling look.

"The Daniels woman is the prime suspect. They have already searched her newspaper office and found anarchist materials. I'm not sure about Serena Towers." Chief Brecken unfolded a piece of paper that he had just been given and had put in his pocket. "But the other one's on this list of women who were on the stage with Edward York when he was killed. Any of the other names familiar to you?"

Plate looked over the list and then handed it back. "No. Just the one. And my sources say- well- it wasn't her."

"As far as we know it was all of them."

"No. Spotlight stayed on during the assassination. There were two killers. I was watching. The other women on stage just stood there like they didn't know what to do, but these two women, the ones that had been kneeling, they had no hesitation when they made their moves."

"That is what the majority are saying, I hear. However, which two was it?" Brecken asked.

"They don't know?" Plate asked.

"Apparently not. This is what I was told. All of the six women standing on the stage when the lights came back up had blood on their cloaks. They all say one of the two killers brushed against them and escaped. Yet the same number of women were on the stage when the lights came back up."

"So the two perpetrators simply did their best to get blood on the other women's clothing while the lights were out, then just stood in place when they came back on?" Plate asked.

"There was a bright spotlight that blinded everybody for a few moments so the feds say."

"I remember that part."

"So could be any two of the six. Or they could all be in on it. Or just some of them as part of the organization. Any of the Lady in Disguise operatives here could be in on it. Depends on how much of a conspiracy it was. Or just the act of two maniacs working together."

"Had to have been somebody else doing the lights."

"True."

"And the attacks on the other three people? What do the feds say?" asked Plate.

"That the attack on Tates can be explained. Right now the feds are looking at the assaults on Peg Brown and the elusive Miranda Watson as somehow part of the conspiracy, until proven otherwise. They have Mark Brown in hand and are desperately trying to contact the Watsons, who apparently are in Europe."

"What you want me to do?" Plate asked.

"The feds consider the Wakefields pretty much above suspicion. Natalie's vanishing and reappearance are still our concern. They haven't exactly ordered me to drop it and I'm not going to ask them."

"You would still like to know the story behind the disappearance of Natalie Wakefield?" Plate surmised. "So would I."

Both of them, he thought silently.

"Exactly," said Chief Brecken. "Fortunately this assassination is not our problem. They changed the laws when Kennedy was shot so the feds have jurisdiction. York was a federal judge, remember? Then he was running for federal office. Assuming the two women injured

220

are connected, we don't deal with that either. Depending on how it goes, it looks like we will be dealing with the Wakefields and the Tates."

"Just where I started from," said Plate. "Except I had been shadowing the Lady in Disguise operations."

"Looks like you were right about them. At least somehow. I suspect the feds will take that over, too."

"Me, too."

"I'm going to ask them to let you go on home. There's plenty of county officers here. HPD sent in a few big shots. They're feeling a little left out. I heard even Galveston is sending a man, just to observe. It is not every day a potential president is murdered in your backyard. I'll try to get your friend, Serena Towers, moved up to the head of the line and I'll tell her it was due to your influence. She wasn't onstage. Should be easier."

"Where was she?"

"Serving drinks, she says. Some of the other Ladies have corroborated her statement. That should square you with her and save you some time. Is this Darica Daniels another girlfriend?"

"No. Friend of a friend. Friend of a trustworthy friend. Daniels doesn't even know me. You don't need to bring my name into anything about her. Yet at least, for my friend's sake, could you just keep me informed as to what they do with her?" Plate requested.

"No problem." Chief Brecken wrote down both names and double checked the spelling with Plate.

"Serena Towers. Darica Daniels," Plate confirmed. "Both journalists, by the way. Like Miranda Watson."

"Don't worry about her. That's the feds' concerns. You go home, rest up and wait for the opportunity to talk to Natalie Wakefield. I will handle the social politics and arrange for you to be at the Wakefield house as soon as possible. Then you and I will have a conference. I want to get this Wakefield matter and the Marvins murder wrapped up and case closed as soon as possible."

"And Emma Tates' murder?"

"Still a priority. Not behind the gates and Tates may now be suspect of a crime himself. But no resident of Sand Waves can be the victim of an unsolved murder that we ever give up on."

"I appreciate that," Plate said.

The chief went back to the York den and sat down once again with the federal agents.

Plate did continue to look for Serena for a few moments. Upon seeing her American flag draped near the fireplace in the den, he assumed the feds had taken her aside as a witness.

Plate left the York estate one more time and went home. Before retiring for the night, he took out all the notes he had taken on all activity he had observed since meeting Serena Towers in the Toy Museum Restaurant that day. He arranged them in hope of making a sensible narrative for the pending conference. But the result was a story as full of holes as Swiss cheese.

He judged it too late to call anyone. He did not feel like conversation anyway.

He turned on the TV but turned it right back off again.

He abandoned making sense of real life in favor of his sci-fi fiction book and fell asleep reading it in bed.

Chapter 47

Less than 36 hours later, Plate sat on the Victorian couch in Natalie Wakefield's blue room. She sat adjacent to him in the gentleman's chair. Ernest Wakefield stood behind her, hovering protectively.

Having her in front of him in the flesh, in this room, after all this time was surreal.

The doors had been restored.

"You were advised you could have a lawyer at this interview," Plate said.

Natalie Wakefield smiled sweetly.

Plate marveled that her physique was slightly more developed than an adolescent child. Her four feet, ten inch frame was almost perfectly symmetrical. She had just the right amount of flesh in all the right places. It was her voluptuous bosom that gave evidence that she was not really a child, along with her finely chiseled features that were so exquisitely formed that her beauty overshadowed a few tiny lines beginning to creep around her eyes and lips.

When she parted her lips in the smile she gave to Lieutenant Plate, he felt his face flush.

"I certainly don't need a lawyer. Lieutenant, I admit that I probably am going to suffer from some latent posttraumatic stress before too long. But right now all I feel is relief and happiness that this ordeal is over and I have finally come home to be with my husband."

Natalie had spent a 24-hour observation period in the local hospital after the ball. Despite all the trauma she had endured, she had been released with a clean bill of health and a prescription for as-needed antidepressants, which she did not bother to get filled.

Wakefield put his hand on her shoulder and she reached up and covered it with her own, gazing briefly up at him with loving eyes.

Her husband started to speak but was overcome again.

"Darling, why don't you go and get us something to drink? I am okay here with the lieutenant alone," Natalie directed.

Wakefield nodded mutely and left the room.

Plate wanted badly to shut the restored bifold doors behind him, lock himself and Natalie in the room and insist she tell him the entire truth about what had been going on.

He knew such behavior would cost him his job. So he leaned back on the Victorian sofa causing it to squeak a little bit as if its joints were tired.

Natalie Wakefield's face froze and she glared at him for just an instant. Then an amiable expression came over her once more.

"I understand you figured out how they got me out of this room when all my guests and my husband were watching."

Plate nodded. He did not quite trust himself to speak.

"I'm afraid it was my own private joke, setting up the closet as secret passage like that. I never dreamed it would be used against me."

"Do you have a theory as to who came in and altered everything after you le- were abducted."

"My kidnappers, of course. They came back and cleverly altered the room to disguise their deviltry. They had my keys and my security code."

"We were all out looking for her. The alarm must have been left off," said Wakefield guiltily, returning briefly to question Plate if he wanted alcohol. "Afterwards, I never thought to change the code."

"If you had, darling, I could not have gotten back in," she said, comforting her husband with logic. "Then I might have missed my moment. I know it was a tragedy later. But in my mind the ball stopped after my performance. I will always see the ball in two pieces in my mind, unconnected to each other. Like the *Titanic* before it sank, a paradise, and after, well-"

Plate said no alcohol and Wakefield vanished again.

"So what more do you want to know?" asked Natalie. "They took me to a location. I didn't know where until I escaped. I was blindfolded for days. In all, they didn't treat me badly considering they were holding me against my will. I was fed mediocre food and drink and may have lost some weight. Like the preachers say, good things come out of everything."

"How did you get away?"

"Sheer carelessness on their part. I think the imminent timeframe of the masquerade ball caused them to simply relax their guard. I have no doubt they were hired thugs, paid by the Watsons simply to hold me long enough to make sure Miranda got to be Marie Antoinette. Poor child. If I had known she would have wanted it that badly I would have traded with her and saved so much pain and suffering."

"What character did she draw?" Plate asked.

"That was just it. She did not draw a character. And I was vain. I confess to a woman's desire to be onstage in spotlighted beauty. I wanted to be Marie Antoinette in the worst possible way. She was undoubtedly the queen of the ball. It was like a miracle when I found out that she was supposed to have been my character."

"You didn't know that until you escaped?"

"Well, I did pick up from little bits of conversation between the kidnappers that my being held hostage had something to do with the characters for the ball. I suspected I had drawn the prize and that being taken captive was someone's jealous revenge."

"And you picked up from those bits of conversation that the Watsons were behind your abduction?"

"Yes and no. The trauma of it all caused me to not really think straight. I'm used to multiple vitamin tablets every day. And the food they gave me was not nutritious and, of course, I didn't get any vitamins. My ability to really think straight was waning towards the end."

"I see."

"That's why when I escaped, instead of going to the police or even trying to contact my husband, I just came right home. My only thought was to take a bath and go to bed. But I walked into my room and there was my Marie Antoinette costume lying on the bed. I think I must've been in a trance when I put it on. After all I had been through, I felt like I deserved to be Marie at the ball."

"You managed to call a taxi to take you to the York estate."

"Yes I, I actually contacted the local limousine service. There was no way I could drive a car in that dress."

"How did you get home and how did you get into your house?"

"Let me think. I got out of the dreadful cabin. I kind of knew where I was. I went to high school here in Sand Waves and had been to those woodsy cabins in the greenbelt on school trips. So I recognized it. But there are so many of them. I had no idea where in Sand Waves I was. I followed the trail out of the woods, realized I was on the outside of the gates but not very far away, right near the church street actually, and I was able to catch a church shuttle taking some members back inside the gates after a support group meeting."

"Did you get the name of this church group?"

"Honestly, I didn't. I'm sure you can find out. It was mostly very elderly people on an outing of some kind. Even the driver looked a hundred. I felt like it would take hours to make them understand what had happened. I just wanted to get home at that point. I told them I had gotten lost in the woods. Told them exactly where I lived. And they were gracious enough to drop me off in front of my house. I had a key hidden behind a rock in one of the front flowerbeds so I was able to go right to it and let myself in the house. Of course, I knew the security code. I was expecting Doris-"

Natalie Wakefield broke off her narrative for a second and shed a tear.

"I was expecting my darling Doris to be there. At that point, I didn't really know it was the day of the ball. I had lost all track of time. As I said I just went upstairs with the idea of falling into my wonderful bed and there was the Marie Antoinette costume."

"That's when you realized it was the day of the ball."

"Well, yes. I consulted the calendar we had hanging up in the hallway. I turned on the television. That 24-hour news channel gives you the day and time whenever you want. It's such a resource! And if it's blinking out, there's the Weather Channel. Time and date are always posted there. Wonderful, this modern era! No more calling a time service on the phone."

"What did you do next?"

"I ran to the kitchen. I grabbed my vitamins, ran back upstairs, and got in the shower. I calculated I had just enough time to get dressed and get to the ball and be Marie Antoinette. Fortunately, Ernest had left the little one-act play instructions and script on the hall tree in my foyer. I did notice, sort of aside, that the house was a bit of a mess. I thought maybe Doris had taken some time off in my absence. I did try calling my husband's office. All the circuits were busy. You know how it is sometimes here in Sand Waves. I know I should've waited a few seconds and tried again but I was just overwhelmed with desire to get to that ball and be Marie Antoinette. I called the limousine service instead. On my way to the York estate I had a few moments to study the script. I tell you, Lieutenant, it was like I had been given a second chance at life. I arrived at that ball, still in kind of a daze, but fresh and eager to enjoy myself as if nothing had happened."

"How did you get past the security? They had already cleared a Marie Antoinette. Of course, they were aware that you had been missing. But it's only fair to them to allow that looking for you to show up at the ball, under the circumstances that you did, would've been a bit irrational on their part," Plate commented.

"I am sorry for all the trouble I have caused the law enforcement authorities. By the time I got to the ball there was a last minute crush of arrivals and I do think they were processing people, not carelessly-I won't say that- but a bit more casually than they probably were at first."

Plate did not reply to this slight of the security procedures.

"I remember I was cleared by an officer- he told me his name-and I remember thinking of the Mafia. What was it? Scarface?"

"Officer Skaar."

"I remember looking at his nametag, now, and thinking he must be Scandinavian. I'm sure he was not lax in doing his job as best he could under such a crush of people. Please don't let me get him in trouble."

"Don't worry about that."

"Anyway, as soon as I arrived, somebody grabbed me. One of the Ladies in Disguise. And she told me I was supposed to be backstage already. They wanted to start the show as soon as the guests were all clear and in the grand room. Didn't want anybody to be bored."

"So you were able to go on stage and do your part after having studied the script for only a few seconds?"

"More than a few seconds. I did have time to memorize it. I have a wonderful, almost photographic memory. Do you want me to prove that to you?" She arched her eyebrows and Plate had no doubt she could prove such a talent without a doubt.

"No. I'll take your word for it."

"And I know you have to ask these questions. I know you don't want to insult me." Her mouth, still smiling, allowed a little pout to creep in.

"No. Quite the opposite. I was watching your performance and it was superb."

Natalie's arms had been crossed across her breasts and at that moment she raised her left hand and stroked her face from her ear to her chin. "Thank you," she whispered.

"That's why I'm saying it was remarkable, considering your ordeal, that you were able to pull it off."

Natalie dropped her arm down to her lap. Her cat came in and jumped up to be petted. The cat's shoulder muscles stiffened and it flexed its claws. The feline looked at Plate, not relaxing at all, as Natalie rubbed the back of its neck. Its mouth opened slightly on either side to reveal the tips of its fangs and its eyes narrowed at the officer.

A snarl seemed imminent.

"Midnight, be a good boy!" said his mistress in a tone of voice that indicated she had no doubts the feline was a candidate for sainthood.

The cat stretched its mouth wide open in a fake yawn to show off its fangs in their entirety. Plate was not unimpressed by the demonstration. The teeth were quite long and looked pointedly sharp.

He looked the other way and cleared his throat.

"As I said, Lieutenant, I know you have to ask these questions. But let me tell you something you might not know. I was a theatre major in college. We had a devil of a taskmaster for a teacher. He was the division dean, so we all had four or five classes under him. He was, and I say this loving the man completely, a bit of a sadist. He would have us undergo all kinds of physical activities which he said enhanced our theatrical abilities and frequently, right in the middle of them, when we were totally exhausted and mentally spent, he would command a performance on the stage. We had to be ready at all times to do our part under any circumstances so that the show could go on. I know I'm sounding terribly cliché. But I drew strength from those college experiences with my Machiavellian professor to go up on that stage and perform my part."

She stopped speaking and looked at Plate for his reaction.

He nodded for several seconds before replying. "Impressive. Indeed. Impressive."

There was a pause. Natalie Wakefield was obviously expecting more.

"There have been reports that Marie Antoinette was seen before the time you are saying you arrived."

"Then that was obviously the other Marie Antoinette. Miranda. Poor child. Any hope for her recovery?"

"Undetermined. Why do you think she was attacked? Do you think her attacker thought she was you?"

"Well now. That seems obvious. Maybe. They tried to get me again through that man Tates during the second skit. Or perhaps Miranda saw something and was about to stop the assassination of Edward York," Natalie said analytically. "Then that would have nothing to do with me."

"If they were after her because they believed she was you, then your abductors must have been at the ball."

"Oh?" Natalie looked at Plate blankly. "How so?"

"Well, no one else would have known you could be there. The Watsons were not there and they seem to be the only people connected to your kidnapping. Who else involved in the crime against you was part of the festivities? Miranda Watson might have attacked you. But who would attack her?"

"Well," Natalie had a ghost of a smile. "Well, perhaps Miranda saw me come in. Contacted her thugs and ordered me to be removed. But when they got there, the thugs mistook her for me and assaulted the wrong Marie Antoinette."

Plate looked Natalie Wakefield directly in the eyes for several seconds. If there were mirth behind her eyes, it was imperceptible. They were steady and clear.

He looked back down at his notepad.

"Your costume was pale blue. Hers was more of a pale blue-gray. There was a difference. Other different details, also. Hairstyles on the wigs were not identical, jewelry similar, also, but also not identical. I do have reports from several people. Both costumes were described as being sighted very early in the evening."

"I'm sure, Lieutenant, if you put the costumes side by side you'll see the difference. But did anyone see both Marie Antoinette costumes at the same time?" Natalie Wakefield's demeanor had slowly and subtly shifted from ingénue to sophistication. She might have been a businesswoman trying to make a sale.

Plate had to admit no witness saw both Marie Antoinettes on the floor at the same time.

"Color is very personal to each individual. What is blue to one person is blue-gray to the other. I don't think you can possibly say that any of the sightings of the Marie Antoinette costume before I arrived, before I say that I arrived, can definitely be proven to be me. Do you have video or photographs?"

"No, there was no photography or video allowed. I'm sure you know that."

Plate did not mention Grace York had surreptitiously taken 16-millimeter footage at random. It was still being developed. There was some hope she had caught the beginning of her husband's assassination on film.

She had dropped the camera when he was knifed.

"Look how close the uniform you are wearing right now is to what you had on that night. Could most people tell the difference?"

"The attackers seemed to know who was who."

"Remember I was attacked myself at that ball. Now, maybe that man Tates was not connected. Perhaps the poor fellow is mentally ill or something. But I was assaulted. Thank the stars, Ernest was there to save me."

Natalie Wakefield had transformed from a trusting cooperating victim/witness to an alert, tense, on guard interviewee. Her cat

230

jumped from her lap, walked around in a circle and slipped under the desk.

Plate was aware of the change and Natalie knew he was aware. She was confident and unconcerned. Her words and demeanor were those of a person who did not care if their actions were questioned and feared no consequences if the truth came out.

This was the most difficult type of interviewee. Plate felt that such a demeanor was equally indicative of guilt or innocence. Or a social status so high that neither moral state mattered.

The cat emerged from under the desk and hopped back onto Natalie's lap. She petted it automatically.

It was time for the interview to come to an end.

Ernest Wakefield, more overcome than he had believed he was, had taken a long time to come back with some refreshments.

Almost as if he were taking the place of Doris, he came in with a tray containing an assortment of liquor and several cans of soft drinks.

Plate took a Coke.

"Darling, thank you. Lieutenant, I would appreciate it if we left this room. We don't normally eat or drink in here."

Natalie Wakefield rose and her cat dived down, its tail twitching rapidly before it ran from the room. Plate got up slowly and carefully made his way around the marble topped tables decorated with porcelain figurines. When he exited the room, Natalie closed the bifold doors behind him and locked them with an audible click.

She intended and he understood that this gesture translated into a demand that he never set foot in that room again.

He endured Ernest Wakefield's sincere thanks for everything as he made his way out of the house. In the front doorway, Natalie stood beside her husband and they put their arms around each other.

Outside on the walkway, Plate turned and looked at them. "And I will be diligently looking for the killer of Doris Marvins," he called back, distracting them from gazing lovingly at each other.

Both of them gave him blank looks before shutting the door.

Chapter 48

"All three of the surviving victims are close to death in Houston hospitals. Peg Brown and Miranda Watson are at the Methodist. Morris Tates is at St. Joseph's."

"None of them are able to communicate?" Plate asked the chief.

"No."

"How convenient. What have the feds got? Shared any more information?"

"Yes. For what it's worth. They gave us a list of items that need more investigation and explanation. They have two discarded Lady in Disguise costumes, one made for a much shorter woman."

"Really?" Plate's eyebrows rose.

"Yes. They have the two real knives used to kill Edward York. They have the prop plastic sword used to cut off Marie Antoinette's head and the fake head and wig. They have both Marie Antoinette costumes-"

"Natalie Wakefield wants hers back."

"So we have been informed. Very loudly, proverbially speaking."

"What else?" Plate asked.

"That's about it. Oh, the wrench used for assaulting Tates. It was abandoned in the restroom where he was found. Apparently all the restrooms had tools for plumbing fixes in the York mansion that got overlooked by security."

"There will be some heads roll for that," said Plate, straightening his tie.

"They were all tools one might expect to find kept near leaky faucets. Common household tools, wrenches, pliers, vise grips and the like."

"Anyone ask if the York bathrooms had leaky plumbing?"

"Grace York said she knew nothing of it. Edward was peculiar about servants and he might have placed such tools where he could easily find them if needed, to use himself, she said. She did not know. They have no permanent servants there anymore. Everyone comes on a temporary basis."

"And I suppose all those are being checked?"

"Yes, it's going to take weeks. Say, Plate, how do you feel about talking with her?"

Plate blinked at the question. Feelings usually did not enter into such decisions in police work.

"I don't think it's a good idea."

"She has asked about you."

"Oh?"

"The feds don't think it is a good idea either, but if she persists, would you?"

"If anyone thinks it will help," Plate said, mildly astonished he was being given a choice.

"It has been mentioned that she might reveal something to you, advertently or inadvertently, that would not come out otherwise, considering your relationship in the past."

"She's not under suspicion is she?" That idea was incredible to Plate.

"No, absolutely not. But still, she may know something. Something she does not know she knows."

"If I'm instructed to talk to Grace, I will. I'm not going to initiate it."

"Okay, fair enough. I'll pass that along and we'll let the feds decide."

"How is she?"

"Bearing up well, I'm told. She had not been reconciled with him very long."

"That makes it worse for her, I think," said Plate. "Anyway, just let me know."

"Congressman Brown has also asked for you. He's threatening to formally ask you to look into what happened to his wife."

"I don't suppose that's going over well."

"No, but he has the authority. Right now he's not up to issuing orders. Only threatening to issue them. But be prepared. Time passes and if this is not all resolved quickly, he's liable to gather the strength to act."

"Thanks for warning me. Meanwhile, I'll just ignore all that and concentrate on finding Doris Marvin's and Emma Tates' killer or killers."

The two men sat in silence for a moment.

"One more thing," said Plate, as he rose to go. "The other stuff at the Yorks? And the film Grace took?"

"What other stuff?"

"The stage, the chairs-"

"All rented and explained. That and stuff belonging to the caterers is all accounted for, been removed. Everything left belonged at the York mansion. Plans had been to rebuild the walls displaced by turning it into the ballroom before bringing their furniture back from storage. But those reconstructions are on hold until the investigation releases the scene."

"The stage is already gone?"

"Dismantled. It was designed that way. To be dismantled and rebuilt at each location. The curtain and its frame system belonged to the prop rental company also. The film Mrs. York took is still in development."

"Is Grace there alone?"

"In seclusion on the third floor in case there was a wider plot. She has some relative with her that has come up from East Texas. Ray- I forget his last name."

"I know who he is."

Plate grabbed his heavy uniform jacket as he left the chief's office. The weather had turned colder.

Chapter 49

Emma Tates was never far from Plate's mind. Neither was Doris Marvins.

But he knew he was really investigating the death of Edward York.

He had no right.

No jurisdiction.

No authority.

But he was sure Emma Tates and Doris Marvins were collateral damage in the wake of the conspiracy to kill Edward York.

He had no idea how, why or who needed them dead to carry out the assassination.

Plate just felt sure solving the statesman's death would also explain why they had been killed. He reflected back on when he first found out Morris Tates was supposed to go to the ball as the character Louis XVI. That was somehow the key.

Why would Tates attack Natalie Wakefield?

And Doris was somehow involved in whether or not Natalie Wakefield played Marie Antoinette. She had talked Wakefield into arranging for a second costume to be available. So she had known something.

Now she was dead.

Someone wanted both the Tates dead, Plate thought.

His first idea- the skit where Louis XVI would be guillotined was a set-up to "accidentally" kill Tates must have been faulty.

It had been scheduled late in the evening, in the middle of the many skits on the brochure.

The party never got past the one act play number two.

And there had been no guillotine, fake or real, delivered to the premises.

"I was wrong about that," said Plate to Daphne as they lunched at the Toy Museum Restaurant. He had called her and told her to meet him there and act as if they had met by chance. "But I was right in that someone planned to kill Tates at the ball. A schoolteacher living outside the gates of Sand Waves. He couldn't afford a ticket.

Somebody might have given him one, that's not impossible, but to give him a character?"

"That was done by random drawing."

"Don't be naïve, Daphne."

"How else did I get a part?" Daphne asked.

"I think your sister arranged it for you."

"Oh."

"You had no idea she was any part of this organization?"

Daphne explained in detail her relationship with Darica and their separate professional careers that never crossed paths.

"I may not know much about her work. But she is not a killer," Daphne insisted. "What's going to happen? My parents are frantic. My brother's threatening to come here."

Plate arranged her narration in his mind.

"She is still being held without communication. I've put in a request to interview her, with some excuse about Tates knowing her."

"I don't think she did know them."

"Who did she know? What did she actually tell you?"

"Nothing. She knew Serena and made a big fuss when you started dating her. Ever since Darica grew taller than me, she thinks she has to protect me. But it's useful sometimes. Playing vulnerable, I can get information from her easily. She told me Miranda Watson worked at *The Sand Waves Whisperer* sporadically. She knew her, too. Something was wrong from the beginning when Darica showed up unexpectedly at my house. There was nothing she really said. It was more the way she acted when the Lady in Disguise woman showed up. Went down the hall, got my gun. I should have told you all about it. But then later you acted weird, too. And- that time-" Daphne bit her lip. "It was her."

"What do you mean?"

"The time you wanted me to let the Lady in Disguise in and I didn't, it was Darica."

"It was her?"

"Yes. I know I should have told you. But she had given me so much flak about you dumping me for Serena, it wasn't that I didn't want you to know she was there, I didn't want her to know you were there. I was embarrassed."

Plate contemplated this for a while and berated himself for a fool.

"Your place must have been misidentified as a contact for the group. Darica led them there by accident. They thought you were a secret supporter. Or that you were a secret enemy. Depending on whether Darica was a comrade or a traitor. Let's go over all the Lady visits you had, starting with your sister showing up that first day. Could you recognize any of them? Were they wearing masks?"

"The one who was desperate for a sale was young and I told you I saw her again at the ball. She was the other Marie Antoinette."

"Then she was Miranda Watson." Plate pulled out a news clipping photo of the blonde journalist/heiress from a folder.

"That is not her."

"Has to be, the other Marie Antoinette is Miranda Watson, she's in the hospital with her parents at her side. There was no third Marie Antoinette. Couldn't have been. That type of costume would have been spotted and could not have been disposed of after the killing. They didn't have time."

"What if more than one person wore the same costume at different times?" Daphne suggested.

Plate sat up straight. "That would explain the extra Lady in Disguise cloak for a shorter woman!"

Plate rose from the table and went to make a phone call.

When he got back, Daphne offered some other information she hoped might help. "Two Lady in Disguise representatives came to see me on the day of the ball. I had a feeling- and I believed it was crazy at the time- but considering what has happened- well, I felt one of them had come to harm me in some way. I was afraid of her."

"The same blonde?"

"No, the crippled woman. Remember I called and told you about her."

"Yes, but you didn't say you felt threatened."

"I didn't want to sound crazy."

"Okay, let's get back to the first woman, girl, you call her."

"She was very young. She fixed my hair."

"I've just gotten permission by phone to let you see some photos of people the feds think are involved. We cannot do that here. Let's go to the station. It needs to look like I met you here and convinced you to come in for questioning."

"Okay. Do we get to eat lunch?" Daphne asked.

"I'll get it to go. Drive your car over to the station. I'll bring the food as soon as they get it ready."

As Daphne and Plate nibbled at their gourmet food in Styrofoam containers, she was also looking over a set of 8-by-10 portrait photos of various quality.

Behind his desk, Plate tapped a pen impatiently as she studied the pictures.

"Well?"

"This is the young girl. I have no doubt." Daphne handed a very professional looking studio photograph to Plate.

"My God," he said.

"Who is she?" Daphne asked.

"First, tell me everything you know about it and I am going to tape what you say," said Plate and he clicked on a cassette recorder.

Daphne retold the story of the first visit of the panicked girl.

Plate changed tapes before she began the second.

"She came back the morning of the masquerade ball to style my hair for the party. And she did do that. It was the same girl who came over panicky that night Darica was first staying the night. She acted very professional this time. She was all business. I had been warned not to let anyone in. But-"

"How did she get you to let her in? You had been told the hairstyling was not going to happen. That's why wigs were included in the costume," Plate prompted her in a professional manner.

"Well," said Daphne. "I guess I let her in because I recognized her. And she is so young! I know what it is like to sell at that age. I just- I just let her in. A fellow saleswoman, I was just feeling for her."

"Was she ever alone in the den?"

"Yes, she was. I had to get my hair wet for her to use the rollers. So I went into the bathroom."

"Didn't you think that was suspicious?"

"I didn't think so. Most hairdressers want the hair wet. But now I see. She must have taken the book that you lent me-"

"I lent Miss Martin an old book that fictionalized folklore about some members of my family in the early 1900s," Plate explained into the tape recorder.

"She must have taken it while I was in the shower."

Daphne stopped speaking and looked at Plate. He shut the tape recorder off.

"You need to come back to my house," she said seriously.

"Why?"

"I may still have that book. I may know where it is." She spoke without thinking.

Then realized- *that's not right. I don't have it.*

"I'll be over after dark."

She kept quiet, making no correction to her previous statement.

"Go inside and lock your door until I get there. Don't let anybody in."

"Is my house being watched?" Daphne asked.

"Yes, for your protection. But still, I am going to wait for nightfall. Go on home. But don't touch anything until I get there."

"What on earth could that old book have to do with all this?" Daphne asked.

"I don't know," Plate said. "Look at the rest of the photos. No, take them with you and study them until I can get there tonight."

Chapter 50

"Who was she?" Daphne was holding the photo of the young blonde at arm's length. "We sort of look alike, I think. Well, she looks more like me than my twin sister. At first glance that is."

Photos of the pertinent women were in disarray on Daphne's coffee table.

"What else do you have to tell me about her that you couldn't tell me at the office?"

From the time she had left his office, until he got to her house after dark, Plate had been debating with himself if Daphne really had more information or was just trying to get him alone again.

He knew she was in love with him.

And she had not found the book.

It was inconvenient just right now.

He kept his vest and gunbelt on.

"The first time the girl was here, the night she was panicking, she left something! I totally forgot about it!"

"My God! What was it? Where is it?" Plate demanded.

"I don't know. I'm trying to remember."

"First, think, what could she have left you and where might it be? Did you get a good look at it?"

"Remember, you messed up my house trying to figure out Natalie Wakefield's vanishing act. Everything got scattered about. But I don't recall ever seeing what she handed me again after that night. I cannot remember what I did with it."

"You have to remember!" Wanting to shake her, Plate forgot his doubts about the value of Daphne's information and her motives for getting him there.

"Just a minute. Let me think. Hush, let me do a reenactment."

Plate waited impatiently while Daphne went to her front door, pretending to answer an urgent summons. She actually opened the door, not unchaining the hook, and mumbled outside, then pretended to take a paper and sign it, almost closed the door, then pretended to be handed something else, then finally shut the door for good.

Then she turned, highlighted by her foyer light, her blonde hair against the blue stained glass, her eyes fixed with intense focus as she struggled to remember what she had done next.

It took all his willpower to stand still.

Daphne rushed over to her hall tree.

"That's it. I put it on the hall tree!"

"It's not there now," Plate observed, still without moving.

"But that is where it should be. You usually find things nearest where they should be. Look, help me move it."

Plate stepped up on the foyer and helped her pull the tall piece of furniture from the wall.

"You should have this secured better," he complained. The bottom heavy piece of furniture shivered a little and its mirror reflected different light as it was forced out of place. "It could topple over on you if you bump into the wrong way."

"There it is," Daphne yelled, as they both spotted a colorful piece of paper jammed between the wall and a section of her baseboard which was loose. Caught between the furniture and the wall, a small hairbrush popped out on the floor nearby.

"It's just a brochure about Lady in Disguise hair care products."

"But it's got her name and contact information. Evelyn Corrigan. And there is something written on it."

" 'The color to order is blood red'," read the handwritten notation.

"And they have no such hair color. That was code," said Plate.

"It was a message for Darica. Darica asked if the woman had left anything and I said no. I thought she meant free samples," said Daphne, "The brochure just didn't register in my mind. I get so much advertising junk."

"She was sending a message to your sister? Are you sure?"

"Yes, but it's obviously too late now. This was a warning of some kind and it's too late."

"Yes, for some. But not for Darica. This will help clear her."

"What? How?"

"The girl you have identified is Lady Evelyn Corrigan. Ostensibly she is a diehard fanatical atheist anarchist, a likely participant in the assassination."

241

"How does this help Darica?" Daphne asked.

"Because Lady Evelyn Corrigan is a deeply implanted double agent. She is originally a British aristocrat but became an American citizen."

"CIA?"

"Maybe. If she was passing a message to your sister, then your sister was aiding her in some way. Maybe unknowingly. But it at least shows that Darica was someone Lady Evelyn felt she could trust in a crisis."

"So why doesn't she come forward and clear Darica?" Daphne asked.

"She was deep undercover. She had not been heard from since the night, the first time she came to your house. It was feared she was dead. She was last seen that night trying to leave Sand Waves, but she did not make it."

"But I saw her, here and at the ball."

"Yes. I believe you did. And she may yet be dead. If you saw her at the ball, someone else might have recognized her also."

"She only had the mask off a second."

"Sometimes that's all it takes. She must have gone into hiding for fear of her life, not knowing exactly who to trust. That means she found out someone we believed was on our side was, in reality, not on our side. Must have been someone high up. They must have gotten her that night."

"It would explain why Miranda Watson was attacked, if they figured Miranda was her."

"Yes." Plate picked up the photo of Miranda. Also a young blonde, she was blowing bubbles at her college graduation, her graduation cap skewed to one side. But it was a posed professional picture.

"Strange ideas photographers have these days," said Daphne.

"Think. Have you ever seen her?"

"No, I'm sure. Darica couldn't get a hold of her after the first night. Then she was told Miranda was gone on assignment and would not be home until the night of the ball."

"That was the story everybody got," said Plate. He put the

242

photograph of Miranda next to the image of Lady Evelyn Corrigan.

"There is something else," said Daphne hesitantly. She pulled out another picture. This photograph was a blown up snapshot of Emma Tates. It was a grainy wedding photo from her outdoor wedding to Morris Tates. Emma was grinning and some of her hair was blowing across her face, which was pudgy from her excess weight and further blurred by a veil.

"Not much to tell about her. Did you ever meet her?"

Daphne hesitated. "Would you think I was crazy if I said she greatly reminds me of the crippled woman who came that day also? The one I was afraid of, sort of."

Plate looked at the picture and at Daphne. "If I didn't know you, I would say so. How sure are you?"

"Not very. But that woman was reminiscent of this bride. Maybe a relative?"

"Emma Tates had no relatives that we can find. In fact, other than your insurance spy records, we cannot find much of anything on her. Apparently she was born at home in East Texas with no birth certificate or Social Security number registered until later. Not unheard of these days, but very uncommon after World War II. Moreover, her driver's license is very recent. We're still checking on her company. It does appear the Watson family owns it and that is now the explanation of why Tates came to the ball and was given a part. The Watsons were sorry for him and wanted to cheer him up. I don't believe it."

"But he identified his wife as dead before that older woman came to my house."

"He did. But he cannot talk now. We could exhume the remains, but there was hardly any in the first place. That's not my decision anyway."

"So Emma Tates could not be Natalie Wakefield's sister?"

"Sister? Why do you ask that? I do remember the odd coincidence of their birthdates being a month apart. That would preclude them being sisters, if the birthdates are correct."

"Maybe cousins then. Plate, they have the same bone structure. I know because that's where Darica and I resemble. Our facial bone structures are very similar. We are different in every other way. We don't even look alike in the face. Her eyes are a different shade. Her skin is a different tone. When we were kids and we grew so different, we used to try to find similarities to prove we were twins. And we measured our bone structures on our face as a last desperation since we could not find anything else similar. And the measurements are close. Occasionally some people look at us side by side and see the resemblance. That's where it comes from. My eyes and her eyes are set in our skulls the same way, our noses-"

"Okay, I get it."

Plate held up his hand for her to stop talking. He picked up the glamorous shot of Natalie Wakefield and put it beside the photo of the stout bride.

"It's not true that all brides are beautiful," Daphne commented.

"No, it is not," he agreed.

Plate debated finally removing his vest and belt so they could relax and watch a show or play a board game.

But it was late. He said goodbye to Daphne and left abruptly.

He took the photos home and spent much of the rest of the night at his apartment kitchen bar with all the pictures of all the pertinent actors in this drama spread out before him, studying them and wondering...

Chapter 51

"Lady Evelyn was my contact to getting past the selling level and finding out what was really going on," said Darica, after she was let out of jail the next day. No charges had been filed against her and she was let go with an admonishment to not leave town.

She was also requested to reside with Daphne and report her movements to Plate.

This caused some tension in the air as the three of them sat in Daphne's den.

Plate had arrived in plainclothes, thinking that would better put Darica at ease. That had failed.

"Later, Serena Towers supposedly recruited me and my official story was that I was not in the group before that. But it was really Lady Evelyn Corrigan who was my entrance into the real secret world of the Ladies in Disguise a little over a year ago. I was indoctrinated in the Dallas group. Then I was sent here to be at the scene of the action after I found out Sand Waves held the heart of the organization."

Plate had been behind getting Darica released into his protective custody. He knew some in authority wanted it to be a ruse to get her to admit damaging details. But he had an insight the others did not have. Moreover, he had enlisted the support of Mark Brown in his endeavors.

No one else yet knew the two women sitting across from him, looking so different, were sisters. Plate wanted Darica cleared before that fact came out. Going on the presumption the women were old friends, federal authorities had accepted Plate's recounting of Daphne's story about Lady Evelyn's abortive attempt to contact Darica at her home.

This had led to the present situation. And opportunity to get more of the truth out in the open.

Faced with the reality of what their organization was and what had been done in its name, hundreds of volunteer and employed Ladies in Disguise were discarding their cloaks and masks and lining up in police stations across the country to talk.

Most of their talk was worthless as most knew nothing.

A trickle of facts was coming in and being diverted from the flood of chatter into a directed stream of information. The flood was keeping police busy across the nation. The stream was flowing to the federal investigators in Texas and ponding in Sand Waves.

The pond was still muddy, but each new flush of fresh insight made it a little more clear.

Plate was hoping Darica could make the waters crystallize.

"Take me carefully through everything that happened from the moment you arrived at the ball until the assassination."

"I want to know, too, dear sister, all about how you got mixed up in this."

"Later, Daphne. Darica, tell me, you've told the federal authorities- what?" Plate asked.

"Not much really. They didn't question me that much. Just threw me in the cell and told me I must have done it. Then came back and questioned me about the Watsons."

"The Watsons?"

"Yes, and I could not tell them much. Miranda's been in the employ of *The Whisperer* on a contingency basis. She spends most of her time pursuing specific stories they assign her. We've been friendly during the short periods she has been in town. I haven't been here long. She hasn't been in town much. Consequently, I don't really know her."

Plate leaned back on Daphne's couch contemplating the appearance of the two sisters as they sat before him in dinette chairs pulled into the den. His thoughts encompassed not only Daphne and Darica, but the numerous other people involved and where they had landed in the fallout from the events of the ball.

Miranda Watson, intensive care unit in Houston. Situation with the Watsons was very delicate. Their daughter was near death and in a near unrecognizable state in the hospital. Despite being in their 70s, they were keeping a 24-7 vigil.

Natalie Wakefield, returned to her husband and recuperating. She was now in seclusion, suffering delayed post-traumatic stress, as reported by her husband.

246

Morris Tates was still in critical condition. His ex-wife on the way from Ohio with his children to be with him. It was unclear if he was a victim or a villain in all this.

Serena Towers, busy with a scoop of her lifetime. Not just reporting the news now, giving interviews on television, talking in depth with star CNN reporters and featured on the nightly news network programs, all three of them.

Forrest Pointpar revving up his campaign- also all over the national news, talking about Edward York's legacy and the country's future.

Peg Brown on life support.

Mark Brown at the bedside of his wife.

Grace York in seclusion at the York estate, on the third floor, still coping with possible danger to her own life.

Darica Daniels now the prime suspect in assassination. Or much more likely, now the substitute patsy in the intrigue.

Lady Evelyn Corrigan- still unaccounted for.

And the dead-

Doris Marvins

Emma Tates

Edward York

The unbidden idea that this list was like the final casting list for the characters at the ball, improbable people chosen for the wrong roles, came to Plate's mind.

A wild idea came to him that the list could change again.

"Daphne, get me a notebook, or sheet of paper would you?" Plate asked.

Daphne immediately rose from her chair and went into her office, which she and Plate had haphazardly restored before Darica arrived.

"You certainly expect her to get up and wait on you don't you?" Darica told Plate with an edge in her voice.

Daphne handed a spiral notebook to Plate. Ignoring Darica's comment, he quickly jotted down the list he had just made in his mind. Studying it, he started toying with the idea of moving the names around just as the names on the masquerade ball character list had been shuffled several times.

"We surmise the ultimate assignation of the characters was nowhere near what was chosen at random. And they actually did go through a mock procedure of choosing them at random."

"Why bother?" asked Daphne.

"Some sort of a ritual I guess," said Plate, "to see if, by chance or voodoo, a name fell into place that was intended to be there all along. Then the first, ideal for the conspirators, set of names was entered. Then someone got in and shuffled those, evidenced by a little computer found burned but surprisingly still readable. Then, there was the under the table trading, which the conspirators did not allow for, as apparently in their world everyone follows the rules religiously. A major error on their part. So then we have the ultimate list of who actually showed up in what costume."

"How do you know anything about the character lists?" Darica asked, with some hostility still.

"You should be nicer to him. He got you out of jail," Daphne observed.

"I'm surprised Serena Towers is not here with us, involved in our little tete-a-tete. Aren't you missing her, Lieutenant?" Darica let open antagonism flourish.

"Darica!" protested Daphne.

"Have you told your sister that you got her the character of Deborah Franklin?" Plate asked Darica with a smile.

"Is that really true?" Daphne dropped her chastisement of her sister for an attitude of surprise.

Darica became defensive.

"You wanted a character so badly. Yes, I typed your name in. I was on the committee that selected the names at random. I drew Deborah Franklin and then I drew a name from the candidates on the spreadsheet. Later, I simply replaced your name instead of the one I actually drew. It is easy to get into these computers with a little manipulation."

"Did you see any of the other names?" Plate asked, still quietly professional in manner. His business-like tone defused some of

Darica's anger.

"What do you mean?"

"Let me ask a different question. Were you all together with the other Ladies also drawing names? If so, what name did you actually draw?"

"It was just an initial and a last name. D. Russo."

"That original list has been found. See, even though you changed it, it was still there in its original form in a different file. So someone noticed what you did," Plate said. "All original names are in no way connected to the crime." He looked at a pocket notebook near also on the coffee table. "In fact, she's on the list of people who don't even live in Sand Waves. Everyone who bought a ticket for the ball has been checked out. Several did not even show up. Young people blowing off money."

"Any other names on the first list look like they were planted?" Darica asked, sounding professional also.

"Well, we are not sure. Chief Brecken's wife was the main one that stood out, besides you, Daphne. And you stood out just to me."

"Maybe Mrs. Brecken's name was really chosen at random," Darica suggested.

"I felt there was something wrong from the beginning," Daphne declared. "I spent hours at the library researching Deborah Franklin. And I came across some of the others in the process. Mrs. Brecken was the wrong age and body type for Molly Pitcher."

Plate and Darica stared at Daphne upon hearing this statement.

"If they were as sloppy in delineating the other characters as mine, and as haphazard in assignations, I don't understand why security forces were not more alert," Daphne continued.

"Daphne," said Plate. "Nobody else researched their characters."

"Really?" Daphne's response indicated this was truly news to her.

"Most people do not have time to take off work and go to a library and sift through thousands of books and articles to gather details about a character they are going to play for a few hours at a party," said Plate.

"If you work 40 hours a week, you barely have time to do your laundry," said Darica.

"I work more than 40 hours a week," said Plate.

"So do I. No matter what, I have to go in tomorrow," said Darica. "And, Daphne, DON'T start in about getting me on at an insurance company."

"There was some attention paid to the character assigned to Forrest Pointpar by authorities," said Plate, getting back to business. "He originally was to be Louis XVI and there was an early notion in security planning that an attempt on his life might be through some type of mock execution scene."

"My skit with Louis XVI didn't involve any violence. It took place at a tea party." Daphne frowned, remembering the inane dialogue.

"Right, before the scripts were released, a skit where he was executed that did involve a fake guillotine was eliminated and that diffused the fears, misdirecting all of us once again. Then at the last minute, it was reinstated on the agenda but by then it was no secret Forrest was going to be a different character."

"How did that happen?"

"I don't have a high enough clearance level to get those details."

"Your security level must be fairly high for you to know all this," said Darica.

"Higher than I would like," said Plate.

"They were planning to kill Morris Tates, that's why the guillotine scene was planned? It does not make sense," Daphne commented.

"These details were all smoke and mirrors, just like the character selections. No performances beyond the second scene were actually planned," said Plate. "Darica, tell me exactly what happened, who you spoke to, where you were, at every given point in time that you can remember."

"As I said," Darica narrated. "I was interested in the group after the lawsuit was filed against them. I decided it would be a good story with a different angle and I could make much more of it, if I could see what was going on from the inside. Why did these women all have to be tall and thin?"

250

"So did you contact Evelyn or did she contact you?" Plate asked.

"I contacted her."

"Why her?" Daphne asked.

"I knew she was not tall, yet she was one of them. I was curious. She told me about those stilt boots they wore if heels were not enough. Near crippling."

"How did you even know her?" Plate asked.

"I had met her a few years ago on a short assignment in London. She was making news then by becoming an American citizen and renouncing her British citizenship, due to antipathy to the monarchy."

"Did you do a story on her about that?" asked Daphne.

"No, that was Miranda Watson. I got acquainted with her at the same time. She helped me get the position I had in Dallas, which ultimately led to my transfer here."

"Did you have any idea she was involved with the organization or that her parents owned the Lady in Disguise brand?" Plate asked.

"Actually no. It was remiss of me not to check out who the real owners of the company were. But that was not the angle to my story. I assumed the rigid physical requirements to get the job had been dreamed up by some press agent or advertising company to maximize publicity. I had no idea they were anything other than a hair care product company. And it's only been in the last couple of months that I realized something more was going on."

"What exactly is going on with that company?" Daphne asked.

"I'd like Darica to tell us what she thinks or knows about that."

"I began to be suspicious when I started getting invited to the meetings where you needed a password. And the meetings seemed quasi-political. Not sales peptalk-type gatherings. And you could listen to a long speech that seemed to say a lot, but when you walked away from it, you had no idea what had actually been said. I've had a lot of English literature classes. I know how to write fluffy nonsense. And that's what all the speeches were."

"They were testing your reaction to certain key phrases mixed in the fluff," Plate said.

"Yes, I can see that now," Darica said.

"Also it is understood now that they were mechanisms to get

251

certain people together in such a way that did not arouse suspicion. Most likely you attended a pseudo-meeting and there was a real meeting later."

"Yes, I'm quite sure that was the case. I never got into the real meetings. That's what got me in trouble the night I showed up at Daphne's. I had lingered after one of the fluffy meetings broke up. That was strictly against the rules. For our safety we were told to go immediately home after every meeting since it was dark and the meetings were always held at those school district cabins in the woods."

"You lingered?" Daphne asked, confused by Darica's behavior.

"Yes. That night I hung around because the meeting organizers never left when we did and I was wondering what did they do after we were gone. When I saw other women arriving, I got a little nervous. I had been in the woods and I decide to go back to my car. Well, it would not start. As I sat there, trying to get it to run, Miranda appeared."

"She was supposed to be in Europe," said Plate.

"She was not. Miranda scolded me for breaking the rules and warned me I could get kicked out. But she said she could take care of it, since her parents owned the company. She drove me to your house and told me she would get the car towed quietly back to my apartment complex. I considered that she was being a friend. Now I guess she must've saved my life."

"Possibly. Go on. What happened next?" Plate prompted.

"I wasn't concerned. Daphne and I had a nice reunion. Then a Lady in Disguise called at Daphne's door at 11 o'clock at night. That scared me to death."

"Lady Evelyn was trying to contact you. She must have followed you and Miranda."

"I hadn't heard from Evelyn for several weeks. That was another worry. Remember, at this time my main fear still was that I would be discovered as an investigative journalist and kicked out of the organization, possibly fired by my editor for incompetence."

"So you were scared," Daphne said.

"I told myself I was being paranoid. Or just plain cowardly. I am an investigative journalist. Some risk comes with the job."

"I can get you on at a good insurance-"

"DAPHNE! That's enough! Anyway, Lieutenant, that was the night I started to have fears that something else was going on besides an old fashioned obsession with women's body issues. I was afraid I had put Daphne in danger somehow. I didn't know what to do, other than just keep attending the meetings, try to cover up my relationship with Daphne as much as possible and follow their instructions concerning the masquerade ball."

"Those instructions were?"

"I was given the time to arrive in the Lady in Disguise costume. Where to go in preparation for my part in the skit. We all arrived early and the six of us rehearsed our position. The two kneeling down didn't have anything to do. The other four of us had to learn the little dance with Edward York."

"Was Edward there?" Plate asked.

"Oh yes. He rehearsed with us."

There was a moment of silence.

"What was he like? I met him but had very little interaction with him. You got to dance with him. What was that like?" Daphne asked her sister, knowing that Plate had known York much better, but wanting a woman's point of view.

"He was charming. Being near him was, I don't know how to say it, electrifying. He had an atmosphere about him, just like they said. It was exciting to be in his presence."

"So, this rehearsal took place earlier in the afternoon. What type of security was there?" Plate asked.

"I don't really know. I didn't really see much security. It was like being in a dress rehearsal."

"Darica and I have done some community theatre in the past," Daphne broke in.

"Everybody was concerned with what they had to do and where they had to be and not paying too much attention to anybody else."

"Do you remember who you saw? Besides Edward and the other women in your skit? Do you remember who any of those women were? Was one of them Peg Brown?" Plate asked.

253

"We were all in full costume. You could not tell anybody apart."

"One of them was shorter," said Daphne.

"No," said Darica. "All six were standard Lady in Disguise women."

"Are you sure they were women?" asked Plate.

"Practically. Might have been a very feminine man in the mix. But I don't think so. That's one of things I had been watching for all along, at all the meetings I had attended. Certain magazines pay really good money for stories like that. I do a little freelancing under a pen name. So I was attuned to that idea. Never saw any evidence of it."

"One of them was shorter," Daphne repeated. "I noticed it right before the skit began, and thinking about them now, I can remember there was a discrepancy that bothered me about one of them and now I realize it was that she was shorter. She had to be."

"If they were all standing up side by side, you wouldn't have been the only one that noticed one of them was shorter," said Plate.

"But that's just it. It wasn't one of the ones standing. It was one of the ones kneeling. It wasn't that obvious that she was shorter. I just happened to look at the proportion of her body. It was different. And I didn't understand what I saw at the time because I'm so used to seeing all these tall thin Ladies in Disguises. But now that I think back, I'm sure. She was shorter," Daphne insisted.

"Which one?" asked Plate.

"The one on the left, my left. So, stage right."

"Excuse me." Plate stood up and went into Daphne's office and shut the door. They could hear him making another phone call, speaking softly.

"Go on." He came right back out and spoke the command before he even sat down.

"That's all," said Daphne. "I'm short. I notice short people, especially amid tall people."

"Okay. Please continue, Darica. What happened next?"

"Daphne's wrong!"

"Just skip it. What happened next?"

"We were all kept backstage during the Marie Antoinette skit. We were told we needed to keep our movements fresh in our minds so we should not watch the first skit. Since we were second on the list, we would be free to watch all the others."

"There were no rehearsals for any other skits, we believe. You had no rehearsal for yours did you, Daphne?" Plate asked.

"No," Daphne recalled. "I just got a copy of the script and was told it would be good if I memorized it. But if I did not, it was okay. I could just hold it in my hand during the act."

"This entire masquerade ball was set up as a framework in which to murder Edward York. The first skit was to throw everyone off guard, we think, so that everyone would be expecting entertaining violence in the showmanship. This would especially throw Edward York, himself, off guard."

"How could you not remember what happened to King Gustav? Don't you recall our grandmother's stories?" Daphne asked Darica.

"I never paid attention to those old tales. History is boring and irrelevant. I live in the present," said Darica. "And I was not expecting murder at the party. There was a ton of security. I thought the cops were on the lookout for drugs or money laundering. I was looking for evidence of revelry and corruption. My attention was focused on getting the story I had come for."

"And the attention of all that security was focused on Forrest Pointpar," said Plate.

The three people were suddenly tired. They were silent for a short time. Then the conversation resumed.

"There was one thing I noticed. The skits seem to happen quickly but they were actually delayed a little," said Darica.

"That has been noted. Remember when we were talking, Daphne, and the music got loud. We could not hear each other, then the music died down again, then rose again when the skit began."

"I remember."

"Darica- what was going on during that time?"

"I don't know. We couldn't see."

"I think it is safe to say that at least one, probably two of the women you rehearsed with, and possibly were kept waiting with, switched places with original members of the dance team before the Gustavus skit actually began. Can you see how that would be possible without anyone noticing?"

"I would say it would be very easy. There was so much coming and going, there could easily have been a shuffle in people backstage."

"We think the two actual assassins did not rehearse and fled as soon as they had struck their blows. So that means the conspiracy went beyond just them."

"I can't believe I infiltrated these women and I didn't pick it up on any of this."

"They were very clever. Almost certainly you were allowed to infiltrate the group and they were recruiting innocent people, people like Peg Brown, who would never dream of participating in such a conspiracy. They were sprinkling such people amongst themselves. A dangerous game, but by pulling it off, they managed to fool almost everyone who did take a hard look at them. As soon as they got wind of any suspicions or investigations, the real conspirators retreated into the background and let their innocent recruits get all the attention."

"That's why you were following me?"

"I didn't know who you were. There were red flags about you that indicated, if the group was up to something criminal, you were probably involved. Some of those red flags, I realize now, were planted. Had I known you were Daphne's sister-" He glared at Daphne. "I would have looked at you from a different perspective."

"No wonder they let me infiltrate them so easily. I was the perfect patsy. I suppose the same is true of Serena Towers?"

"Let's leave Serena out of this for the time being," said Plate.

"I suppose she's some sort of secret CIA operative," said Daphne.

"I said leave her out of this discussion."

"I'm bound to see her again, even after this clears up," said Darica. "What do I say?"

"Nothing. And I'm sure she will not bring up the subject."

"Just act like nothing happened? We know nothing about it? Even though she's feeding her career with it and will probably come out of it more important than Barbara Walters?" Darica was incensed.

"That's right."

"You probably won't see much of her, if that's the case, anyway," said Daphne. "She'll be in New York all the time. Never come back to Sand Waves." *What a happy idea,* she reflected. Then a cold wave gripped her, *suppose Plate uses this to forward his career and he leaves, too.*

"You are probably right," Darica sighed. "I finally get a break and I dare not use it or I'll wind up in the federal penitentiary."

"You can always write your memoirs 30 years from now," Daphne said consolingly.

It was Darica's turn to glare at Daphne.

Chapter 52

Daphne was wrong.

Serena completed her business in New York in record time.

She then returned to Sand Waves.

Serena announced her plans to write a book about the assassination and at once had several publishers express interest. One came up with a healthy advance.

Serena did move out of the Watson home, saying she felt like she was intruding on the family in a time of stress. But after she had made the rounds of the national television talk shows obligatorily promoting the coming book, she announced she felt she could best complete her manuscript in Sand Waves.

No apartments were available for rent so she asked Darica if they could become temporary roommates.

While the joint project they had originally planned was now defunct, Serena did offer Darica the opportunity to contribute a forward to her upcoming book.

Darica declined this consolation prize. Her transfer back to her original position in Dallas was pending.

"I'm going to be staying with my sister for a while. In fact, I am already there at official request," Darica told Serena. "Just take the apartment. I'll get my stuff out. I expect to be back in Dallas very soon."

This was perfect for Serena. The apartment was a furnished unit. Serena moving in and Darica moving out was easily accomplished. Daphne found herself living with another human being for the first time since she had graduated college.

It was not the person she had anticipated.

She felt invaded.

"You know, we could contact Scott and maybe he would visit," said Darica, when she showed up at Daphne's front door with her small set of luggage.

"Don't push it," said Daphne. She had spent the day before her sister's anticipated arrival hiding everything she did not want Darica to see. Fortunately she had a spacious attic. "And don't you dare say anything like that to Mom and Dad when they come over for dinner tomorrow night. Any family reunions need to take place at their house. Scott doesn't need to come to my house. It will just cause jealousy between us."

"I think you just want to keep him away from Plate," said Darica. "I don't know how you can still be friends with that cop after all this. You know he's now living in the same complex as Serena."

"I still haven't sold him any insurance yet," said Daphne.

"And how can you be friendly to her?"

"I haven't sold her any yet either."

Plate was continuing his public romance with Serena unabashed. Due to the publicity and Serena's social connections, they were now a frequently invited couple to affairs behind the gates. But his long hours on the job meant there were many days Serena flitted about Sand Waves unaccompanied.

It would have unnerved her to know that Plate watched her in an unmarked police car, not wearing a uniform, whenever he could get away with it.

The satisfaction he gained from watching her innocent comings and goings was diminishing as time passed. She showed no signs of any activity with any other women, much less men.

She went to the movies sometimes and he did not follow her in. The theatre in Sand Waves was small enough he could spot any single man coming and going from the building. He never saw anyone. Families with children, couples holding hands abounded.

Serena was usually the only person there alone.

She spent a fair amount of time at the library. Researching her book, Plate surmised.

Now living outside the gates, she never once went back inside surreptitiously at any time Plate had her in his sight.

Instructions had come down, however, that was going to divert him from spying on his girlfriend for a day at least.

He was going to have to start visiting the sick.

Chapter 53

Daphne was surprised when the doorbell rang early the next morning. Darica had already gone to work. Still in her bathroom and slippers, Daphne's feet made a padding sound on the marble tile as she crossed her raised foyer to the front door.

Peering out the clear section of the stained glass, she almost expected to see another Lady in Disguise out there wanting to sell her something.

It was Serena Towers.

Daphne opened the door wordlessly, surprise keeping her silent.

"May I come in?" Serena asked politely.

"Oh, my, of course."

Daphne stood back and let Serena pass across the shining floor, noting the condition of the journalist's shoes as they stepped onto her white carpet.

Serena left no tracks.

"I came to return a couple of things that your sister left in the apartment," said Serena.

Daphne noticed for the first time a small bag in Serena's hands.

"Thank you. I'm sure she wouldn't have minded picking it up. She has to drive right by there to get to work and back from here."

"I confess I could have called her. But I wanted to come by and speak to you about a couple of things."

"Me?"

"Yes, I'm going to be doing a book on the assassination. I understand you had prior relations with Edward York-"

"Not really," Daphne hastily interrupted. "I was nominally acquainted with him. That's all."

"Still you must've formed impressions. They say he was quite incomparable."

"I would say that is correct." Daphne realized she was slipping into the role of interviewee almost beyond her control.

"What would you say his most outstanding trait was? What impressed you most about him?"

"I really don't know that I want to be part of your project, Ms.

Towers," Daphne said, in an effort to regain control of the situation.

Serena calmly handed her the bag of Darica's forgotten possessions. She glanced around the house, letting her eyes fall from one piece of furniture to the other.

"You have exquisite taste in furniture," Serena observed.

Daphne felt a rush of pride against her will. Furniture was one of her passions.

"I'm a furniture junkie," she said lightly.

Both women laughed.

"Maybe if a little time passes," said Daphne. "I don't know why, Perhaps it's because I was there and witnessed it, but Edward York's death has affected me, maybe more than it should have."

"The trouble with letting time pass is- someone else will get a book out before me," Serena said frankly. "And look how much time has gone by so fast since the killing."

"I could see that. Still, I'm not quite ready to talk about what happened at the masquerade ball."

"All right," said Serena. "I'm going to be in Sand Waves for a while. Would you consider getting together with me anytime in the near future?"

"Perhaps."

"And there is one other thing. I'm on the trail of an old book that may be connected to all of this. I know you are friends with Sinclair. He had a copy but he's misplaced it. He's trying to find the book for me and I was wondering if you had ever seen it or maybe he had mentioned it to you? Maybe he lent it to you and forgot?"

Daphne stiffened. She gazed at Serena more alertly. Did this woman think she had Plate for her own now?

"No," Daphne replied and her voice had grown cold.

Serena was perceptive enough to know she had outworn her welcome.

"That's okay. It was just a thought. Well, we will probably be seeing each other around. Please give these items to Darica and thank her again for agreeing to move out and let me have the apartment. She was a lifesaver."

"I'll give her the message." Daphne walked pointedly to her

front door. Serena's heels clicked as she followed.

As wordlessly as she had opened the door when Serena arrived, Daphne held it ajar once again.

"Thank you," said Serena, somewhat awkwardly. "And do you thank your sister again for me. Funny how I knew her all those years and never knew she had a sister."

With those words Serena stepped out onto the concrete and Daphne closed the door behind her, turning the key in the deadbolt lock with deliberation.

Chapter 54

Tending the sick in Houston was a tedious chore.

Plate had to take an entire day off to go to downtown Houston if he was going to spend any time there. First he would have to spend up to an hour and a half in morning traffic on the Gulf Freeway just to arrive in the vicinity. And that was if there were no wrecks that impeded the traffic flow on the route he took.

He accomplished this chore, arriving shortly after 9 AM.

Then he had to negotiate the downtown traffic, find a place to park and make his way through the morning crowds of arriving office workers to the skyscraper hospital where two of the victims of the violence at the masquerade ball were being treated.

The intensive care unit that held Peg Brown and Miranda Watson in the downtown Houston hospital was circular with the nurses' station in the center and patients occupying abbreviated pie shaped rooms all around the edges save for where the wide doors provided entry and exit. Thick hinged vinyl curtains could be drawn to provide a little privacy but their standard position was open so that the patient could be reached as quickly as possible by the nurses if there were a crisis.

The air was cold so mechanized life support systems functioned better.

Houston police provided policewomen at the side of both ladies stricken at the ball. The security personnel sat at the foot of the beds at the edge of the rooms and would have to actually get up and move for the curtains to be closed for either Peg Brown or Miranda Watson.

Mark Brown sat with his wife further inside the room but still visible from the circular walking space that divided the nurse's station from the patient's living quarters. A multitude of equipment surrounded Peg Brown as it did Miranda Watson.

The Watsons sat deep inside her room and were barely visible to Plate as he walked around the area. Three other intensive care patients had no armed security, just their families at their sides. Two stalls were empty.

After courtesy word to Mark Brown, Plate approached the

Watson room.

The Watsons were petitioning to have Miranda taken off life support.

Plate wanted to have a word with them before their final decision was made. They stepped outside into the little walking space but refused to leave sight of Miranda. They did seem deeply and genuinely grieved and confirmed their request that their daughter not suffer anymore.

Plate only spoke with them for a few seconds, offered his sympathy and then turned to leave. He was out of their sight before a hospital physician, seeing his uniform was different than Houston police, approached him and asked him what authority he had concerning the two women wounded at the masquerade ball.

Plate suggested that the physician confirm with Congressman Brown his identity and let the congressman vouch for him and the extent of his authority.

The physician asked Plate to wait, spoke with Brown, and came right back.

"I would like to tell you a few things that concern me before you leave the hospital," the doctor said to Plate as they walked into the main corridor leading away from the intensive care unit.

The next day Plate visited Morris Tates. He had been transferred to the comparatively small one story Sand Waves Medical Center and was in the intensive care at that facility, a smaller version of the big city life saving environment. At his bedside was a county officer standing guard and his ex-wife, holding vigil with a Bible in her hands.

Frieda Tates had filed a legal petition to be appointed as guardian of her ex-husband. No one objected and it was granted. His condition had stabilized with a diagnosis of permanent brain damage that would require constant care but was no longer life-threatening.

Plate introduced himself to Mrs. Tates and chatted with her about Tates' imminent transfer to a rehabilitation facility. She accompanied him to the waiting room nearest intensive care but it was full. So an office was made available to them by the hospital staff so they could speak in private.

Tates was not technically under arrest since Natalie Wakefield, still in seclusion but, speaking through her attorney, was declining to press assault charges. Natalie, considering the man's condition and the chaos at the ball, claimed she was no longer sure Tates meant to attack her. Perhaps he mistook her for one of Edward's attackers, or Peg Brown's assailant, or just lost it all in the confusion, due to the stress of recently being widowed himself.

Tates was still under consideration for possible independent charges but nothing had been decided yet.

Authorities were inclined to let his transfer proceed without any interference or supervision. Since he would be living in an institution for the foreseeable future, he would be readily available if Powers-That-Be changed their minds.

Plate conferred only briefly with Mrs. Tates who informed him the transfer was scheduled for the upcoming Saturday. Weekend transfers were easier on everyone involved usually and gave the patient time to rest before weekday routines began.

Plate confirmed the details with Mrs. Tates and then left to make his own arrangements.

The local press, hungry for information about anything concerning the tragedy at the ball, somehow were notified in time and were waiting that Saturday morning outside of the fairly open facility. The large parking lot was relatively empty as the hospital had only a small weekend staff. Today, Tates would be released from the hospital and taken to a rehabilitation center in Houston in a private van equipped with a wheelchair lift with his ex-wife at his side.

The press had previously noted in an advance story that the Sand Waves Police Department would no longer be providing security for him since his injuries had rendered him in such a condition that he could no longer be a threat to anyone.

Similar to a stroke victim, Tates was able to recognize people but not speak much. No one was quite sure how much he understood. And when presented with the scenario of the masquerade ball he only gave them completely baffled looks. Police department resources could not continue to be spent on providing protection under such circumstances.

The morning of the transfer, several reporters made their way into the hospital, only to be stopped at the entrance to the intensive care unit by hospital security, who were unarmed and more schooled in public relations than safety, Sand Waves being considered one of the safest places to live in the nation.

The reporters were escorted politely to the area by the front door designated for them. Nearby in the spacious parking lot, the white van could be seen waiting and it was plainly going to be impossible to stop them from photographing Tates as he exited the building.

But another van, a more somber gray, was waiting out back of the hospital where deliveries were usually made.

Inside the unit, Tates was being prepped for his transfer. The presence of his ex-wife was very comforting and the nurses were doing their best to make the transition as smooth as possible for him.

He was looking much more alert than his condition would have indicated as he sat in his wheelchair, looking around the circular area as his ex-wife and the nurses gathered his few personal belongings to bring out of the room he was leaving.

A short stout woman came through the massive doors unnoticed. She carried a camera and a notepad and had a journalism badge on her shoulder. Morris Tates looked delighted when she bent down to speak to him. Busy with the transition details, no one seemed to notice when she slipped around to the back of the wheelchair and started to push him away.

The look of happiness on his face combined with an expression of bewilderment caused everyone they passed on their way out of the hospital to see a mentally challenged man very happy to be attended to by someone he loved.

The woman flew the wheelchair by the press members before they could think to react to the possibility that one of their own was getting a scoop interview with the target of their upcoming stories.

Suddenly the gray van in the rear raced around front and blocked the white vehicle. A man in a blue uniform jumped out.

In the front parking lot, the wheelchair was already on the back of the van lift, which was going up, when Lieutenant Plate drew his gun and stepped in front of the pair.

"I have the right to take him," said the woman, gritting her teeth.

"It's Emma! Lieutenant, it is Emma!" Tates was saying with more coherency than he should have. The woman still gripping his wheelchair looked down at him in alarm.

"My Emma has come back for me!" Ernest Tates laughed happily. "There's no need for a gun!"

From the passenger section another uniformed man came through the empty van and grabbed the wheelchair, pulling it inside, shutting the doors.

"No, no, put your gun down, Lieutenant." The woman looked around in alarm and backed away from the vehicle. By now, members of the press and other security personnel were headed in their direction.

"Don't try anything, Mrs. Wakefield. I have orders to shoot you if you resist." Plate said. "And I'm sure you know that killing you would save a lot of people a lot of trouble."

Officer Willhouse rapidly drove the white van around back where medical personnel were waiting. They quickly took Tates back into the facility where the wife who really cared was still waiting.

Willhouse had substituted himself for the original driver of the getaway van, the latter detained as soon as her partner had entered the hospital doors.

It all happened so fast, the frightening gun came out so rapidly that the legitimate reporters and photographers at the scene only got brief glimpses and blurred pictures of the attempt to abduct the injured schoolteacher, before each one either took cover or were restrained by Officer Jordan, depending on their risk level.

His gun also drawn, Skaar stepped out of the crowd to back up Plate.

Still looking around, as if hoping for some deliverance from somewhere, Natalie Wakefield slowly raised her hands. Plate walked around her and put handcuffs around wrists that normally wore diamond bracelets.

Chapter 55

"So tell us what happened?" Darica Daniels spoke for everyone.

Three women were at the table in the Toy Museum Restaurant with Lieutenant Plate.

Daphne Martin, Darica Daniels, and Serena Towers.

It was a triple lunch date. Daphne had Officer Jordan as an escort and Darica was on a blind date with Officer Willhouse.

The men wore casual shirts and no ties. They were technically off-duty, yet Jordan and Willhouse were acutely monitoring their behaviors in the presence of their superior. They knew just what he expected of them.

Serena Towers was with Lieutenant Sinclair Plate. She was dressed in a long red one shoulder satin gown, though there was no need for formal attire. Daphne was dressed in a sienna pantsuit and Darica was wearing jeans.

Yet Serena did not look out of place. She would have preferred the smoking section of the establishment but she had been outvoted by the nonsmokers present, everyone else except Jordan. She looked very natural and exotically beautiful without drawing undue attention to herself.

In the same environment, in the same wardrobe, Natalie Wakefield would have sparkled like a rare jewel. Serena managed to be subtle atmospheric décor.

Plate could not keep his eyes off her. Without any self consciousness, he watched her every movement to the exclusion of all the other women there.

"Natalie Wakefield and Emma Tates were the same person? How can that possibly be true?" Serena's low purring voice almost disguised the demand element within it.

Plate hesitated to give an explanation.

"Tell us," Daphne piped up. "How did she do it?"

"Remember what happened? Natalie Wakefield appeared magically in the first skit, then disappeared at the next. But not before sending Ernest to get me. While Ernest and I were looking for her, sent in separate directions by different Ladies, Edward York was killed. Next we see of Natalie, she has been attacked by Morris Tates and rescued by Ernest."

"How did that happen, Lieutenant?" asked Darica.

"After some Ladies in Disguise pointed out her true location to the frantic oilman, Ernest finds her in a bathroom with Tates. She cries out and, along with another helpful Lady in Disguise, Wakefield goes to her aid. The bewildered Tates is battered and left for dead. Wakefield, thinking he had rescued Natalie, then escorts her out into the ballroom."

"Yes," said Daphne to Plate. "I remember. You sort of confronted her."

"That was the end of a long and complicated scenario where Natalie played wife to both men at the same time," Plate said with finality.

This satisfied no one.

"How could she possibly have pulled that off?" Darica persisted, speaking for everyone at the table.

"And Morris identified Emma as the dead woman. Why did he do that? And how did you find out he had lied?" Daphne added.

"Yes, I'm very interested in the answer to that question," said Serena Towers. "Not for any journalistic reason. I am just so curious."

"It will all come out anyway," said Darica.

"Not yet," Plate warned both reporters.

"We understand," said Serena. "Not a one of us has leaked a word."

"Yes, for Miranda's sake, we are cooperating," said Darica.

"Continue, please," said Serena. "Is Tates coherent?"

"Because he is recovering his memory and brain functions slowly, Morris has only been able to tell us a little at time. But we have the basics from him. As he returned from Ohio, called back by me to identify the body, Morris received a message from Emma, carried to him by a Lady in Disguise representative. He turned into his driveway and there she was," said Plate.

"How did they know exactly when he would turn in his driveway?" Daphne asked.

"They had to be watching the house," suggested Officer

269

Willhouse.

"Of course," said Jordan.

"It was imperative the message reach him before he identified the partially burned body as not being his second wife," said Plate.

"Have you seen this letter, Sinclair?" asked Serena.

Sinclair! Daphne silently exclaimed to herself.

She reached and took Officer Jordan's hand and placed it on her knee. The policeman jumped.

"We found Tates' letter at his home. A vital piece of evidence. It is very persuasive prose, convincing him Emma was in the employ of the CIA. She had never been an insurance adjuster- which was true- all the times she had been gone for weeks at a time, she had been in the service of her country," Plate said.

"And when she was with Tates? What did she tell Wakefield?"

"She came up with the usual rich women activities. Health spas, trips to Paris to view designer clothes. Wakefield suspected she was cheating on him. He was so in love with her, he didn't ask too many questions. He was getting annoyed, but his patience had not run out yet."

"Is he standing by her?" Serena asked.

"No way. He has turned against her now. That is what this sale today is all about," said Plate.

"And Tates had previously believed she was just working in a job that required a lot of travel?" Serena asked.

"Yes. Having him believe she was really missing was a great psychological ploy. His concern exponentially grew the longer she was gone. Now, to his relief, he was presented evidence she was alive and she was calling upon him to join her in a patriotic cause. The letter claimed she needed to appear to be dead for the sake of her own safety. He must identify the charred body as his wife, Emma Tates."

"So Tates knows nothing about the organization?" Serena asked.

"Nothing. He believed he was being recruited into the service of the CIA. Tates decided that he would be true to his country and identify the body as Emma. After all, if later it was proven otherwise, he could claim he made a mistake under extreme stress. There was very little of the body to see," said Plate.

"So even if he makes a full recovery, he has little information that will help with the capture of the other assassin," mused Serena.

"Right. We suspect only Natalie Wakefield knows the true identity of her accomplice. Tates was just a tool to be used in the most profitable way. At some time, Natalie Wakefield actually telephoned Tates to convince him the communication was genuine and give him further instructions. Apparently, based on what she told him, at the ball he expected to be reunited with her and they were going somewhere to assume new identities, like the federal witness relocation program," said Plate.

"So all along, it was only one woman playing both parts?" Darica asked incredulously.

"Are you just now getting that?" Daphne asked.

"Why was that so difficult to ascertain?" asked Serena. "I would think dozens of clues would have alerted the authorities. Pulling off a dual identity might have been easy back in the olden days, but in 1983? I would think it would have been as plain as the nose on your face, so to speak."

"She was very clever about it. Almost brilliant. She is petite. Only four-foot-eleven. She can dramatically change her appearance by losing or gaining 20 to 25 pounds," said Plate.

"Less than that," said Daphne. "I'm five-one. And I look drastically different if I gain 10 pounds."

"As Emma, she wore no makeup, was overweight, wore low heel shoes and dowdy clothes. That's what gave her away to me at the ball," said Plate.

"How?" Serena asked.

"I saw a box of old clothes in her closet in her blue room. They were clothes she had on hand for an emergency transformation into Emma. The shoes, though, were a transition between the two characters she played. They were elegant and bejeweled but with short heels. She never wore them as Natalie or Emma. She couldn't take that chance. They were too low heeled for Natalie and too fancy for Emma. But she loved them, they fit her personality so well and fit in with all the blue collectibles she had."

"So she kept them and wore them to the ball, where she needed a more practical heel length in case she had to move quickly," Daphne concluded.

"Right. The night she came back for the costume she got those shoes also. When I saw them I knew who she was."

"Incredible. A pair of shoes," said Serena.

"Amazing," said Daphne dreamily. "Inside the gates of Sand Waves she is a glamorous socialite. But why not, as Emma, feign membership in the volunteer disaster group that travels to remote areas of the world instead of just an adjuster job? That would also explain her absences when she is Natalie."

"You would fail miserably at leading a double life," Plate observed. "It was vital she not be associated with the Ladies in Disguise or their charity, in any way, as either woman. It would have been risky for her to be a customer if they had not blanketed the entire area with so many saleswomen that being a customer became the norm."

"I heard it appears there were times when she actually did go and do disaster relief work," said Darica.

"Oh, yes. Times when she was gone as Natalie and as Emma simultaneously. Mostly in countries with anarchist or extreme anti-American views. She was a real believer in her cause," said Plate.

"Who was she really?" asked Serena, in a light tone of voice that indicated she found all this great entertainment.

"She was Natalie Wakefield. She was legally married to Ernest Wakefield."

"I mean before. She had to have a maiden name and come from somewhere," Serena persisted.

"Her name was really Natasha Bratonn," said Plate.

"Bratonn?" Daphne frowned. Plate glared at her.

"Let me finish," he said. "Natasha Bratonn is an anarchist with ancestral family ties going back to terrorists before World War I."

"Was she gone to a disaster these last weeks when both Natalie and Emma were reported missing?" Willhouse asked.

"No, she was needed to plan and execute Edward York's death. That took a lot of time, creativity, and management skills. She was too busy to be either Emma or Natalie."

"The plan seemed to be fairly simple," Serena observed.

"No, it was far from simple. And it was changed significantly as it developed, with drastic changes even at the very end," said Plate.

"Oh, how so?" Serena asked.

"From various communications, now linked together, we think the first plan went something like this- In the initial plot conceived over two years ago, Morris Tates was the intended scapegoat for the murder of Edward York," said Plate.

"That would make sense. Why include him otherwise?" Jordan commented.

"Tates was spotted as a vulnerable man in the perfect position to be set up. Creating an identity as Emma, Natalie sets up her make-believe position as a traveling freelance insurance adjuster, seduces and marries Tates. Recently divorced, lonely with children, living nearby in Sand Waves, he is an easy target. Natalie-slash-Emma goes about her job with enough coy hints that there might be something else to her work besides just insurance adjusting so that when she disappears and a body is found that might be hers, it doesn't seem outside the realm of possibility to Tates that she has been some type of a government agent all along," said Plate.

"That worked brilliantly," said Jordan.

"To fool Ernest Wakefield, Natalie set up fake signs of having a lover so her frequent disappearances were connected with that ruse, when she was actually playing the part of the dowdy Emma. She would gain weight just before appearing as Emma, then crash diet and lose it when she returned as Natalie," Plate continued.

"When the time comes, in order to protect her, Tates is more than willing to misidentify the burned body as Emma," said Willhouse.

"Afterwards she calls him, she sends him a paid-for invitation and instructions to attend the ball and meet her there," said Jordan.

"The original plan was- She lures him to the ball and persuades him to dress up in the same Lady in Disguise costume and be caught as a man when she kills Edward. But since the marriage, Tates has gained a lot of weight. So that plan is scrapped. Instead of a pivotal player, Morris becomes a loose end that has to be dealt with," Plate finished.

"There is one problem with that theory," said Serena. "How did they know there would be a body to identify?"

Plate stared at Serena and his mouth opened a little

"Good question!" Darica exclaimed with some enthusiasm.

"Oh, I guess it really is a silly question," said Serena hastily.

"They had that planned from the beginning. I bet," suggested Skaar. "Some body would have been stolen from a medical center. Brought in to be identified as Emma Tates to stop the law from digging into her existence any more."

"No," Plate said slowly, still gazing at Serena. "The maid Doris was meant for that part. She was to die as Emma. But she was not needed. So she was left out of the masquerade and got the privilege of dying as herself."

"So ultimately what did they decide to do to Tates? Why did they bring him to the ball? And not kill him when they saw he wasn't going to be used for the original purpose?" Willhouse asked.

"Another outright murder? Remember Doris has been killed the day of the ball. No. it would be better if his death came as part of the cluster at the ball," Jordan analyzed.

"This is what we think," said Plate. "The plan then becomes to dress Tates up as Louis XVI, kill him quietly at the same time Edward York is being murdered, thus confusing the situation even more."

"How could you know that?" Serena asked.

"Just guessing. But they failed to kill him. He switched the costumes with the priest, confusing everything. When the priest was found to be wearing the Louis costume, he was not harmed. And they had the extra and unexpected Marie on their hands at that point."

"There was no third Marie Antoinette?" Daphne asked.

"No, only two," said Plate. "The short cloak was Natalie's."

"I was wrong. I guessed three," said Daphne.

"It was a great shock to Natalie Wakefield when she found herself face-to-face with Morris Tates on the stage when the first one act play began," said Plate. "The organization's cruel little joke of assigning the character of Robespierre to Father Thomas backfired on them badly. They never considered that a priest would break their

274

party rules and switch costumes."

"Priests are stereotyped as obedient," said Jordan.

"It was an equal shock to Morris to see his Emma, slimmed-down and dressed up as Marie Antoinette and also claiming to be Natalie Wakefield at the same time," Plate continued.

"I'll bet," said Darica.

"He had just seen a different woman as Marie Antoinette, bumped into her in fact and fell down. She was nothing like Emma. He had been told that Emma would be at the party but that she would be in a rather plain costume and would contact him when it was safe. The organization didn't expect to have to deal with him until after the assassination," said Plate.

"Yet there he was on the stage for the first act. Instead of Father Thomas as they expected," said Willhouse.

"What did they do?" Serena asked.

"Adapting quickly, Natalie convinced Tates right there on the stage. Daphne, remember the repartee between Marie Antoinette and Robespierre? She convinced him on the stage that this was all part of the plan, even the priest was involved in initiating the costume switch, and Morris needed to go through with the skit as written. It must have been a mix up that no one told him that she would be Marie Antoinette. She was also standing in for the missing Natalie Wakefield due to a vague resemblance between them."

"More than a vague resemblance," Daphne said, smiling.

"He was thrilled and gave a great performance," said Plate.

"And after?" Darica asked.

"Naturally after the skit was over he followed her off the stage. The co-conspirator waiting to help her change into the Lady in Disguise cloak was there to help her deal with him. They lured him into a restroom marked out-of-order, reserved for such an emergency, where the organization had planted various innocuous tools, towel bars and other metal household items, easily used as weapons that would hopefully be overlooked by security. They told him to wait there for Natalie. She was going to change in a working facility. She would be right back in ordinary clothes and they would be on their way."

"So what went wrong?" Darica asked.

"Another complication quickly arose," said Willhouse.

"Maddening for them, no doubt," said Serena.

"In the glare of the spotlight, expecting the substitute Marie onstage- he had also seen her and spoken to her- instead Ernest Wakefield had seen his wife. He had been clinging to Doris' ethereal prediction that Natalie would appear at the ball as Marie Antoinette. So he was looking for her to be Marie Antoinette. And there she was! Ecstatic that she was alive, he was in the process of rushing to her side and, by the time he got there, he saw her going into the other restroom with a different Lady in Disguise," said Plate.

"What did he do?" Daphne asked.

"Stop interrupting him," Serena commanded. "Let him finish."

Plate took a deep breath before resuming.

"He followed her into the room, where Natalie embraced him and sent him after me. If he had not gone, he surely would have been killed right then. Natalie was desperate to get changed and back to the stage. The second skit could not begin without her. She convinced Wakefield to go get me, telling him to be unobtrusive. It was a dangerous gamble, but she was counting on it taking enough time that she would be able to change costumes and slip back to the stage."

"They had a lot of women in on this," Jordan said.

"Yes. As soon as he left, the accomplice and Natalie quickly communicated plan changes to the other women involved."

"We're still sifting who was innocently used and who knew what was happening," said Willhouse.

"She slipped into her Lady in Disguise robe. The Marie dress and wig were transferred to the bathroom where Tates was being stalled. This also helped placate him."

"Keeping him confused also," said Jordan.

"Natalie made her way to the stage for the second skit. The murder of Edward York came off just as planned," said Plate.

"Then?" Serena prompted.

"Natalie then rushed back to the out-of-order bathroom. Inside, Tates knew nothing except there had been a power failure. He must have been confused when she slipped back into the Marie costume but

I'm sure she sweet-talked him into complacency. Meanwhile, still searching for Natalie, Wakefield was directed to the out-of-order bathroom by a Lady co-conspirator, and Natalie let him in.

"Wakefield still had no suspicions of Natalie," said Willhouse.

"As soon as Ernest entered, Natalie cried out to Wakefield that Tates had kidnapped her and now was attacking her. To Morris, she whispered this was part of the drama to get them away into the witness protection program. Melodramatically she threw her necklace at him," said Plate.

"Later claiming that was what injured him," Jordan scoffed.

"As Natalie further distracted the now confused Morris, her compatriot and Wakefield actually worked together to attack him. Wakefield grabbed him and the Lady in Disguise struck him with the wrench. Wakefield believed he was protecting Natalie. By this time a few other people had heard the commotion, so the women didn't dare attack Wakefield. Instead they convinced him to be quiet. Tates was some kind of nut and the least fuss made the better."

"Natalie is talking. Must be for you to know so much in detail," Serena observed.

"No, she is not. We have pieced this together from the other innocent women used by these vultures. And we have Wakefield, an eyewitness. Many ordinary Ladies in Disguise were used in the framework of this crime without their knowledge. Tates' other female attacker was not part of the conspiracy, just an overzealous obedient supporter. She is now telling everything she knows as are the other women on the stage who were not part of the plot," said Plate.

"These women know they were used," said Jordan.

"Their indoctrination techniques have failed. The Ladies devoted to the cause are rushing to the other side. People usually do when confronted with prison." Plate paused. "Any questions?" he asked.

"So what happened next? We know what she did after the murder of Edward York. But what actually happened on the stage?" Daphne wanted to know.

"After distracting both husbands and shedding the French queen costume, Natalie slipped back to the stage, took her place and on her

277

signal, the one act drama featuring Gustavus III began. Everything went wrong in the first skit, which should have been just fun and illusion, but everything went right in the next play, which was planned murder and sedition," said Plate.

"That's the way life is, even for assassins," Darica commented wryly.

"During the ritualistic dance before the assassination, Ernest Wakefield was busy searching for Natalie again with me as his helper. It must have amused the mastermind behind all this to point me in Grace York's direction to look for Natalie Wakefield at the very period in time that Edward York was being killed."

"Maybe that was a different Mastermind. If this was all meant to be, maybe she needed you there," said Daphne.

"I'll never believe this was fate," said Plate. "It could have been prevented."

"Go on with your story," said Serena calmly. "What did Natalie do next?"

"Instantly after Natalie had struck her blow to Edward, Natalie fled the stage and, as planned, another accomplice took her place kneeling in the dark, same procedure with the other assailant."

"Do they know who that is yet?" asked Jordan.

"They think it may be me," said Darica.

"Nobody believes that," said Daphne loyally.

"The evidence against you was planted," said Willhouse. "They know that now."

"We'll get her," said Plate solemnly. "She apparently had no complicating husbands around and made a complete getaway unobserved by anyone."

"Perhaps you will find some clues at the sale this afternoon," said Serena.

"Are y'all all going?" asked Officer Willhouse.

"I am," said Daphne. "I am so curious to get inside the Wakefield mansion. Natalie was my client but I never got to meet her."

"Isn't that unusual? Selling insurance by mail?" asked Darica.

"Yes, it will never catch on," said Daphne. "But it happens once in a while."

"So Ernest Wakefield wants to sell everything that reminds him of Natalie? I'm surprised he is letting people come into the house. Why not move everything out on the lawn and have a garage sale?" Serena asked.

"This is illegal in Sand Waves," explained Officer Jordan.

"You're kidding," said Darica. "You mean you cannot even have a garage sale here? Can't you get a permit?"

"No, there are no outdoor sales or with open doors, such as garage doors, allowed anywhere in Sand Waves. Every year the colony federation has a huge community sale in a public parking lot. Residents are allowed to rent parking space size areas and bring tables to sell personal items," said Daphne.

"Technically, it's not really legal here to have a garage sale inside the house. But there's some difficulties with the Constitution that stops the authorities here from preventing what's called private sales within the home," Jordan said.

"I imagine that keeps them up at night," Darica said.

"Knowing that there is a Constitution keeps them up at night," said Willhouse.

"Wakefield is smart enough to walk the fine line of the legal points on this issue," said Plate. "So long as he's acting as a private individual within his own home, that he is the owner of- not a renter, there's nothing the authorities here can do to stop him from letting people come into his house and selling them his personal property."

"As long as he doesn't advertise a sale," Jordan said.

"So that means there should not be very many people there," Serena remarked.

"Just those who know about it by word of mouth," said Plate. "Like us. We had inside information."

Chapter 56

Plate was the only one of the men that drove from the Toy Museum Restaurant behind the gates to the Wakefield mansion. The other two police officers reported for shift duty. Serena rode with Plate. Daphne and Darica went in Daphne's car.

Serena was right. There were few people there. But those few people represented quite a bit of money.

"I want to see the blue room," Daphne told Ernest Wakefield when she arrived.

A little taken aback by hearing it called that by a stranger, Wakefield nevertheless quietly led her from the front foyer through the den around to the parlor.

Wakefield looked like a man in mourning with still some remnant of shock about him. He was very quiet and businesslike to all those who were in his home. Most were women living behind the gates who were combing through the racks of Natalie's clothes that were set up in the den. Few of them were finding much they could actually wear.

It was all too small. Those with underdeveloped teenage daughters were picking up a few pieces.

Few were interested in the furniture. Most did not like the style and Wakefield was asking retail prices. A few dealers had already come and gone empty handed and peeved.

"Only this furniture is for sale and bedroom furniture upstairs," Wakefield told Daphne.

"It really is like my house," Daphne whispered to Darica. "I'm not interested in bedroom furniture," she added to Wakefield.

"What is it you're interested in buying?" Darica asked.

Daphne did not reply but ran her hands over the carved mahogany of the Victorian sofa. She looked at the little price tag that was pinned on the arm.

"Mr. Wakefield. I would like to get the sofa," Daphne called.

"Heavens! Daphne!" Darica had also seen the price tag.

"I want it," Daphne insisted. "Is there anyone that can deliver it for me?"

"I can probably get it home for you," said Plate to Daphne, as he came around the corner. Serena walked slightly behind him. "The department has a pickup truck. The federation has a flatbed truck that I can get access to. What are you buying?"

"Actually I am interested in all the furniture in this room. I'm just not sure I can fit it all into my office room. Does anyone have a tape measure?"

"I'm sure there is one around here somewhere," said Wakefield.

"I'm buying the sofa," Daphne told Plate.

"That will take the flatbed truck," said Plate.

"Is it not against the rules for your authorities here to let public vehicles be used for private purposes?" Serena asked.

"We're here to serve," said Plate. "This is a small community. Everyone pays a high annual assessment on their property by the federation board. So using a truck that belongs to the authorities for a minor service is acceptable. May I use your phone, Mr. Wakefield?"

Wakefield showed Plate the location of the den phone and then returned to take Daphne's money.

"I wish I could buy the matching chair but I am not sure I have room for it," said Daphne, dubiously walking around the piece. "I should have brought the tape measure."

"Why don't you take the sofa home and see how it fits and come back for the chair?"

"I'm afraid someone else will buy it," said Daphne.

"I will hold the chair for you until you can get to your house," said Wakefield. "Call me when you find out."

"How are you going to manage moving it around?" asked Serena, placing her hand firmly on Plate's arm as soon as he came back.

"It's real light," said Darica, picking up one end. "Daphne, you and I can carry it together with no problem."

"Is that flatbed truck clean?" Daphne asked Plate.

"I will get an old sheet for you to wrap the piece in," said Wakefield, and left briefly to procure the covering.

Shortly after the two sisters left with the truck carrying the sofa, Plate found himself in the blue room with Ernest Wakefield once more. Serena was the woman with them now.

"Are you interested in any of this furniture?" Plate asked Serena.

"I hardly think so," Serena said. "I spend most of my time in hotels. I have a miniscule apartment in New York where I can land from time to time. But I am usually always on the road."

"Must make for an interesting life."

"I am getting tired of it, quite frankly," said Serena, looking Plate up and down as if viewing him for the first time.

He was running his hands over the Pulaski desk. With a decorative frame across the back containing an etched mirror and carved wood spindles, the corners were topped off by glass finials. From each side a sloping scalloped frame contained etched opaque glass with shorter posts at the front, also boasting finials. The desktop was a leather rectangle area inside a square of dark wood. Three drawers on one side had apothecary décor with glass ball drawer pulls and a door on the other side opened with a brass handle. The back panel covered the entire desk bottom, allowing the desk to be placed anywhere in a room.

Plate looked at the price.

"Can you come down on this price?" he asked Wakefield.

Wakefield looked at the man who had exposed his wife as an anarchist and murderer. But for Plate's intervention, he and Natalie might have gone on for years, for the rest of their lives, and he would never have known.

And he had loved Natalie very much.

Plate was still running his hands over the top of the desk, feeling the coolness of its leather island.

"You really want this desk, Lieutenant?"

"You said you lived in an apartment," said Serena. "Have you room for it?"

"I can make room," said Plate.

"Take it," said Wakefield. "It's yours."

"I could not possibly do that. Thank you, but I have to pay for it."

"Make an offer then," said Wakefield.

Plate knew ethically that he should pay full price to avoid any

282

suspicions down the road. But he could not come up with $1200 all at once.

"I suppose you could not take a loan either?" Serena asked sweetly. She noted his hesitation with interest and wondered what it must be like to not be able to come up with such a paltry sum of money.

"Absolutely not!" he told Serena, then turned to his host. "Mr. Wakefield, could you take off 10 percent?" Plate had bought enough at resale and antique shops to know that was standard and could be defended.

"Certainly," said Wakefield.

Plate hesitated. He still did not have enough. But he got paid again in two days.

"Could I give you half today and pick it up day after tomorrow and pay the balance?"

He would have to reach into his savings account.

"Of course," said Wakefield. "I will put a sold sign on it."

That matter settled, Plate and Serena followed the trickling small crowd of people up the stairs to look at Natalie Wakefield's bedroom furniture.

They viewed the ostentatious room in silence. Serena showed much more interest in the items in the room. Opening all the drawers and doors, opening Natalie's empty jewelry box. Turning it upside down and thumping it with her fingers.

"Wakefield probably sold her jewelry to a jeweler," said Plate, watching her as he picked up a long wooden cylinder with brass at one end. At first he believed it was a spyglass but when he looked through the peephole he saw a dazzling array of colorful beads.

It was a kaleidoscope. Not a child's toy but a collector's item. Elegant and expensive. He held it gently and looked at the price. He wanted it very much but it was too expensive. He put it back down on its holder.

"Undoubtedly. What about the Marie Antoinette costume?" Serena asked, copying Plate's actions with the kaleidoscope.

"That can't be here. It's being held for evidence."

"What will happen to her? What do you think?"

"I don't know. I don't actually worry about them after they've passed through my hands."

"She might get the death penalty?" asked Serena thoughtfully.

"Maybe. They'll certainly try for that, if she doesn't cooperate, especially."

"She'll never cooperate," Serena said firmly. Then she dropped the kaleidoscope on the bed. "I mean. What I meant was- she doesn't seem the type to ever cooperate."

"I got that impression as well."

Plate noticed the other shoppers had left the room. Serena looked around as if she were aware of this also. Before he could react she walked quickly over to the door, shut it and flipped its inside lock.

"We're alone here. This type of privacy lock won't let anybody in." She pulled a small latch near the bottom of the door. "We are alone in here with this lovely bed."

Serena had already taken off her jacket before Plate could get close enough to touch her. He put his arms around her waist and drew her close to him.

"You always wear your bulletproof vest?" Serena asked. "Even off-duty? They're a bit of a damper, if you know what I mean?"

"Whenever I'm in public. And I've never off-duty."

She thrust her arms around his neck and kissed him passionately.

"We cannot possibly," said Plate, after they had slightly disentangled.

"That's absurd. Of course, we can." Serena was struggling in his arms to get closer.

He held her tight and kept her arms entwined as he thwarted her efforts.

"I can't go around doing things like this in other people's homes or in public places. I'll lose my job."

"How can this possibly have anything to do with your job?"

"This is Sand Waves. I'm a public servant. I have to be discreet in how I live."

Serena relaxed and he let her go.

"Put your jacket back on," he instructed her.

He walked over to the door and unlocked it.

"So you're telling me you never get to have any fun? Any thrills? Take any risks?"

"I'm afraid you just have to understand my idea of fun is relaxing on the couch with a science fiction book."

"There's a whole world out there. I can show it to you," said Serena. "I will be leaving this area soon if you don't give any reason for me to stay."

"I sincerely do not want you to leave Sand Waves," Plate said truthfully.

Serena smiled. "I hope that's not just because you think there might be trials I need to testify at. After all, I am somewhat of a public figure and not hard to track down. I can always fly in if I'm subpoenaed."

"I am not worried that you won't be able to avail yourself when it comes time for you to go to court," said Plate, picking up her jacket and handing it to her.

"Then you're going to have to prove it to me. You're off this weekend?"

"Not completely." He unlocked the door and opened it slightly. There were a few people in the hall.

"Friday night? Saturday night?"

"I can arrange to be off one of those nights if necessary."

"It is necessary for our relationship to continue. You can pick one of those nights to take me out to dinner and then I want you to spend the night with me."

More people started coming in. Serena and Plate departed the bedroom and went back downstairs, still talking as they descended the staircase.

"Saturday would be better," Plate told her, wondering how he was going to come up with the money for an expensive dinner and pay for the desk at the same time. Maybe there was money in the petty cash fund at the department.

He watched Serena look at the desk as they passed it on their way out. The sold sign remained intact as they went out the Wakefield front door.

Chapter 57

Before his paycheck came on in Friday, Lieutenant Plate had another opportunity to prove he deserved every penny.

Chief Brecken was complaining.

"How long are we going to have to keep Natalie Wakefield's arrest out of the papers and off the TV news? We cannot hold her much longer incommunicado. The press is cooperating in suppressing the story but that cannot last. That sale Wakefield is having is not helping either."

"Wakefield's sale is still by word of mouth. No one is going to call the Watsons as they sit in the intensive care unit at their dying daughter's bedside and invite them to a garage sale. The press is keeping the story quiet in the interest one of their own. Miranda Watson was their colleague."

"I'm not sure this is going to work anyways. What excuse are you having for being there?"

"I am an independent witness."

"Hmm. I don't like it." Chief Brecken was fussing about the first step in the plan to unmask Natalie Wakefield's killer accomplice.

"It will all be over this afternoon," said Plate. "I don't want her arrest upsetting the Watsons at this point in time, considering what they are having to do."

"Okay, but we cannot put personal considerations above the law indefinitely."

Not two hours later, Plate was watching Miranda Watson's parents enter into a small private room with the injured girl and medical personnel with the authority to pull the plug.

Mrs. Watson was weeping almost uncontrollably whereas her husband was a tower of strength, never taking his eyes from the bedside of the blonde girl, but continuing to give support to his wife as the procedure began.

"Could we just have a few moments alone with her?" asked Mr. Watson, his tone of voice as tragic as any father who had ever lost their daughter.

The two medical personnel looked at each other. One of them spoke to the Houston policewoman standing at the doorway. She nodded and the woman motioned to her coworker. The three of them exited into the adjacent hallway leaving the door to the death room open.

Immediately Mrs. Watson ceased to weep and the two elderly people bent over the woman in the bed.

As the man pulled the electric cord from the wall they were concentrating on the reaction of the patient in the bed.

Used to the constant presence of uniformed personnel to serve their needs, they failed to see Lieutenant Plate and the Houston policewoman slip back into the room and were astounded when the male officer grabbed Mr. Watson and the female officer grabbed Mrs. Watson, pulling the elderly couple away from the bed.

The Houston policewoman forced open the hand of the elderly woman in which there was a syringe filled with liquid.

The hospital medical workers rushed back into the room. They removed the dummy breathing tube from the patient and wiped her face with a cold cloth and placed an oxygen mask over her mouth and nose.

The Watsons stopped struggling and looked at each other in shock.

"Let us go," cried Mrs. Watson. "Can't you idiots see these medical technicians are trying to murder our daughter?"

Sudden movement within the bed captured everyone's attention. Still rather weak, the injured woman reached slowly and pulled the mask from her face.

"I'm not your daughter," she said hoarsely.

She rose slightly but fell back and one of the nurses went to comfort her while the other nurse went to the head of the bed and pushed it out of the room, back to the intensive care where the doctor who had conferred with Plate previously was waiting.

"You're under arrest," Plate began the routine speech, which varied at only at the next part, depending on the perpetrator. "For the crime of attempted murder of Lady Evelyn Corrigan, you have the right to remain silent…."

Chapter 58

Plate was rewarded with Saturday off but remained on weekend call and had to be in uniform if he left his apartment. He arranged for the desk to be picked up from the Wakefield home, having taken the balance of the payment late that night in cash to Ernest Wakefield.

He compromised on his date with Serena. He wanted another get-together for dinner and a movie but promised her his entire attention after it was over. It was another triple date. Daphne had Officer Jordan as an escort again and Darica and Officer Willhouse knew what to expect from each other this time.

It was pretty much mutual dislike.

"Why are you cops, all three, in uniform this time?" Darica asked.

Plate explained his situation.

"Actually, we are still on duty," said Willhouse, indicating himself and Jordan.

"We are sort of playing hooky with permission," said Jordan, with a grin, winking at Plate simultaneously.

With some self-righteousness, the three women looked at Plate for an explanation.

He was the senior officer.

"We get away, sometimes, with a little fun and games at the public expense," said Plate in a conspiratorial manner. He winked also.

"Look at what goes on with most people," said Jordan. "They filch whatever they can, time or money."

"It's the killer criminals that you really have to worry about," said Willhouse. "So we have dinner with you lovely ladies on the public time. So what? We would eat anyway."

"I thought we were going to the show again," Serena commented.

"We are," said Jordan.

"Certainly we will be there," said Willhouse.

Darica indicated her disgust without speaking further.

"We can always deny it," said Jordan. "You have to catch people

288

red handed these days to prove anything."

"Like the Watsons," said Plate.

"Who would have dreamed the Watsons were criminal traitors? Hell, I've known them for years." Serena lit a cigarette before remembering they were seated in the section of the Toy Museum Restaurant that was no smoking. She quickly put it out.

"The Watsons were old easy targets. They'd always been a bit liberal and they loved their daughter a great deal. She grew up to be an anarchist and convinced them to turn their commercial organization over to a group of people with similar beliefs," said Plate.

"How is the girl in the hospital?" Serena asked.

"Back in a medically induced coma before she could tell us anything. But they think she will recover. Time will tell. They are hoping no brain damage, hence the coma, it helps prevent it."

"I cannot believe you bought my desk," said Daphne.

Five blank looks fell on the insurance agent at this radical change in topic.

"I was trying to keep the furniture pieces together," Daphne continued seriously, oblivious to their reactions.

"It was not your desk," said Plate, smiling a little.

"Did you get it delivered?" asked Serena, turning to Plate in such a way that Daphne could only see the back of the journalist's head.

"Yes, I did. And they dropped it on the steps."

"Oh no!" Daphne exclaimed. "That beautiful desk!"

"It just had a slight crack in the glass on one side," said Plate. "Otherwise, it was all right."

"Movers are so careless," said Darica.

Serena and the two patrolmen vehemently agreed.

"I've never had any trouble," said Daphne.

"You've only moved once," said Darica.

"Twice, one from Mom and Dad's to my apartment and then from the apartment to my house."

"Guess what else happened when the desk was dropped," said Plate. "It had a hidden compartment which popped open."

The announcement caused everyone to completely focus their attention on Plate.

"And it had writings from Natalie Wakefield inside. A history of the anarchist movement she was writing, a copy of the genealogy unearthed in the name of Emma Tates by Morris, and details about who was really in the conspiracy."

"Indeed?" commented Serena. "Who did it name?"

"Well, the genealogy is in English, of course. But part of the writings and all of the detailed information about the group is in the Old Russian alphabet. It's being translated as we sit here. A Russian translator in Houston is working overtime to get it back to us by Monday morning."

"Will it reveal all the names of those who were really in on the conspiracy to commit murder?" Jordan asked.

"It appears she kept everything about the group. What she didn't have in the way of documentation she wrote it all down. That's the part that is in Russian," Plate answered.

"Who would have considered she could write Russian? Or that she would have her family history traced," Serena mused.

"I'll bet Natalie was expecting fame and fortune as a result of the group and wanted her genealogy available to the masses," Daphne said.

"No, I think she planned to get away with it all and go back to being Natalie Wakefield," Plate responded.

"But all that organization and all that planning, just to kill one man! They could have created nationwide anarchy as complex as their structure was," Darica said.

"They intended to do this crime and get away with it. Get back to their routine lives, except Natalie would no longer be Emma. Just go back to their lives before it happened, just like we are doing."

"Is that what you think happened with Miranda? She was part of it. She got away, that is?" Darica asked.

"Possibly," said Plate. "We have not found her. That is why we need the true story suppressed just a little longer. She may have been innocent. She may be dead. We're hoping the other girl will be strong enough to talk in a few days when she is scheduled to be brought out of the coma."

"You can count on us to keep it quiet as long as needed," said Darica.

"Fortunately you were able to accomplish the Watson arrest without anyone else knowing yet," said Serena, with some admiration in her voice.

"I am counting on you two to maintain professional silence," said Plate to Darica and Serena.

"All the better for my book that I can prepare the information in advance like this," said Serena. "I have stopped all activity related to the assassination in lieu of my book release. Publisher's orders."

"I only hope, guilty or innocent, Miranda is alive somewhere and she will be found," said Darica.

They were all was silent at this sobering idea that another person might be lost to the anarchist cause.

One so lovely and young as Miranda.

Plate took a deep breath and everyone turned to him.

"Now we're six friends here, out for dinner and a movie," said Plate. "Let's forget all this murder and mayhem just for tonight and have a good time."

Chapter 59

The movie was good. The party broke up. Darica was staying with Daphne still, so the two junior policemen took the sisters to her house and returned to duty.

The senior officer offered to take Serena Towers to a hotel. He was not ready for the relationship to end.

This evening she wore another flaming red formal dress with a matching cape longer than the dress. She carried a matching shoulderbag that was obviously custom made and very expensive.

"Our apartments are near," she told him, flaring her cape about her shoulders.

"Your place or mine?"

Serena put her arms around his shoulders and kissed him sensuously.

"I'd really rather come to your unit."

"Okay. I'm surprised. I figured you would want to go to a hotel."

Technically it was still winter but this was Texas. The unpredictable temperature had suddenly turned warmer and it was actually a nice night.

This was somewhat of a shock to the couple when they exited the restaurant.

Plate had his heavy uniform jacket off and Serena draped her cape over her arm, allowing her bare shoulders to reflect the moonlight. "All the more better if it's a little bit messy. I get to know you better, seeing what messes you tolerate."

"You've caught me off guard, I'll say. As I recall I haven't left my apartment too much of a mess. But it's small."

"I don't think we'll need much space," said Serena. She kissed him again and this time ran her hands down his chest and around his back.

"Okay, let me check in. I'm on call."

"Don't tell me you've already left word you would be at a hotel tonight?"

Plate laughed a little guiltily. "I had one picked out. Won't take me a minute to correct the information. I have to let them know which

292

direction I'm going."

He went to the pay phone outside the theatre and made a short call.

"We don't have to go yet, you know. We could see the second show or go to an all-night bar," Plate told Serena when he returned to her.

"Are there all-night bars in Sand Waves?"

"Of course not. We would have to go to Houston. Even there, they are supposed to close at two in the morning. But I know a couple that don't."

Serena paused for a second and once again put both her hands on Plate's shoulders. Slowly he lifted his own hands and put them around her waist. She looked deep into his eyes.

"I really do want to go to your apartment. I appreciate what a gentleman you are. It's a true rarity in this day and age. But as you just said, we are two single consenting adults. I'd like to get my hands under that vest."

Plate made no more protests. He drove to the apartment complex.

He allowed her to go first at the outside metal stairs to his door. But at the door she suddenly turned and faced him.

"Can I change my mind?"

"Of course," he said, swallowing hard, allowing a little disappointment to creep in his voice.

"Oh, I don't mean- I mean I don't want to see your apartment. I'm afraid I will see too much. Too much about you that is. If I see your laundry and your dirty dishes, well, I may not live behind the gates of Sand Waves but that's only because I don't live permanently in Sand Waves."

"What do you suggest?"

"I want to, terribly," said Serena, caressing his arms and letting her hands fall to his buttocks. Instinctively he covered his gun with the palm of his hand while holding her with his other arm.

"Where should we go?"

"I want you," she whispered to him. "I want you. Let's go somewhere else. Anywhere else. A different hotel maybe. A little side

293

street motel down the highway? Surely there's one you know about."

"I know a place we can go. It's a little cottage just before the gates. I have a key. The police department owns it and well, makes it available to us for when we need to, you know, go beyond the call of duty to keep the peace. The school district doesn't own them all."

"Really?" She laughed scornfully.

"Now you must not let on that I ever told you. I'll lose my job."

"I only freelance important stories. I won't give your department's dirty little secrets away. How far is it?"

"Come with me. It's a short drive."

"I don't know how you're going to drive. I don't think I can let go of you."

Clinging together, they made their way down the stairs. Plate was correct in that it was a very short drive and in just a few minutes they were inside the little cottage, which was indeed very elegant and clean.

"It's not perfect but it will have to do. At least no one knows we're here. We won't have any interruptions?"

"The place doesn't even have a phone," Plate grinned. "It is designed for no interruptions. All I have to do is turn my pager off."

"Wonderful! I've a surprise for you. I bought you that kaleidoscope you were fondling at Natalie's."

She handed him the gift, taking it from the shoulderbag.

"I should not take it." He handed it back.

"Don't be silly. There's something special about it. I'll show you afterwards." She sat it down on the nightstand.

"Let's get down to business," he said.

Serena immediately slipped out of her gown and tossed it with her cape at the foot of the bed. She wore a silk slip under the dress, even more beautiful than the gown.

"Get out of that vest. I want to put my hands on your skin," she told Plate.

He removed his shirt and vest, took off his gun holster and started to unbutton his pants.

"Let me wash my hands."

He stepped into the bathroom which was just off the bedroom

and closed the door and turned on the sink faucet. Peering through the door he could see Serena was completely naked now. He flipped a switch on the wall and a small light came on.

He drew a sharp breath at the sight of her, stretched across the entire length of the bed. She was so tall. He walked back out into the room.

"Oh, come on," she said, laughing. "Take your pants off! I think you must be the most modest police officer in the world."

"I imagined I would let you take them off for me," he said calmly. He cautiously climbed on the center edge of the bed, remaining on his knees on the soft mattress, balancing himself above her.

She laughed again and reached her long arm up towards his torso without even having to rise. But her other arm was sliding in a different direction, causing her body to shift towards her clothing.

He blocked her from proceeding in that direction.

Alerted, comprehending at once, she reacted swiftly, reaching for the kaleidoscope and aiming it at him. She activated its concealed mechanism and a bullet whizzed by just as he ducked.

Infuriated, she threw the device at him. He ducked again and it hit the far wall. Its false head broke and plastic beads showered the room.

With a single motion he fell down on top of her, his left arm across her belly holding her down as her arms and legs began to flail. With his right arm he reached and grabbed the scarlet dress and cape and threw them off the bed.

The knife they had concealed clattered to the wood floor.

"You really were going to," he gestured with his free hand. "First? Or afterwards?"

"You bastard," she snarled at him, fighting to free herself. "Before? After? Ha! During!"

He let her up and she jumped out of bed and made a grab for the knife, clutching it on the floor. He jumped aside and got around behind her, pulling her arms back tight and causing her feet to fly out from under her. The knife fell back to the floor.

"During?" he asked her, as he reached into his pocket and got

295

his handcuffs. She was still kicking so he threw her down face forward and pulled out his tie wraps and bound her feet.

"You would have felt your pleasure morph into pain," she rasped at him. "I am an expert."

"You may well be an expert. But if you don't stop struggling, I will hog tie you with these special tie wraps. They are bare metal and if I pull them tight they're going to slice your skin open. So stop fighting so I don't have to hurt you. I am not into that."

Serena looked like a wild animal naked and bound on the floor. Plate pulled a sheet off the bed and covered her.

"It's your word against mine. You attacked me," she hissed at him. "If you were a real man you would at least see it through."

"I don't think so. What do you want to bet you are on the home movie Grace York took at the ball, defying your rules?" Plate reached up and uncovered the camcorder that the switch in the bathroom had activated. "And this seems to be working properly. You are on tape again."

He pulled a phone out of the nightstand and started dialing, keeping his eyes on the furious woman on the floor who was still combining her anger with skewed looks of lust.

"This place really does belong to the police department but I lied about the phone," he said with a smile.

Then his expression became grim.

"And I don't tolerate any messes," he stated somberly.

Chapter 60

"How did you know it was her?" asked Darica. Plate and Daphne were seeing her off to her new position in Dallas. She was catching a 5 AM bus in Humble, a small city north of Houston where a bus depot was located.

A bus leaving from this location would have fewer stops and take a more direct route.

"It was either her or you," said Plate to Darica. "There was no other option after all the investigation was done. But there was no evidence against her. We couldn't find anything. To make her show her hand was the only way to get her."

"I thought it was Miranda Watson," said Darica.

"No, I knew it couldn't have been her." Daphne stood next to Darica and they both faced Plate.

Darica thought he looked unassuming in blue jeans and a pullover sweater. Daphne thought he looked wonderfully normal.

"Why? She's unaccounted for, even still, right?" Darica asked.

"No, she's not, Darica. She was the women burned in the cabin, wasn't she?" Daphne declared.

"Officially, I cannot tell you," said Plate crisply.

Darica's bus was called for boarding. She embraced Daphne and shook hands with Plate.

"I don't care. It's not my story anymore," said Darica. She waved goodbye. "I'll be back on the society beat in Dallas."

She didn't look behind her as she climbed aboard.

"She still doesn't like me," Plate said to Daphne, as the bus pulled out of the Humble depot.

"Miranda Watson was the burnt body, right?" Daphne persisted, once they were in his car and headed towards the highway. He had insisted on taking his personal car even though it was older and less comfortable than hers.

"Do we have to talk about it? I'd like to enjoy my one day off."

"You said it was a long drive to East Texas. So yes, we either have to talk about it or listen to the radio. And I don't like country and

297

western music. It will have to be classic rock since we won't be able to find anything else."

Plate pushed her hand away as she reached for the radio control. "Well?"

"Yes, Miranda Watson was the corpse."

"Lady Evelyn killed her."

"How could you know that?" Plate asked.

"It's logical. The only explanation. I'm sure it was self defense in the line of duty and all that. She is a federal agent, right?"

"Yes, she is a federal agent."

"So, what happened?" Daphne asked.

"After catching Darica attempting to spy for a story angle, Miranda took pity on her and took her to your house that night. She kept watch, though. When Evelyn showed up, Miranda knew who the traitor was. She blocked Evelyn from leaving Sand Waves, followed her to the cabin and they collided. Evelyn killed her. The next night Evelyn came back and set the fire. That was the night Natalie chose to vanish. I actually saw the fire trucks as I was leaving the gates after being at the Wakefields."

"Just one more question," said Daphne. "Was there a real Lady in Disguise Corporation and what happened to them?"

The streets of America were empty of tall thin women in long gray robes with red trim for the first time in two years. As they had driven through the Houston suburban streets towards Humble, both Plate and Daphne had been aware of how deserted the roadways looked.

"There are really several levels of Lady in Disguise entities. There really was a hair care sales company owned by the Watsons that sold hair care products door to door with the gimmick of having costumed saleswomen with an air of mystery about them. That section actually went bankrupt."

"So that part became a sham?"

"The anarchists created a charitable organization to act as a façade and money laundering mechanism. Instead of just keeping a shell sales group, they had the much better and more misleading idea of showering the country with young saleswomen, all looking very

298

much alike, all paid a living wage regardless of whether they sold anything or not, just giving them a territory to cover."

"Wow! A foot soldier quota, so to speak," Daphne said.

"Yes, to make sure that they became both a household word in every suburban neighborhood and a benign acceptable and familiar presence on the streets of America," said Plate.

"And fix your hair if you wanted. In your own home," said Daphne.

"It was a brilliant concept, don't you think?" Plate asked, as the car sped up to 55 miles per hour, the maximum speed limit on the highway. "Products were actually sold occasionally. They were harmless normal ordinary hair care products with fancy names at exorbitant prices. And add in fixing hair on demand at random."

"They had to fight the current style of long straight hair," Daphne noted. "The prevailing hairdo since the 1970s."

"Most of the women employed were happy to have such a well-paying job that allowed them to have time with their families, dress up in a nice costume, and be part of a social sisterhood," said Plate.

"I know women like that."

"Likewise, those women chosen to be part of the charitable organization upper-class were high society wives of prominent men with time on their hands looking to do fulfilling work that got them social status and praise and, again, a sisterhood to belong to," said Plate.

"In my job, I've met many women lonely for other women. A sisterhood that makes money is very appealing, especially if you get to keep part of the money."

"There was a small number of women who ran the organization and planned for its real purpose," said Plate. "Again that was handled brilliantly. These women rarely broke the law. They worked behind the scenes to incite trouble between naturally antagonistic forces and create civil disobedience."

"Now you've put them out of business for good," Daphne said with admiration in her voice.

"I certainly can't take credit for that. I played a small part in the overall operation."

299

As they talked, Daphne gazed out the window at the changing landscape as they sped down the highway.

"Have you never been this way before?" Plate asked, noting her fascination as they left the urban areas behind. Only small towns and a couple of mini cities were between them and their destination.

"No, I have not," said Daphne, looking at the long lines of trees only occasionally broken by a small house or business facing the highway. The highway had turned into two lanes on each side with a big green area between them.

"I don't know how you can live in Houston all your life and never go to East Texas."

"Very easily," said Daphne. "We always vacation in Galveston. Or in Dallas, before they built Astroworld. We had no reason to come up here."

"Didn't you ever go to camp or hike or just go fishing?"

"I camp only in fine hotels. I do not hike or fish. My idea of recreation is an elegant affair where I can dress up in a formal gown."

"I know that. I was with you at the ball, remember?"

"You took Serena, and you were having quite a time at that ball before the murder."

"I was at work."

"Did you suspect Serena then? Really, from the beginning? Why?"

"Her name was on a list of people to suspect. I told you I cannot take that much credit. As I told you from the beginning, I was under instructions to get to know her and attempt to form enough of a relationship with her that I could either be her date at the affair, or at least meet up with her there without her suspecting anything. That was my part."

"So she arrived with you, as Betsy Ross, with her Lady in Disguise costume in a bag wrapped up in the American flag, the murder weapons inside, and changed into her assassin's clothes right there under everyone's nose. She probably would have killed you if you had searched her bag."

"I had no authority to do that. My orders were to accompany her and then leave her alone. I had no authority to search her bag. I did

300

what I was told."

"So somebody high up vouched for her?" Daphne asked.

"Yes. His actions are being reviewed. But it appears he was innocent of any knowledge of what she planned. Her part was simple, really. When it was over, Serena only had to abandon the outer cloak and mask and reappear as Betsy Ross. She had the easier deception than Natalie Wakefield with all her husbands."

"What did Natalie tell Wakefield? He must have demanded an explanation." Daphne noted with amusement how quickly Plate wanted to focus on Natalie at the expense of talking about Serena.

"The same nonsense she told me about escaping from her fabricated kidnappers. And about a magically appearing group of elderly churchgoers, out and about, finding her and bringing her home. Notice she was clever enough to emphasize their age. There was bound to be a church activity that day. There are nearly every day in Sand Waves. She wanted to make sure that the fictional participants she created would be so old it would be plausible they would likely not remember her, in case we tracked down a church social. And that story about graduating from college with a harsh drama professor and going to high school in Sand Waves, all fantasy," Plate declared.

"Was all that long story, about the sequence of events and Natalie's behavior at the ball, that story you narrated in front of Serena, actually true?" Daphne asked.

"Exactly as it happened. I wanted Serena to know I knew everything there was to know. Except, of course, that she was the other assassin. Especially that I saw Wakefield and Natalie coming across the ballroom with the police beside them. Remember?" Plate asked, as they stopped on the highway for a red light at a small town.

As they exited that small town the road became two lanes with only stripes of paint in the middle to divide oncoming traffic.

"I do. She looked ashen in her face. And the man with her looked so happy," Daphne recalled.

"Natalie was shaken. She had been through quite a bit. Wakefield was relieved and happy to have her safe."

"I remember you told her you had to talk with her soon. She flinched. Murder must be stressful even for the dedicated."

"At that moment, I think she was convinced she had truly gotten away with it. The Ladies in Disguise who were actually members of the real terrorist group, were so devoted to her that she had no fear of any of them betraying her identity. Most of them didn't know who she was anyway. Only the Watsons and Serena knew the leader was Natalie Wakefield, the other few entrusted with an identity believed she was Emma Tates. And Emma was officially dead."

"Serena knew?"

"Serena was second in command. Few knew her identity either. Miranda was only tolerated as a necessity. She was considered a dangerous child by Natalie and Serena. We have documents detailing their plans for her. And they were not good. Her death at the hands of Evelyn was probably merciful."

"It is hard to imagine. And all that time we were socializing with Serena, you were trying to entrap her into admitting something that would give her away."

"She almost did, several times. I was surprised at how close she came to slipping up. But our time was running out. We had to deal with Natalie's arrest. And now she would be Serena's target."

"Natalie went from the top to the bottom in one instant," Daphne observed.

"And it was quite a fall from her supreme triumphal moment."

"The Watsons knew their daughter was dead already? Or had Natalie and Serena deceived them about that?" Daphne wondered.

"We don't know. They have lawyered up. We only know they covered for her absence and identified Evelyn as Miranda for the sake of the cause, planning to kill Evelyn whenever they got the chance. Fortunately there is no privacy in modern day intensive care."

"Natalie knew so long as Evelyn and Morris were quieted, she was safe. She must have worried when they didn't die right away. God does have a hand in these things."

"I can see where the Watsons might have felt they had a chance to pull the plug on Lady Evelyn. We were surprised Natalie fell into our trap so easily. Natalie must have known she had very little chance of kidnapping Tates successfully."

"No, I don't know about that," said Daphne thoughtfully. "I bet

302

she relished the challenge."

"Think so?" Plate stopped at another small town red light.

"Look at it from her perspective. She had won all that she dreamed of. Then reality set in. The ball was over. Her lifelong goal met. Her job was done. What was she going to do with her time?"

"Anything she did other than being Wakefield's ornamental wife would be suspect," Plate agreed.

"Somewhat of a letdown just to go back to the Wakefield mansion and sit around in the blue room, I would imagine. No more Doris to adore and serve her. No more Lady in Disguise meetings. She dare not remain Natalie Wakefield and go back to any type of subversive activities. No more clandestine adventures. Or exotic costumes, except on Mardi Gras or Halloween. No wonder she wanted that book as a souvenir of her heritage."

"Still, retirement with Ernest Wakefield did have its appeal over prison," Plate pointed out.

"I'll bet somewhere in her nightmares she was more afraid of being stuck as Emma Tates than she was of going to prison."

"She had not shed Emma yet. Her supposed seclusion for post-traumatic stress was actually hiding out so she could gain weight to become Emma again so she could get at Tates," said Plate.

"What actually happened to Peg Brown?" Daphne asked.

"We don't know for sure. We think Peg must have put a few things together. She brought it to the attention of the wrong person."

"And that Lady in Disguise lured her into a trap," said Daphne.

"That's what we think. She acted swiftly, attacking Peg, but did not make sure she was dead."

"Who?" Daphne asked, as she watched the light turn green.

"We don't know yet." Plate stepped on the accelerator.

"No one saw?"

"Those out-of-order signs for the bathrooms were effective. They had been prepared in case a sudden private space was needed and they could float around," said Plate.

"That speaks of efficiency."

"The whole plan was incredibly efficient. Think about how difficult it was to recreate the escape closet in Natalie Wakefield's blue room so that it appeared to never have been touched. And to do it under Ernest Wakefield's nose without his noticing."

"How did they do it?"

"There was a set of women carpenters attached to the charity that helped repair homes for the poor in foreign countries. They had other duties as well."

"The maid was in on it from the beginning?" Daphne asked.

"Yes, Doris died for her loyalty. She just knew too much. I think Wakefield would eventually have met with a similar fate. Although he knew nothing."

"Remember I told you that Natalie wearing blue was important?"

"Yes, and you were right."

"I have wondered about that. I've no idea why I said it."

"Natalie- and Serena, by the way- were experienced assassins. Other international deaths are now being traced to their movements. Natalie knew small details were vital in extravagantly planned killings. She needed just the right gown to slip in and out of easily. It needed to be blue to blend in with the Marie Antoinette costume. Doris did away with the other gowns to confuse me."

"And the other stuff you found in the closet?"

"Just junk to distract us. Only the old clothes were important. Natalie kept some in there to change into in case she needed to make an emergency escape as Emma Tates. Or, if there was a complete meltdown, she could get away on horseback."

"Where would she get a horse?" As she spoke those words Daphne noticed clusters of horses and cows in pastures along the roadside.

"The Watson estate. They kept horses just for such purposes. She availed herself of one the first night I was watching the Ladies in Disguise. Ironically it was Wakefield who first reported suspicious activities related to them due to their primitive methods of passing messages in code in people's mailboxes."

"Is it accurate to say the Watsons were behind it all?"

"Fairly accurate. They were the money. Serena Towers was the popular engaging public relations slash recruitment officer. Natalie

Wakefield was the brains, the genius ritualistic organizer. The blue room, the disappearance, Doris' devotion, all evidenced a brilliant fanatical charismatic personality."

"Natalie wanted Evelyn killed because she was actually usurping her role as Marie Antoinette? How macabre! Did she know it was not Miranda?" Daphne asked.

"Natalie and Serena suspected Evelyn had killed Miranda shortly after fire. But they were not sure. They could not have it known publicly that Miranda or Evelyn was missing, too much investigation was risky at this crucial time. So it was decided to lure Tates into identifying Emma as the dead body. After all, Emma did not really exist. Killing her was very convenient."

"Evelyn then did not know who to trust, she had found out Natalie's background and that the corrosion reached high into upper society."

"That goes on from years and years past. Well, you know what we have found in that genealogy report Tates dug up on Emma."

"How did he run a genealogy report on Emma without finding out she was Natalie?"

"Because he never questioned Emma's identity. He did not check on contemporary people with contemporary records. He took the names she gave him as her grandparents and researched back in time. If he accidentally turned up a cousin named Natasha Bratonn, that meant nothing to him. The name Natalie Wakefield meant nothing to him before all this."

"So he did find Natalie's real ancestors?"

"Oh yes."

"What about Serena's background?"

"We don't know."

"Don't know?"

"Her background, which no one ever checked due to her stunning success and fairly widespread renown as a journalist, was completely faked. We have no idea who she really is."

Chapter 61

"Well, we are here," said Plate, somewhat hesitantly.

He had pulled up on a red dirt road that ran off the highway up a slight hill then back down to the highway again. But he had stopped at the crest of the hill and made a right-angled turn off the road onto a narrow bumpy driveway that led to an old large rambling house needing a coat of paint.

He stopped his car at the foot of the front porch, so high off the ground that the porch would have gone through the windshield if he had attempted to drive beneath it.

No such destructive thoughts seemed possible in this very country setting with scraggly woods approaching the house and a few chickens strutting about the unfenced yard, which held a pickup truck and a Cadillac parked at random angles near the path to the porch steps.

As there was no railing on the steps, Plate took Daphne's elbow as she negotiated the wooden planks with her two inch heels.

"I told you to wear tennis shoes," he said.

"I don't have any," she replied.

The door opened and a slim middle aged woman of medium height with a 1960s bouffant hairstyle and no makeup stood in the doorway.

"Peter!" she exclaimed. "How wonderful."

She embraced him violently, then released him abruptly and turned to Daphne. "And you must be Miss Martin. My dear, how nice to meet you."

"My mother, Vivian Plate," said Plate formally.

"Hello, Mrs. Plate." Daphne held out her hand.

"Come in." Instead of shaking it, Plate's mother took Daphne's hand and led her inside. "Peter said you couldn't stay long so let's not waste time outside. Peter, did you have anything you need to get from the car?"

"No, Mom. No luggage. We really have to make this a one day trip."

"I have my briefcase," said Daphne.

"Oh, get that for her, Peter, in case she needs something from it," insisted Mrs. Plate.

"Miss Martin is an insurance agent," said Plate.

"Licensed for the entire state of Texas," said Daphne brightly.

Mrs. Plate gently pushed Daphne ahead of her and looked back quizzically at her son as he closed the front door.

"Insurance? Well, we- uh- let me get your father, Peter. He is in the backyard working on the tomato plants."

"No selling," whispered Plate to Daphne, as his mother went out the back door. He and Daphne went further into the house and were now in the living room.

Daphne was looking around at the charming country house. "Antiques," she said, her eyes widening in delight. "Everywhere."

"They are not for sale," he warned. "No selling. No buying. This is a socialize-only occasion."

"Drake Plate," said a loud voice. A man who might have been the Plate she knew now- in 30 more years- came towards Daphne, his arm outstretched.

"Oh," she said in surprise, shaking hands with him.

"I know. It rhymes," Drake Plate laughed. "My mother had a strange sense of humor."

Daphne and Plate caught one another's eyes and almost burst out laughing together but a large cat took that moment to jump from a high perch onto an antique chair, startling everyone.

"Tomcat!" scolded Vivian Plate, coming back into the room. "Tomcat, you know better than that!" She looked at Daphne apologetically. "He only acts that way when we have company."

She grabbed the cat and tossed him out the front door.

"That's what you used to say about me," called Plate to Vivian, as she slammed the door behind the feline.

"I wish I could have tossed you out the front door back then."

"Sit down," said Drake Plate, as he plopped down in a large easy chair himself. "We are dying to hear all about the assassination. I understand you were both there."

"Drake!" Vivian addressed her husband in the same tone she had used with the cat. "They just got here after a long drive and need

307

some time to rest, eat something-"

"No! Mom, no. We don't have time to rest or eat. We came for the book and we have to get back as soon as possible."

"You want that book?" asked Drake Plate, pushing his easy chair in position so that his legs rose up. "That is my property."

"You don't even know where it is, Drake," said his wife.

"Nevertheless, no talk, no book," said Drake Plate, with a confident smile.

"Sit down, Daphne, we may be here a while," said Plate resignedly.

Daphne laughed. She had no reason for the trip to be short. She wanted it to last as long as possible…

Chapter 62

"The book was actually at my house when all this began," said Daphne. "Pl- I mean, your son had lent it to me. I read it some time ago but had not gotten around to returning it to him. When they figured out I might have it, two of them came after me at my own home to try for it. On the actual day of the ball."

"Natalie knew her time as a clandestine operator was drawing to a close. She had a copy of her real genealogy. If she did not get a copy of the book before her only identity permanently became Natalie Wakefield, it would be too risky for her to procure one later. Her outlet for obtaining anything that might throw suspicion on her was going to soon be blocked forever."

"It is hard to find old books," said Vivian Plate.

"Natalie came to Daphne's that day to try for it but was unsure she was at the right house. Evelyn had already conned Daphne into letting her in and had swiped it. Thinking it vital to a murder plot, she burned it."

"She didn't con me. I trusted her by instinct. Things might have been different if she had trusted me," said Daphne.

"The book really had nothing to do with it?" asked Vivian, disappointed.

"Nothing," said her son. "I'm getting it so that I can let the person who almost died for it read it."

Several hours after they had arrived, Plate and Daphne had the senior Plates so involved in the story, the older couple almost felt like they had been there.

After a tasty brunch, they were all sitting in the living room of the old country house. Tomcat had been let back in and was purring on Daphne's lap.

"So are you sure, son, that Wakefield is totally innocent?"

"Sure as can be, Dad."

"And the women assassins! I cannot get over that," said Vivian.

"Serena and Natalie had been the two women kneeling at either side of the stage. Natalie had slipped out of her Marie Antoinette costume and into the Lady in Disguise costume. Only Daphne had

309

noticed the discrepancy in her height," said Plate, a little pride creeping in his voice.

"But it did not register." Daphne complained at her own lack of perception. "I knew something was different but it just did not click at that moment."

"Lady Evelyn had been attacked just before the first skit. I'm not sure they knew then if she was Evelyn or Miranda. But a spare Marie Antoinette was a grave danger, whoever it was."

"And this was the federal agent? How did she get so herself so vulnerable?" Drake asked.

"She's very young. She played a lone hand when she ran out of people to trust. She almost pulled it off but she was attacked. Peg Brown may have witnessed this and that's why she was also attacked. We're still speculating on when and why she was attacked. She is still in a coma. We just found out her condition is complicated further."

"That was the congressman's wife?"

"Yes, Mom."

"How is her condition complicated?"

"They have found out she is pregnant. Very early stages. Apparently undiagnosed. Mrs. Brown may not have known herself."

"How sad," said Vivian Plate. "Maybe they can save the baby?"

"We don't know, Mom."

"Continue with the crime story," Drake demanded. "These two necessary attacks were the first things that went wrong for the criminals, I presume."

"Right, Dad. But the second skit goes right. Natalie and Serena kill Edward. The spotlight is out. They leave the stage, dropping the knives. Two co-conspirators step into their places. The other Ladies on stage are stunned and in darkness. Natalie and Serena attempt to get blood on them, especially Darica. The others are merely housewives, one drafted at the last minute to take Peg's place. Only Darica has an interesting profile, so she's the designated scapegoat. The group has planted evidence against her in her newspaper office."

"That's a terrible thing to say about housewives," Mrs. Plate protested. "What do you think most of my generation is? What do you think I am?"

"I'm sorry, Mom. I didn't mean to insult you."

"Vivian, I'm sure Peter didn't mean anything. After all, he's young and speaks impetuously at times."

Daphne looked at Drake in astonishment. *Impetuous!*

Daphne did not see Plate in that light at all.

"Tell me what happened on the stage after the assassination?" insisted Drake. "Let's get back to that."

"During the darkness, two other Ladies in Disguise- unwitting or unquestioning contributors to conspiracy- we're still gathering them in and sorting them out- walked onto the stage and knelt down in Natalie and Serena's places."

"Where did the assassins go then?" asked Drake.

"Natalie quickly gets back into her Marie Antoinette costume. The costume was cumbersome to move about in but it had been designed to practically jump in and out of. Serena had her costume under her cloak all the time, so she simply sheds her cloak."

"And goes to Plate's side," said Daphne.

"Really?" exclaimed his mother.

"That's another story, Mom."

"I heard how they tricked that poor schoolteacher."

"Yes, and Ernest Wakefield as well. As you heard, shortly after, Tates is discovered injured, as is the second Marie Antoinette, who was really Lady Evelyn."

"I heard that part on the news, too," said Vivian Plate. "And how, still trying to keep up the pretense that Miranda is alive, she was misidentified by the Watsons."

"We knew the Watsons," said Drake.

"Really?" Plate was exclaiming now.

"Long story, tell you some other time. Long time ago," said Drake, with a very serious light in his eyes.

"The death of their own daughter did nothing to stop the Watsons from their madness," said Plate, eyeing his father's reaction to that statement.

"They are from a line of anarchists going back to the eighteenth century itself. The death of one of their own means nothing. Some type of elevation in their atheistic history lessons, that's all," said

Drake Plate. "I'll tell you all about it some time. Go on."

"Drake, this is more than just a crime story," said Vivian. "Daphne, how did your sister get so involved in all this?"

"My sister was investigating them for discrimination and possible criminal activities such as money laundering, drug running, and prostitution," Daphne said proudly.

"That's what I was convinced they were all about at first," said Plate, knowing it would be useless to ask his father for more.

"What made you suspect them?" asked Drake.

"Wakefield and others behind the gates had reported costumed women walking the streets at night."

"What on earth were they doing?" asked Vivian.

"Communicating by coded brochures. They feared the phone system. One would leave the message, another get it after dark."

"They should've known nightowls and insomniacs would spot them. How far in it were you from what point in time?" asked Drake.

"Remember, Dad, when I say 'we' I don't mean I knew all of this from the beginning. I was just part of local police helping out, not privy to everything. The feds had suspected this group of subversion for more than two years but were only spying on them through Lady Evelyn. Resources were under allocated, you might say."

"Actually Lady Evelyn had already gotten Darica in the group but Darica kept quiet about that," said Daphne.

"That was one of the things I was not told," Plate glared at Daphne, thinking- *and the other was that she was your sister.*

"Could y'all get on with the story?" said Drake.

"They would get a lot further without your rude interruptions," said Vivian.

"I tried being polite," Drake said to Vivian.

The younger Plate ignored his parents' repartee.

"After leaving Daphne's that night, Evelyn killed Miranda and entered Miranda's name as Marie Antoinette on the character list, removing Natalie's. In her capacity as headmistress, Natalie must have discovered it the next day. Seriously worried- this change involved herself- Natalie put her contingency plan to disappear into action. Her dinner party, already planned for that coming night, was the perfect backdrop. Just my analysis. Maybe not perfect."

"Sounds good to me so far. Go on, son," Drake commanded.

"Natalie Wakefield's disappearance was a brilliant move on their part. Another distraction from their real purpose. This also pointed to her as the possible victim."

"No one, not even experienced agents, suspected her?" Drake wondered.

"This is what I was told. They were convinced she was a target. With her disappearance, experts watching the whole scenario decided it seemed as if plans for any hostile action at the ball had been called off. The perpetrators, having achieved partial success and seeing how Pointpar was guarded, had just dropped it for another time and were going on with the ball as a fund raising event."

"Even with an unidentified body on their hands? Sounds like they missed the mark."

"Shut up, Drake. Let Peter finish telling this."

"No one knew at this point if Miranda or Evelyn was the burnt corpse. Serena and Natalie knew one or the other was a traitor. Only our side ever seriously suspected Darica Daniels."

"Which was absurd," commented Daphne, scratching Tomcat's ears.

"Serena Towers covered for Miranda's absence by telling everyone Miranda was off on assignment," Plate continued, "and by telling the others at the paper that Miranda had gone undercover for a story unexpectedly, without the ability to get word back."

"You have to understand, my sister never told me any of this."

"Letting either Evelyn or Miranda being labeled missing publicly would have jeopardized the ball. If one was proved to be the corpse, the disappearance of the other could also come to light. So they covered it up and used it."

"Even though Darica knew I was going to be at this ball," said Daphne, distracted by Tomcat abandoning her lap for a favored rug.

"Lady Evelyn had been given up for dead. But our side wanted no attention brought to that possibility either," Plate continued. "Before disappearing, her last message sent indicated the intended victim was Forrest Pointpar and or Natalie Wakefield. Or both. It was feared Evelyn had died in a partially successful attempt to thwart the plan, Natalie had been kidnapped and probably killed, but with vigilance on our part, nothing would happen to Forrest at the ball."

"They were deliberately led astray from then on," Daphne spoke up again, "by the constantly changing character lists."

"The list of characters was influenced by the planned murder but also by the personalities involved. The list drawn by Natalie was the real list but it was only a few pertinent characters. They merged it with random list altered by Darica who added Daphne. Evelyn switched Marie. Forrest insisted on being Napoleon. Morris Tates was conned into coming as Louis XVI. But, not knowing it mattered what character he was, he changed costumes with the local priest."

"No one took it seriously enough," observed Drake.

"When Evelyn added Miranda's name as Marie, it gave credence to the idea that Miranda was alive and Evelyn dead. Feds knew about the Pointpar change. Then Darica checked the computer and found the list doctored again. We think Natalie could not resist changing the character of Marie Antoinette back to herself. Her determination to be the French queen was one of the weaknesses of the plot. This time the list was deliberately leaked by the editor and could be changed no more. Also time was running out. Notifications had to go out to the paying guests."

"A mistake to bring in a civilian. Every time," said Drake.

"Darica?" asked Daphne, her eyes widening.

"She was making sure you were still listed as Deborah. And she believed she was leaking it to her editor. But actually it was being passed to federal agents. The editor was cooperating."

"Does Darica know this?" Daphne asked Plate.

"Um. No," Plate said.

"Don't ever tell her," Daphne warned him.

"Continue, Peter," Drake requested politely.

"Drake, this is Daphne's story too. What else happened on your end?" Vivian asked Daphne.

"They sent a notice canceling the hairstyling aspect," said Daphne.

"Daphne was the only one who got a style."

"I can't wait to see the pictures," Vivian commented

"It was lovely. But no pictures were allowed," said Daphne.

"Back to the story," interrupted Drake, gritting his teeth a little and provoking a silent glare from his wife.

"Natalie was caught by the Marie character change. As headmistress, she could not speak about it to anyone she did not wish to suspect she was Natalie Wakefield. After all, finding a substitute was logical. Natalie was officially missing. So she could not safely change it back."

"But she could not resist. She did change it back," Drake speculated. "And that spooked our side."

"That's my thought also. Everyone was distracted by these historical characters. Everyone feared the scene where Louis XVI faced the guillotine. That's where we saw the danger. That was the part Forrest was given first. It really did look like they wanted to kill Natalie Wakefield and Forrest Pointpar."

"It seems you had enough information to figure all this out and prevent this tragedy. You or someone," said Drake Plate.

"The changing list kept us all confused. Since all these women were in disguise all the time and no one knew the truth about more than two or three others, nobody knew who was targeted, dead, missing, or in hiding. I was not officially privy to the lists until the very last minute."

"Then everything changed again at the ball itself," Daphne said.

"Yes. They staged Marie Antoinette first. Suddenly Natalie Wakefield was back. Like a magic trick, Natalie reappeared as Marie. Then vanished just as promptly before the second act. There was no time for us to properly analyze what was happening. It was initially feared they would get Forrest back into the Louie costume. Or rewrite the script where Napoleon did not die in his bed. As our concern was alleviated when the first drama was proved to be faked, we let our guard down, distracted by the Cheshire Cat act of Natalie Wakefield."

"Too much concern for the Wakefields and Pointpar," Drake observed.

"Right. And I was worried about the coincidence that my chief's wife had drawn a character."

"Killing York was always the plan. The whole event, including the skit, designed as a vehicle for that crime," Drake concluded.

"Right. York was cast as Gustav and given a revisionist lesson in Swedish history so he would not be alarmed when they came at him with knives, dancing slowly in the rehearsal. But they wanted to kill York quickly in the real skit."

"Why wait? Why not kill him in the rehearsal?" asked Vivian.

"A nuance of psychology. York would have been more on guard in the rehearsal, not knowing exactly the blocking of movement the first time the script was dramatized. The first time he might have flinched, or otherwise somehow thrown off their steps. They needed him to be exactly where they wanted him, expecting their aggression."

"Catch him unawares," concluded Drake.

"Right. For the lethal blows they moved just a little differently enough to confuse him."

"When they moved differently he would have feared he did something wrong," said Vivian sadly.

"If he had known the history, he might have been more leery, like with Louis and the guillotine, or Caesar and the Ides of March," said Drake.

"I thought politicians had to study history in college," said Vivian.

"No. They study political science and law," said Drake.

"Doesn't political science teach them history?" Vivian asked.

"No, it teaches them how to get elected," said Daphne.

"Oh. No wonder they don't know how to govern anymore."

"Besides, history classes don't cover Gustavus' assassination. No one knew the history behind his character," said Plate.

"I did. Darica should have. Darica forgot what being Gustavus at a masquerade ball meant. They feared his popularity with the people in the 1700s so they killed him."

"It was Edward York they feared today. He was so charismatic, so devoted to his faith, people loved him. It was a combination they did not want to see in a President," said Plate.

"You knew him, Peter? What was he like?" Vivian asked.

"Enigmatic. Sounds cliché, I know, but that describes him

perfectly. He was everything everyone said about him. Yet, there was something about him that most did not see, I believe. What used to be called melancholia."

"Really? So he was not a happy man?" asked Vivian.

"That's just it. He was, in a peculiar way. Not happy like, well-like us, right here and now in a normal way, but joyful in an ethereal way. I think his joy did not extend to earthly life. It was reserved for God."

"I didn't know him nearly as well, but that does sum up what I observed," added Daphne.

They were silent. Tomcat rose and stretched. He looked at the strangers in the room. Then sat back down warily on his rug.

"Let's get back to this list of characters," said Vivian. "Were you always on it, my dear? What happened with your part?"

"My sister manipulated it so I would be Deborah Franklin. And that never changed."

"Deborah Franklin?" Drake looked puzzled.

"Ben's wife."

"Benjamin Franklin had a wife?" Drake asked.

"Yes, dear, all great men have a wife," said Vivian.

Plate glared at his mother. And not because of her confused grammar.

"Let's get back to how the feds did not see York was in danger and how they assumed Miranda Watson was still alive impersonating their own agent, when it was the other way around. Somebody should have seen this coming," said Drake.

"York was in his own home, amongst people who adored him. He had not officially announced for the Senate yet. There had only been minor threats against him that were vague in nature and sourced back to the Northeast. York was not considered significantly at risk."

"What a loss," said Vivian Plate.

"Who will take his place?" asked Daphne.

"No one," said Drake Plate.

And the others in the room were surprised to see tears in the older man's eyes.

Tomcat jumped into his lap and began comforting him.

317

Chapter 63

"I don't understand," said Drake Plate. "Why can't I tell her?"

"That's right. It's nothing to be ashamed of," said Vivian.

Daphne was freshening up in the bathroom before she and Plate started the drive back to Sand Waves. Plate was with his parents in their living room, trying to say goodbye.

"I just don't want her to know yet. She's urban, raised in the city, never lived elsewhere, never even been to the country before. I don't want her intimidated."

"I don't see where that is so intimidating," said Drake.

"It can be," said Plate.

"She doesn't look that modern, she looks like she stepped right out of *Tammy Tell Me True*," said his mother.

"And she's not like that. I know she hasn't said much but she's intelligent. She has a degree in economics," Plate said.

"As I recall that character was quite intelligent also, despite being from the country."

"That's just it, you don't know what ridicule characters like that get now. You haven't kept up with modern times, Mom."

"She has to know eventually. Don't you think she will understand?" Drake Plate asked.

"Of course, just let me tell her in my own time," Plate said.

Daphne emerged then and Drake Plate gave her the book they had come for.

"You will come back and see us when you can stay longer," said Vivian. "Escape from the modern world."

"Yes, Peter's friends are always welcome here," said Drake. "You don't have to bring him if you don't want to."

"Right, just let us know you're going to drive up and we'll be here for you," said Vivian.

"Thanks," said Plate. "Mother, Father, I love you, too."

"Thank you. I might just do that," said Daphne.

"Want me to find your parents and visit them without you?" asked Plate when he got Daphne in the car and was driving out of his parent's yard.

"They live in Katy. Houston for all practical purposes. They would not let you in."

"I'll get a warrant."

"My father's a salesman also," warned Daphne.

"Oh my God, what does he sell?"

"Cars," said Daphne.

"Oh, that's not so bad. And your mother?"

"She's like your mother."

"A housewife?"

"That would be- homemaker."

"Yes, right."

"We do have one thing in common concerning our parents."

"What?"

"I think they are about the same age."

"Mine were in their late 30s when I was born."

"Mine, too. About that."

"Well, that's something. Would they have much in common?"

"Maybe. Probably."

"I wish your Swedish grandmother had been around to help with all this."

"She still would have had to have known what costume Edward was wearing. Actually, I could have helped if I had known."

"I didn't know. I could not have told you in time. I was not in the level of 'need to know' to get that information until very late in the game. I think Brown got me clearance after a brief meeting with him because of something his wife told him. Little good it did them."

"Darica knew what character Edward was cast as. And Darica was never much of an academic, except in English and journalism. She has trouble with American history, much less Swedish."

"Why do we only study Louie and not Gustav, do you think?" Plate asked.

"School teachers have to try to make this stuff make sense. These two kings were both executed with a few months. But one was killed as the result of the uprising of the peasants while the other was killed by the aristocracy that spawned him. That's too complicated for

319

teachers to explain so Gustav got left out of the school book history text. That's what I think."

"I don't think that's it," said Plate. "Was Gustavus a devout Catholic like Louis XVI and Edward York?"

"No. Their common ground was being kings, not religion," said Daphne. "So why do you think we learn about one and not the other?"

"Sweden is not nearly as important as France?" Plate then added, "I don't think the Swedes would agree."

"My grandmother would not have agreed," said Daphne. "And it's other than just different nationalities. Like we all know about certain women historical figures but no one knows about Deborah Franklin."

"You know what I think?"

"What?"

"Hollywood did not make a movie."

"That's a depressing thought."

"That we may only learn about those things we first see as entertainment? Yes, I agree."

"You are probably right."

Daphne leaned her seat back.

"Are you going to sleep while I drive all the way back?" Plate asked.

"Yes."

"I'll listen to country and western music," he threatened.

She sat back up.

"What shall we talk about?"

"That's better," he said, and sped the car up quickly as they reached the open country.

"I should get to pick the subject if I have to stay awake and keep you company."

"You could drive."

"I am done driving all over creation. I did that to make a living before I moved to Sand Waves."

"What do you want to talk about?" Plate asked.

"I want to know how close Serena Towers came to killing you."

"Really? Do you want to really know that?"

"Yes."

"Not very."

"That's not what I heard."

"We had cameras set up in all three locations, my apartment, Serena's apartment- set up before Darica moved out- and in the cottage. Jordan and Willhouse were following me and available for backup at a prearranged signal, which was not needed. I am somewhat physically competent. I can take care of myself."

"How did you know she was going to kill you? Why did she want to kill you? Why didn't she just leave?" Daphne asked.

"She knew Natalie's writings would give her away once they were translated. She feared Evelyn waking up. And I gave her every reason to suspect that the feds were on to her. She thought I was too dense to put it together. She didn't take it seriously that I was shadowing her every chance I could get. A serious error for a seasoned operative. She should have just tried to flee. Then we would have moved in on her. I don't know why she played it out as long as she did."

"I do. She fell for you. She believed your stalking her was the action of a lovesick jealous boyfriend. She may have suspected you logically, but her emotions told her what she wanted to hear. That you were in love with her."

Plate did not disagree with this assessment. "So it was decided I should show my hand. Let her know she was on the verge of being found out."

"Having led her down the garden path, she was furious when she was faced with proof that you were insincere in your affections. She decided to kill you before trying to make an escape. I can empathize."

"Why can't women just settle for being friends?"

"You know the demographics show our generation had about 12.8 women for every 10 men."

"Yes, I am quite aware of that."

"So that does leave a significant number of women without even-aged partners."

"I suppose it does."

"And when you count gay men and take away men who are undesirables for various reasons, like being drug addicts or criminals, the eligible population dwindles even further. Whichever way we women look at it, some of us are going to wind up alone."

"Or with other women. Or marrying a divorced man."

"Well, one man can service several women in modern day society, just not at the same time."

"You can go after older or younger men," Plate suggested.

"I think the demographics cover several years over and under our generation. At least seven."

"You don't have to be restricted by seven."

"I can go for older than that. Or younger. A 19-year-old would be interesting," Daphne agreed.

"There's no shame in remaining a single woman. I have a maiden great-aunt who's never married. She's a well-respected member of the community and an important member of the family."

"Oh yes there is. Times have changed. There's a stigma to being a single woman these days. And a duality of expectations that are without precedent in our society."

Plate was silent, unable to avoid imagining Daphne with an amorous 19-year-old boy at her side. He rejected the scene, resolving the fantasy by mentally arresting the teenage playboy and throwing him in jail.

"That takes care of that," he said aloud without realizing it.

"What?" Daphne yawned.

"I suppose it would be okay if you napped a little," said Plate.

"No, absolutely not, I shall stay awake whatever it takes."

"Do you like classical?"

"Yes, some."

Plate deftly fished into his bin of cassette tapes, found a Mozart, and popped it into the player without taking his eyes off the road.

The slow music began softly.

"Go ahead and lay your chair back a little," said Plate.

And she did.

Daphne did not wake up again until they reached her home in Sand Waves.

Chapter 64

Lady Evelyn Corrigan was well enough to be in a private room. Daphne and Plate visited her after having recovered from their East Texas trip.

The British aristocrat was still guarded by HPD, so Plate drew no notice in his uniform. Daphne dressed professionally also, despite having little prior success at selling life insurance in hospitals.

It was usually too late by then.

Evelyn had happier news.

"I am expected to make a full recovery, but there is going to be therapy for some time. I will have some time on my hands. And they won't let me smoke here, they won't."

"Then this is just what you need," said Plate, handing her the remaining copy of *Murder as the Organist Plays*.

The blonde girl in the bed laughed as did the one standing by the bedside.

"Why did you come to my house that night?" asked Daphne. "The first time, I mean. Was it in search of the book? How would you have known I had it?"

"No, I knew nothing about the book. I did happen to see it lying on your hall tree and something about it stuck in my mind. I am trained to observe. No. I was after Darica. By that time I knew she was the only one person in the organization I could completely trust."

"Why her?" Daphne asked.

"Because I had brought her into the organization and I knew she was the one that was going to be set up for whatever crime they committed at the ball."

"So why didn't you ask for her?"

"Your dialogue about a hubby and all that threw me off. You were like an actress. I was suddenly uncertain what I had stumbled into. I thought you were covering for Darica and she was long gone out the back door by then."

"You and Serena both recruited Darica?"

"Serena believed it was she behind Darica having been lured into the organization under the pretext of doing a joint story

323

undercover. Serena was a true believer in the atheistic anarchist cause and she was sure she could convert Darica."

"Convert Darica? Ha! She only listens to herself," said Daphne.

"Nobody thoroughly investigated Darica. She was seen as a middle class reporter on a small community newspaper so she was totally underrated by both sides," said Plate.

"If anyone had checked, they would have easily found out Darica is a Christian," said Daphne.

"Easily?" Plate asked.

"They could have found out somehow," said Daphne.

"I knew Darica was a Christian from way back," said Evelyn.

"Why would you trick Darica into such a dangerous position?"

"Understand the fear from high up was that Forrest was the target, as he was originally supposed to be Louis XVI and also, whoever was chosen as Marie Antoinette would also be a victim. Forrest Pointpar was determined to be Napoleon so that threw a kink in their plans, we thought. When the wife of a prominent oil company executive was named as Marie, it seemed that our original fears were well founded. She would die instead. Just the right person to make their profound statement by action. Or whatever they call it."

"We know all that. I still don't see how this involved Darica."

"Darica approached me with her legitimate undercover reporter idea. I saw an opportunity to get someone inside who I knew would reject their principles. I was confident they would not seduce her. At least pretty confident. I needed someone I could go to if I needed help. Not one of our other operatives could get anywhere near the group. If I had not responded to her, she would have found another way in. I still pretended I was really one of them and Darica pretended she was interested in the cause as well as furthering her career. I pretended to believe her. Darica had no idea how I really felt about it all. I knew she was not taken in. Serena did believe in her."

"It was better for her to be vouched for by two trusted members of the group than just one," Plate said.

"Right," Evelyn agreed. "When Serena approached the headmistress with the same scenario that Darica thought she had with me, it was almost amusing. Keeping details and plans from one another was a key to the group's methods."

"They were very good at that."

"Miranda was trying to catch me in the act of betraying the group. She must have confided her suspicious to Natalie because they changed the password."

"After your confrontation with Miranda, how did you get away?" asked Plate.

"I took her car instead of mine, ditched it in Galveston, took the bus, then a cab back to Sand Waves. I laid low for a day, terrified Miranda would be found along with my car. Luckily no one went there that day and I hiked over after dark the next night. I set the fire and got my car. Took me most of the night but no one saw and I got away before dawn."

"Yes, I saw the fire on my way out of the gates, leaving the Wakefield house," Plate commented.

"When I heard that Natalie had vanished, I was terrified even more. I decided the only way to hide was as a common ordinary Lady in Disguise saleswoman. A new hire, recently homeless due to the recession, needing shelter. It was a good backup plan. But it was hard, I had to wear those boot stilts all the time."

"But you fooled them?"

"Not only that, I was selected at random from the destitute Ladies to act as a servant to the headmistress and Serena Towers one day when they had tea. Truly God's hand in all this, what? I still had no idea Natalie was the headmistress- the disguise was very good and Natalie's voice was not well-known to me- but that's when I found out how high Serena actually was and when I overheard about the book. I believed the book was vitally important. That's why I risked going back to your house the day of the ball to steal it. I remembered it and just took a chance I could get it. I didn't know you were Darica's sister. I forgot Daniels is not her maiden name. She was married when I first knew her. I had no idea. What do you two do? Keep each other a secret?"

"Yes," Plate said. "They do."

"Our careers sort of conflict so, he's right. Sort of. Yes."

"I would have trusted you if I had known. I had found out what you do. I figured you were her insurance agent. And nobody- " Evelyn bit her lip.

"And nobody trusts insurance agents," Daphne finished for her.

Everyone laughed.

"Selling insurance beats door-to-door selling. I get to go inside people's homes from the beginning. I don't have to stand out in the weather, beating on the door," said Daphne.

"I usually didn't have to pound too long before people let me in or ran me off," said Evelyn. "I did sell quite a bit of hair care products. Sales is a line I could fall back on."

"If you ever want to get out of the spy business, I know several good insurance companies."

"Do you get a kickback if you come up with a recruit?" Plate asked Daphne.

"Actually-"

"Never mind. I don't want to know."

"I'm terribly sorry I destroyed the book. I was sure it was going to somehow be used to set up someone to be killed if it surfaced."

"Don't worry about it," said Plate. "Let's get back to your story. If I have to write a report, it is not going to be as long as this book but I need every detail."

Evelyn picked up the book and flipped through it.

"So Natalie wanted this book? I had no idea she was behind it all. When Natalie disappeared I was frantic at first. Then, I was able to use it. I managed to convince them, that as daughter of the owners, Miranda was insisting on becoming Marie now that Natalie was missing. I decided I had to arrive as Miranda in the Marie Antoinette costume at the ball. Either I could make contact with other federal agents or, as a decoy, I would at least expose any violent plot during the first skit. That failed. I never got the chance."

"How did you get the costume?" Daphne asked.

"I stole as it was delivered to the Watson home. I couldn't believe I got in and out of there with no one catching me."

"Up until they were needed to mis-identify you, the Watsons were not told Miranda might be dead," said Plate. "The organization feared the Watsons' reaction would disrupt the ball."

"What happened when you got to the ball?" asked Daphne.

"I never made it to the stage. I knocked some man down and drew attention to myself. Then I spotted Natalie as Marie behind the stage curtain, I went to warn her. She attacked me."

"Do you remember anything else?" Daphne asked.

"Not until I started coming out of it at the hospital."

"You were not found until after Edward York died," Daphne told her.

"The organization now was sure it was Miranda who died. But they wanted her death kept secret even more. Serena identified you as Miranda on the scene. The Watsons were pressed into service to confirm the identification and behave as concerned parents should. That was the only way they were going to have future access to you," said Plate.

"As I slowly came out of it, I saw they were there so I kept pretending to still be unawares. They never went away and I had to listen to them try to persuade the doctors to remove my life support and listen to the doctors' confusion as to why I did not respond when my vitals indicated I should have. The damn doctors and nurses poked me hard and it took all my training to keep still. Finally, I just decided to give up. I told the Lord, it's my time to go, what? So be it, then. The Watsons sitting there, hating me so, wishing me dead was just unbearable. I think I actually took a turn for the worse then."

"No, you improved. That's when the doctor talked to me," Plate corrected Evelyn. "But you are right in that he did not understand why you did not respond and feared you were somehow suicidal. He told me he explained to the Watsons he was optimistic you would eventually recover but they still wanted to pull the plug, had even hinted that you should be helped to leave this world if possible. And hinted cleverly, without incriminating themselves, that they could make it worth his while to accede to their wishes."

"Can I ask a personal question?" Daphne inquired.

"Of course."

"How old are you?"

Lady Evelyn smiled. "Nineteen."

"I cannot imagine letting anyone so young take on so much

risk," Daphne said.

"This group was very hard to infiltrate. You almost have to be born into them. They have been raised from birth to believe the hatred. It was however, very flattering to them that a sixteen-year-old British aristocrat would come to them as a convert. I have some Irish heritage as well. All the better, they believed. That and being so young put me above suspicion so to speak. I did nothing but participate in their charitable activities, actual good works really, until this."

"You should know you have played a significant part in exposing Natalie Wakefield and the Watsons," said Plate.

"But Edward York is dead. We lost."

"I don't think anyone is going to blame you," said Daphne.

"Oh, I have already been told I am being promoted to 'training'. So my espionage career is over. That is the kiss of death professionally."

"It must have been quite an adventure," said Daphne.

"At first I had a wonderful time acting the part of the alienated teenager, struggling with parental control, finally breaking free and renouncing my birthright. It soon got old."

"What will you do now?" Daphne asked.

"Now I'll go back to England with my parents. Get my British accent back. They are on their way over here. I have already spoken to my mum. Knowing the truth means so much to them. They were under the impression I was a disgrace. Then they were told I was probably dead. They are so happy. It will be nice to have my family again."

"I can write policies for foreigners as long as the policy is actually written in the state of Texas," Daphne informed her. "So if, before you leave-"

"Daphne," said Plate with a warning tone. "I think WE had better leave."

"Thank you, I'll keep that in mind," said Evelyn. "My parents are arriving at Houston Intercontinental very early next morning. I'm a fast reader though. I'll have this book read by then."

"We will let you get to it then. Just leave the book with your Houston police guard and she will get it back to me."

As they left her room, Evelyn reached for the book and started reading…

Plate dropped Daphne off at her house, telling her he had to go back to work. Actually he went back behind the gates of Sand Waves.

He drove to Ernest Wakefield's house.

Unofficially, the sale was still going on. The mansion was almost empty. What had not been sold was in the midst of being sorted for packing or storage.

Wakefield was going to Asia for an extended stay. He was still selling whatever he could until his travel date arrived.

"No returns on the desk," he said lightly to Plate, as they shook hands.

"No, I love it. I was wondering if any other objects from that room were still available. Namely the painting."

"Actually yes. Someone bought it and paid for it and never returned to get it. Called them and they said forget it. Isn't that amazing? Younger generation. What are they thinking of?"

"I'd like to buy it."

"Name your price. It's already made me money."

Plate looked at the painting. Sized 36-by-24 inches, it had every color of blue imaginable in it and, save for white, no other hue was present. Snowy mountains in the background and a white blanket of snow in the foreground, with a stream cut through the middle and frozen bushes on the side, made for a frosty image.

The most interesting part was a huge tree to one side with such intricate and dark branches that only by shining a light on it could the details be seen.

It was nicely framed in brown.

"Fifty dollars?" Plate ventured.

"Sold, Lieutenant, if you take it with you."

The painting was worth much more, actually the frame cost three times that price, but Wakefield was eager to see it go. The youthful buyer had paid $800 for it and then blew it off.

That was half its real worth.

It was so distinctive it would not sell easily at its just retail price, his antique dealer had told him. People wanted art that fit with their décor.

Few people had an all blue room.

"One more thing," said Plate. "If it is not spoken for. I saw an advertisement you put about it in the paper..."

Plate told Wakefield what else he was interested in.

"Lord, yes! Free, absolutely free," said the oilman, and ran to track it down.

Chapter 65

As she promised, Lady Evelyn had left the book with her police officer guard when she had started her journey back to England with her parents. A couple of days later Plate planned to meet Daphne for lunch to give the book back to her. She wanted to reread it.

"I don't have time for a long lunch so it will have to be McDonald's," said Plate.

"Why don't you just lunch at my house? I'll fix a sandwich for you."

"Sounds good. I think I can sneak away."

Plate was in uniform but since he was staying for lunch he removed his belt and vest this time.

"So this is how the genealogy connects, or does it connect depending on your point of view?" Daphne asked, as they munched on bologna and potato chip sandwiches with mustard.

"This is sort of like being in my sci-fi book," said Plate, looking at his sandwich after a swallowing a crunchy bite. "But it's good."

"That historical book of yours is the next thing to sci-fi, if you ask me," said Daphne, crunching also.

"Don't tell me the ending. I've never finished it. If you have to tell me how all this is involved, give me a chance to read the book first."

"I don't have to give anything away to tell you."

"I know. One of the characters in the book was reportedly based on a real person who was Natalie Wakefield's great-grandfather."

"It's not the same character as the one that was your great-grandfather."

"Thank goodness."

"It would be more interesting if you and Natalie Wakefield were related."

"Well, we're not. Banish that thought from your head."

"Are we sure it was somehow connected to people she descended from?" Daphne asked.

"Who knows? But we have Tates' work. My family book was only about her father's side. Her great-grandfather was a mysterious character and other than this book, which is fictionalized, we don't know much about him. On the other hand, from her mother's side, Tates traced her ancestry back to France and Russia, where she is descended from, not one, but two families with radical ties going back to the 1700s."

"You know, we hear all about building a family tree, finding our ancestors who helped found the country, fought in the Civil War or immigrated to Ellis Island. But what if you find out you came from long line of criminals?" Daphne wondered.

"And the definition of criminal varies a great deal from time and place."

"Yesterday's criminal is today's activist for freedom."

"Yesterday's police hero is today's civil rights abuser."

"The Sicilian Mafia were heroes during World War II."

"Really?" Plate raised his eyebrows.

"Yes, they fought against Mussolini and the Nazis and were quite invaluable to the allied War effort. After we won, of course, they went back to being criminals, both here and in Italy."

"We think the assassination of Kennedy and Lincoln are the major political killings of all time but many history changing murders have taken place among world leaders for centuries," Plate said.

"That's what I'm saying about researching your family trees. You wonder whatever happened to all the descendants of the atheists, anarchists, revolutionaries."

"Yes! Natalie Wakefield. Look, she had everything capitalism offers, but it meant nothing to her," Plate said contemplatively.

The potato chips made more crunching sounds as Daphne and Plate ate. Then Plate continued on the same line of thought.

"I think most descendants of anarchists and other violent types just grow up and live normal lives and assimilate into the population just as all the descendants of most people. But there is a fringe group, just as some of the Civil War types, both sides, still raise their children to fight for the cause, so is there a small culture of anarchists, communists, even Nazis still who keep their cause alive generation through generation. And sometimes a generation comes along that rises up and causes havoc."

"So at any given moment, there is a set number of people, literally programmed from birth to grow up and destroy our society."

"Yes, and it is actually the law abiding nonviolent ones that are the most dangerous."

"How do you say that?" Daphne asked.

"Look at the Lady in Disguise movement. With the support of so many prominent women, the group was untouchable. Edward's death was the first time they had ever let domestic violence brush them. Suppose it had not been co-opted by the violent fringe. It could have gone on for years, gained the public's trust, become an American institution, as trusted as any major organization. Kept the money coming in from the business end as well, ended up, not just door-to-door sales, but parties and gatherings in people's homes. Slowly indoctrinating more and more people, especially women. Women who raise the children and teach them. Women who make the bulk percentage of school teachers in this country. Mark Brown said their first move on Peg was to convince her to drop her Bible study group, which she had been part of for years, in favor of their activities. Had the Lady in Disguise movement people been patient, kept going, been persistent, they might have indoctrinated millions." said Plate.

"So they didn't see this?" Daphne asked.

"This particular sect didn't see it or didn't care. They were getting on in years, the older section like the Watsons. They wanted action in their lifetimes. It's those that have near infinite patience that are really to be feared. Those who, despite believing in nothing after death, nevertheless are so dedicated to their cause they are willing not to see the end. They keep building generation after generation of vipers chipping away at our culture and lifestyle. Growing more and more organizations that seem innocuous, beneficial actually. Calling them by names opposite what they stand for. And continuing to gnaw at the fabric of our society. Taking a little more each year from us until all our liberties are gone."

"You believe that is going on? Here in America? Here in Texas?"

"Yes, I do."

"Plate! You're scaring me. What can we do?"

333

"That's just it. All we can do is live our lives and keep faith with our causes and beliefs. Try telling people, any of your clients for example, try telling most of them this and they will say you are crazy. You'll wind up in the mental institution."

"You're probably right about that. I never talk politics with my clients. Most of them don't want to talk about that. They talk about their personal lives. How unhappy they are. How unfulfilled. How lonely. Those that are happy, fulfilled, and companioned don't talk that much, they just buy insurance and send me on my way. That is why I was troubled by Wakefield's purchase of insurance by mail for his Natalie. I thought he was hiding an unhappy wife."

"It was probably her that did not want to see you. She dealt with few other professional women not in on her cause. Natalie Wakefield was not lonely, unhappy, or unfulfilled. She had a reason to get up each day. I suspect she rose each morning filled with enthusiasm."

"That really is scary. I'm pretty happy and busy, but I could not say I'm ecstatic every day of my life."

"She had her blue room for inspiration."

"That is so strange. What was the real story behind those missing doors?" Daphne asked.

"The real story was me. They counted on my perception and I had a blank disconnect about those doors. The witnesses all told me they were staring at Natalie through the doors when the light went out. It just didn't register. For, at the same time, I was thinking about how this new style of building houses with a minimum of walls and no doors on any room, except bedrooms, is really asinine."

"It is. I wish I could close off the living and dining room."

"Would that give more purpose to your life?" asked Plate.

"I don't discount the effect of a nice environment on productivity," said Daphne, recalling an economic class lesson. "But I think you have to be a fanatic like Natalie to be totally entranced by atmosphere. Natalie was a fanatic, I take it?"

"Yes. So was Serena Towers. She always had a sparkle in her eyes that was a little too bright whenever I took her out. I would say some things that should have perked her up, some that should have taken her down, but she reacted the same to all. I felt like she was

334

eyeing me in preparations to devour me."

"Environment cannot be everything if Edward York was really so depressed all the time as they are saying now," Daphne said.

"Yes and no. I think people are trying to justify his death in some way. He was depressed so someday he might have committed suicide so his being murdered is not so terrible. That kind of thing."

Daphne's cat entered, stretched with her behind in the air and then fell at Daphne's feet.

"I sometimes think Catherine suffers from melancholia," said Daphne.

Plate stared at her, then at the cat.

"Oh, you think so?"

"Yes, she is so serious some of the time, not playful, just drapes around the house like a limp rag. Think it's lack of self-esteem?" Daphne asked.

Plate looked at the cat, which had promptly passed out on the floor.

"She does look in need of counseling," he commented. "All that stress about which cat food is best and how she is going to convince you to buy the right one."

"You are being facetious. But I worry about her."

"Maybe you can find a kitty psychiatrist in the Houston yellow pages."

At that moment, the cat woke back up and stood on its tiptoes, then jumped on the Victorian sofa, eyeing the two humans curiously from Daphne's office doorway.

Suddenly the feline began to scratch hard on the arm of the couch.

"STOP!" Daphne screamed, lunging at the animal. "STOP that! You vixen! Scratch my new couch again and you're dead meat!"

She grabbed the cat, smacked it on the behind, and tossed it into the garage.

When she returned to the den, Plate was smirking as he sat watching.

"I don't see where this is going to help her self-esteem," he commented.

"Tough love," said Daphne, dusting the palms of her hands together.

"Guess the visit to the psychiatrist is off. He may report you for cat abuse. Speaking of love, does Catherine have a boyfriend?"

Daphne glared at him. "Of course not, she's been fixed."

"Would she like a companion?"

"She absolutely hates other animals."

"Even other cats?"

"Especially other cats."

"Oh."

"Why?" Daphne asked.

"Well, I have a little problem. Wakefield was going to send Natalie's cat to the pound. He advertised for someone to rescue it before he left for Asia or it would have to be taken away. It is such a beautiful animal. All black and sleek, with those green and yellow eyes. It sort of captivated me. And it being an older tom, well, I was afraid they would put it to sleep. I sort of took it."

"Wonderful. A good cat to live with will do you a world of good."

"I live in an apartment. No pets. I'm in violation of my lease, having to hide the animal under the bed. I was hoping you would consider taking him. He is a real beauty."

"You know we're only allowed one pet per household."

"You could apply for a hardship exception. I know some people. I could pull some strings."

"Absolutely not. Catherine would never accept him."

"Just give it a try. Please. At least, let's introduce them."

"You know nothing about cats."

"True. Tomcat did not come into the family until after I left home. We only had dogs when I was growing up."

"You have a lot to learn."

"I'm counting on your help."

"Are you going to be writing your reports on the case? Need my help again?" Daphne asked. "Of course you do. You could come over this evening and we could get started."

"I'm not going to be doing any reports for this case. I'm too low down on the lineage. Even the death of Doris, which was my case from beginning to end, has been taken out of my hands. Robert- Chief Brecken- will be doing all the reports."

"Oh," said Daphne, with disappointment.

"I could not come over this evening anyway. I have another engagement. How about tomorrow night? We have some unfinished business that I would like to get out of the way."

"We do?" Daphne was blank.

"We do. But tonight I have to go see Grace York."

Plate watched as Daphne visibly flinched at that declaration. However, she straightened her shoulders and held her head up and he couldn't help but admire her.

"I've been summoned," he said lightly.

"Indeed?"

"I don't have to go, of course. Answering summonses such as this one is optional. Civil-service laws protect me if I don't cooperate."

"You want to go."

"Yes, that is true. I do want to go. I have unfinished business with Grace York as well."

It is Grace York who would devour you if she could, thought Daphne.

Chapter 66

At the same time as Daphne and Plate lunched at her house, Forrest Pointpar stared at the small group of men seated with him at one of the round tables in the Toy Museum Restaurant.

The same group of people he had met with the first time were nearly replicated.

The leader was back.

Conversation opened with remarks about the tragedy. Grief was expressed for Edward. Shock was expressed that Serena Towers was part of the conspiracy to kill him. The Watsons were denounced all around. Curiosity about Natalie Wakefield crept in.

All this conversation was dignified and subdued.

At the side of the leader sat Grace York.

She was properly attired in black, with a long mantilla veil capped by a black hat. Her simple black dress came slightly below her knees. She wore black transparent hose and pumps, one of which rested gracefully upon the other as she crossed her legs at the ankle.

"Forrest, I wanted to thank you for what you did," she said in a soft voice.

"I was only acting on instinct," Forrest replied with uncharacteristic modesty.

He realized he was going to need that modesty as the topic of the conversation became clear. After everyone had expressed their condolences to Grace York, the talk turned to which candidate would take her husband's place as nominee for senate.

Forrest had suspected that was why he had been called to this meeting. He had allowed himself to entertain the idea that he would be the choice.

Already deep in his campaign for the congressional nomination, he had the mechanism in place. He bristled with anticipation.

Then the group got down to business. The reason they had come together one more time in Sand Waves.

"History shows that when the widow, able and willing, steps into her late husband's shoes under these circumstances, the result is almost always positive," said the leader.

"I have no political experience," Grace reminded them.

"We don't think that is going to be a detriment," replied the leader.

"I am here to give support to Mrs. York?" The near interruption of the leader by Forrest caused everyone to jump, then sit back in some astonishment.

"My boy," said the leader. "You know your time will come. We don't want you to feel any pressure. I know you're in the midst of a campaign against Congressman Brown. You feel like your own effort is going well?"

Forrest hesitated. At first his announcement of his candidacy had caused a wave of support to come his way but he had slowly seen it erode back towards the incumbent. Now Peg Brown was an object of prayer and sympathy by most constituents. Forrest felt helpless about his own prospects.

"Sir, I don't know."

"I like that honest answer. Suppose we tell you that circumstances can be made to conform to a situation where you get the nomination for the seat in congress."

Forrest stood up, then sat back down again.

The other men at the table all glanced at each other with bemused expressions and a couple chuckled.

"Yes, we can do that," said the Wall Street man, with calm confidence.

"Of course, we cannot guarantee against unexpected events," said the past adviser to presidents.

"I am still in absolute shock about Serena Towers," said the journalist, and the look on his face confirmed his statement.

"But all in all, most of the time…" The leader left the statement unfinished.

"I've known Congressman Brown for a long time," Grace spoke up. "But, Forrest, your actions the day my husband died were-"

She broke off with genuine emotion in her voice indicating she could not continue.

"Gallant." The leader put the tips of his ten fingers together in front of him.

"Yes, that is an excellent word, Mr. Pre- I mean, Richard," said the journalist.

Grace recovered her speech. "Yes. Gallant."

Tears came to Forrest's eyes. "I wish there had been more I could do."

He was quite sincere.

Everyone else concurred.

There was a brief silence and the ghost of Edward York seemed to hang over the gathering.

Grace was sure she felt his presence. Briefly, then he was gone.

Gone to higher callings, she reflected. *How like him, a brief glimpse at me and then his attention is diverted so easily by the ethereal. The celestial, it must be now.*

You may be dead, Edward. But you haven't changed any," she said silently to him, and smiled secretly to herself.

"I'm sorry gentlemen. Mr.- I mean, Richard. My emotion strayed for a second."

"We completely understand, my dear. Give some consideration to the idea of a candidacy for yourself. We can count on your support Forrest?"

"Yes indeed."

"What will we tell Mark Brown?" Grace asked.

"Leave the congressman to us. His primary concern right now is his wife. How is she, Joe? Any report,"

"Sir, unfortunately, her condition seems to have plateaued. She hangs in the balance, neither in nor out of this world. We are praying for her and her unborn child," said the former adviser.

"I thank God that was not Edward's fate," Grace said truthfully. "I could not have endured it."

In proper words, the gathering agreed with the widow. The rest of the meeting consisted of the men attempting to find ways to help her and themselves understand the ways of such a world in which such a man as Edward York would be considered such a threat to the dark side that such elaborate steps would be taken to eliminate him.

Despite being the subject of the conversation for the rest of the afternoon, Edward's ghost never again made his presence felt. Grace often thought, even years later. that those few moments of the brief fluttering of his spirit was his farewell to the world that had kept him perpetually sad, despite offering him the best of everything it had.

Edward no longer wants anything to do with any elements of the earth. He is happy now for the first time.

Those words came to her mind at that moment and, for the rest of her life, Grace never saw any reason to challenge that conclusion.

Chapter 67

"Are you completely alone in this house?" Plate asked Grace as she greeted him in the front foyer of the York mansion.

Grace reflected that Plate had no idea what it was really like to be alone.

First a member of my family took my husband, then after I got him back, my friend murdered him...

Embracing Plate, looking around at her reconstructed house, Grace was in as much shock at the environment around her as at her husband's death.

Except to enter and exit, she had hardly been downstairs since the killing and in her mind the house had reverted to its pre-masquerade ball status.

A short time ago the front and back yards were completely divided by a fence which ran from the further most edges of the east and west wings to each of the side fences.

It had been torn down. The two driveways piercing the fence to allow access to the four cottages were still there but all the elaborate fencing had been removed. The family had used those drives to access the backyard. All comings and goings had gone through the back door.

Now the front door was opened, the dogs relocated.

The huge den taking most of the back of the house, once divided by a closed foyer from the kitchen and hallway where the elevator was located, was now almost completely open to the hall.

Walls had been removed and the divisions were gone. Even a small portion of the wraparound kitchen at back was accessible. A large picture window still looked out at the yard from the kitchen, as did a couple of smaller windows in the den.

Plate and Grace sat at the kitchen table and he felt it was eerie now to be able to both see out the window and into the heart of the home at the same time.

"I'm interviewing live-in servants," Grace said. "Ray is actually staying in one of the cottages. I decided it was better decorum that he not actually live in the house with me. He's gone into Houston tonight."

"He's planning to stay for good?"

"You never liked Ray, did you?"

"I have ambivalent feelings about him. He was a suspect in a murder investigation. Some of his actions, not only broke the law, but I feel, were questionably dysfunctional."

"They wouldn't have been in the old days."

"This is not the old days. This is the 1980s."

"It doesn't matter. He's not going to stay. I want him to. He's going to stay as long as I insist on it. But I'm not Regina. I will eventually give in because he will be miserable and won't be able to stand it. So I will send him back to East Texas. As soon as I can bear it."

"It's no longer the old days in East Texas either."

"Whatever. Ray will not be your concern. However he behaves." Grace smiled knowledgeably. "No more than Forrest Pointpar will ever come under your jurisdiction again."

Plate's eyebrows shot up. He almost asked her what that meant. It only took a brief second for him to decide he did not want to know.

"Why am I here?"

"Because I wanted to see you."

Plate gave her no response.

"It was not necessary for you to come in uniform. You can take off your gun and vest if you would like to get more comfortable."

Plate remained silent. He shook his head no.

"I'm alone again in the world."

He still gave her no answer.

"There was a time I was alone again in the world and you were there."

"That was a long time ago."

"Actually, it was just last year."

The accuracy of her words astounded him. It did not seem possible that just last year he considered his relationship with her so serious that he had proposed to her.

"I think I took our relationship more seriously than you did at the time," Plate said. "That was my error."

343

"Our timing was off."

"That happens in life."

"You're being very cold to me, you know."

"What do you want, Grace? Our relationship ended and you've remarried Edward. I'm deeply sorry that he is dead. I admit I never understood the man. I came to see his appeal before he died."

"He could have made a real difference in the future of this country."

"I believe that."

"They're now telling me I could make a difference."

"They?"

"Don't ask. Just they."

With his arms folded on his chest, Plate walked around in a small circle. Grace could not see the barrier between them but he saw it plainly.

"What do you want from me, Grace? My support? Are you going to be a candidate? As a Sand Waves police officer I can't openly support you, but I certainly can't imagine voting against you."

"I'm not sure what I want. I think I just want reassurance that you will be on my team. If I need you, I can call on you. Remember how often you told me that."

"Yes I do." Plate recalled his flowery words with regret. His poetic impulse grew from a desire to impress, failed to bloom, and died.

"You said you would always love me."

I told you that I would always love you. But I left unspoken the last part of the line- if you will also love me. And you did not, Plate thought.

"So, I suppose what I'm asking for now is confirmation of that reassurance."

Plate was silent. Grace shifted.

"That was then, of course. Irrelevant now. I guess I just want some confirmation that I have a special friend that I can call on."

"I have professional duties," said Plate haltingly. "And I hope we can always be friends."

"That's not what I mean," Grace said, a little nervously. "Maybe

344

I am not making myself clear. Naturally, it's far too early for me to think about men in a romantic or sexual way. If I'm going to become a politician, my life will be even more of an open book than it was as Edward's wife. I'm talking about something else, types of relationships that people like me need if we go into public life. Edward had that odd connection with Mink Tanem. I'm not saying that's a good example. I'm just trying to explain to you what I'm talking about."

"I am at your service to the extent my profession requires. I consider you a friend. I hope you also consider me a friend."

Grace started to resume her explanation of the type of relationship she wanted when the look on his face told her that lack of comprehension on his part was not the problem keeping him from giving the answer she wanted.

He looked her in the eyes and then dropped his gaze.

"I see," she said lightly. "Your answer is no."

He did not reply.

"Just for curiosity. Did you think I was calling you to ask to resume our romantic relationship?"

"I did not know what to think."

"Would that have made a difference? What if I told you that if it weren't for one thing I would say yes to your marriage proposal? What would you do? You never retracted the proposal, you know?"

Plate tried to collect his thoughts.

He had believed the proposal was negated by her remarriage to Edward.

In his world, common sense said any romantic relationship was ended by someone's marriage to another person.

Apparently Grace felt like his proposal remained in perpetuity unless formally withdrawn.

"You're wondering what that obstacle is?" Grace persisted.

Plate shook his head. "I would be prying if I asked that question."

Grace stopped herself from telling him. He took advantage of her hesitation.

"Grace, do not tell me about parts of your life that you will regret telling me about later on. Let's leave a simple friendship intact if we can."

He left unspoken the words, *it might come in useful to either or both of us.*

Grace collected her emotions and had practically the same identical thought.

Plate noticed Ray Cathare's pickup truck had returned by the time he descended the steps off the porch.

There had been many people in the world willing to serve Edward York if he had continued his ascendancy. Plate wondered how many of those people would serve his widow. Fewer than she believed, he would bet.

He wondered if he himself would have denied this call to serve if Edward were still alive and still the rising star.

He was not sure he would have said no.

Chapter 68

Two days had passed, with two broken appointments, but Daphne firmly expected Plate tonight.

It had been almost a week since their trip to East Texas and she had only had the brief lunch with him.

He promised the whole evening tonight.

She planned to make him keep that promise, no matter the consequences.

To pass the time waiting for him to come, Daphne had eschewed all work and gone shopping for furniture.

She'd gone to the Finger's furniture store on the Gulf Freeway. Unlike previous visits, she had not come home with a new and beautiful item for her home.

Instead in the appliance department, in the middle of the washers and dryers and refrigerators, a new counter sat with the new product- home computers.

Daphne left, $2200 poorer, with a new Franklin Ace. After a chat with the computer salesman, who had an ethereal glow in his eyes when he talked about the technology, she stopped by a small strip mall establishment that he had recommended and purchased a Brother printer for another $300.

She brought them home and sat the computer on her spacious fireplace hearth, opened the box, and spent the day putting it together. She had to open the top of the computer and carefully and correctly insert the proper cards into the correct slots.

The printer was already completely assembled.

After three hours of studying and test runs, she had the new machines going strong.

Now that it was all over, the problem was where to put all the stuff. There wasn't any room on the desk in her office. She left it all sitting on her fireplace hearth.

Daphne had high hopes for a quiet romantic evening with Plate. But when he arrived in his uniform she knew he must still be on call. He took off his gun belt and vest as usual and sat on the couch in the den. But he had an all business like aura around him.

"What's going on now? Another case? I was hoping we could have a nice fun evening. You know, like play cards. A game? Something? Monopoly?"

"I'm on call, but just for show. Actually Skaar is covering for me tonight. Just if anything major happens, I have to show up. That's why I'm in uniform. What is all this on the hearth?"

"See my new toy."

Daphne demonstrated the computer. She booted it up and showed Plate the word processor and spreadsheet.

"It has 64 kilobytes. The old models only had 32."

"Do you know what kilobytes are?" asked Plate.

"No. But, look, if you make a mistake you can correct it before it prints. If you want to change something, like a name, it will go through your entire piece and change everyone automatically. "

"Unreal. How much did this cost?" said Plate.

"Less than $2200 with tax. And the printer made it $2500."

Plate flinched. That was more than he made in a month. Gross.

"It is the latest. Expensive, I know, but I'll never have to buy another. This one will last me the rest of my life. Look here, the spreadsheet will automatically add up rows of numbers!"

Plate sat on the carpet in front of the hearth and pulled out a list.

"Can I type this in and see if I can print it?"

"Sure."

"It's a copy of the real random set of assigned characters."

He studied the computer a moment and then started a file.

"The department is going computer in a few weeks," he said, as he typed. "Everything is going from paper to floppy disks. It's going to be a nightmare."

"Are they going to hire someone to do it?" Daphne asked.

"Ha!"

Plate finished the list and turned on the printer. "Nothing's happening."

"You have to give it a command. Press these buttons here," Daphne instructed.

The printer ball began striking the paper.

"It's like a player piano typewriter," Plate laughed. "With no keys. I've seen a lot of this type of stuff at various departments and businesses but to have it work in your own home like this. Wow."

"Everybody is getting one. We've been behind the times, I think," Daphne said.

"I've no idea what we are getting at the department. Something like other larger police facilities, I hope."

"This makes the computer at my general manager's office look obsolete. It is so cool. But his is a giant thing that connects to outside information. This is just for me."

Plate pulled the list out of the machine.

"The real first list of people chosen at random for the characters. Just a partial list. I only typed in the characters that finally mattered. They were listed only by last names and first initials and will never know how close they had come to being a part of history."

Daphne and Plate gazed at the list, each holding one side of the paper.

Bates, F.- Betsy Ross
Brecken, B.- Molly Pitcher
Brown, N.- Empress Josephine
Carlick, J.- Louis XVI
Cryer, T.- Gustavus III
Johanna, C.- Marie Antoinette
Russo, D.- Deborah Franklin
Salvatore, R.- Napoleon
Samuel, C.- Robespierre

"So your chief's wife did draw a character at random! Where did you get it?"

"It was in Natalie's desk, in yet another secret compartment," said Plate, his eyes glowing. "Don't ever tell anyone."

"Fascinating," said Daphne.

"First favoritism influenced the list, then the list was changed due to a killing, a name was added out of love, then the movement out of fear manipulated it, finally money changed hands."

"Money? Really, new information, about that?"

"No, I added the money part," Plate admitted. "But it sounds good. My point is if there had been no conspiracy, no intrigue, no favoritism, this was the list that would have stood. Ordinary people, maybe a little better off than most, or maybe just like you, someone splurging for once, just wanting to go to a masquerade party and have a good time. Instead Edward York is dead."

"A good time. Those are rare, you know. Life is short, they say. Edward York had a short life," mused Daphne.

"He had a charmed life. Good looks, success, plenty of money always."

"Wonder what his life was like before he met Grace?"

"From what I have heard, he spent his youth accumulating many accomplishments."

"A charmed but short life," said Daphne, somewhat repetitively.

"Which would you rather have?" asked Plate. "A short life in which almost everything goes extremely well until near the end? Or a difficult struggle through this world blessed with longevity?"

"Are those the only two choices?" Daphne protested.

"I think I would take the long struggle," said Plate.

"I'll let you know later. I will have to think it over," said Daphne. "Meanwhile, I'd like to research other configurations."

"Well, there is the hard difficult life that ends abruptly at a young age," Plate commented.

"You're going in the wrong direction there," said Daphne. "Let's just drop it and cut the computer off. How about a movie tonight?"

"We haven't finished. This is a business discussion."

"It is?" said Daphne, with resignation.

"It's late February. Almost March."

"So?" Valentine's Day, with all its possibilities, had come and gone unnoticed. Daphne was resigned to the disappointment.

"Remember we had an appointment in February for me to buy some life insurance?"

"Oh that."

"I assume I don't have to come to your office or meet you in some public place? I know you have all the papers you need here."

"I always have all the papers I need wherever I am," Daphne said smoothly.

"Great, let's do it."

"All right." She went to her desk in her office and pulled out the life insurance application.

"I'm going to need you to help me fill it out," said Plate, when she handed it to him with a pen. "In fact, I want you to do the writing, except for my signature, of course. I have enough hand written paperwork at the office. My hands just ache sometimes and now is one of those times."

"Okay, no problem."

Daphne took out her clipboard first, then attached the application to it and started writing. She filled out his name and address, birthdate, and all other pertinent information that she already knew by heart. When she came to the medical questions, he told her she could just check no to every one. He was in excellent health, had consulted no doctors in the past few years and had no medical conditions to report.

"Face value?"

"Is 500,000 too much for me? I know I don't make that much money. But I think I make enough to live on and provide a pretty good life."

"That is the outer edge for your income. But since I know you personally I don't think it will raise any questions. Particularly if we don't add double indemnity. That would cause the premium to go up quite a bit in your profession."

"Am I going to have to pay a higher premium?"

"Maybe a Level I rating. I'll try and get it through without a rating but I cannot guarantee it. You may have to contribute a statement saying that you're primarily a traffic cop and you don't do undercover, all that type of stuff."

"That statement might not exactly be true."

"Then I suggest you just accept the rating that goes with your job. Just pay it. It's not that much more."

"Do you get a higher commission because of it?"

"Yes, only because it's more money. I get a straight percentage of whatever you have to pay."

"Okay, well then, we won't worry about the rating."

"Good. Next- beneficiary. I know the names of your parents but I'm going to need their complete full names including your mother's maiden name."

"They've got long names. My hand feels better. You've done enough work. Here just give me the clipboard and I'll write it out myself."

Daphne handed him the clipboard.

"Show me exactly where to put it here."

"Right there- where it says 'beneficiary'." Daphne sighed with exasperation. "And then the line right beside it says 'relationship'- you can put both your parents' names on the beneficiary line together- and then on the relationship line, put 'parents'. And on the lower lines, if you want contingent beneficiaries, you can put the names of your brothers and sisters. That might be a good idea since your parents are significantly older than you. Like mine."

"Okay. Let me just write this out carefully. Now watch me while I'm doing it, so you can make sure I don't mess it up."

Daphne sat next to him, her knees under her so she could hover over him a little. She leaned over his shoulder and watched the letters appear as he started writing the words in the section designated for the primary beneficiary.

'Jeanne Daphne Martin.'

And on the relationship line he wrote- 'fiancée'.

"There," he said, looking at her very seriously. "Did I do it right?"

Tears came to Daphne's eyes and she could not speak for a minute.

"You told me back when we were trapped in Innovations that a fiancée was a valid beneficiary even though there was not yet a legal relationship," he said, completely serious and businesslike.

"Plate-" Daphne began, but she could not say anything else.

"You should call me Peter from now on. You will be related to other people also called Plate. It will get confusing at family reunions," he said.

And he could no longer suppress his smile.

"Peter," Daphne managed to say but got no further.

352

"I think the application is complete. I assume I sign by the X."

He wrote his full name- Sinclair Peter Plate.

Daphne was weeping and laughing simultaneously openly now.

"I know I don't make as much money as you do. But I can live with that. It will be hard on me. I'm pretty strong guy. I can do it," he grinned.

"I love you, Peter," Daphne managed to say. "I love you so much."

"I love you, too, Jeanne. Jeanne Daphne," he said laughing softly. And he held her in his arms on the sofa until she stopped crying and then he started to kiss her.

Published by Ruskras Corner

By Deborah DR Kralich

Fantasy

*A Cat Whisperer** humorous futuristic murder mystery romance

Historical Fiction

The Mystique Woven in Our Land 1792 murder mystery
Murder as the Organist Plays 1904 murder mystery thriller
Interlude of Carelessness 1930s intrigue romance espionage
*A Spy Come to Town** 1950s intrigue espionage thriller
The Mystery of the Missing Persons 1960s cultural drama

Lt. Plate in Sand Waves Mysteries

A series of mysteries set in the 1980s

An Innovative Murder for the Season traditional cozy
The Ruler of the Toys murder mystery cultural drama thriller
A Kaleidoscope of Masquerades traditional mystery thriller
The Unknown Puppeteer traditional murder mystery romance
Poised Like a Knife short story anthology including 2 Lt. Plate stories

I Lift Up My Heart a book of Christian poetry

***

By Carl S Kralich

Young Adult Science Fiction Series
Karl Sabers Space Knight Adventures:
3748 A.D. The Return of the Cat
Auction of Worlds
humorous adventure with space pirates, princesses and feline
***

Available on Amazon and Kindle

* Published under the pseudonym Deborah Denise

www.ingramcontent.com/pod-product-compliance
Lightning Source LLC
Chambersburg PA
CBHW071215250626
47159CB00001B/321